BEYOND THE PEACE RIVER

by

Virgil Griffis

PublishAmerica
Baltimore

First printing

ISBN: 1-4137-5023-0
PUBLISHED BY PUBLISHAMERICA, LLLP
www.publishamerica.com
Baltimore

Printed in the United States of America

I dedicate this book to my father, Leo, his father, Thomas, and his grandfather, Charles. All my ancestors who bared the Griffis name into an untamed wilderness called Florida in the 1800s, the time period depicted in this story. Because of the courage and determination in their blood, they were able to carve a new life for their families. It is that same stubborn Celt blood passed down to me, enabling me to complete his work. I am grateful for that, because without it, I surely would have failed in this endeavor. For a lifetime, my heart will be filled with gratitude toward them and the God they followed.

ACKNOWLEDGMENTS

It gives me great pleasure to acknowledge my family, all my children for their tireless support given me while writing this book; it was ever so helpful. I surely am indebted to all my friends and co-workers, who offered encouragement through their wonderful interest. Last and most importantly, I must acknowledge my loving wife, Melody Lee. For without her knowledgeable assistance in subduing a computer run amuck, and for her steadfast encouragement, I may not have completed this book. I thank you all very much.

To Harry, Elwin
I hope you enjoy
Thanks

Virgil Griffis

CHAPTER ONE

Miz Penny always sat in the only rocking chair on the back porch of the big house. Not the usual rocker prevalent to most Georgia farm homes, a crude homemade rocker. No, sir. It was a store-bought "Peerless Home Comfort Rocker" from Atlanta. Will Nash, Miz Penny's husband over twenty years now, conceded that she deserved to sit and rock in the evenings weather permitting, if she took a notion. And generally she took a notion, especially now in the cool October evening of 1858. The frail small woman sat with the soles of her worn, plain black shoes barely off the floor. By habit, she allowed her thin freckled arms to rest on the arms of the chair after readjusting the white cotton shawl draping her slight shoulders. Occasionally she would cause the chair to rock by stretching a leg, and with the tip of one shoe push the chair slowly back, holding it for a moment, and then allowing it to drop forward. After a few minutes she would repeat and continue the process many times over, before retiring for the evening.

Will sat on the unpainted yet smooth floor of the porch, one leg crossed over the other exposing a sockless pale thin ankle. His other foot resting comfortably on the plank step below, a small portion of bare toe showing through a hole in the end of his worn brown brogan. By choice he preferred the floor, not bothering to use the long crude bench against the wall. Both Miz Penny and Will were childless, each in their second marriage. She being widowed, after losing her husband to the last marauding Indians in Georgia, after only a few months of marriage. That happened thirty years ago, around the same time Will's young wife Sara died from the slow sickness, along with their unborn child. Sara's death left Will and his two younger brothers, James eight years, Luke six, along with their father, but no woman on the place. Realizing a problem, before his grieving son had time to consider it John broached the subject.

"Boy, we in need of ah woman on tha place ta look ta thangs," was the way his father put it, only weeks after Sara had been laid to rest. "It ain't ah matter of ah lack ah love fo' Sara, Lord knows thet wuz plain fo' all ta see. It's ah matter ah need," John explained to his son in the days following. "It's James an' Luke, them young'ns need ah woman's hand," John added.

The reluctant Will, still wearing his black armband, chose for his wife "ta look ta thangs," a neighbor and widow, Penny Claxton. With not the slightest pretense of true love in their very brief courtship, the union developed an abiding respect, lasting through and up to the present, over the years. Both young brothers long affirmed to be men, grew straight strong and proud. The majority of credit for their principled up bringing favored Miz Penny, as she had always been referred. As expected, they remained on the land they were born. Later additions included Polly, James' wife and their two children. They formed the typical southern farm family lacking little in necessities for life. And never found guilty of beseeching God for extras.

"Needless thangs," as Miz Penny always classified the items considered extras.

Few words passed between Miz Penny and Will since establishing their places on the porch some thirty minutes earlier, mostly they just sat. In past fall evenings it would have been a pleasant experience, watching the changing colors on the far hills. Now however, it was not, especially not now. Even the lingering sun cloaked in long thin crimson strands of placid clouds produced no noticeable pleasure. Its unyielding persistence creating a wonderful profusion of bright hues in the distant sky yet failed. All divine intervention not requested by neither party on the porch. The enlisted legions of tall trees casting long shadows, presenting belts of dark and light, stretching the breadth of the far hills and fallow fields, failed. What would help if an immense canvas painted by the very hand of God were of so little use? They could not see it, their minds totally bankrupt and their eyes blind to color, from the best God would proffer.

This collection of fall colors and gentle cool breeze in the past usually made Georgia evenings priceless. Producing conversation and mirth, easing if not lifting the burdens of a hard day for a son or daughter of the land. Instead, the approaching dusk signaled only the end of a day and inducing the listlessness hovering about them. Even the devout Miz Penny could not bring herself to relish God's masterful work splashing the sky before her. But before overcome by sleep this night, she would, while on her knees, pray for God's forgiveness and strength to bear their burden.

In lieu of conversation, she and Will continued watching the mostly unmoving figures gathered on a distant knoll, on the far side of an already harvested field. Only as silhouettes now, they clustered in the shadow of the large oak, resembling a huge dark umbrella over the low rise. No words from the serene gathering on the hill reached the two inactive observers, even as a gentle breeze carried in the direction of the big house. The distance was too great. Besides, no requirement existed. It was known their hearts were equally as sorrowful as those on the porch. Miz Penny knew well that enough of their tears were falling, for washing the feet of Jesus.

An elusive whippoorwill made a shrill musical call from a cluster of pecan trees somewhere near the barn, and was immediately answered by another farther away.

"Listen ta them ol' birds, they ah knowin' it's too early fo' all thet callin'," Will fussed, while refusing to turn his gaze toward the sound. Knowing such an act futile, a waste of energy, seeing the bird was impossible anyway. In all his years he had never been able to see one, even when he felt like looking, and tried.

Instead, he kept his focus on the small group in the shadows. In truth, Will harbored no resentment toward the whippoorwill, actually he was quite fond of them, and well aware that it was indeed their usual time for calling. Simply, he had grown weary of the silence and felt like saying something. Not wanting to speak about the assembly they watched, but knowing full well that shortly he would be obliged to do so. At least attempt to talk to them one more time, when they returned to the house.

After mulling his remark about the whippoorwills over in her mind, Miz Penny gave a delayed response, "Will Nash, I reckon them birds got good reason 'nough ta call early if'n they take ah notion. 'Sides it's whut God wants. An' if God wills it, then thet ol' bird start his calling right after breakfast, or jus' mayhap skip tonight an' take it up tomarrer. An' them owls too." An after-thought. Even though they had heard no owls, and Will had not mentioned them, and had not the slightest intention of doing so.

Her rebuke of her husband was mild, because of her full understanding of his gloomy mood. But to Miz Penny, any questioning of Gods work would always bring rebuke, no matter the mood. While on her knees later she intended on bringing rebuke to herself. Rocking her chair back again satisfied that she would hear no further grievance over one of Gods creatures the whippoorwill. Gods will covered just about anything and everything according to Miz Penny, and she used every available opportunity to testify for the Lord. Her unshakable belief in Gods will included the four headstones reflecting the last rays of the setting sun, yonder in the shadow of the oak, and reason for the assembly being watched.

"Reckon so, Miz Penny. Reckon he do." Will agreeing only in part

Delaying for a moment, his conformation of a secret selected portion of her statement, knowing it prudent after thirty years of marriage. Reaching down and with a callused finger and nail in need of attention, he poked at his exposed toe, as if noticing for the first time the hole in his shoe. Stalling…should he say more? No, sir, he would not. Not even bothering to clarify his last statement. He was in no mood for further preaching from his wife. Not this evening. He carried more than ample weight on his shoulders and troubles on his mind, to be further burdened by Miz Penny's thoughts concerning God.

Will Nash's beliefs often clashed with those of his wife over such matters as God. Quietly of course. Sure he believed in a creator. What else could one believe when seeing the sun rise every morning in the east, and set every night in the west without fail for a million years? When man could do something as simple as planting corn and beans, and be a fool if he supplied a promise of them producing. But he felt sometimes…that, God just left some things up to man and birds, to do as they saw fit. Call now or call latter, plant now or never plant. Will harbored the belief that God had more pressing things to be concerned over. Assuring the sun did what it was supposed to do for instance. If man or birds did something wrong, there would come a time for their atonement. Atonement, now that was something in which Miz Penny was more than well versed. Quietly Will disagreed over the four stones on the hill, as being the work of God. His notion was, sometimes, bad things just happened. Like his first wife Sara dying from slow sickness for instance, or bugs eating the collards.

He didn't like wearing himself out thinking on it. Nor had he spent much time calculating how a whippoorwill might atone to God for calling at a bad time, or bugs eating to many collard leaves. Hell, he couldn't even vouch that it was a sin in Gods eyes. A nuisance certainly, but mostly just a riddle that man had no proper answer. Miz Penny would surly have an answer. She often preached how man would atone and he was unwilling to hear it again. Especially not now. And he sure as hell rejected any inclination of questioning how a whippoorwill might. No, just let it be. Wait until the folks returned then maybe talk on other things.

The amicable feeling surrounding the assemblage at the graves, clashed with the underlining sadness hovering about them, as surely as the approaching dusk brought the enduring whippoorwill calls.

"Ain't them colors purty, Momma?" Kara Sue pointed a thin finger toward the granite stones. Praising the accomplishments of the reflecting sun, which the others ignored.

It didn't phase the blond, pigtailed, seven-year-old that she had not received a response from her mother. The objects of the little girls scrutiny were the four grave markers. All being the result of God's work according to Miz Penny. Or just bad thing happening according to Will's reasoning. Each stone identified the eternal resting place of a loved one, under a low smooth mound of red Georgia clay. The last placed there only two days ago, its polished gray marble lacked the coating of green mildew, so prevalent to the others. It had taken two weeks to get the latest gravestone from Stone Mountain, marking the final resting place of John Nash. The previous head of the family and father to the Nash brothers of Augusta County. Hardly an evening passed that some portion of the Nash family didn't pay their respects. Those who didn't make the sojourn to the diminutive bit of tranquil ground remained on the porch, just as Will and Miz Penny were now. But seldom so gloomy, discounting the days when a new stone would be added. It had been so, since Sara, the first buried there. God's will? It depended on who was asked.

After tonight though, their lives would change. James, Polly and their two children, along with Luke, were leaving Augusta County. Lanky fifteen years old Jimmy D. and sister Kara Sue ten years old, considered plans for traveling through an untamed country exciting. Entertaining visions of great adventure. But not right at this very moment, their thoughts as did the adults remained on the graves. The very last one ever, very special, very sad, leaving the tiny graveyard behind.

"Momma, look at them shadows. They look lak li'll angels dancin' an' all, don' they?" Kara Sue, falling under the spell of a child's imagination, studied the slow smooth movements. The dancing figures on the face of the tombstones were created by shadows from wind blown moss, hanging long from low limbs of the covering oak.

"I reckon they do chil', they purly do," her mother agreeing this time. She along with the others watched the animated figures against the reflected colors on the stones. "It's real purty right 'nough. Reckon God wants us to have ah real nice visit, on 'count it our last one an all." Her words were soft, somber. Eyes misty. Dull, instead of the usual bright blue.

With his wife, James sat on the short bench he had constructed from oak planks, a couple of year's back. Earlier, Polly had entertained the thought of taking the bench with them, but decided against it. It should be left for Will and Miz Penny; everything here belonged to them now, as it should be. James tenderly squeezed his wife's hand, as they leaned back against the huge oak. Ignoring the roughness of the crusty gray bark with its one hundred years of growth.

"Yo' right 'bout them dancin' angels, Kara Sue. How they moving over Matthew's stone," Jimmy D. expressed his agreement with his younger sister's description of the shadows. "Dancin' right on them grave markers," he added, leisurely laying his long arm over her slight shoulders. In silence Polly read the carved inscription under the gliding shadows on the nearest stone. On every single visit, it was the one that usually caught, and held her attention for the most part.

Matthew James Nash
Beloved son and brother1844-1856
Now in the loving hands of Jesus

The distance across the open field seemed much father on their return trek toward the big house. Allowing time for the brightly colored markers, only a few minutes before, to be consumed by the shadows and darkness of the giant oak.

Speaking first, but unsure of what to say, as they approached, Will simply asked a rhetorical question, "Everythang tha same?"

"It wuz ah real nice visit," James replied with what he considered a reasonable statement. Especially sense he wasn't even sure if a question had been asked.

"Ah might sad though," Polly added. Saying nothing else...

Silence lingered momentarily, only noise from the surrounding forest drifted to the porch. Mostly from the same whippoorwills, that had earlier caused Wills admonishment. Lighting now was meager and they continued their talk in reflected light, leaving the tree tops visible only as silhouettes, their lower portion's concealed by the drifting fog.

Once again Will interrupted the silence speaking in his slow southern cadence, the same drawl possessed by the others. "Reckon they's no sense talkin' on it no more," Will lamented again rhetorically. Not bothering to look up this time. Not wanting to hear the answer. But he received one just the same, from Luke.

"Naw, they ain't. 'Sides y'all ought ta sell out once we get settled an' come too."

"It ah fac' Will, y'all ought ta leave. Y'all know tha talk, 'bout tha trouble thets brewin' between tha north an' south. An' if thet scalawag Lincoln gets hisself 'lected, it'll come to more than jus' talk," James argued, kicking at the ground once, sore at the thought

"Awh, James, they ain't no cause fo' frettin' on such. It ain't gonna come tha no shootin' war." Unwilling to admit himself, especially after having spent much time fretting on the very subject.

"They's already lots ah meanness goin' on between Missouri, Kansas and Arkansas right now, with them border troubles an' all." James was more than willing to argue his point.

"Tha south ain't gonna stan' fo' all them port tariffs tha north's tryin' ta push down our throats. All tha while claimin' it's all over slavery, 'cause ah thet ol' crazy fool John Brown, an' them other 'litionist," James spoke defiantly. "An' it could mean Yankee soldiers right here on this place."

"It's ah fac', Will, only thang Europe values from this country is cotton, an' tha south is where tha cotton is. Thet boils down to Yankee tariffs." Luke taking up the argument. "'Sides Lincoln made ah speech las' week on how tha nigras and whites cain' live together. How they all gotta be shipped back ta Africa, Liberia or some such. Wuz in tha paper."

"It don' matter if Lincoln gets 'lected or not, Buchanan already sent over two-thousand federal troops against them Mormon's out in Utah, 'cause ah their religion," James added.

"Whupped good by them Mormons too," Miz Penny said, smiling at the thought of government troops being put to the run.

"We ain't got no slaves, an' we ain't Mormons. It's Lincoln's wife, whut got slaves. Mayhap he ort ta start cleanin' his own house. Let'm come. I'll be right here waitin' on'm jus' lak them Mormons," Will defiantly added. "I ain't runnin' from tha laks ah no Yankee trash. Nash's ain't never run from nothin', an' I'll burn in hell befo' I'm tha fust," he said, spitting in the dirt.

"Will Nash! Thet's blasphemy an' I ain't 'llowin' it! No mo' than yo' 'llowin' Yankees on this place!" Miz Penny proclaimed loudly, glaring at her husband. All the while siding with his philosophy. Taking exception only, with the verbiage of his declaration.

"I'm sorrowful fo' tha rough talk. Jus' tha same, I ain't runnin' from no John Brown, Yankees, or no other trash whut crawls south," Adding to his already taken stand. "Ain't ah matter ah runnin'. An' thet ain't whut me an' James is studyin' on. If we got ta fight', we c'n make ah better fight in them

Florida swamps, lak them Indians do than open fields here." Luke, supplementing his argument with sound military tactics.

"'Nough of all this war talk, an' whut ta Yankee's gonna do. Special Pa still cold in tha ground," Miz Penny interrupted. Knowing the statement about their father would hush the negative conversation. "Ah body would have no idee, it's ta be our las' day together." She was determined not to hear any further unpleasantness over war.

"Reckon yo' right, Miz Penny. But our minds set on our leavin' jus' tha same," James stated. "An' ya'll know we been studin' on leavin' fo' more than two year now, an pa's passin' ain't responsible fo' our goin', war either. 'Cause if Georgia 'ceeds, Florida will too," he added as an afterthought.

"Reckon thet's all true right 'nough. Jus' tha same, yo' an' Luke orta let me pay y'all more fo' ya'll's share." Will switching the conversation to something other than war with the Yankees.

"Naw ain't so, yo' paid us fare an' square, 'sides, it's whut we all 'greed on befo'. It wuz yo' an' pa whut built tha place. Done mos' ah tha injin fightin' an' all. Me an' Luke wuz just butt'ns, 'cept fo' tha end of it. Ain't thet true, Polly?" James looked at Polly for conformation of his statement.

"It ah pure fact, Will. Miz Penny tol' me stories 'bout yo' an' pa diggin' stumps an all, an' them two wantin' ta he'p, but they too little. Sayin' they hardly big enough ta tote tha tools."

Satisfied that Polly had well supported his argument, James added, "So yo' see, Will, ain't no cause fo' sayin' we got mo' commin'.''

"Sides even if yo' did, ain't no way ah gettin' it to us. I allow they probably ain't no more than ah dozen post offices in the whole of Florida." Polly really had no idea as to the number of post offices in the state. Even though she was quite certain, there could not be many."

"I 'spect they ah whole lot more injins an' varmints whut will eat yo' lak as not, than they is post offices. It ah awful harsh an' godless land y'all goin' ta." That was the first remark Miz Penny had been willing to make, regarding their leaving. Except for mentioning that they would be greatly missed, and the federal soldiers being beaten by Mormons, and her small body shuddered as she did so. She had no reason for speaking further about it; it was all in the hands of God. And as far as Miz Penny was concerned, it had always been so.

"Well, Miz Penny, it 'pears we ah trifle out numbered, don't it?" Will reluctantly surrendered not inclined for further comments on the subject.

"I reckon so, it lak James sez. Ain't no sense talkin' on it no more. All's I c'n say is, thangs ain't ever gonna be tha same." A tear trailed down her heavily freckled cheek, and she gently wiped it away with the back of her dainty hand.

"Lord he'p us baby Jesus, we gonna miss y'all too." Polly hugged Miz Penny's petite frame, both crying unashamedly. Which started Kara Sue crying.

"Now look at y'all, carryin' on lak thet, yo'd think somebody up an' shot our rooster. Whut say we go in, Miz Penny done made ah fresh pot ah coffee earlier," Will suggested after the crying ceased.

"Good, an' we c'n cut thet pan ah ginger bread I baked up earlier," Polly added.

They left the porch's dim light, its source, the single lamp in the parlor near the window. Inside Polly poured hot coffee into porcelain cups Miz Penny insisted on, instead of the usual tin cups. Miz Penny cut the sweet dark rich cake, placing a large portion on each plate, from the same special set as the cups. Before the first bite Will said grace, one a bit too brief for Miz Penny's approval, bringing a glare without comment, thinking it sufficient for now. On heir last night together, she believed God would overlook her husbands' weak petition. Later before sleeping though, she would add that to her already long list of things to speak to God about. Mostly over Will's carelessness, in dealing with his repeatedly straying soul.

"Bes' we break up this frolic an' try ta get some sleep, we aim on getting; ah early start," James spoke, stretching his arms wide.

Sleep failed to overcome Polly and James as quickly as both had hoped for, their minds cluttered with thoughts of the past, the present, and what might await them. A picture of Matthew's gravestone cold and grey, splotched with green mold. Eventually the picture was slowly erased from her mind, and the dancing angles drifted away in the fog, one by one. Slumber overtook her.

Sleep was slower coming to James as feelings of self-doubt plagued him. Everything that they had ever known was being left behind. He made mental inventories of the trappings they were taking. Soon though, he followed Polly in sleep, almost satisfied in his conviction.

The hours allotted to them for sleep somehow seemed mysteriously stolen away. The repetitious musical calls of the bashful whippoorwills, the sounds they had fallen asleep by, no longer echoed. In its stead, the low mooing of cows demanding to be milked, along with the offensive loud crowing of the rooster perched atop the split rail fence, screeching news of the coming dawn. Had anyone bothered to look, it presented a beautiful picture equal to the evening just past. A glow appeared through the trees behind the rooster as the sun fought the damp fog for dominance. The proud crimson cock stretched his neck long, continuing his harsh sound for another twenty minutes.

Assignments had already progressed as if it were an ordinary morning before the rooster's self important crowing began, and blended with other normal farm sounds. Hay was pitched to the penned cows, seven in all readied for travel. The four heifers plus two young cows would follow the sound of the copper bell strapped to the neck of an immense steer. Tater, the brindle cow dog, would be indispensable in helping control the small heard, especially the first day, because of their proneness for turning around and returning to the corral. One of the older heifers was sure to be slower than the others, but James felt she could keep within sight of the slow moving wagon, or require being secured to the wagon. Luke fed and hitched the four mules to the wagon. With the stock ready, the men sat on the fence, talking about old times, watching the animals eat.

In the house the women cooked breakfast as the shrill crowing of the rooster renewed his assault their ears through the kitchen window.

"Would yo' listen to thet no 'count bird, ah squawkin'. Lak as not he'll be at it till noontime. One ah these days, I'm gonna take ah axe to 'em, an' put 'em in my stew pot."

The aroma of the meal being cooked brought the men, as Miz Penny's complained with mock irritation over the rooster.

"Be proud ta ring his neck fo' yo', Miz Penny."

"Jimmy D. Nash yo' lay one hand on my rooster, an' I'll take ah broom handle ta yo' backside," smiling and shaking her finger in mock warning.

Fine fare it was, eggs fried on both sides in bacon fat after the bacon had been cooked. Biscuits fitting a man's hand, grits, plus a platter of thick ham slices. Then there was pure golden honey, peach jam, and plenty of black syrup if preferred for the biscuits, and sugar for the coffee. After all were seated, Will, to the satisfaction of Miz Penny said an especially long blessing, compared to his deficiency the previous evening. Included in the usual thanks was a special mention of a safe journey for the departing family. Will suffered no change of heart as far as long prayers were concerned; it was just his way of delaying the inevitable. Through the entire meal, there was not one example of low spirits. The family seemed satisfied.

"I baked up extrie biscuits an' put 'm in ah cloth with some meat fo' each of tha men ta tote in their war bags," Miz Penny declared, being well aware of the inconvenience of travel.

"Ain't likely we goin' ta get ah meal lak thet fo' ah spell."

"Lak as not we won't even be able ta get dry firewood everday, fo' cookin." Kara Sue, adding to her mother's statement. Gathering firewood was one of her duties.

"Don' worry, little girl, we'll make do." Luke patted her head.

"Papa, kin I take ah biscuit out ta Tater, an' mayhap them left over eggs?"

"Thet's up to Miz Penny, son."

"'Course thet be fine Jimmy D. Take whut's lef' fo' Tater an' yo' pig."

The pig referred to by Miz Penny was a half-grown sow named Bakon. Raised from a baby, by Jimmy D. and Kara Sue. They had not mentioned anything about bringing Bakon along. It was assumed there would be no objections and a sure certainty that Miz Penny and Will didn't want the swine for butchering time. After all she was a pet.

When the wild piglet was found a year ago, James objected. "I don' hold with makin' no pet out'en ah pig. It ah farm animal pure an' simple."

But by the time Jimmy D. and Kara Sue had raised it to a shoat eating on its own, they were attached to it. James had no heart for further protest over the small black and white sow.

All along Polly had been in favor of them keeping the pig. "After all they did fin' her, an' raised her." Defending Bakon's right to become a pet, and allowing her to follow the children around, wherever they went on the place.

From the porch they tossed the food, watching as, Tater and Bakon quickly and happily consumed their meal. Ending the meal. Beginning the adventure.

Polly and Kara Sue boarded the wagon, Bakon followed, taking a spot underneath between the rear wheels. There she stood swinging her corkscrew tail, waiting for the wagon to move. Bakon had long since learned to take full advantage of shade provided by the wagon, when following Jimmy D. into the fields last summer. Although, the sun was not yet up, it probably would be another thirty minutes before it would successfully burn away the slow retreating fog. Everyone including the pig knew that, the late October Georgia sun would soon heat up. Not unbearable, but uncomfortable, when subjected to it for extended periods. Traveling would place them in just that situation, and they were sure that the discomfort would increase as they proceeded farther south.

James, Luke and Jimmy D. mounted. Their horses snorting clearing their nostrils, stamping the bare ground, anxious to be moving.

"Well I reckon it's time."

"I reckon it be thet," Luke answered his brother.

"Whip 'em up, Polly!" James yelled toward the wagon, both driver and passenger concealed by the faded tarp covering.

"Ya hiya! Get on there! Pull Rhyme, pull Reason, yo' too Moses an' Plug." Polly commanded loudly, calling out the names of the four mules.

Slapping the reins lightly produced a popping sound over the animals. Slowly they started moving, easing back on the left set of the long leather reins, caused the mules to change direction toward the trail, that would lead them to another, pointing south and many more after that. Miz Penny walked beside the slow moving creaking wagon for a short distance, holding onto Kara Sue's outstretched hand, then stepped clear of the wheels.

"God be with y'all," she called, with a farewell wave, as the loaded wagon pulled slowly away.

"Pull yo' stump heads or I'll see yo' to tha glue factory when we get ta Florida."

"Thet Polly, she comin' ta be ah regular mule skinner ain't she?" Miz Penny standing next to her husband bobbed her head. Together they watched the wagon make a last turn onto the hard clay road.

Kara Sue took a couple of small pebbles from a tin pail on the floor, tossing them at the tail end of the nearest mule. The small projectile hit its target, the rump of the brown mule Moses. The second, she tossed hitting the lead mule named Plug on the rump. Rhyme and Reason twin grays, were next, feeling the lightly tossed pebbles.

"I knows y'all kin pull when y'all ah mind to," Kara Sue yelled in her deepest little girl voice possible, after tossing the last stone, causing the reluctant animals to increase their pace a little.

Waiting until the wagon was on the main road, the three mounted men made their way toward the cow pen. Jimmy D. opened the gate wide. "Move'm outta there, Tater!" James commanded the dog. The first step, many would follow.

The mixed breed yellow cur began barking and nipping at the slack cows at the rear of the pen. At first the cows refused any suggestions from the dog to leave the pen, instead, preferred staying where they were chewing hay. But Tater was the more determined, seemingly enjoying his responsibility, and knowing it well. Seeing the cows' opposition, he changed tactics, ceased barking, and eased his way around the obstinate cows. In a low a crouch, as if not wanting to be seen, made his way to the very front of the small herd where he spied Bo. Bo was short for Bovine the giant muddy red steer, an

18

awesome looking beast. Creamy white ivory horns tipped in black, curved out from his head, spanning almost five feet in width. This, with his ringed nose, made Bo an inspiring frightening sight, but the massive animal was as gentle as a kitten. Tater continued his slow approach, coming in behind the big leader. A couple of low barks persuaded the steer to move toward the gate. The resounding tarnished copper bell, attached to the leather collar around his thick powerful neck, announced to the heifers, it was time to move.

Tater returned to the rear, where a couple of nips and barks hastened the departure from the pen. Jimmy D. urged his gelding Cherokee, alongside of Bo, and gently guided the gentle animal toward the trail, following the wagon. The cows followed, slowing once they had caught the steer. Little trouble was expected in keeping the small herd moving. They knew that wherever the four mules took the wagon, Bo could follow with the rest on his tail. The cows would supply more than enough milk for traveling, plus extra butter and buttermilk for trading. Except for Jimmy D. assuring that Bo would go the right way, when intersecting another trail, Tater could do the rest. The mounted men headed south following the ruts of the wagon leading away from the house.

They rode slowly over where Will and Miz Penny stood. "Boys y'all wuz young, but yo' seen 'nough injin fightin' ta know. Y'all gotta pro-tect them girls at all cost. God be with y'all."

"Yo' c'n count on it, brother." They stopped long enough to shake Will's hand and quietly saluted Miz Penny by touching their hats, a final farewell. Standing together watching until all had disappeared; even the road south appeared to have ended. Only the sound of the bawling cows reaching them through the thick cool, morning mist. With a slight trembling hand, Miz Penny cupped an ear, thinking she had heard a faint clinking of the steers copper bell. Coming back? No, of course not. A ruse designed in her own mind, enough to prevent her turning her back on her departing family for another moment. Then realizing it a fraud, the devils work, she turned for the house, unwilling to wait until her bedtime to pray, she would do it now. And still unwilling to share her feeling with Will, yet by her side. An absolute dreadful feeling. A feeling she would not ever see her loved ones again. Only God could relieve her heart and mind. Plagued with his own similar secret feelings, Will, in his own way would attempt to gain God's ear. Surely God would take notice of a broken hearted sinner on his knees in a barn in Augusta County Georgia.

Riding some distance behind, James and Luke stayed within sight of the wagon, sound of the bell, and bawling disagreeable cows. It was necessary that the beeves be allowed to move along slowly.

"No sense burnin' all tha fat off 'em. Movin' this slow, they c'n grab ah mouth full ah grass by tha trail."

"Thet outta keep 'em satisfied till we bed 'em down tonight," Luke added.

Tater would prevent them straying, should they see grass that might appear more tasty.

The brothers agreed that, for the next three weeks at least, everything should be quiet. It would take that long following the old Coffee Trail to reach Valdosta and on to Troopville, allowing them valuable time for getting used to travel, especially the animals. For now there would be little to worry about, as the roads were easy traveling. After Troopville and especially in Florida it would be different.

"Luke, ain't lakly we gonna hit any kin' of river whut ain't bridged or easy ta ford long as we in Georgia least ways."

"Right as rain, brother. They several rivers ta cross near Valdosta, an' we knowin' tha army built bridges there."

The brothers intended to take full advantage of every opportunity for relaxing. As they suspected, things were basically uneventful, almost boring except for seeing workers at different farms they passed, along with occasional wagon's heading for market especially as they neared the developing town of Valdosta. One day pretty much like the rest, a hill lower or higher than the last, always-red clay. For two weeks they followed the same trail, as others ahead of them bound for the wilds of Florida, sometimes turning left, another time right, but always leading south. After progressing to within a day's travel of Troopville, James Luke and even Polly welcomed the tediousness so far.

Troopville, Georgia, a tiny community, boasting itself to be the jumping off point for Florida. Now however the flow of travelers had all but stopped. Stories of Indians, bandits, assassins, slayers of all sorts, discouraged such travel. Not to mention swamps and other natural obstacles to hinder or even take their lives. Always in the back of their minds, a major concern for the adults of the Nash family, watchfulness and fear would very soon replace their so far dry-as-dust travel.

But for now they continued on, passing many farms that appeared prosperous, some large some small, many were just like the one they had left behind. For the last five or six miles they had been passing large previously harvested fields, indicating they were near a plantation.

"Look, Momma, they's somebody coming yonder."

"I see them chil'. 'Pears ta be two people walkin'."

Drawing closer they identified them as two Negroes, a man tall and thin, and a stout woman with a small black-and-white spotted dog. Kara Sue was first to notice that the little dog sported a bandanna loosely tied around its neck. The same red and white cloth material as that tied under the round-faced woman's chin, securing her old straw hat. The two stopped moving off the roadway as the wagon approached, both greeting the travelers in the wagon politely, the old man removing his hat exposing a head of white hair. The large bosomed woman bobbed her head, thick lips forming a lame smile. Polly noticed the chunky woman's spotless white apron, at the front of her long black dress. Even though their clothes evidenced a great deal of wear they were very clean, and evidenced regular repair. Both lacked footwear, not uncommon for many residents of the south. White and black saved their shoes for winter.

"Mornin' ta yo', Mistiss ma'am an' li'l Miss." Continuing to hold his hat against his chest, flashing a genuine smile displaying a missing tooth.

"Mornin' ta y'all." Polly pulled back on the reins, the wagon rolled to a stop.

The woman quickly picked up her shorthaired dog, holding it in such a way so as not to soil her apron and dress.

The man spoke. "Yo pig got shet ah his line, Mistiss. He ain't tied or nothin', ma'am," observing Bakon under the wagon. "Yo' lak, I be proud ta tie him if yo' got ah line, ma'am."

"Naw suh, it don' require no line, it's my pet," Kara Sue explained with unexpected politeness. "An' he ain't aimin' to harm yo' li'l dog neither," she added, trying to ease the woman's fear over her dog being harmed.

"Thanke, li'l Miss." Still eyeing the grunting pig.

"Now ain't thet ah pure caution, ah pet pig," smiling wide once again. "By yo' leave, ma'am, we bes' be own our way, ma'am." His ragged hat still crumpled against his slender chest. "Good day ta yo', Mistiss an' li'l Miss."

"Good day ta yo' Uncle...Aunt," Polly bid them respectfully, the criterion way of addressing elderly colored folk in the south.

"C'n I throw ah biscuit ta yo' dog?"

"Li'l Miss, she be right proud, yo' wuz ta do thet," the woman answered, smiling wide showing rows of white teeth for the first time, returning the little dog to the ground.

Kara Sue watched the little shorthaired spotted dog snatch the biscuit up as soon as it hit the ground, it's nub of a tail rapidly vibrating.

"Thank yo', li'l Miss." He called back, both waving to Kara Sue in the rear of the wagon.

"Wonder where they goin', Mamma? They ain't got no grip or tha lak. Thet wuz ah right purty li'l dog they had."

"Cain' say chil'. 'Spect they live here 'bouts though," Polly answered as the wagon rolled once again.

As before, the couple stepped from the road allowing James, Luke, Jimmy D. and the cattle to pass. Again the tall lean Negro exhibited respect by removing his hat before speaking. "Mornin' ta yo', Massa suh, young Massa."

"Mornin' Uncle." James stopped his horse, respectfully returning his greeting.

"We from Whittfield Plantation Massa suh." The old man volunteered. "Dis here's my woman, an' we be on our way ta Massa John Rolling place down de road here." Further explaining without being petitioned. "It bein' Sunday an' all, we gets ta he'p out fo' wages fo' Massa Rolling. 'Spect y'all pass his place ways back." Continuing his explanation. "We's got us ah note if'n yo' care ta see it Massa suh." Lightly patting the breast pocket of his tattered coat, indicating the location of the important document.

James removed his hat, wiped his shaggy brown hair and stubbled face with a cloth, before speaking. "We passed his place right 'nough, Uncle, but ain't no need ta see yo' note. We be bound fo' Troopville. Y'all know how far it is?"

"Sho' do, Massa suh." Answering Luke's inquiry. "It mayhap twenty mile straight down dis ol' road suh. Y'all be thar by dark suh. It ah real 'spectful town too, got three churches. One fo' colored folks too," he added with pride.

The chubby woman picked up her little dog after seeing Tater behind the cows.

"Our dog ain't gonna harm yo's Aunt, he ain't mean," Jimmy D. assured the woman.

"Thank'e, young Massa suh." Still reluctant to return the short tailed dog to the ground just yet.

"Oh Uncle, we got ah ol' heifer whut is troublesome keeping up. Yo' would be doin' us ah great kindness yo' wuz ta take her off our hands. No cause fo' leaving her fo' bears an' wolves an' tha lak," James said.

The man looked at his wife in a puzzled fashion before answering, "Yeah suh, Massa, be proud. Massa John back at tha place, be ah kin' man. Let us keep ah good cow fo' butter an' tha lak. Be thankin' yo', Massa," he said.

22

"No cause, Uncle. She's ol', but will serve yo' well."

"'Spec' we's bes' be on our way Massa suh," almost apologetically. "We's gots lot's ah work ta do fo' Massa Rolling. Lawd willin' suh," he said, untying the cow.

"Why sho' Uncle y'all go on. We bes' be movin' too."

Replacing his hat and gripping the tired heifer's rope, he gave his farewell. Jimmy D. watched them for a minute, thinking that was the first time he had ever heard a Negro speak. He continued watching as they walked away leading the aging milk-cow with the little dog following.

"Well come on, boy, we gotta catch up some."

"Yeah suh." Calling Tater, encouraging the dog to move the cows toward Troopville.

Short the slow heifer their progress seemed to increase, and in no time at all the travelers were passing the large open fields of the Whittfield Plantation, where the old Negro called home. A dozen Negro men and women along with a few children could be seen in an already picked cotton field. They appeared to be scrounging the field for any remaining cotton. The travelers could tell from the road that the pickings were scanty. But perhaps enough of the white balls could be salvaged, snatched from the plow only days away, to sew a small blanket or coat for a child, or store away until more could be had.

Riding ahead Luke reach a road junction and a sign indicating the Troopville road leading northeast, the other veering west, no doubt for Tallahassee yet the sign failed to indicate such. Guiding his horse following the direction of the sign, he rode another few miles before stopping and dismounting beside a small clear stream. Both rider and animal drank freely before allowing Red a taste of the tall dark green grass, once again mounting and riding back toward the others.

The sun yet an hour from setting by the time Luke returned with his family to the exact spot he had just left, and with supper behind them and the stock taken care of, there was still ample time for relaxing before turning in for the night.

"Good spot, Luke," James said, as he sat hatless by the fire. "How far yo' calculate ta Troopville?"

"My guess we ort ta make Troopville in ah couple ah hours tomarrer, been easy today, but lak yo' say this ah good camp, water, feed an' all."

Passing the cool evening they chatted while enjoying the music from Jimmy D's harp, with last pot of coffee ushering in the darkness. Sleep came easy that night under a clear sky.

Luke's judgment about the little town the night before proved correct. Within two hours under a still cloudless sky, they met their first resident of Troopville. The wagon with James riding next to it first passed a little shack just off the road. A lack of smoke coming from the stovepipe was an indication that the shack might be abandoned, but the place didn't appear overgrown. The next turn provided answers for any questions they may have conjured, concerning the shanty.

"Howdy pilgrims," The one-legged potbellied man called out, having stopped when he heard the wagon and team behind them. A black and tan flop-eared hound trailing him had been aware of the wagon, long before the man. But paid little mind, just turning his attention from them and sniffing the edge of the road.

"Mornin', suh." James returned the greeting, after the man using his one crutch, awkwardly turned himself to face them, taking care staying on the hard packed red clay.

Past middle age and wearing a threadbare blue military coat, a little to snug about his waist, recognized by James to be cavalry. His gray hair reached past his collar under his faded military hat. The coat and hat were clean, as was his white shirt underneath. His loose fitting trousers were not military however and appeared homemade.

"Troopville, how far, suh?" James noticed the dull yellow chevrons on the long sleeves of his coat. The neatly sewed triple stripes denoting a sergeant's rank.

"Yeah, suh, mayhap ah mile."

"Well then, Mista, yo' might jus' as well ride. Could be ah might faster."

"Lak my pa always said. It ain't prudential ta walk when yo' got ah in-vite ta ride, but as yo' c'n see I ain't much fo' climbin' these days." The one-legged man slapped his homemade crutch lightly.

"Don' fret, Mista, ain't gonna be no chore ah-tall. My brother Luke an' me c'n boost yo'."

"Names Dew, Homer Dew." After he was seated, next to Polly.

"Proud ta make yo' acquaintance Mista Dew. My wife Polly there and tha young'n is Kara Sue. I am James Nash, an' my brother Luke here."

With the quick introductions completed, the wagon was rolling once again. Homer Dew didn't bother calling his dog, there was no need, after sniffing at Bakon, the well-fed long eared dog followed behind the pig in the shade of the wagon.

"From tha looks ah all y'alls trappin's it 'pears y'all bound fo' Florida." Mister Dew made the statement, without expecting any ratification

"Right as rain Mista Dew, we from Augusta County Georgia," James answered, his horse close to the wagon, near Mr. Dew.

"My pa learned me not ta meddle in other folks doin's, but it will be real troublesome fo' me if'n I don' try." he stated, lifting his blue hat, showing the top portion of his thick gray hair, then replacing it, scratching and then smoothing his thick whiskers of the same color.

"How so Mista Dew." James glanced at Polly, seeing her puzzled look.

"It be ah hostile land, ain't fit fo' livin'," he answered without hesitation, as if anticipating the question. "Only injuns, gators an' snakes an' tha lak in them swamps," he added. "Truly hellish," he added as an afterthought.

"But they seems ta be lots ah folks still tryin'." Polly looked over at Mr. Dew

Deep in thought, his eyes on the rear of the nearest mule and not looking at anyone, like he was not even riding in their wagon. It appeared he didn't expect her attitude of defiance. And seemed to have suddenly sent him far off, deep in thought. It did, and he was, because she reminded him of someone else. Polly had provoked in him a past deeper than he had intended visiting, and she knew it. She wished she had not done so, after seeing his face. He, on the other hand, was convinced even more they should turn around, and not venture into Florida. He would at least try, presenting more facts, until someone squealed they had heard enough.

"True 'nough, ma'am. But it's ah barbarous and ferocious place' lak yo' ain't never seen." Then he added, "Jus' as many don' make it," his own mind confused over butting in, or preventing a great deal of grief, for kind people. "Tha lucky ones go back ta where they come from. Them thet ain't so lucky, don', an' gets buried sooner than ex-pected." His explanation again was quick in coming, but spoken slowly and surly, adding. "I know, I fet two injin wars there. Chasin' them varmits from one place ta 'nother. After thet under tha Bounty Grant, I claimed me one hundred and sixty acres ah faulty land," he said, then went on to explain where things went wrong, his turn of bad luck. Thet's how it happens. And he harbored no doubt it would befall them. He continued slowly.

"My dear wife took tha vapors," after an uncomfortably long pause he continued with a softness in his voice, "she died, four year ago next July. Lord res' her soul."

Once again taking on that far away look, a definite sadness in his voice that almost choked him, but he continued, "Ah place called Merritt Island, over on the east coast, Brevard County, it wuz. Ah split off from Muskeeter County. Ain't fit fer growin' nothin' but snakes, skeeters an' more gators then yo' c'n count. I seen tha skeeters so thick my las' spring there, they choked tha stock," he said, clutching hard at his throat with rough fingers from both hands, underscoring his point.

Both Polly and Kara Sue at first thought he might choke himself to death, after seeing his face turn red and his eyes swell. But then he released his neck as if it were only because of a lack of oxygen, and he continued on.

"Them pore animals sucked 'em right up they noses, an' throats, plugged up they breathin'," he took a breath himself. "Lost this ta ah rattler," he stated matter-of-factly, as if feeling his point about the mosquitoes had been well made, and hoped taken.

Then he patted his stump of a leg, missing just below the knee. No sadness though, it was something else, Polly couldn't be sure. But she didn't consider it to be fear. Attrition? Could be. As if regretting he had ever attempted to settle in such a godless land, especially taking his wife there.

Then he went on to Explain in detail about his leg, "Rattler got me in late afternoon on my way to tha privy. Ah champion rattler if I ever seen one too."

He continued with his tale of how his wife in a small mullet skiff, had rowed more than two miles across the Banana River, then walked another five through rough brush to Cape Canaveral for help, adding, "Makin' fo' tha light house at tha ocean."

"She fetched Capt'n Mills Olcott Burnham, him an' his boys maintained tha beacon. There yet, if tha injins ain't kilt 'im an' burnt tha light house, lock stock an' barrel."

Polly and Kara Sue were wide eyed now. Saying nothing, wanting him to continue. Homer Dew went on to explain how, his wife, Captain Burnham along with a son of Burnham's rode back to the river on mules. And in a larger boat under sail made their way back across the Banana River to where he was laid up in their shanty on the Island.

Further explaining, "When they come in tha cabin it scairt me bad. Thought I wuz ah goner, an' they wuz ghost whut come ta present me ta tha devil hisself. Them white flour sacks over they heads, an'eye holes cut in. Fever an' all I reckon," he added, shaking his head as if it had all happened yesterday.

"Lordie Mista. Dew! Whut ever they got sacks over they heads fo'?"

"Skeeters litt'l lady! Skeeters," answering Kara Sue's question. "My po' wife wuz eat up real bad gettin' over. Face all swoll red an' all," describing his wife appearance.

"Capt'n, tol' me later, he ain't knowed how she crossed thet river after dark, it so thick with gators an' all. An' thet skiff so small, an' tha skeeters eatin' on her lak they wuz. Said when she got ta him she wuz ah fearful sight, had her long hair all pulled down over her face ta keep tha skeeters off, clothes ragged. Some ah her undergarments she tore off and wrapped 'roun' her neck an' hands." He explained, the sadness returning to his voice again as he described his wife's dreadful ordeal and appearance.

Her body quivered a little, and she felt her daughters doing the same, when she hugged her. Still saying nothing, allowing Mr. Dew to continue.

"But nary ah whimper. Little bit of ah woman she wuz, heart bigger'n thet animal," Homer said, pointing at the nearest mule, he shook his head slowly, back and forth several times. "Don' reckon she ever actual got over it all, it all run her down dreadful. Capt'n Burnham calculated it ain't actual the swamp whut cause tha vapors, he figurin' skeeters whut doin' tha injury." It was apparent he was unable to prevent that far away look of attrition masking his bearded face.

Listening intently to the story, Polly could not help but admire the courage and determination of Mr. Dew's wife. Could she, herself have been so heroic? Yes, for someone in her family, or maybe anyone else's. She hoped she would try anyway; she would be compelled to do so. Then, as if under some extreme moral compulsion, asked.

"Her name? Martha Jean…used ta be ah Tucker," he added as if that bit of information might mean something to Polly. "Anyways after thet I sold my place ta ah man name ah Charles Griffis, from Clinch County Georgia. Had ah wife an' three half growed up boys. Kindly folk, stayed with'm till I could catch ah supply schooner from tha lighthouse back ta Jacksonville, then home. Miz Griffis looked after me till then, an' pledged ta look after Martha Jeans grave. Flowers an' all if she wuz able ta grow any. Soil so po' ain't lakly Martha Jean ever gonna get them flowers," his face showing an expression of sadness now. Seeing Polly's own unsettled expression from his story, the old soldier looked away, damp eyes, wishing maybe he had followed his fathers advice, but it was too late for that.

"Mamma, we still goin' to Florida?" A quick shiver jerked her small body.

"'Course we are, girl. Mista Dew wuz at a different place then where we goin'," James answered the question for Polly, having heard the whole story.

"Thet's right, littl' lady, some folks do jus' fin'." Now Mister Dew felt resentful at himself, his talking so much for their sake as well as his own. He gave her a friendly pat on her knee.

"Reckon I jus' talk out ah turn too much. Ah moral de-ficiency I'm plagued with, I reckon. Jus' too ornery ta be 'round decent folk, ain't got no body but thet no 'count dog," he lamented.

"Don' fret, Mista. Dew, yo' wuz only tryin' ta let us know whut we facin, so's we don' fin' ourselves out on ah limb when we get there," James said, refusing to be hard on the one-legged former soldier.

"Welcome to Troopville," the weathered rough wood sign, invited. Welcome was not exactly what she was feeling, as she pondered Mr. Dew's story over in her mind, sad, yet; fascinated. But this instance fearful too, for once past this town, who knows. They stopped in front of the general store as Homer had requested.

"How far ta Florida, Mista Dew?"

"Yo' c'n be out ah Georgia by dark, Luke," he answered as they helped him down. "Want notice much difference in tha land though, but yo' know yo' there. Come to ah ol' rail spur whut use' ta run between Jacksonville an' Tallahassee. Haulin' timber an' turpentine an' tha lak, ain't in use now though, injins burned out tha bridges," he explained.

James spoke after mounting. "Mista Dew, we be thankin' yo' fo' tha information. Got ta keep movin though."

"Obliged fo' tha ride Mista Nash, Miz Nash Miss." He touched the stiff black leather bill of his cap. "Pay min'." He waved to Jimmy D. and Luke, who had returned to the cows, as they rode by. Then called out to Luke. "Mista Nash, lak I say, yo' pay min' 'bout them swamps an' all. Vapors be ah fearsome plague, ain't no known cure. I be knowin'," he cautioned again, feeling compelled to give one final warning, before watching them leave. He stood supporting himself on his crutch, waving his hat.

"Will pay min, Mista Dew. Obliged."

They left Troopville behind adding another five hours of travel since leaving the town, with dusk fast approaching. And Luke still had not found the rail track that Homer Dew had mentioned, indicating Florida. James decided they should make camp. From here on out he knew that mind, body and soul would be tested greatly, and he had to be ready, and be assured the others were too. Doubting himself would have been easy had he allowed it, especially when looking at his wife and young daughter. How badly had he placed them in harms way? What torment or worse might he have subjected them to?

"Stop thinking on such things," almost saying out loud.

"Reckon them tracks ah might further than Mista Dew figered."

"Reckon so, James. But I'm guessing they ain't far."

As the nights before, this one passed quietly, they talked on other things though, mostly the past. As if by not talking on the future, they could deal with it easier. By not speaking of bad things they might prevent them. The fire was comforting it would be their last for a while, and when it died they turned in. Polly at first was restless, with thoughts of Homer Dew plaguing her delaying her opportunity for sleep right away. All that time, wishing they had never met Mr. Dew, and hearing those awful things. But then just before sleep, feeling his pain, understanding why he had returned to Georgia his old home. What sadness he must have felt leaving his wife in a grave, in a place that had driven him away. A beaten man? A coward? A battered man he appeared to be, Polly decided, but Homer Dew was no coward, he had done his share of trying to build good place to live for himself and others with the courage to follow.

It was an unlucky bite from a rattlesnake that killed his loving wife. No the snake's fangs hadn't penetrated her flesh snuffing out her life, as it did his missing leg, just the same, its venom killed their dreams. Plus the blood-sucking insects in dreadful numbers, and the revolting charge by Captain Burhnam, that it was the mosquitoes that carried sure death called swamp vapors. She understood his retreating from such a place. When dreams die, it's hard to live. She moved closer to James and fell asleep. Not soundly however.

CHAPTER TWO

Not bothering to eat a cold meal, Luke instead packed some smoked mullet in his war bag and rode out before daybreak, expecting to run onto the track by full sunup. Occasionally in the dim morning light he saw sign indicating someone had crossed the path he followed. Hunters'? Could be bandits, or renegade Indians. However he went on, confident he was on the old military route, even though the overgrowth witnessed a lack of routine travel. Determined to continue until reaching the abandoned tracks before turning back, he walked his horse another thirty minutes, and before being aware, suddenly he was there. Dismounting on the slightly elevated bed he studied the landscape and realized the rails, having long battled nature, still resolved to serve. Now as an agency, a guide, performing its duty as an invisible wall, segregating a savage untamed land from it's opposite to the north. Posting notice to the foolhardy, that perhaps they should not cross into this savage place called Florida.

As Mr. Dew had mentioned, the forest changed little, oak, pine, and black jacks dominated the higher terrain. Raking his boot across one of the rust coated twin rails, as if determining if they were actually real; he suddenly resisted the tendency to duck. For no reason other than realizing he was there. In Florida, and it abruptly made him a bit jittery, a feeling that eyes were watching him. Silly, he looked at his hands for signs of shaking, but they were not. Even if he had been seen, then it would be too late for hiding, however ducking a little lower, yet able to observe about, wouldn't do any harm. Caution. Once again on Red, he backtracked toward a shallow stream he had crossed earlier. It was thick with cypress and cedar in addition to the great quantity of tender grass for the stock. Knowing well that James would be there by now for the noon meal, having followed his tracks and discovered the tree, with it's bark cut. The distinctive three marks, signaling he had passed through and would return to that location. They intended making a meal of the extra bacon Polly had fried from the last fire they had enjoyed and sweet potatoes.

"Papa, I seen ah horse-backer 'cross thet field."

"Where, boy?" reaching for his long gun.

"Yonder," his own rifle in hand Jimmy D. pointed in the direction of the rider on the far side of a palmetto thicket.

"It's Luke," James declared, holding his hat up shielding his eyes from the noon sun. "Thankin' injun mus' ah got 'em, 'xpected him back befo' this," he teased.

"James Nash yo' hush thet kin' ah talk," Polly chastised him.

"Jus' funnin' Polly, jus' funnin'."

Luke cantered Red across the field through narrow openings in the high thick palmettos into camp and dismounted, still holding his mount.

"Be obliged fo' ah cup ah cold water, Polly," removing his wide brimmed hat, before taking the cup. "Obliged." His disarranged sweaty hair appearing darker than the almost blond stubble covering his unshaven deeply tanned face, effecting a deeper shade of blue to his eyes.

"Anything interestin' up ahead, lak ah rail line?" James asked.

"Yeah suh, run on'm jus' lak Mista Dew said, they ain't been used fo' ah spell. Seen some sign thet we ain't tha only ones about, cain' tell who or whut though, don' 'pear ta be injuns, far as I kin tell," he explained.

"Yeah we seen some too, I 'spect we in Florida," James said matter-of-factly.

"Jimmy D. I'd be obliged if yo' walk Red ah cool 'em down give him ah handful ah oats, an' water 'em. Don' let him drink too much, danger ah founderin' been riddin' him real hard an' all," he said, handing the reins to his nephew, then watched Jimmy D. lead his already unsaddled horse away, Kara Sue walking next to him, drying his flank with moss.

"James we got ta be on tha alert from now on out," Luke warned, after Kara Sue was farther away.

"Got any special reason fo' sayin' thet, Luke?" James asked, looking over at Polly.

"Well it's them pony sign I seen, they shod right 'nough. But I ain't smelled no smoke, 'speciall it mornin'. Don' allow they homesteaders here abouts, not ta be cookin' breakfast an' all this mornin'," Luke explained.

"Sounds right, Luke, mayhap we ain't got much, but our goods 'n stock be worth alot ta bandits," James said, drinking the cold water from his cup. "An' more then thet we got tha girls ta think on," he added, glancing over at Polly.

31

"We ain't ah half day from thet rail line an' 'nother full day to the Santa Fee River, whut runs east to south off tha Suwannee," Luke explained, turning and looking toward the north as if looking for something. Then added, "Word is them marauders wuz operatin' this far east, out 'en ah place they call Hell Swamp between tha Aucillia River ta our west an' tha St.Johns ta our east.

"Thet's ah considerable area," James added, expecting his brother to understand his meaning.

He did. "Yeah big bunch ta cover so much territory."

Luke knew what was expected of him, waiting only long enough to consume a cold, cooked sweet potato, and Reds cooling down.

"Yo' pay mind, Luke Nash," Polly said, as she handed him a handful of cold corn-doggers for his pocket.

"Will do thet Polly girl. An' y'all do tha same," he answered, lightly nudging the sides of his horse with his heals, he rode off.

Cantering Red toward a trail through the trees on the far side of the wide palmetto field. Polly continued watching until he had reached the trees, flushing a large covey of bobwhite quail ahead oh his galloping mount. The wings of the small brown birds reflected the light from the noonday sun, as they scattered in a multitude of directions seeking safety.

"Well I guess we bes' get ta movin' ourselves," James said.

Tater's barking and the ringing bell alerted the girls the cows were moving. Not bothering to look back but thinking only of dangers ahead, Polly guided the team south following Luke, at first the brush closed in close on the trail, barely allowing room for the wagon. Experiencing a hint of anxiety she touched the cold gray steel of her double-barreled shotgun once the mules were settled. Glancing at her young daughter, she took some comfort in the fact that the gun was in reach. Added consolation in remembering that the men were well armed, even Jimmy D. Each carrying a forty-four revolver, the latest and best Sam Colt offered, in addition to saddle guns.

Before mounting James tightened the cinch strap of the saddle on his dun colored mare, as he passed instruction to Jimmy D. as the boy rode slowly by him. "If trouble comes yo' leave the cows an' go ta tha wagon, we got ta protect yo' mamma an' sister above all else. Boy, yo' hear me good?"

"Yeah, suh, I hear Papa," the boy answered. Reckon them wuz bandit or mayhap Indian tracks Uncle Luke seen, papa?" The boy exhibited confidence even in the face of possible danger from brigands or Indians.

Almost smiling but held it, instead answering and advising. "Don' know,

son, ain't no way ah knowin' such. Jus' be alert, an' 'member whut I said."
Suddenly he felt a great pride in his son.

"Yeah, suh."

Riding slowly, they erged the cows closer to the wagon as it cleared the
palmettos and entered the forest of pine trees. Following the deep shapeless
tracks left in the white sugar sand from Luke' horse, in the now not so
confined wider trail. Soon weary of riding on the hard board seat, Kara Sue
entertained herself by imitating the whistle of the bobwhite quail. The same
covey Luke had scattered earlier, were calling to each other attempting to
regroup. Back in Georgia, Jimmy D. had taught her to answer their calls.

"Mamma, kin I walk with Bakon fo' ah spell?" After unpuckering from
another whistle and slightly irritated at not receiving an answer in return.

At first Polly was reluctant to grant her permission as she quickly glanced
around, not really expecting to see anything. The thought of her daughter not
being right by her side at first frightened her. But she recanted knowing James
could see her, and allowed the girl her wish, with a warning.

"Stay inside tha wheel ruts, yo' hear me?" she cautioned

"Yes, ma'am," she answered, making her way to the rear of the wagon,
passing the wooden keg and taking a handful of hard tack biscuits and putting
them in the pocket of her apron.

Effortlessly she dropped to the soft ground from the slow rolling wagon.
Bakon oinked her pleasure at seeing Kara Sue, especially after getting a whiff
of the unseen biscuits tucked away in her pocket.

"Here, Bakon, have ah snack," she said, holding one of the hard biscuits
in the palm of her small hand, pushing it toward the grunting pig. Quickly
Bakon sucked up the unexpected treat, swallowing it without chewing,
voicing her great pleasure with a deep snort, at the second and third. The last
two-she tossed to the side of the trail, knowing Tater would discover them.
She knew that he had after hearing his bark, bringing a smile to her face.
Skipping along following the wagon between the ruts, as her mother had
instructed, stopping and scratching Bakon's ear on occasion, also enjoying
one of her favorite recreations of late, searching for doodlebugs. Because of
the mule tracks most of the small cone shaped indentation in the sand were
few and far between.

Eventually she did spy one, not between the wagon tracks yet not far off
the trail. Picking up a tiny short stick after dropping to her knees, she stuck the
end of the stick into the sand at the edge of the small impression, home of the
tiny bug. Moving the stick slowly around and around, quietly singing,

"Doodlebug doodlebug, yo' better come out; yo' house is on fire, so yo' better come out."

Continuing to move the twig around the rim of the small hole, until the wee bug showed itself. With her small fingers she gingerly picked the tiny gray harmless bug from the sand, after inspecting it, she returned it unhurt to its sandy home. Seeing the wagon had gotten ahead, she ran to catch up with Bakon by her side. Having captured a doodlebug, she would ride now, easing her mother's mind.

After four hours traveling just as Luke had said, Polly caught her first glimpse of the Santa Fee River, to her, more a stream. And there was still sufficient light for enjoying its natural beauty. The water was clear and cold and very swift, yet inviting.

"Kara Sue! Fetch tha dipper from tha keg les' give it ah try," she called as the girl jumped from the wagon.

"Yes'm," she said, quickly walking for the waters edge, the long handled metal dipper in hand, dipping it full she passed it, watching as her mother swallow the cool refreshing liquid.

"Thet's real good, spring water," she declared, handing the dipper back. Kara Sue dipped her own.

Jimmy D. and James came up ahead of the bawling cows, drinking their fill before bringing the animals over, further down stream. James instructed Jimmy D. to leave the mules hitched until he returned. He intended locating the tree he was sure Luke had marked as he passed through. He quickly found it and returned just as the sun was disappearing behind the tall oak and hickory trees.

"We'll stay on this side of tha Santa Fee tonight, it don' look lak much trouble fo' crossin' here. But it ain't prudential ta cross so close ta dark," James said, then added. "'Sides Luke may have a better crossing."

Along with the dusk came a slight chill in the air, with a hint of rain. November nights could get cold and they would be more comfortable with a small fire, but the comfort would not be worth the gamble.

"Bes' we camp close ta tha water leave some open ground between us an' thet tree line," James said, as if reading Polly's mind.

"Yeah, I know it's bes'," she agreed, bringing out a sack of jerky and another of smoked fish, for their meal.

"Yo seem ah bit on edge." James saw a look of concern on Polly's face.

"It's jus' thet I'm fearful 'bout Luke. He shoulda been here by now, he said sundown."

"He'll be along directly," James assured her. "Mayhap by tha time tha young'ns take care ah tha stock," he added, this time reassuring him-self more so than Polly.

Jimmy D. along with Kara Sue hobbled the mules for grazing after giving them a ration of corn, and the horses were secured to a picket line closer to the wagon after their ration. Polly could hardly keep her mind on her work, for wishing to see Luke ride in. Her movements were all mechanical with as little thinking as possible. James and Jimmy D. strung a canvas cover between some trees next to the wagon; it would allow them some protection against the drizzling rain that was now falling. With the cooler air moving in with the rain, it would be best to stay as dry as possible. The wagon lacked enough space for them all to sleep underneath, and James knew that if it rained hard, even Tater and Bakon would soon be under the wagon.

The cows wouldn't stray with the green grass they were now enjoying, besides they were pretty tired and Tater would hear them moving. The evening seemed almost bearable even with the cold rain, but after another hour had passed Luke still had not returned.

"James, somethin's wrong." Polly spoke in as normal a voice as she could muster fearing upsetting the youngsters, yet; it wasn't enough to cloak her concern from James.

"Yeah', seems ta be," James agreed.

After Kara Sue was out of earshot, she had taken a smoked ham hock to Tater who continued watching the cows. And as always a few biscuits for Bakon to supplement the grubs she had been rooting for all evening.

"Ain't no sense in searchin' in darkness, 'sides won't be no tracks with this rain, cain't see 'em even if they wuz," James lamented. "We got ta believe he's alright though. Luke's mighty good out there, it would take ah mighty good man ta get up on 'im. Do 'im harm." James delayed the last few words of his statement not wanting to think on it, but still trying to placate Polly at the same time. "But, jus' tha same we got ta take precautions. Me an' Jimmy D. kin spell each other, stay awake tonight," he said.

"Yo' jus' add me inta thet too James Nash," Polly levied herself for sentinel duty, with her husband and son. "Me an' my scatter gun kin guard too, jus' as well," she added.

James decided it prudent to reconnoiter their back trail for a while, at least an hour or two, after pondering the situation in his mind. But undecided if he should go, or stay and send Jimmy D. After thinking hard on it, he concluded that he should remain, and he instructed Jimmy D. to backtrack their trail maybe a half-mile. To dark for seeing the concern on Polly's face, only feeling her anxiety, mostly her lack of protest. He spoke to her.

"Ain't nothin' else ta be done, girl," he declared. "We got ta consider we been discovered."

It was a most arduous decision, a father sending his son into possible harm's way, and he felt Polly's distress, yet knowing there was nothing he could say to erase it, but also believing she trusted his judgement fully. At any rate he attempted to refine his decision for her, even at the risk of increasing her anxiety.

"Polly, Luke could be in troubl, mayhap worse," he disliked saying it as much as he knew Polly would hated hearing it. He almost couldn't finish the statement, and chose his words.

"Lord knows, it's jus' thet," she turned away from him.

She didn't complete what was on her mind as she watched her young son saddle his pony, and hearing James reminded him, his instructions. Of making no effort for challenging anyone, but to warn the camp, and stay off the trail, only close enough to observe and hear what might be moving about. Ringing her hands, she almost wanted to scream, feeling such fear for her son.

"Yo be mindful boy if'n trouble comes, it likely to come from yo' direction, knowin' we on this trail. If anythang movin' out there on ah night lak this, it sho' ta be calamity. I'll spell yo' in ah couple hours or soon as Luke shows," he said, endeavoring to ease the mind of the boy. Wanting him to concentrate on the task at hand, not on his uncle.

"Anythang move down thet trail other than animal, yo' fire one shot with yo' revolver, then break fo' here. But not on tha trail boy," emphasizing the point strongly, just in case he had not mentioned it before. Unmindful that he had, and was repeating himself. Had he caught himself doing so, he would have taken steps to better cover his anxiety. God only knows what those steps might have been.

He resumed his final instruction, "Thet will be plenty ah warning fo' us. It's ah painful thang ta say boy, but they's more at stake here than Luke. Hear me, boy?"

He had heard, and required no further explanation. Standing closer James saw his own determination reflecting from the eyes of his son, the same blue as his own staring toward his mother, as she clutched his little sister to her breast. Even thought the darkness prevented her seeing Jimmy D's eyes, Polly understood maybe for the first time, the depth of love, her son held for the rest of the family. She felt proud, but said nothing. She was afraid to say anything, otherwise she would cry openly, instead of within.

He spoke, "I hear clear papa. Fire ah shot n' circle back here quick."

Jimmy D. mounted and adjusted himself in the saddle, more from nerves than discomfort in his seating. Adjusting the collar of the black rubber slicker to his neck, he touched the dripping brim of his hat toward his mother, slowly wheeling his horse, walking the sorrel pony north, disappearing in the dark and rain. Turning a last time in his saddle, but it was too dark, and they failed to see his wave or his nervous smile. Glumly they stood together under the canvas cover, watching until horse and rider was completely absorbed by the black curtain of the night.

Polly shivered, not from the cold damp night air, or even the dreadful call of a nearby wolf, but the imbedded memory of her son being devoured by the night, as an alligator would snap up a careless animal drinking from the stream on an equal night. For the sake of her daughter she blamed her shaking on the cold, all the while wishing James would squeeze her hand tighter, feeling somehow it would prevent her shaking.

"Come girl les' get yo' under ah blanket, this dampness'll pain yo' bones."

She wished her son and Luke back in camp, warm, dry and safe. She wanted to cry but didn't dare, only to herself, deep within. She petitioned God to return them, as she held her shivering daughter snuggly to her bosom. Sheltering her from the unseen perils behind the curtain that isolated her son from the rest. Angry with herself for allowing him to go, but not at James. Decisions had to be made if they were to survive and reach their destination and live once there. She felt unable to make them, but she could carry them out.

Moving from the shelter and standing in the rain, James stared at the spot where he had lost his son to the darkness, feeling he should go after him and bring him back, thinking their must be something he had neglected to tell him. So many things a boy should know, there had to be something, maybe like keeping his horse quiet, anything. "No sense in frettin', tha boy is dependable. He'll do," James thought. Convincing himself there was no alternative.

Pulling the wide brim down a little lower, making an effort to shield his face from the now steady rain, Jimmy D. realized for the first time that his hands were shaking, he had heard the wolf too. On the trail previous weeks past he had heard wolves, and had been fascinated by their dejected wailing, now it seemed different. Spooky. When he listened for other sounds, he heard the rain falling on his stiff slicker, and the top of his leather hat, but nothing on the trail. Taking a deep breath he tried steadying his nerves, telling himself it was merely a chill, and that he would warm soon under his coat and slicker. Through the wet blackness and brush he made his way to the long curve in the trail, the location that his father had described earlier. Close to the trail and shielded in a clump of blackjack oak and high thick palmettos he reined his slow walking pony to a stop.

Visibility was nearly impossible, he would have to depend on his hearing for now, hoping that he would be able to hear larger forms moving on the trail that he could not see. And right now he was hearing all manners of night sounds, the continuing rain beating the palmetto fronds surrounding him and the dead leaves falling from the oaks carpeting the ground. A dead limb or pinecone dropping from a nearby tree startled him. Desperately making an effort to sort out each and every noise, and realizing the safety of the family depended on him staying calm. He wished all noises would stop, especially the tree frogs, their chirping drowned out other noises. Between his wishing over noise and being plagued with doubt, it allowed him time to became lost in thought, drifting away in darkness like the cry from the wolf. At first he wanted to think on the wolf, instead fought it, along with his apprehension over Luke. No later perhaps, he was losing sight of his mission. Now he must concentrate on the sounds closing in all about him, excluding the ones he had been hearing, the pesky frogs, and consider new ones.

It had been less than thirty minutes but to Jimmy D. it seemed forever when totally unexpected, he was almost jolted from the saddle. A hideous scream sharp and piercing echoed through the darkness. The turbulent scream bore into his ears, his brain and shocking his very bones, making him instantly colder than he was.

"My God! Mamma!! Kara Sue! Has to be them. Who else?" he thought.

There couldn't be other women around, not in this wilderness. But it seemed closer, maybe even another direction, actually having no idea where it came from, or how close or far. He had to admit that much. He battled the fear and confusion being forged in his brain from the horrifying scream. A woman's scream that made his skin crawl, and the hair on the back of his neck stand straight. In all the confusion, there was one thing he had no doubt, no one could have gotten to his mother or sister while his father lived. His own fear transferred to his pony, and it pawed the wet ground, perking its ears to better hear. He leaned over the animal's neck softly rubbing its nose and speaking quietly, an act of calming himself as much as his horse. Should he fire a shot and make his way back to his family? No, What good would that do now? Deciding that he would hold where he was for now. If his father was already dead, and he feared that was the case he had to help his mother and sister, if it were not already too late for that. But they or one of them screamed that meant that, at least one was probably still alive. He had to think more clearly. Devise a plan. Determine who and how many he was up against. Suddenly now he seemed unafraid, at least for himself. What good was he if they were all dead?

The second scream sounded closer than the first, and like before, there was no chance of pinpointing the direction. And his state of mind would not allow him to consider it was not his mother or sister. He considered the chance of another woman, a captive maybe being tortured. "Very little chance he determined." Almost certainly the piercing screams had come from the direction of the camp. Shaking badly not from fear, but as a steel spring coiled ready to strike out, but holding his jittery pony in check at the same time. And weighing what evil doings could be taking place forcing such terrifying screams. He couldn't imagine, and he didn't want to think about it. But how could anyone or anything get into their camp and kill his father? There was Tater maybe it was to far to hear the dog barking, but he had heard no shots, he must return to camp or at least try. Afraid of what he might find even if he made it that far. A warning shot would not be necessary, actually ill advised, stealth was in order he somehow concluded. His mind dashed in every direction, adrenaline moving him now.

Drawing his pistol he urged his pony from the deep shadows of the trees, and onto the trail. Vigilantly he moved trying to concentrate once again on the noises about him, and hoping that he would not have to endure more terrorizing screams. His judgement told him that death would stop the screams, he almost wished it, his or the screamer. That thought added guilt.

Because of his anguish over the screams and the certainty of them coming from the camp, he failed to see the other horse. And rode fully into the path of the animal before realizing its presence. Total confusion erupted as the shadowy like figures collided. In his derangement he must have kicked his mount too sharply by accident, causing the sorrel pony to leap high in the air. In the darkness Jimmy D. failed to see a rider, only the ghostly figure of the other horse. The mysterious horse reared, making heinous sounds as it rammed into his pony. Everything appeared in slow motion as the panicked lad and his mount went down, slamming him hard onto the earth, knocking him almost senseless. Nearly blind because of his mud-covered face and rain, his already panicked mind raced for a plan to fight. Even more disadvantaged now because he had lost his pistol in the confusion. Unarmed he had a

39

sensation of watching the vexatious scene from above, outside his own body, leaving him almost helpless. Frightening cries from the horses mixed with other sounds, his screams perhaps. He didn't know, and it didn't matter. Forcing himself, he rolled over the ground feeling for his pistol. If it was for him to die this night, as it appeared his family already had, he would at least attempt to answer his death, and theirs with a fight of his own. Just as he was sure his father and uncle would have done if given half a chance. Knife stone fist and teeth.

Still searching for his own weapon he listened for the metallic click of the assassin's pistol, hammer striking the copper cap bringing a flash and deafening blast. Would he be able to brace himself against the lead ball that followed? Tearing its way into his flesh, crushing his bones as it ripped through. He didn't hear the exploding pistol, instead a voice coming from behind him. At first not understanding the words, too confusing to be sure.

"I said don't move or I will send yo' straight ta hell!" The mysterious voice repeated what had not been heard clearly before. Jimmy D's mind seemed to have allied against him, playing tricks?

Because of his plight he determined to become even more hostile than the blowing wind and cold rain in his face. "Lets finish it, your deadly game," he thought. Voices again. Now he thought that he had heard Luke's voice in the darkness. But how and where? He was too muddled. The bandits must have Luke for once again the heard the hidden voice. Luke? He would not be taken in. In the darkness, he continued to crawl searching about for his revolver, until he felt his heard jerk sideways, and the pain that followed the snapping of his head. He couldn't see the boot coming that landed square on his chin, knocking him once again on his back. He regained a portion of senses to the same voice, and someone vigorously slapping his face.

"Jimmy D! Jimmy D! Snap out of it, boy."

Uncle Luke's voice and plain too.

"Yo' alright, boy?"

"Uncle Luke? Whut happened? How did yo'?" the bewildered boy asked, rubbing his sore jaw.

"I kicked yo' in tha head."

"Yo' most kicked my head clean off," he lamented, moving his head around limbering his neck.

"Boy, whut yo' tryin' ta do, get yo self kilt?" Recognizable irritation in his voice, but quickly changed after seeing the boy rubbing his chin. "I ain't knowed it wuz yo' holt up in tha brush."

"I declare, Uncle Luke, I sho' thought I wuz ah goner," the boy said with great relief, after realizing it was his Uncle Luke and not an assassin.

"Yo' near wuz, boy, I 'most dropped tha hammer on my pistol, but kicked yo' instead," Luke explained.

"I'm sho' proud I ain't shot, but thet kick sho' is hurtful," still lightly massaging the side of his head, with muddy shaky fingers. Jimmy D. retrieved his pistol and holstered it without wiping it of mud, before getting to his feet.

"Jimmy D. whut wuz yo' doin' out here in tha dark? An whut cause yo' got coming' out lak yo' done? Not knowin' whut yo' wuz up against?"

"Los' my head I reckon, Uncle Luke, 'cause ah thet woman ah screamin'," he said, trying to justify his actions. "Yo' hear her, Uncle Luke?" Starting to quiver again at the thought of the piercing shriek. "Feared it ta be mamma or Kara Sue, an' whut might be happenin' ta them," he explained. "Bes' we hurry an check," he said reaching for the reins of his pony.

"Hol' on, boy," Luke said grabbing the anxious boys arm. "Firs' place it weren't yo mamma or no other woman ah screamin'.

"But it wuz, I tell yo', heard it plain."

"No." An almost stern voice.

"It weren't? Then whut wuz it?" the perplexed boy asked.

"It wuz one of them big cats, ah panther," Luke explained. "Follerin' tha scent ah them cows on tha trail, or lak as not yo' pig, got vexed on 'count of tha rain washin' tha smell away. Them big cats normal quiet hunters, but I reckon thet's whut all tha screamin' wuz over, losin' tha scent," Luke explained, as he mounted his horse.

"Them big cats mus' be awful mean, I allow I don' won't one of 'em on me," Jimmy D. said.

"Yo' right there, boy, they lak straight outta hell. Me an' yo' pa met ah man whut wuz caught by one of 'em . Said he right glad ta be 'live, even if he is short one arm an' one eye, an' all scared up," Jimmy D. didn't notice Luke shaking his head, at the memory of the man. "I declare he wont even get near ah barn cat now. Ah growed up man runnin' from ah small cat, an' screaming lak ah little girl." Luke shuddered picturing the disfigured victim. Remembering at a frolic in town once, when some drunken men, threw a small cat on the drunken man, and how he ran away screaming and crying. Pathetic.

Jimmy D. didn't want to picture such a thing, a big cat, or a one eyed one-armed man, running from a small barn cat, squalling like a girl. The rain had

41

stopped as they walked their horses on the trail toward camp, they talked quietly giving Jimmy D. a chance to collect himself.

He asked, "Uncle Luke, how is it yo' wuz ah foot when I come on tha trail an' run into Red? How yo' know ah body wuz in thet scrub? Pay mind ta yo' horse boy, it was Red whut tol' me," Luke answered, barley able to see the boys mud caked swollen face in the darkness.

"How?"

"Watch his ears, boy, when he lays 'em back or sticks 'em up yo' know he hears something, smells somethin' too,"

"I declare Cherokee wuz tryin' ta tell me, he wuz actin' real funny lak. I wuz jus' too scairt ta pay mind. Reckon papa's goin' ta be ah might vexed, 'bout the way I done. Ain't he Uncle Luke?"

"Ain't no need he be ah knowin' boy. 'Sides yo' learned yo' lesson 'bout what yo done wrong. Thet's tha whole of it," his uncle explained. "Yo' learned."

Now mounted the two rode slowly along the narrow trail, Luke described how he had quietly slid from the saddle when he heard Jimmy D.'s horse give a low whinny. And went on to explain how he was off the path in the brush when Jimmy D's frightened pony bolted into the path of his own horse.

"I declare I would've been a goner for sho'. I learned right 'nough, Uncle Luke," a detectable quiver yet in his voice. His hands still shaking, and he spoke in a voice slightly louder than necessary.

Luke could not bring himself to further admonish the boy, knowing that in a few minutes he would settle himself down. Besides they were approaching the camp. Tater emitted a low growl and looking in the direction of the approaching riders, well before they were visible. Recognition at first by smell, the vigilant dog vigorously began wagging his tail, and shot from concealment of the wagon and ran in their direction. Bakon realizing something was happening, but not quite sure what it was followed Tater.

"Two riders comin' in, got ta be Luke an Jimmy D." James said watching the two shadows approach and the excited animals running to greet them.

"Thank tha good Lord fo' thet," Polly said, with transparent relief in her voice.

She leaned her shotgun against the wagon, as did James his rifle. Standing close together, they waited for them to ride in, followed by Tater and Bakon.

"Near gave yo' up brother, but awful glad ta see yo'," James said, reaching out his hand.

"I figured yo ta be frettin' me bein' late an' all, but I wanted ta check our back trail after dark jus' in case," Luke explained. "Thets how me an' tha boy here run inta each other," he explained, grinning at Jimmy D. after they had dismounted. "Kara Sue fetch some oats fo' our animals," Luke requested, as the two unsaddled and began brushing their wet mounts with handsfull of moss.

"Wish we had some hot coffee, but water will have ta do," Polly said, first handing the dipper to her son, then froze, after getting a closer look at his muddy face and puffed jaw, as the moon broke free of the clouds. "Son! Whut happened ta yo' face, all dirty an' swollen? Yo' hurt!" Almost dropping the dipper after closer inspection in the dim light. Reaching out toward his face.

He turned his face away, "Naw I ain't hurt Mamma."

"Whut happened to yo'?" she asked a second time, attempting a better look at his face in the darkness.

"Tha boy jus' took ah tumble. Cherokee slipped in tha mud on tha trail, thet's all, don' fret Polly." Luke answered for him, knowing Jimmy D. would not have lied to his mother.

As far as Luke was concerned, a small lie covering his nephew's mortification wouldn't do any harm.

"Here, son, I'll do thet, yo' wash up," James said taking the balled up moss from Jimmy D.

James and Luke discussed the events or lack of events of the evening. Luke, of course, leaves out the details of his, and Jimmy D's encounter. James believing there was more to the story than what was being told said nothing, letting it drop. Knowing Luke had his reasons.

"Ya'll hungry?" Polly asked.

Both declined any food, feeling more tired and cold than hungry.

"Well I reckon we bes' try an' get some shut eye," James said. " I'll take firs' watch, Polly, I'll wake yo' in ah couple ah hours, yo' kin spell me then Luke next," James said, assigning the duties for the night guard until daylight.

Later after the others were asleep, James rested his back against a pine tree, near the trail, his rifle across his knees. Looking up at the sky somehow drawing peace from the few stars that fought their way through the mist, silently hoping that the remainder of the night would pass uneventful. And being sure that God had heard his silent thoughts of gratitude. The explanation Luke presented concerning Jimmy D's. swollen face crossed his mind, but he would never bring it up, still confident of his brothers reason. He continued his watchful duties and thinking on other things from the shadows until relived by Polly. So it went for the rest of the night, the whippoorwill's singing from the forest, just like in Georgia, but this seemed so far from Georgia. Polly thanked God they were at least together, if not totally safe.

How long would it be before they could feel safe? If ever. Daylight was slow in coming.

Luke rubbed a closed fist across his tired eyes, facing east seeing the first glowing signs of light. Almost paralyzed for a moment by the beauty around him, Luke stood letting his eyes follow the river east, until it disappeared into a bright mist where the sun would rise. The yellowish light soon burned brighter melting away the resisting mist left by the night. The clearing sky and the warmth of the rising sun was a welcomed substitute for cold night. And as James had predicted the night before they had no trouble crossing the river, after a quick meal of smoked ham and the last of the three-day-old corn cakes. One could have easily fallen prey by the beauty surrounding them, becoming negligent to unseen dangers. They did not however, instead remained ever vigilant. The sun had yet to display its dominance over the sky and fully warm them, bringing them a greater degree of comfort, before Luke rode out.

Following the banks of an unnamed shallow rivulet south, he calculated eventually it would intersect the Oklawaha River running southwest. The others soon moving in the usual marching order easily followed his well-defined trail over the ground.

After the first three hours, there became a noticeable absence of hardwood trees, such as oak and maple. In their stead, cabbage trees of assorted heights growing close forming island hammocks, throughout the wide savannah of tall saw grass, and divided by the often-dried stream he followed.

Luke thought out loud as he gazed upon the vast expanse of lowland, that, "This has to be the area known as Payne's Prairie."

These marshes and their slightly elevated islands provided home for an abundance of unseen wildlife, affording them shade from the scorching summer sun, or protection from cold winter winds. This unchanging picture would stretch out before him for the next ten miles, following the meandering unimpressive stream on its way to join the bigger and more impressive Oklawaha River. Deciding to holdup on the last high ground and wait for the wagon, Luke unsaddled Red and rested in the shade of a small stand of oaks. Hours later relieved and less fearful in the open flat grassland, they rolled up to the spot where Luke waited. From the seat of the lumbering wagon, Kara Sue and Polly took in the great and beautiful panorama. Consisting of flocks of white birds numbering in the thousands gliding low and high over the distant prairie. The darker shades of green of the nearest trees making up the hammocks turned a lighter blue green further away. With the far distant clusters eventually disappearing into gray clouds on the horizon, until the eye could not separate trees from clouds. To Polly, the human tongue could not have described such a magnificent picture.

After an hours rest for the animals they were once again moving following Red's tracks. Stealing a glance at Kara Sue, Polly could not help but smile at the happiness showing in the young girls face, almost shinning in the bright sun. Her daughter was eager and wanted to see all of it at once, but could not. Still the young girl could not help clapping her hands happily as she bounced on the seat. The mostly dry streambed that they had been following now carried water, so the wagon diverted slightly following a path toward the river. A great blue heron nearby squawked a loud disapproval, as its long yellow ochre colored legs propelled the big bird from its log perch into the air. It sailed smoothly on slow flapping outstretched wings just off the water's surface, to a more solitary fishing spot, free of intruders farther down the river.

Watchful, yet the long-necked bird was easily surprised, forcing avoidance from unexpected danger, its unwelcome flight, prompted thoughts in Polly's mind of what possible dangers could be awaiting them. Just as the great blue heron they too could be caught off guard, and escape for them, surely would not be as graceful, and probably not as painless as the birds. She shuttered thinking of such things, and how easily one might forget and grow slack in such a place as this. Indeed, looking out across the vast sea of deep grass, it seemed a true paradise. Polly refused to dwell on the toll one might be accessed for such a lapse of attention. Such as that extracted from the Georgia citizen, Homer Dew. Perpetual proof. The dead he left in Florida where he once was, and the living in Georgia where he now was. Becoming once again wary as they rolled along.

Soon picking up an old military trail as it changed their direction veering more southwest, distancing them from the river again. And the ground became less muddy, but still allowing the wagon wheels to sink. The wiregrass that had been a solid waist high carpet for miles grew now in intermitting clumps. Further along the narrow, little used trail, became only deep gashes into a thick forest. The tracks in the sand left by Luke's mount, were easily followed, trailing through the tall pine rising high over dense tall beds of palmetto, both suited for the sandy higher elevation.

"Mamma, kin I walk some?" Kara Sue asked, finally recovering from the excitement of this land, and its great beauty.

"Well. I reckon," Polly answered, pausing and extra moment to consider the question.

As before she reminded Kara Sue to remain within the boundaries of the easily defined wheel tracks, left in the sand. Kara Sue made her usual departure, and as always snatching a handful of hardtack biscuits, pushing one toward the snorting pig, and quickly pulling her hand back still holding the treat. Bakon snorted louder in protest.

"Oh no yo' don't, yo' li'l fat pig," she said, after seeing the pigs face, caked with mud from rooting for grubs in the blue-black muck they had just passed through. Instead, she dropped the biscuit on the ground; Bakon discontinued her mild protest, and promptly devoured the morsel. Smiling upon hearing Taters bark as always, after discovering his treat in the grass. The dirty-faced pig now expected to enjoy her usual dose of ear scratching, and trotted for Kara Sue, but instead and unexpectedly she backed away, keeping her arms straight out shielding herself from the muddy animal.

"Yo should be 'shamed gettin' yo'self so dirty an' all, yo' naughty pig an' yo' ain't gettin' thet mud all over me," she proclaimed, playfully backing away attempting to escape becoming equally as dirty as her pet.

Out of the corner of her eye, she saw movement in the shadow of a palmetto clump. Then a whirring noise, a sound she had never before heard, but fully understood it's meaning, a distinct warning of a deadly diamondback rattlesnake, assalted her ears. The terrified child didn't hear herself screaming, had not intended screaming, thinking only of fleeing from the danger. Screaming would only delay her departure, increasing the danger. Yet her intense fear rendered her incapable of movement, and instead, the horrid involuntary shrieking escaped her throat after seeing the coil of death. Petrified she saw the wide flat head larger than one of her own shaking hands. The two small round, black diamond like eyes were fixed on its intended target, herself. The purple forked tongue further mesmerized the terrorized child, constantly flicking, investigating smells from its victim. Completely overcome and blind with terror, Kara Sue was helpless, and in an instant would feel the fangs sink into her flesh, injecting the clear liquid of death. Polly stopped the wagon with the first terrified scream and with a natural flow of adrenaline assisted her movement from the wagon, scatter gun in hand. Kicking their mounts James and Jimmy D. raced headlong for the screaming little girl, scattering the cows as they passed.

The brightly colored six-foot-long reptile coiled its fat body tighter, mouth wide displaying its lethal fangs. Kara Sue's shrill shrieking failed to screen from her ears, the hissing and the audible warning from the end of its vibrating tail. To Kara Sue the rattle mimicked that of a child's toy, like small buckshot in a dried gourd, vibrating faster than the eye could manage, as was the strike. Tumbling backward, Kara Sue landed on her fanny in a sitting position on the ground, legs wide apart.

The viper's diamond patterned body shot out with almost invisible speed, its first strike hit but barley missing flesh, as the attacking rattlesnake miscalculated the loose multiple layers of her long clothing. Preparing itself for another strike, the huge deadly snake quickly recoiled between the spread legs of the terrified girl. Offering to the snake, an unclouded target of either bare leg from knee to her shoeless foot. The next strike was certain to produce an agonizing lingering death for the child, far too small to survive the amount of venom the viper would inject. The second like the first was only a blur, with its mouth wide, the two long curved deadly fangs already leaking death. With her eyes shut tight, she refused watch, as her piercing cries of death mixed with that of her mothers own terrifying screams. Close to her daughter Polly was frozen wide-eyed, only seeing a flashing of color. Dismounting at a run, James and Jimmy D. reached them as the panicked Polly was attempting to examine the location of the child's bite.

"Tha chil' been snake bit, James! Rattler," she managed to cry over the terrified girls wailing.

"Lord God chil'! Where'd it get yo', girl?" the panicked James asked, attempting to inspect her kicking lower limbs and twisting frame for puncture marks. But he failed to find any sign that the snake had bitten her. "Jimmy D. get this damned pig outta here," he yelled, trying to push Bakon from between them. "An' where's tha snake?" the confused and excited James called to Polly.

Loud squealing added to the confusion, as Jimmy D. grabbed the excited Bakon's hind legs and pulled him free of the pile.

"Don' know, but I'm 'llow mayhap Bakon kilt it," she answered as she examined the child's jerking arms for marks.

"Talk ta me, girl, whut happned?" her desperate father asked, realizing that if she where to have any chance at all, eventhough a slim one at best, treatment was of the essence. James attempted to control his shaking shaking hands and then realized his shaking didn't matter.

"Don' know, but I feelin' no hurt though," she answered, her voice quivering as she tried to compose herself and answer her father's questions. "I 'llow he got Bakon 'stead ah me. Is Bakon gonna die 'stead ah me mamma?" The muddy-faced girl asked, with a slight quivering in her slim body.

"Naw, girl, ain't either yo' gonna die, it 'pears yo' ain't hit, an' ah snake cain' kill no pig, his hide to thick," James answered for Polly. Shaking his head with a deep sigh of relief that she had not been bitten.

Polly was right, for in all the confusion, flying dirt and dust, the terrified woman failed to see that the usually docile swine had turned ferocious. The deadly intended strick landed square on the shoulder of the pig as it jumped between the screaming girl and sure death, clamping the reptile between her sharp teeth while swinging her head wildly severing the snake in half. Its head still showing deadly fangs went in one direction, the rest of the body in another. Even though the danger was passed the excited pig again forced her way between a now calmer Kara Sue and her still shaking mother and father, refusing to move. They had no intentions of removing her again, for surly she had earned the right.

"Ah miracle tha chil' ain't harmed, nothin' short. God has put his hand on our girl taday." Speaking faintly almost frail, then as if concentrating not knowing what to say, feeling drained to a point of exhaustion but realizing their deliverance from anguish. "I ain't never seen tha lak ah size ah thet snake," she said quietly, as if thinking out loud.

Polly pulled her shaken daughter very close, constricting. Knowing how very close she had come to watching helplessly, as her daughters' life ebbed slowly and agonizingly away. She couldn't abide the thought, leaving her little girl covered with sand, in this alien place, as Homer Dew had left his wife. Then she did something totally unexpected by anyone, even herself. Grabbing her yet weeping daughter by both shoulders, she started shaking her, almost violently.

"Why did yo' disobey me! Why! Why! Why! Yo' 'most wuz kilt!! Screaming in the girl's face, tears streaking her cheeks for the first time. Continuing to shake her. The same question over and over, louder. She almost collapsed, but did not.

Kara Sue began to cry louder, and tried to answer between sobs, even though she didn't quiet understand the question. "I'm sorry, Mamma, I'm sorry!! I didn' aim to!! I jus' forgot thet's all." Still unsure of what her mother meant, and exactly what she herself had forgotten, that had caused her to be nearly bitten by the rattlesnake, almost killed.

"Polly it all right, our girl ain't hurt," James said, in a soothing voice, sliding an arm between the two, preventing any further shaking.

It calmed Polly, enough for her to think more clearly now, and she pulled back, but left a hand on her daughters shoulder, realizing for the first time her trembling little body. Taking a corner of her apron, she gently wiped the mud and tears away from her daughter's eyes. They both cried, and she hugged her shaking daughter, very gingerly this time. Speaking to her quietly lovingly, "I'm sarroful honey, I wuz jus' so awful scairt fo' ah while. I reckon I thought." She didn't complete her statement, but continued holding her daughter close. "Oh God. Oh God," she repeated quietly, then again.

James wrapped his arms around the two hugging them. "Everythang alright now," he stated, "we bes' get yo' cleaned up. Jimmy D. les' get them cows bunched."

"Yeah, suh, papa. Kara Sue's fin' now, ain't she?"

"Yeah boy, she's ain't bit."

Together they walked their horses in the direction of the scattered cattle, both shaking their heads, but saying nothing. What could they say? Neither wanted to think about what might have been or how close they had come to loosing Kara Sue.

"Mamma Bakon saved my life, is she alright? Did she get herself bit?"

"Reckon she did chil'. But it lak yo' pa said, ain't no snake fang gonna get through thet hide," she explained, helping the girl on the wagon, after cleaning her of most of the mud. .

Polly urged the mules into a walk and to her relief, they seemed willing to follow the trail with little guidance. Kara Sue didn't toss any stones from her pail, she just didn't feel like it. Wanting to just set there, not talking, not even thinking about walking or doodlebug hunting. They both wanted that. Saying nothing even when two fat does' noiselessly bounced across their path, their dun shading blended with the brush, and they were gone. Even with her usually sharp eye Kara Sue seemed not to have noticed, nor did her mother. Both unwilling to converse for the next couple of hours as the wagon moved slowly south down the overgrown trail.

"Thet were ah sight, it purly wuz," Polly said, finally able to speak of it, and her hands no longer shaking.

"Whut, Mamma?" Kara Sue unsure if her mother might be referring the earlier unmentioned deer, or something else.

"Tha way thet ol' pig done, an'," Polly answered, finaly able to discuss it.

"Yeah, I thought I wuz snake bit, fo' ah fac', an' thet wuz ah awful big snake mamma, but Bakon saved me. Kilt thet ol' snake. Saved my life." Repeating the actions of her pig.

"I ain't never seen tha lak of it. Thet wuz tha biggest snake I eva seen, over six feet long, if it wuz ah inch I reckon. Don't get near thet big in Georgia," Polly said, a chill going through her as she spoke.

"Reckon it wuz ah snake thet big whut bit Mista Homer Dew, an' they had ta cut his leg off?"

"Reckon."

"Mamma, c'n I give Bakon ah treat, fo' savin' me an' all," she asked.

Kara Sue would always use any and every excuse for treating the pig, and she could think of no better reason than the saving of her life from the rattlesnake. She tossed the tasteless hard cracker underneath the rear of the wagon, listening for the grunt that came almost instantly. She watched as Tater located his, and happily barked his approval. James and Jimmy D. had yet to talk. There just didn't seem to be anything to say, or maybe they didn't know how to say it. But they were thankful. Very thankful, and they kept that in mind as the day wore on, hoping to hear from Luke soon.

CHAPTER THREE

Long before Luke heard the noise from the chopping axe, he smelled the smoke drifting from the opposite side of the river, here the Oklawaha River was narrow maybe only forty yards wide. And from the sign Luke could tell this spot was used as a ford, or had been frequently in the past. Not because it was shallow, it was deep and running hard, but the narrowness of the river. The mostly hardwood maple and cabbage trees closed tight against both banks of the rapid, clear water. Moving slowly and cautiously for the waters edge constantly scanning the brush in all directions for movement. To him the beating of his heart seemed louder than the noise of the rushing water or the gentle rustling of leaves by the wind high above in the maples. Reaching the waters edge he stopped, staying concealed in the brush, he quietly dismounted and gently rubbed Red's nose, speaking in a soft voice calming him. Red's ears signaled that he had picked up the scent of strange animals and would want to clear his nostrils. He didn't, because of Luke's light hand on his nose.

After moving about fifty yards paralleling the water Luke could hear them, but could not distinguish their words plainly over the rushing water. Moving his head around he saw, partially hidden by trees on the far side, a portion of canvas covering for a wagon similar to that of his families. Listening more intently, he distinguished the voice of a woman along with at least two men; still he could not see them. They were camped at a point where the rarely used military trail would normally lead across, but heavy rains north had brought the water up, increasing the peril of crossing. He allowed they could be pilgrims planning to cross, and hoping the water might drop before the attempt. But how could he be sure? Could even be bandits with a female hostage, very likely. If they were pilgrims, they were very careless indeed with their safety. If bandits, they could be strong enough in numbers and weapons making security moot, except in case of an army patrol.

Deciding the best way to get answers was to cross the river and attempt to get close enough for a better look. Knowing Red could swim the river, but to do it quietly and undetected was another thing altogether, his attempt would have to be made farther away. Again following the river he backtracked north for about two hundred yards, there he located a suitable crossing point. The river was narrow, but appeared very deep, and extremely swift. He mounted and quietly and slowly walked Red through an opening in the brush, and into the water.

It amazed Luke that the waters depth instantly dropped to well over eight feet so near the bank, requiring the also surprised gelding to extend his neck long, keeping his head above the surface. The current too was deceptive, far stronger than expected, as was the extreme cold temperature of the water. Stifling his desire to scream out, and releasing the reins he slid off the already kicking horse and into the swift running water.

"Swim, Red, swim." Quietly instructing Red to swim Luke was towed across by holding a firm grip on his horse's tail.

Releasing the tail only after feeling an abrupt leap indicating Red had touched bottom, less than ten feet from the desired bank. There gaining his feet Luke experienced yet another surprise, in discovering the bottom to be hard packed white sand, and he followed Red up the opposite bank and into cover. After listening for any sign of having been discovered, and believing he had made a favorable clandestine crossing, he reloaded his pistol and saddle gun with dry powder, having no idea what he would be facing. They very well might be bandits with a woman captive, a more than common occurrence. If that were the case, he had no choice but to attempt to liberate her. Alone if possible, if not, he would have to wait for support from James and Jimmy D. In any case his weapons had to be dependable.

Leaving the jittery Red untied should anything happen to himself; the horse might make his way back to their wagon. Drawing his revolver and carrying his rifle, he crept closer toward the sound of the camp. Suddenly Luke froze. Through the brush, someone or something was moving in his direction. Squatting low in concealment, he saw who it was, a young light skinned Negro boy slowly making his way out of thicker brush to a small clearing in the trees. In silence Luke continued observing the boy who he judged to be about twelve years of age. The slight seemingly carefree lad took a dozen more steps before turning and facing a tree not five feet from where Luke was hidden. Spreading his legs, and firmly planting his bare feet in the sand, his back to Luke, he yielded to a call of nature against the tree. Waiting until the boy had almost emptied his bladder, but not totally. Luke stood and stealthily eased up behind the boy. Leaning his long gun against another tree and holstering his pistol, he quickly reached for the boy covering his mouth with one hand, while securing him with the other.

"Don' yell out, boy! I ain't aimin' ta do yo' harm. Jus' ask some questions." Letting the boy know his intentions in a low voice.

At first the frightened boy thought to resist by pulling at the hand covering his mouth, but quickly realized the strength of his captor, and instead relaxed.

"Yo' ain't gonna yell out if'n I let yo' go, are yo', boy?" Barley easing the pressure over the boy's mouth after the lad attempted to shake his head, indicating no.

Turning the boy to face him, yet prepared to silence him if he thought to sound an alarm, Luke looked into the youngsters' eyes. His round dark eyes displayed defiance not fear as Luke expected, but the boy made no move toward resistance.

"Who yo' be, boy? Lak I say, I don' mean yo' no harm. Thet is, if yo' don' call out."

"Be called Cork, Massa suh." The boy stuttered, looking at Luke through large eyes, as he reached up and quickly snatched his stiff felt hat from his head, clutching it to his chest.

His subdued behavior somehow didn't match his challenging eyes. Luke feeling the boy might not stay calm decided it necessary to tell him again. "It all right boy, won' harm yo'," reassuring him further, especially after noticing the boys trousers were wet in front, mostly because he had not quite completed his call before being grabbed. Luke allowed the boy to button his britches.

"Who yo' be with, boy?"

"Be wiff, Massa Randle Thomas suh, an' Misstis Caroline Thomas, suh," he answered.

To Luke, there was something strange about the boy's answer. Not what he said exactly, but something in the way he said it. Planned or somehow rehearsed, overly cautious perhaps, Luke couldn't put his finger on it, just a feeling he had. This boy was not reacting, as one would think a twelve year old should, after being seized alone in the woods. Luke found it impossible to gauge this boy.

"Thet all, boy?" To Luke, the meek answers he was given didn't match what the boy eyes were saying. No this young Negro boy had fight in him, but was smart enough to realize his great disadvantage in strength against a man.

"Yas suh, Massa. 'Ceptin fo' ol' Uncle Caeser, he useta be a slabe lak me, but he be free man ah color now. Massa Thomas say so, an' give him ah paper wid' writtin' on it too." Still submissive yet presenting pride in knowing such information. "He keep dem papers in ah box wid his possibles in de wagon."

"Where y'all bound for?"

"Don' knows dat Massa suh, ah no count Nigger slabe lak me, got no reason fo' knowin' such I reckon. Mayhap Massa say but, reckon I jus' fo'gets. Mistis Caroline say I always fo'gets thangs." Looking down and scratching his bare big toe in the dirt, as if he had done something wrong, then looking up directly into Luke's questioning eyes, a look of defiance again. Luke kept his grasp on the bib of the boy's canvas coveralls. His clothes looked new, strange. In the past Luke had seen slaves before, but never one with good clothes, usually hand-me downs. Harboring a feeling that the boy was lying; he meant to find out.

"Thet alright, boy, no cause ta fret, we jus' go an' fin' out fo' ourselves." Loosely holding the suspenders from the rear, Luke guided the bare-foot lad toward the camp. Keeping his rifle at the ready, remembering the boy's eyes. The boy could be lying, and leading him into some sort of a trap.

"Randle! There's a strange man with Cork."

Luke could not hear what the pretty woman with long red hair had said, but knew only, that she had warned the young, hatless, darkly tanned man. The man around Luke's age quickly reached for his rifle and held it across his chest at the ready, but not in any threatening fashion. They waited for Luke and the boy to approach closer before speaking.

"Who are you, suh, and what business might you have with us?"

The man asked the question in such a way that surprised Luke. Polite, not angry, but clearly expecting an answer, while with his arm, motioned the well-dressed woman to move behind him. The man's speech and manner caused Luke to reason he was facing a southerner of breeding. A gentleman, not the normal traveler one would expect run across in this wilderness. Out of the corner of his eye he saw an old tall and lean, Negro man, no doubt the one the boy had mentioned earlier, Uncle somebody, a free-man. Normally Luke would have considered the old Negro harmless, but not now, after seeing the double-barreled shotgun, even though he didn't appear stout enough to fire it.

"Ain't no need fo' thet scattergun, I mean y'all no mischief, ain't no robber or tha lak." Unruffled but a little uneasy as he pointed toward the old Negro man with the shotgun, yet keeping his eyes on the younger man. "Names Nash, Luke Nash, I got family comin' south on thet trail other side yonder, maybe two, three hours yet," he explained, pointing across the river. "Smelled yo' smoke, thought ta 'vestigate. Cain' be too causious, bandits assinss an' tha lak" Explaining why he was there, still watching both armed men. Mostly the old Negro now, thinking if the mans nerves got the better of him and the gun fired accidentally, it could cut a man in half.

"Yes, you are indeed correct, suh. I suppose we were a bit careless in letting you approach without challenge," the gentlemanly man said. "Uncle Caeser, you may lower your weapon if you please, Mista Nash means us no harm." The olive complexioned man appeared to be reading Luke's eyes, as he presented more a request than order to the shotgun wielding Negro. He quickly judged Luke to be harmless; a judgement under other circumstances could be a deadly mistake. But the man to Luke did seem quite capable in his ability to judge a man.

"Sorry to be so inhospitable, we have come across so few travelers." Lowering his own weapon and walking toward Luke, extending his hand and Luke accepted it firmly. "The names Thomas suh. Randle Thomas, and this lovely lady is my wife Caroline."

She was indeed lovely. Luke could not help but notice, as she walked toward him her own hand extended. The light from the sun reflected off her shoulder length red hair that closely framed her beautiful face. Her slightly blushed high cheeks, added color to a light creamy skin tone, leaving her a healthy appearance. The well-tailored apparel was not the usual cotton frock worn by most womenfolk he had been acquainted with. And Luke could not definitely identify the shinny green material making up the long dress adorned with white lace. Silk, he thought, and it was probably called a gown, not a dress. Nor was the shirt and trousers worn by the man homespun as his own, he was sure they was broadcloth, he had seen such clothes in a Savannah store. Very nice clothes; but to his thinking should not to be considered suitable for the trail, especially the ladies clothes.

"Yo' servant, ma'am." The best impression of a southern gentleman he could muster after removing his hat, and taking the delicate hand extended him.

"You must allow me to apologize once again for my rudeness, Mista Nash."

"No apologies, suh, yo' were right ta be cautious Mista Thomas." Slightly mortified, that he may have held the soft gentle hand longer than necessary. No one noticed.

"Randle suh. You must address me as Randle. I insist."

"Randle it is then, and Luke fo' me."

"You are correct, Luke, about never being too cautious."

"I am, suh, yo' mus' stay alert at all times in this land."

"My brother James an' me, we been special careful since we crossed inta Florida. An' ain't run on no trouble so far. But, tha trails here, 'peers ta be prime fo' bandits an' assassins."

"Your advice is well taken suh, in the future we will extend ourselves more caution."

"Well, I do declare Mista Nash, we have taken complete leave of our manners," Caroline Thomas expressed. "I suppose we have been in this lovely wilderness far to long already," being careful in not making a disloyal charge against the land, as her quality upbringing warranted, yet denouncing their absences of manners. "We insist you share our meal suh. Modest fare to be sure, fried bacon and hoe cakes, but it is quite filling."

"Be proud, ma'am, ain't had much ta boast on fo' quiet ah spell, not even coffee."

"My goodness me. It is barbarous of me to inquire but is your family completely impoverished and depleted of food?"

"Huh?" Poor? Maybe they are, but not believing his family to be that big word she had said. "Oh, no, ma'am, we ain't considered wealthy or the lak, but got plenty ah found. Only we been cold campin', no fire nigh on three days now."

"Why?" Randle Thomas appeared truly surprised by what Luke had told them, and shot a concerned look toward his wife as she poured them coffee.

"It 'cause ah them tracks I seen cuttin' our trail, two horses, could be trappers I reckon, but no way ah knowin'. But I do know this is prime bandit an' injin country."

"We've seen so very little of anyone. However, we did encounter one wagon early yesterday, a freighter by the name of Dilbert Smith a freighter, and his wife Mary." Randle Thomas spoke while his deep dark eyes, watched Caroline place fried meat and corncakes on their plates. "Mista Smith seemed a harsh man, but well acquainted with the area and free with information. He informed us that he was bound for settlement called Honey Tree." Speaking in a slow pleasant voice before placing a piece of bacon in his mouth.

"Honey Tree? I ain't never heard nobody mention thet place before."

Luke had no recollection of such a place, not even from the old soldier Homer Dew. But that was not so surprising, considering the governments Armed Occupations Act in effect, new settlements were springing up everywhere, especially near military installations. Many families were taking advantage of the offer of 160 acres of land, free for the taking. The only requirement was live on it and protect it by use of arms if necessary. Or acquire their land under the Bounty Grant, for military service, against the Indians.

"Mista Smith described it as a new and very small colony on the West Bank of the Oklawaha River, and was a camp for a detachment of soldiers, but he indicated they had left. The goods he was transporting was for a merchant there, by the name of Holder," Thomas explained.

"My guess from his description is that the settlement should be about a day, maybe two, south of this crossing. Actually, suh, we were preparing to backtrack our trail, to the cut off where we encountered him. The ford there was not good, even wider but now it seems a more suitable crossing than what we have encountered here, The water here seems to be running faster," he lamented.

The dejected tone in Randle's statement did not go unnoticed by Luke, as he gulped his coffee washing down a large bite of dry hoecake before speaking, with little pretense of quality eating habits that would have earned correction from Miz Penny.

"Yeah it rained hard north ah here yesterday, lots more water now," he said after being able to speak. "But jus' tha same, ain't no cause fo' y'all t ta cut back though, y'all c'n cross here right' 'nough."

As Luke spoke, the boy called Cork stepped over with two tin plates and helped himself to a healthy portion of bacon and cakes. After taking them to the old man sitting on a log a short distance away, he returned with two cups and poured coffee adding a heaping spoon of sugar, then another to each.

"Thank yo'. Ma'am," he said politely, and then nodded toward Luke before turning away with his cups.

"Tha boy said tha ol' man is free?"

"He is, suh, my daddy before he passed years ago, freed him. I was just a girl myself then. The boy is also free, actually born free, because his mamma was given her freedom at the same time before his birth, and both have documents stating so. Uncle Caesar is Cork's grandfather," she explained.

"But tha boy ain't said nothin' 'bout being free his-self, only tha ol' man," Luke said, surprised at the news.

"That's because he's been instructed not too." She spoke quietly, glancing over at the two setting together on the log.

"How come?"

"It's because some folks few in numbers however, can't accept the idea of free nigras. Knowing he's free might very well bring on maltreatment. But, believing he is someone's property might be cause to value him. Uncle Caesar, well he's so old nobody pays him mind, one way or the other."

To Luke, the explanation given by Mrs. Thomas made sense. He silently pondered her statements for a moment, as he looked over at the two. The Nash family had never been slaveholders, but he could clearly understand what was being said, and he knew of people that fit such a description, as she had just mentioned. People full of meanness and hate, and more than capable of doing harm to the boy; for no other reason than him being classified as a free person of color. They explained that after reaching "Two Rivers Plantation," their destination south of Tallahassee, Uncle Caesar and Cork would be on their own, with fifty acres of land deeded to each them, with a small cabin already in place.

"Of course Uncle Caesar is much too old for common labor, but Cork would be assigned work for wages. We will assign others to assist them whenever needed, they will make out just fine," she explained. "Following Uncle Caesar's advice, Cork will do very well, he has considerable education, and reads and writes very well." Mrs. Thomas smiled and glanced toward them with affection after speaking.

"Uncle Caesar has declared we could get the wagon across by floating it on logs. We have briefly discussed it but decided against such an attempt," Randle Thomas stated, wanting to return to the subject of the river crossing. "Uncle Caesar's judgment is becoming a bit cloudy I'm afraid, I suppose it's his age."

After mentioning it, only briefly, Randle explained his opposition to Uncle Caesar's plan. Such as the banks being too steep, and the water far to swift and deep. Luke knew exactly what the old Negro had been thinking, and knew it could be done. The idea was presented to the Thomas' in such a way, as perhaps the old man had not. It required first cutting two pine logs at least a foot in diameter, and as long as the wagon. After moving the wagon to the water's edge, a log would be secured to each side. Next it would require swimming the oxen to the opposite side.

"Goodness me, Luke, I would be quiet fearful of the wagon overturning." There was a noticeable degree of fear in her voice and eyes.

"Ain't lakly, ma'am, them logs lashed ta tha sides will steady the wagon, it won' turn over or sink," Luke explained with confidence.

"Then Uncle Caesar was correct," Randle, declared, feeling a little more confident and with a small degree of embarrassment over his doubting the old man.

"Right as rain." Gulping the last of his coffee, before speaking.

"'Member I said yo swim them animals over Fust, thet so they c'n pull tha wagon over usin' ah block an' tackle." Pointing to the far bank as he spoke.

"Well then, I am afraid your plan is doomed to failure from the start, suh," Randle lamented.

"How so?"

"We have no such equipment in our possession."

"But we do, an' we got plenty ah rope too."

"Well Mrs. Thomas I believe with Mista. Nash's assistance we will take our evening meal on the west side of the Oklawaha River." For Caroline there was no need to hear more.

Cork, who had been paying close attention to the conversation, realized that they had completed the meal, and approached. The old man was still setting on the log, and still sipping from his cup.

"Would yo' like me to clean up now Miz Caroline?"

"Yes, Cork, thank you. Luke, would you care for anything else?"

"Uh, no ma'am, I'm as full as ah tick. Uh, I mean I'm satisfied, ma'am," rephrasing his answer, a little embarrassed for his vulgarity in the presents of such a quality lady.

"Well, Cork, in that case continue, we are all full as ticks," she said, flashing a wide happy smile at Luke, erasing any self inflicted mortification he had gained from his statement about ticks.

Cork gathered all that had been used, except the cup that Uncle Ceasar held, and headed for the river. The conversation then turned once more to the river crossing.

Luke explained that by securing one end of a long stout rope to a large tree upstream, and the other end tied to the wagons, tongue, they could float the wagon across.

"Of course! The rope will prevent the wagon from being taken away by the current. Capitol, Luke, absolutely Capitol!" Randle Thomas was now very enthused.

"Yeah, suh, learned thet little trick when me an' my brother James wuz fightin' tha Creeks in Georgia. Them animals there c'n pull'r right 'cross ta tha other bank with 'nother rope, an' tackle blocks, slick as ah whistle," Luke added. "Won't take much pulling neither, 'cause the current will do most of the work. She'll come over jus' lak a pendulum on ah grandpa clock," he explained, smiling and swinging an arm simulating a moving pendulum.

"I declare." Caroline was amazed picturing the procedure in her mind. It seems so simple.

"Then it's settled. We c'n get y'all over by dark if we get on it," Luke declared.

"Fust thang, yo' gotta cut an' trim them logs fo' lashin' ta tha sides. Then get tha wagon close to tha water as yo' c'n get it, but not total in tha water," Luke explained. "While yo doin' thet I bes' go an' hurry my folks along. I will be back in sight ah three hours, an' I thank yo' fo' tha chuck, ma'am." Touching the brim of his hat toward Caroline, then shaking hands with Randle.

As he turned to leave he noticed Uncle Caesar had picked up an axe and head for a tall straight pine nearby, apparently intended on chopping it down. Randle also saw the old man.

"No Uncle Caesar, no need for that," Randle called out to him, "Cork and I can handle that chore.

"Thet's right Uncle. But they is ah powerful need fo' yo' ta keep ah sharp watchful eye, an' keep thet scattergun ah yourn close. Tha sound ah thet axe will carry ah far sight in tha woods.

"I sho c'n do thet Mista. Luke. Ain't nobody walkin' in on us no mo," the old Negro said, showing a wide toothless grim toward Luke, before handing the axe to Randle and grabbing his shotgun.

"I will be back real soon, an' y'all pay min'," Luke warned once more before touching his hat again and walking through the brush toward Red.

As Luke reached the tree line, he turned to wave one final goodbye, and noticed Randle Thomas wielding an axe already busy at work on the pine, no doubt leaving the trimming of limbs for the boy. Caroline Thomas returned the wave as he disappeared into the brush. The sharp whacking sounds of the axe echoed through the woods as he urged Red once again into the frigid water. Before doing so he drew his pistol, intending on holding it out of the water, while being pulled across by his swimming horse. The tactic worked, it would be unnecessary to reload his revolver.

Horse and rider made the second crossing as effortlessly as the first. Luke's body shook and his teeth chattered from the cold water as Red pulled him to shallow water. He mounted and rode north, to link up with the family. His body quickly warmed after urging his mount into an easy lope. From the position of the sun he had ample time to guide them back to the Thomas' camp. After two hours of cantering, a light pull reined the gelding to a walk, both now sufficiently warm, even though his clothes remained damp.

Thoughts of the Thomas' flashed through his head, how the young boy Cork was so careful in not declaring his standing, being free.

And Randle Thomas had refused to allow the Uncle Caesar to chop down the lofty pine tree. Luke knew the old man lacked the stamina to bring the tree down, but it surprised him that Mr. Thomas would display such respect in the presence of another white man. Could be that, Randle Thomas was indeed a quick judge of men, for it seemed they both had taken an immediate liking to him. To his knowledge, there were very few slaves in Augusta County, where they had come from, and the family had never had any close contact of any sort with slaves. Sure he had seen slaves on the road passing by their farm, walking or sometimes being transported in wagons with their white guards. Though he remembered once years ago, seeing a group pass by with an armed and mounted black man along with a white man guarding them. Mostly coming from Florida's panhandle, where they had been trained for special jobs, such as masons, carpenters blacksmiths and the like, and the females for house chores.

Little mind was paid when they passed, even to the runaways being returned after their capture by men termed paddy rollers. But one could tell the difference between the white owners and the bounty hunters, the latter being, always foul in appearance and speech, and the captives more harshly treated. Often they stopped for water, at those times he couldn't help but notice, the animals were cared for first. The adult males always constrained by a long chain linked together, with the women and girls unrestrained, except by ownership. All were made to drink from the same trough after the animals. And he remembered Savannah's slave market where, just as cattle, they would be sold and taken away, chained in a wagon, their value too great for walking. In many cases, families were split, and taken away by new masters to unknown places. Luke had always known and seen those things, but he had never dwelled on them. He and his family didn't necessarily approve of such things, but it wasn't their doing and besides there was nothing to be done. No, he didn't think on them then and he wouldn't now, his mind would dwell on more pleasant subjects instead, and he allowed himself to relax and enjoy his surroundings. He thought he heard the thudding sound of an axe, but just as quickly discounted the thought; he was well out of hearing range of Randle Thomas' axe.

The scrapping of limbs interrupted the stillness along with the swishing of leaves created by an occasional lift in the wind, or assorted sounds from unidentified birds. Luke was experiencing what Polly had suffered earlier, the same stealing away of cares, being stripped of all prudence in regard to danger. He allowed his eyes to lift upward, toward a cloudless sky of light blue, "Clouds as rare as coins in a poor mans britches," was how his daddy used to describe such a sky. A hawk that flew into his view broke his semiself induced hypnosis of gazing into the sky. It circled then dove toward the earth escaping his sight. He wondered if it's intended prey had escaped or become a victim in nature's food chain. All things were subject to the whim of nature, or the will of God, as he briefly thought of his dead parents, and of Miz Penny and Will. Brushing them from his mind and twisting his mouth, he created a clicking sound, which sent Red into a swift smooth gallop, backtracking north toward his oncoming slower moving family.

On the seat of the wagon, Kara Sue was in the process of recorking the canteen, the hardtack cracker she had just consumed left her with a dry mouth, and she cured it with a swig of warm water, after first offering it to her mother. Polly refused, calculating the trail would take a turn back in the direction of another stream soon, and they could enjoy more of the clear cold water like they had taken from the Aucillia.

"Mamma! Look, it's Uncle Luke, an' he's ah pushin' Red hard," she said, shading her always sharp, blue eyes from the sun, and portraying the way her uncle was riding as her father would have described it. There was no need to point Luke out as they had all expected him to be coming from the south, but it was however, unusual for Luke to be running Red in such a manner. Polly felt chilliness, an acute sensation that something must be wrong.

"He comin' fas' right 'nough. Maybe trouble ahead," Polly said calmly, not wanting to alarm her daughter unnecessarily, as she had experienced quite enough excitement for one day. Polly tugged on the reins bringing the mules and wagon to a stop.

"Poppa!! Uncle Luke's galloping in fast," Kara Sue yelled, standing on the seat, leaning around the side of the canvas top, and waving an arm wildly.

"Move 'em up close, boy," James ordered, and with his heels prodded his dun gelding, sending him into a lope to reach the standing wagon.

With Tater's help Jimmy D. as instructed, moved the uninclined cows forward at a hastier gait, bawling their displeasure as they moved along. James galloped past the wagon to meet Luke calling out, "Be ready," as he passed. James like Polly suspected trouble, he didn't like the feeling.

"Trouble ahead, Luke? Whut's tha reason fo' yo' great dispatch?" he asked the second question before his brother could speak, and reining his mount next to Red, as the two animals snorted their own greetings.

"Naw no trouble, sorry if I alarmed y'all though," he apologized. " Jus' run onta some pilgrims on tha far side ah tha Oklawaha River, they needin' our hep ta cross," he explained. "One wagon, man name ah Randle Thomas an' his missus, an they got ah couple ah darkies with'm," Luke explained in a quick report, as he removed his hat, wiping a sleeved arm over his sweaty tanned face.

Polly put her shotgun down, after recognizing her husbands' wave of his hat in the air as a signal that there was no trouble.

"How far ta tha river?" James asked.

"Ain't far maybe five mile, I calculate," he answered. "Thet's why I wuz ah hurrin', so's we kin get'm' 'cross 'fore dark," Luke added, looking down the trail leading toward the river.

"Well, yo' get on an' I'll get us up quick lak'," James said, looking back at Polly, and motioning them forward with a swing of his arm.

"Will do brother, I had Mista Thomas cut logs ta lash ta tha wagon," he said, as he wheeled Red for his return to the crossing point.

Holding his position beside the trail until the wagon reached him, then explaining the circumstance to Polly as they moved along trailing Luke.

"Mercy me I ain't never figured on ever meetin' nobody on this trail, seem lak we tha only ones here in this whole land," Polly declared, as much to herself as to Kara Sue, after James rode back to report to Jimmy D.

Anxious to meet the pilgrims and find out about them, where they had come from and where they were bound, just to talk to strangers, especially another woman, Polly encouraged the mules forward, wishing Luke had taken the time to tell James more about them. She was starved for company of another female, Kara Sue on the other hand wanted to tell her uncle about her encounter with the rattlesnake, eventhough meeting other people would be nice.

"Momma, I ain't had no time fo' tellin' Uncle Luke 'bout thet ol' snake, an' how Bakon saved my life," Kara Sue lamented.

"I know, sugar, but there will be time for thet later. But, yo' gotta 'member yo' manners, when growed folks is talkin' an all," she reminded her daughter. Growed ups get vexed at rude young'ns," she added.

"Yeah'um, I will, Mamma, I will ask if'n anybody wont's ta hear 'bout it fust." she promised, accurately tossing another small stone at the mules rump.

Polly smiled at Kara Sue's statement, as she herself was beginning to feel her little girl's excitement. She popped the long leather straps, moving the mules along a bit faster.

"Mamma, Papa said them folks got darkies with'm, I ain't never seen none up close, 'ceptin them what passed our place, an' then papa made me go inta tha house. Reckon I kin talk to'm?" she asked, her blue eyes wide with interest, as she stared at her mother.

"Don' know, sugar, I jus' don' know how them folks might feel 'bout such thangs, lots ah folks awful funny 'bout they property," she explained.

"Mamma, how come they don' make them slaves get thet wagon 'cross tha river? They'd have ta do it if they tol' too, wouldn't they, Mamma? 'Cause they get whupped if'n they don', ain't thet right, Mamma?"

The questions persisted from the inquisitive little girl, questions that Polly had no suitable answers. Neither she nor James bothered themselves with such things. Drought floods or grasshoppers in the corn, or spring fever that had taken Mathew, were the concerns that had occupied their time. Not questions of human bondage. After all they, like most of Augusta County, had always been, and voted Democrat. It was the northern abolitionists that continued to make slavery a false issue, when taxation was the true issue. They all knew that much.

"Kara Sue, I don' know if'n they gonna whup'm or yo' 'llowed ta talk to'm, we'll jus' have ta wait an' see. Me an' yo' pa don' know 'bout such," she answered, delaying as long as she dared before doing so, and knowing her answer didn't satisfy the girl.

Detecting a slight irritation in her mothers' voice over her question's Kara Sue stopped probing her further over the issue of slaves.

Unwilling to answer anymore questions about the Negroes. The frustrated woman declined to think on such things any longer, and redirected their conversation, "Mayhap we c'n git yo' papa an' Uncle Luke or even Jimmy D. ta make some music after supper. Papa might feel it safe fo' ah cook fire," she said steering the conversation to lighter subject.

"Yeahs'm I got ah powerful cravin' fo' some fried bacon an' mayhap ah big skillet ah cracklin' bread, an' sweet sorghum," she stated, licking her lips and rubbing her little tummy.

"Uh huh, thet soun's good don' it? An' we will too! Thet is if'n Papa calculates it safe. I crave ah steamin' cup ah coffee myself," she added.

For the next thirty minutes they rode in silence, thoughts of hot food replaced those of Negro slaves and the politics of dealing with them. It felt good allowing them to think of such things as a fire and hot food now. Polly glanced at Kara Sue and smiled at her bright eyes, tanned cheeks and excitement on her face. It could be that James and Luke might still declare no fire tonight. She hoped not, for Kara Sue's sake, if for no other reason. The little girl had, had a very trying day already, considering her run in with the rattlesnake. Polly thought, without mentioning it to the little girl that a sweet potato buried in the hot coals for cooking, would be another treat they might enjoy with supper.

"Mamma, smell!" she said, stretching her neck and taking another deep whiff through her nose.

"Whut?" Polly questioned, shocked at Kara Sue's action, and appearance. Her eyes were bugging out, as she strained sucking in more air through flared nostrils.

"Smell, Mamma!" she cried out, expelling the air she had drawn in.

Polly did as Kara Sue had twice suggested, drawing in a more than ample quantity of air through her nose.

"Why chil' thet's smoke! I smell smoke!"

"It sho' is, Mamma, mayhap Uncle Luke's already got us ah fire goin'," she said excitedly. "I c'n smell thet bacon fryin' already" she said.

"Now jus' yo' be patient, we ain't even there yet," she cautioned the girl.

One more turn in the trail brought the wagon to the edge of a clearing edging the river, and in sight of the wayfarer's wagon on the opposite side of the Oklawaha River.

"There they are, Mamma!" Kara Sue said, pointing toward the wagon, the smell of smoke still in her nostrils.

CHAPTER FOUR

Polly pulled the team up in an open area, being sure to avoid the area where she anticipated the soon to be floating wagon should land. A man whom she assumed to be

Mr. Thomas, and Luke urged the pair of oxen into the shallow water with the wagon in tow, stopping the wagon at the waters edge long enough for the woman, the old Negro man and the boy to climb into the wagon. The woman waved to Polly and Kara Sue before disappearing from view in the wagon. Polly would have loved watching the crossing, but there was much to do before dark.

"Come girl we gotta get us a fire goin', thet smoke we smelled wuz commin' from over there," she explained.

Kara Sue proceeded first by chopping on the deteriorating exterior of a nearby pine stump, expertly exposing the interior hard wood, knowing it to be heavy with pitch, and more suitable for starting the fire. Her effort was quickly rewarded for very soon she had more than an ample supply of the thin strips called lighter. On the ground she discovered pieces of broken limbs that had fallen from an oak, and quickly had the fire burning. Jimmy D had been minding the cows but promptly left the chore to Tater, after smelling the smoke, certain the fire to be theirs, confident that the dog would keep the cows bunched with little effort, as they were belly deep in lush grass. Without being told he took up the duty of sentry, positioning himself in the shadow of the trees allowing a full view of the camp.

Unmindful of the crossing, Polly and Kara Sue busied themselves with the preparations of supper until the shrill scream. It caused them both to drop what they were doing and run to the riverbank. Just as the wagon floating in the center of the narrow river was saved from being carried away in the currant by the rope. The rapid water had caught the wagon causing it to tip precariously to one side, bringing an alarming scream from the frightened woman inside. Uncle Caesar was compelled to calm her and prevent disaster by keeping them in the center of the wagon. He succeeded in his attempt and they settled, allowing an improved balance to the wagon. Clinging to the log that had been secured to the wagon on its high side, James and Randle Thomas enabled the wagon to stabilize itself, and the strong current did the rest. With the danger of the wagon overturning past and secured by the forward rope it swung, as Luke had suggested, like a pendulum on a clock. To the relief of them all, especially those in the wagon, the wheels settled on the bottom in shallow water, on the intended opposite bank, and now could be pulled to solid ground. The two oxen that Luke had crossed over earlier were secured to the wagon and the crossing was finalized by pulling it out of the water.

"I declare that was just a most awful and frightful experience, I feared for a moment that we would all be lost to that wicked river," Caroline said after being helped from the wagon. "I'm Caroline Thomas," she introduced herself while brushing loose strands of long red hair from her face, and extending a delicate hand toward Polly.

"How do, I'm Polly, an' this here is Kara Sue," Polly said smiling, putting on arm around Kara Sues shoulders, and taking the extended hand, feeling the soft but cold skin.

"My my what a lovely young lady you are, mistress Kara Sue," she said in her soft southern drawl, she released Polly's hand and took Kara Sues.

"Thank yo' kindly, ma'am." Kara Sue flashed a big smile at the pretty lady.

"Goodness me, yo' must come over by tha fire an enjoy ah cup ah coffee, dry them wet shoes an' warm some." Remembering how cold Caroline's hand felt.

"Kara Sue, pour Miz Caroline ah cup,"

"We got fresh milk ta' add to it if yo' crave it," Kara Sue said handing the tin cup to Caroline. "An' sugar too, if yo' ah mind," she added.

"Oh how wonderful, we have not tasted milk since St. Augustine. Thank you very much, just a touch of milk will be just fine," she answered cupping the hot vessel in both her cold hands for just a moment.

Not long ago she would have thought it a little queer, being served in a tin cup, as Cork or Uncle Caesar would be. But what did that matter now? The coffee was hot and tasty, and she was quickly growing accustomed to the crude life of the wilderness. She trembled slightly as she sipped from the cup, more from excitement than the chilling breeze with the approaching dusk, replacing the warm winter sun. Settling down in one of the rocking chairs that had been placed near the fire, she blew across the surface of the cup before gingerly sipping the hot liquid. Polly did the same after chunking a piece of oak limb on the fire. After seeing that all the men had coffee Caroline removed her wet shoes and stockings, placing them near the heat to dry, but not too near.

"Believe it's gonna work up ah right fair chill by sunup," Polly declared looking over at Caroline, her wonderful lace trimmed store bought dress. How pretty they both were. She thought that she would like to own such a dress one-day, but probably never would. Caroline returned her glance making her feel a little self-conscious. Lightly with her hand, she attempted smoothing the wrinkles from the unornamented frock draping her lap. Caroline's smile relieved the unworthy restive feeling she held over her clothes, especially after watching Caroline place her bare feet on a log toward the fire.

With the animals taken care of, the men came to the fire, except Cork and Uncle Caesar they remained near the Thomas wagon.

"I instructed Cork to build a fire for them to dry out," Randle said glancing toward the two by the wagon.

"No need fo' thet, they's plenty of room 'round this fire, 'less yo' require otherwise," James said.

"There will be no such requirement then, I just didn't want to offend anyone," Randle answered.

"Kara Sue go fetch'm, tell'm they welcome at our fire, an' eat supper with us too, if thet's satisfactory with y'all," James said.

"That will do just fine, and we thank you for your kindness," Caroline said, suddenly feeling right at home, rubbing her bare feet.

Kara Sue ran toward the two Negro's, eager to deliver the invitation. "My papa said y'all come dry out by our fire, an Miz Caroline say y'all ta eat supper with us too, ain't no sense ta tote more firewood," she added, returning the toothless smile from Uncle Caesar with her own wide grin.

"Dat be jus' fin' li'l miss, be right proudful ta do so, Cork yo' fetch our plates an' cups, ta eat wid," the aging man said, pointing toward the rear of the wagon.

"No need fo' thet, we got plenty ah plates an' all," she explained.

"Then I reckon we bes' get on over there an' get at them rations," the old man said, flashing another smile on his wrinkled face. The three of them made there way to the fire, with Cork supporting Uncle Caesar. The old mans wet feet already affected by the cold, causing pain to his joints.

"This is Uncle Caesar and Cork," Caroline said introducing the two. "Uncle Caesar, this is Mr. James and Miz Polly Nash, Mistress Kara Sue and Master Jimmy D," she completed the introductions.

"Me an' tha boy here, be proud," Uncle Caesar said after removing his hat as did Cork.

Cork helped the old man remove his shoes and placed them to dry before either had taken a plate of food. Everyone was at the fire now, including Jimmy D. Tater was left to tend the cows, and other stock. Jimmy D. had taken a double handful of hoecakes for Tater and Bakon soon they all had had their fill of grits, fried ham plus baked sweet potatoes from the coals, along with squash cooked soft with onions. Polly had fried an extra amount of hoecakes, which they topped with peach jam.

"Polly that was a delicious meal, and we are most grateful," Caroline said, her bare feet still toward the fire.

"Thank yo', ma'am," Uncle Caesar said, tapping Cork on the shoulder and pointing toward the dirty dishes.

"Yes'm," the boy said, quickly jumping up to clean the dishes and utensils, and with the help of Kara Sue it was quickly taken care of.

For the first time in a while, James and Luke felt as though they might make use of the occasion for relaxing, yet still be watchful. With the addition of the Thomas wagon, added to their own, they felt a little more secure. For awhile they all sat with their bare feet toward the fire, until all the foot wear was sufficiently dried.

By now the Thomas' and Nash's' had accepted each other as fast friends, and followed the normal pattern of story telling around the fire. Caroline decided with her husband's approval to relate the story of his family's history in early Florida. His uncle was the owner of a large plantation where the Santa Fee and Suwannee Rivers juncture in northwest Floria. His uncle recently became quite ill and found himself unable to maintain the holdings. We agreed to sell our place in Carolina and relocate there after he wrote us of his plight. Randle is his last surviving relative.

"Do yo' have any idea whut tha place even looks lak?" James asked.

"Some, we have been communicating by mail, it is quite large. An overseer has been running it all since my uncles illness two years ago. It's taken us that long to arrange our affairs," Randle explained.

"Oh and I must tell you the story of Randle's grandfather taken hostage in eighteen ten by a band of pirates, who came down the Suwannee intent on holding him for ransom." Caroline sipped her coffee before continuing, wanting to divert the conversation to something thought to be more entertaining. Plus waiting for any approval.

"Lord he'p thet had ta be ah wicked experience," Polly said

"Yes, it was, but he was rescued by a band of friendly Timmican Indians, and returned home safely to the family. Are they any pirates still in Florida?" wide-eyed Kara Sue asked excitedly.

"They are thet girl, an' worse, thet's why we always got ta be watchful," James said.

They talked until well into the darkness, the sun having long since moved far to the west dragging the last of it's glow, leaving behind a coldness dropping the lowest since leaving Georgia. Yet around the fire it was quite comfortable with the wind barely moving the cold air, allowing the smoke to twist straight up into the star speckled sky. On rare occasions the breeze, still gentle, would lift only enough to carry the delightful sounds of the whippoorwills to them from the trees. At times Uncle Caesar's head would nod unceremoniously, allowing his chin to tough his chest as he sat on the ground, his back against a pine. On one such occasion his half-empty cup fell harmlessly from his twisted fingers, the spilled cold liquid missing the blanket underneath him. Kara Sue, Jimmy D. and Cork sat a little farther away from the fire taking turns scratching Bakon's ears as she lay between them.

"Ain't they purty? They look jus' lak fallin' stars, but it's ah lucky thang they ain't," Kara Sue said about the lightning bugs bouncing among the trees, just over the top of the tall grass, being falling stars. Kara Sue as always had ways of looking at things, seeing them as no one else, like the dancing angels on the stones in the grave yard, back home in Georgia.

"They sho' do, I reckon I ain't never seen so many befo'," Cork said as his eyes tried to keep up with the luminous tiny flying bugs. "But how come yo' sayin' it's lucky they ain't fallin' stars'?"

"'Cause my grandpa tol' me thet ever fallin' star yo' see, means somebody gonna die."

"Oh lordy! I seen three since dark set in!"

"Three? Well don' yo' be ah frettin', Cork, since we lef' Georgia I seen mayhap ah half dozen, it jus' ah ol' darky sayin' anyways. I, ah, ah." Suddenly disconcerted by what she had just said, she covered her mouth and opened her eyes wide. "Well I ain't never heard it, an' I'm ah darky." They both laughed at their private joke.

Later the mellifluous sweet soft tones from Jimmy D.'s harmonica drifted through the cool night air, as he blew melodies of old spirituals, the ones that pleased his mother so. Everyone was well ready to turn in, and did after a couple hours of his entertainment, coupled with the warmth from the dying flames.

By the time dawn broke and the drowsiness washed from their eyes, their preparations were being carried out for another days journey over a satisfying breakfast of sourdough pancakes, covered with black syrup. And hot coffee, maybe the last they could expect for awhile. After the meal Randle approached James and Luke with a business proposal they could not refuse, the idea of an even swap of his four oxen, for their four mules. His reasoning being that the faster gait of the mules, against the slow but steady pace of the oxen, would be to his advantage. Delbert Smith had said the trail was better suited for travel once the river was crossed. The military trail leading west toward Tallahassee from St. Augustine was more frequently used, and they were anxious to improve their time. The trade was agreed too after taking a few minutes to weigh the offer, believing the oxen would be advantageous in the swampy land further south where strength, rather than speed would be more worthwhile. The swap was completed, with a note explaining the transaction for each family, and sealed with a handshake in true southern fashion. The two families parted, the Nash's continuing south, and the Thomas' moving west, waving their final good-byes until the trees separated them. Jimmy D. took his place, walking his horse to the left of the slow moving oxen, guiding them along the trail. At first Kara Sue wasn't happy with the big ugly lumbering beasts. It was no use to toss stones at them, they only had one speed, slow.

"Yo' could hit one ah them rascal right between tha' eyes with ah big rock, an' it won't make no never mind ta him," Jimmy D, chided his little sister.

Working the cattle together along with Tater, James and Luke rode in the warming sun, which became even more pleasant as the morning wore on. Yet they guarded against becoming overly complacent about the dangers that may lay ahead, especially after their relaxing night with the Thomas'.

"Ain't this nice, now we kin walk together," Polly said, laying an arm over her daughter's shoulder.

"Yeah, an' Bakon laks it too," she answered, taking a hardtack cracker from her pocket bending down as she walked, and allowing the pig to take it from her opened hand.

Looking at each other, they smiled after hearing Tater's yelp from behind them.

"Thet Tater, he's ah real caution, ain't he mamma? Reckon that ol' hound'll fin' thet cracker if'n I chunked it right ta tha top of ah tree," she said, bragging on Tater's nose, and growing more fond of the sluggish oxen. The trail even though sandy and deep in places displayed signs of being a little more used, indicating a settlement nearby. The Thomas' had mentioned that colonies were popping up everywhere in Florida, and being abandoned just as quickly for reasons known and otherwise. But in this case the trail showed definite signs of regular use, and no reason for Luke to ride out ahead. Excitement increased along with more evidence of a populated area ahead. Especially after Jimmy D. held the wagon up and motioned his father and uncle forward to investigate a queer set of tracks that seemed to have come from nowhere, and turned south onto the same trail. Leaving Paralleling furrows wide apart, with human tracks centering the deep twin ruts, plain enough that anyone could follow.

"Ah travois, heavy load too, no animal. Queer, ain't it?" James added, speaking of the exceptionally heavily loaded rig being pulled by a lone man.

"Right brother. Barefoot man, but from tha length ah his stride an' size ah them tracks, he don' require no mule or tha lak." Both agreeing, they had never see a man with a foot that large. Footprints almost twenty inches long imbedded deeply into the sand, measuring a good four feet distance between.

"I ain't never seen tha lak, ah giant if they ever wuz one," Luke exclaimed.

"Ah pure fac' brother."

They continued on, the same mode as before now with a clear trail ahead, anxious to see the man that had left the bare prints in the sand, as deeply as the hooves of the oxen.

Taking advantage of the slow moving wagon, Polly and Kara Sue moved to the front jumping from one deep rut to the other, or one footprint to the other without falling, until they tired. Then taking turns kicking fallen pinecones from the path into the brush. Now, even the men could allow themselves to relax, feeling the security of a nearby town.

"HONEY TREE, pop 56," painted blackish gray, with a slash painted through the population number "56," and altered to read "55." The information was coarsely painted on a weathered board and nailed to the trunk of the immense oak tree, it's long twisted moss draped limbs extended far beyond the trails opposite side. Besides being a convenient place to hang the sign, it created a wonderful ingress to the quaint little village. Jimmy D. was first to see the sign, taking note of the faded lettering with the exception of the latest population revision. The substituted population number and the slash were freshly painted in red, with a slackness of care. After the sign, next to capture his attention, was the sight and sounds of bees, in which thousands maybe more of the insects swarmed around a dark cavity high above the time-bleached sign. Feeling no threat from the assiduous buzzing insects, he moved past the tree, guiding the oxen and wagon toward the sandy main street, his mother and sister following along with Bakon.

"Look at all them bees, Mamma," Kara Sue said of the buzzing mass. "An' ain't thet ah queer name fo' ah town? Honey Tree. It ah right purty name fo' ah town though," she added.

"Ain't much of ah town, but it's all we've seen fo' ah spell, an' I 'spect it's named proper, thet ol' oak with them honeybees an' all," Polly said.

The herd of bawling cows bringing up the rear was eased into a patch of high grass edging the river, marking the rear boundary of the town. With good grass and clear water, James knew there would be no danger roving from the tired cows. After lapping his fill in the cool water, Tater trotted after the men, sounding a few yelps, signaling he was following. Tater stopped and sniffed at the base of the tree, then quickly caught James and Luke walking down the sandy street into town, heading toward the wagon in front of the largest of about a dozen mostly unpainted, wood structures. James could see a man and woman both wearing aprons, standing on the porch talking to Jimmy D. A third person, setting on the floor, in the shade of the overhang, appeared to be a boy about Jimmy D's age.

"Where you folks hail from, boy?" the man asked looking down the street toward James and Luke.

"Georgia, suh, Augusta County, this here is my mamma, Miz Polly Nash, an' my sister Kara Sue," he answered pointing toward his mother and sister, touching his hat toward the lady.

"How do, ma'am, young lady," the tall, thin, slightly balding man politely greeted them, nodding toward the two and snapping his head for a double take of the pig under the wagon.

"Proud to meet y'all, I'm Abner Holder, an' this here is my missus Betsy," he said in a slow mellow voice.

"Tha pleasure is all ours, suh, this here is my son Jimmy D. there, an' this here's my husband James an' his brother Luke," Polly said, pointing out James and Luke, as they reached the wagon.

The storekeeper moved to the edge of the porch, reached and shook hands with James and Luke.

"Betsy, how about you take the women folk in an' sho' them the goods, mayhap they're in need," Abner Holder hinted, without turning toward her.

It was clear to both James and Luke, that the merchant had something on his mind, and preferred the girls not hear it.

"I allow you folks met with no trouble on the trail." A questioning look on his face as he spoke, staring at the two of them.

"Nothin' ta speak of," James answered, looking over at his brother, both realizing there had to be a reason for the expression the storekeeper presented.

"It sounds lak yo' a little surprised thet we ain't," Luke added.

"I am, suh, I surly am…It's because of Indians, they're on the roam again," he answered before either could ask why.

"How so, they been trouble 'bouts?" James asked once again, looking straight into Luke's eyes.

"Plenty, a bunch hit the Willoughby Tillis place four days ago, that's about ten miles east of here. Didn't do much damage to them, but wounded a young Negress that Miz Tillis keeps. Slight scalp wound, but she'll be fine. And they drove off a cow or two," he added, turning, looking back assuring the women were not close. Then continued. "It was a mounted army patrol out of Fort King, that came to help that took the blunt of the damage. Their lieutenant was killed along with two troopers, and one bad wounded. The Indians suffered one killed," he added.

"Yeah thet sounds bad, right 'nough," James exclaimed. "And takin' on thet army patrol lak they done means they well armed, and smart lead," he added, again staring into Luke's eyes.

"That's just the start of it, we have a woman inside, a Mary Smith, a hunter brought her in yesterday," he said pointing a thumb back over his shoulder, without looking back.

"Unfortunate woman's been treated real wicked," he said, this time pausing to look behind him. "I suppose it a miracle she's survived at all, but I don't allow she will ever have her mind back. They violated and scalped her, and cut her nose almost off. Dreadful mischief…Just dreadful." He paused as if thinking about it, shook his head side to side, slowly, then continued speaking. "Left her for dead," he said, still shaking his head, staring at the floor. "It seems her man had no chance for making a fight of it, even thought Dell Smith was always known to be well armed, and more than efficient in their use.

"Del! Yo' mean Delbert Smith tha' freighter here 'bouts?" Luke exhibited shock, interrupting Abner's description of the incident.

"Why yes. Are you acquainted with Del Smith?"

"No, suh, we never had tha pleasure, but we met some pilgrims back at tha ford north ah here, they mentioned him, James explained.

"He tol' them 'bout yo' town here an' said he was freightin' goods fo' yo'," Luke added.

"Well that's him all right, and he was bringing in a load of goods for my store, all gone now though, they took what they wanted, especially whisky and burned the rest. That's his place over there, or was," Abner said, pointing a finger toward the livery barn across the street. "SMITH'S LIVERY and STABLE" in aged neat lettering over the wide opened door of the large unpainted wood structure.

"A trapper and mail carrier by the name of Acre Foot Johnson found what was left of the wagon, with Del's burned remains tied on top. Said he was burned alive, him being tied an' all, his voice quivered. "Acrefoot Johnson's very knowledgeable about such things. He calculates the attack was a total surprise, maybe even jumping on Del from trees, clubbing him down before the poor man had a chance. Tying him up, and having their way with his missus."

"Sounds 'bout right, them injins ain't gonna take time fo' tying no dead man," James agreed.

"How many this Johnson fella calculate they wuz?" Luke asked, looking over at the livery barn for no particular reason.

"A dozen maybe took part in the attack, Dell managed ta kill one with his knife and another bad wounded before they took him. The wounded one, according to Johnson, left ample blood enough to be dead by now. Soon after Johnson killed two more that were too liquored up for traveling, so the others left them, and he came up on them. It's only on account of his dog that he found Mary, her in the shape she's in, found naked, cut up an' all."

Mr Holder did not further elaborate about her being cut up, nor did anyone ask; they had heard enough about the unfortunate woman.

"Lord he'p tha poor lady," Luke lamented.

"Johnson figures that it's only because of Mary's age that she was left alive, if one can call it living. Because the Indians don't make captives of older people, especially only the young and strong."

"He's right as rain there," James agreed, sweat beading up on his face, thinking how lucky they had been so far, and other possibilities. "Could be too that, them two Johnson kilt had min' ta dispatch her later, after more ah their meanness," James added as a second thought.

"Could be."

"I reckon they run off with his stock though... Mules, were they?" Luke asked.

"Yes, like I say the heathens took what they wanted, weapons, powder and shot, liquor, and used poor Mary the way they did, God help her," he said shaking his head again looking down once more.

"This Acre Foot Johnson, he ah 'bout anywheres?" Luke asked, looking around.

"No, suh. He took out for Fort King after dropping poor Mary off. He's a Christian man; he even brought Smith's remains in for a proper burial. Drug'm both in on a travois that he crafted.

"That explains the drag tracks we been seein' whut cut inta tha trail leading inta town some ten mile back. But them tracks showed he wuz afoot." Luke scratched his head as he looked at his brother, mirroring his own puzzled look.

"Yes, suh, that was his tracks y'all followed, Johnson is never mounted," he said without explanation. "After that he quickly lit out, had to make a report to the army, and drop off their mail bag. He's a first rate woodsman."

"I'd say he's ah sight more then thet, he's got ta be one hell of ah man." James still anxious, and couldn't wait to meet such a person, remembering his tracks.

"Acrefoot Johnson is a giant of a man, suh," he offered, but once again with no further explanation. They didn't ask for one. "Say y'all meet other travelers?"

"Yeah, suh, man named Thomas an' his wife with ah couple ah darkies. Free darkies though, ah boy an' ah ol' man, makin' fo' Tallahassee. Reckon it don' look real good fo' 'em," James said, rubbing callused fingers over his suntanned face, showing concern regarding the Thomas' safety.

"It looks bad all the way around at this point, and we have no true numbers of the savages or where they have gone. There was certainly more than the ones that Del and Johnson killed, but don't know how many," Abner said anxiously.

The three men continued discussing their concerns over the situation, but James and Luke considered only briefly, the suggestion they delay any further travel. Movement on the trail was chancy at best, and none could deny that fact. But with consideration given that Fort King was only forty miles farther south and they intended to take the trail leading there. Also, having had some experience in such things they were certain the army would be patrolling in strength. Especially after the casualties they had taken after the Tillis raid.

CHAPTER FIVE

As Jimmy D. completed his task of caring for the animals, he attempted to keep an eye on the boy setting with his legs hanging over the edge of the porch. The lad appeared remote, paying little or no attention to the goings on about him. The hatless and barefoot boy, kept his hands busy weaving a second hat from the palm frond strips. One having already been completed, was laying on the floor in the doorway of the store, so that anyone wishing to enter would have to step over the unique looking, head gear with its wide brim. The homemade hat to Jimmy D. appeared more suitable for womenfolk than for a man. With a substantial supply of green pliable strips at his side ready for weaving, his speed and production amazed Jimmy D.

"Howdy." Was all he said as he approached the diligent youth with the shaggy red hair.

"How do," the boy returned the greeting without taking his eyes from his rapid moving hands.

"Name's Jimmy D. Nash, how yo' called?" he asked contemplating a handshake, but not wanting to impede the fabrication of hats, instead sat down next to the boy. Being careful so as not to disturb red handled "Barlow" pocketknife sticking in the plank floor next to his supply of material.

"Called Jojo. Jojo Stroughby," he answered politely, looking at Jimmy D. for the first time. And to Jimmy D.'s surprise he momentarily abandoned his hat making and extended a hand, which was accepted firmly.

"Them's fin' lookin' hats, they purly shine. They fo' girls ain't they?"

"Yeah, they girls hats right 'nough, an' I thank yo' fo' sayin' they fin'. I do tradin' with folks whut comes through, iffin they be of ah mind. Been slim pickin's of late though, on ah-count ah them injins on tha prod again," he explained, matter-of-factly.

"How much."

"Most folks agreeable fo' ah nickel," he quoted before proceeding with the production. It seemed to Jimmy D. presented as; make an offer, rather than a set written in stone price for the hat.

"'Pears ta me, thet's ah right ah fair price fo' ah fin' hat. How'd yo' learn ta make ah hat lak thet?"

"Nigger John, he learned, ah, ah, taught me. Miz Anna sez I should say taught," he said correcting his grammar, and then added the last twist and ties needed for completing the second hat.

"Nigger John, who's he, an' who' Miz Anna?" Two questions at once, thinking he might forget one, if not asked at the same time. There was something about this boy that told him, there would be a lot of question, time permitting.

"Nigger John wuz my frien', ah half breed thet use' ta live down at Big Cat Slough," he answered, placing the newly finished hat on top of the other, before looking over at Jimmy D.

"Thet ah right queer name, reckon he ah nigger, huh?" Just as he had thought, he forgot about his inquiry about Miz Anna. The name Nigger John fascinated him too much.

"Part, his momma wuz ah 'scaped slave. He claim he wuz ah great gran' son ah ol' Chief Cowkeeper, thet ol' Seminole chief way back. My pa sez it ain't so. Say he weren't no kin ah Chief Cowkeeper. Said he weren't nothin' but jus' ah regular half-breed," the boy explained.

"Wuz?" Jimmy D. asked, picking up on the key word after hearing it several times from the boy. Wanting to ask questions about Chief Cowkeeper, but was forced to wait until the redheaded boy answered the "was" question.

"Yeah, he ain't nothin' now. 'Ceptin maybe food fo' tha varmints," he answered, almost angrily.

"Varmint food!!"

"Yeah my pa kilt 'em. Mista Abner there, gave me tha loan ah his ol' mule Jerico an' I toted Nigger John's body clear over ta tha Big Cat. Nigh five mile too, fo' buryin'. Jus' me an' ol' Jerico at his funeral, 'cause me an' pa wuz tha only folks ta take ta Nigger John. My pa wuz too drunk fo' he'pin' with tha burrin' an' all'," Jojo explained, his voice almost cracking as if he might cry, but didn't.

"Dang, if thet don' beat all! How come yo' pa done it? Kilt Nigger John I mean."

"Over ah card game. They wuz both liquored up an' all. Mos' ah tha time they wuz anyways," Jojo lamented. "Pa said Nigger John wuz cheatin', but I ain't never knowed Nigger John ta cheat or steal." Jojo defended his dead friend. "I weren't there ta vouch, I wuz with Miz Anna. Nigger John pulled his blade fust', least ways pa said. But, thet don' make no nevermind, 'cause my pa's real handy with ah knife, real handy," he repeated. "Ain't no man alive c'n take my pa with ah knife," The boy declared confidently. "Folks say pa split Nigger John lak ah ripe melon. Fell dead right in his own guts in tha dirt, right over there at tha barn," pointing toward the livery

Jimmy D's slim body quivered slightly allowing the name of Miz Anna, to once again to get passed him.

"I declare if thet story don't shine more'n any I ever heard," Jimmy D. said, unable to contain his excitement of a knife fight, and a man dying, even if he was just a half-breed.

He was at a loss as to why Jojo wasn't showing some degree of excitement, while recounting his story, and he had every intention of hearing more. It was clear to Jimmy D. that the boy after the ripe melon analogy was finished with the knife-fighting tale. Because he renewed his hat weaving with out speaking further about the knife fight, although not necessarily the death of his friend Nigger John. But Jimmy D. would have none of that, thinking Jojo might stop talking altogether, and he was thoroughly enjoying himself. He wanted to hear the boy talk more about anything, anything at all.

"Y'all gett'n any honey from thet ol' tree we passed north ah town," he asked quickly, unable to think of anything else, yet; unwilling to allow Jojo to cease talking.

"Yes'm. Nigger John used to, 'till me an' Jerico buryed'm, but now I do fo' tradin' an' such. Honey is good fo' thet, as well as eatin'," he explained. "Tha Romans use ta use honey ta pay they taxes," the red headed boy added, matter-of-factly.

"Romans? They live in Honey Tree or here 'bouts?"

"Naw. Romans don' live in Honey Tree, they lived across tha ocean long time ago. Two thousand year I reckon, when Jesus was living," he explained.

"Ain't so," Jimmy D. made a statement of interest more than argument.

"Is so. Ain't certain, but I thank it wuz them Romans whut kilt Jesus too," he added.

"Dang! Yo' sayin' them honey traders kilt Jesus? I always thought it wuz them Jews whut done it. Ah traveling preacher back in Georgia said it wuz Jews whut done it." But Jimmy D. had no intentions of arguing over who had killed Jesus, he only knew it had been done, everybody knew that much. "How yo' ah knowin' all this?" he asked, shaking his head in amazement, at this latest development of information from the red headed boy. By now Jimmy D was close to considering the boy a talking schoolbook.

"Miz Anna," he answered. "But I cain' re-collect fo' sho' her ah sayin' who kilt Jesus," he confessed his confusion over the matter of Jesus' death.

"Miz Anna? Who's she?" Finally the familiar name popped up again.

"Ah school teacher, lives south ah town. Use' ta be ah teacher anyways, till them injins went on tha prod again an' folks moved away ta Fort King. Now we ain't got 'nough young'ns fo' schoolin'," he lamented.

Now Jimmy D. wanted to hear more about Miz Anna, and fully expected too. But it didn't happen.

"I got me ah leather-back. Yo' know whut thet is?"

Right out of the blue, Jojo switched the subject as if he didn't want to talk about Miz Anna, honey traders, the death of Jesus, or Nigger John any longer; instead he started taking about leatherbacks.

"'Course I do, it ah long neck turtle whut lives in creeks an' such, 'ceptin they ain't got no hard shell lak ah regular turtle, it lak leather kinda," Jimmy D. answered, with his best description of the soft shelled reptile. Deciding he would discuss leather backs if that's what pleased his saggy-headed friend, so he added, "An' they right smart eatin' too."

"Right as rain, yo' know yo' leather backs right 'nough," Jojo said.

"Where is it?"

"'Round back in ah barrel, got 'em in water too, so's he don' dry out none."

"C'n I take ah gander at 'em?"

"Okay, come on back then," Jojo answered, after retrieving, folding, and pocketing his Barlow, before leading his new acquaintance around the corner to the rear of the store.

"Whut yo' mean?" Jimmy D. asked, as the boys started for the back of the store.

"Whut?"

"Yo' said them letters 'O' and 'K,' whut yo' mean?" he asked a second time.

"Dern, yo' don' know whut okay means?"

"No. Jus' plain letters is all I know."

"It means lak, yo' ah sayin' alright, or thet's fine," he explained.

"Dang, thet sho' is ah queer way ah talkin', sayin' okay, I ain't never heard such before," Jimmy D. said. " How come yo' talk lak thet?"

"Miz Anna tol' me 'bout it, she say it started way up in Washington, where tha president is. Miz Anna say purty soon everybody be sayin' okay," Jojo explained, but not to Jimmy D's satisfaction.

"Well, I don' know if I ever be talkin' lak thet. Who would start such as thet?" Jimmy D. asked, being more than a little confused by this boy.

Every time the boy opened his mouth, Jimmy D. could think of a dozen more questions to ask. And he was yet to be fully satisfied with any of the answers he had received from Jojo Stroughby.

"I think Miz Anna said it started when ol' Andy Jackson wuz runnin' fo' president of tha United States again' somebody named Van Buren or some such name. Said this Van Buren wuz from a town called 'Ol' Kinder Hook,' so everybody started callin' tha town' 'OK' for short."

"Andy Jackson won tha 'lection. Thet's why they named Jacksonville after him I reckon. Ain't thet ah caution we got ah town named after ah president," he added.

"Yo' ever been there?"

"Naw, my pa did once," the strange boy answered.

Jimmy D. had only been aquatinted with this strange boy for less than twenty minutes, and was now so confused he didn't know what to ask next, or even think. He was talking about Nigger John, Jesus, leatherbacks and Romans, then before he could say jackrabbit, he switched to, ok, then somebody named Van Buren, President Andy Jackson, and a schoolteacher named Miz Anna. All this and he still felt he was not even close to seeing the leatherback. So he decided to stop asking questions and just follow the red headed boy to see the turtle. Feeling as if he had run onto a walking talking book with red hair, but he liked him just the same. The plan worked and Jimmy D. couldn't believe what he was seeing, when the boy removed the boards covering the top of the drum.

"Danged if thet ain't the biggest turtle I ever laid eyes on! I ain't never seen no real leather back befo', only ah picture in ah schoolbook," he confessed.

"Yeah, suh, his size sho' do shine, nigh ta forty pound I calculate," Jojo boasted.

"Reckon yo' folks ah min' ta have leather back fo' supper?"

"Reckon, how much yo' askin'?" Jimmy D. was prepared to dicker for the turtle.

"Two bits, an' I'll clean 'em fo' ten cents mo'," the business minded boy said bargaining for another ten cents.

"Come on, I 'llow thet ah right fair askin' price fo' sho' fine leather-back,"

Jimmy D. agreed, enthusiastic over the price, plus the fact that, he had never eaten any leatherback before.

"Okay."

"Okay," Jimmy D. said, flashing a big grin at Jojo.

The boys closed the impending transaction with a handshake, on the understanding that Jimmy D. would approach his folk on the matter of the turtle. The verbal contract being contingent on what his folks had to say concerning the enormous long necked turtle. That consideration was being discussed as they walked toward the front of the store. After reaching the edge of the street Jojo suddenly stopped as if he had walked into a fence post, his head snapping in the direction of the street leading south out of town. A strange look masked his face, and his complexion changed to a sickly ashen tone.

"Yo' bes' leave me be now," Jojo said in a very serious voice, never taking his eyes from the street.

"Who's thet?" Jimmy D. asked, after seeing the man at the far end of the windblown street. It was his appearance that had caused his friend Jojo's sudden change in attitude and behavior.

"My pa. An' it's lak I say yo' bes' get away now, mayhap yo' c'n take them hats inta yo' ma, see she might have a min' ta dicker. An 'bout thet turtle too," he said anxiously, not looking at Jimmy D. instead watching the approaching figure of his father, at the far end of the street.

As he was asked, Jimmy D. picked up the hats, but at the same time continued watching Jojo's father walk toward his son. Backing through the doorway and into the store, Jimmy D. watched from the shadows, as the man made his way directly toward Jojo. His heavy boots kicking dust with each deliberate step. In his right hand Jimmy D. could see that the man Jojo called his pa, was carrying a coiled bullwhip.

"Boy," he said gruffly, stopping in front of Jojo. "I come ta fetch yo' home, but firs', I got ta learn yo' ah lesson, 'bout payin' min' ta what I say." Slurring his words in a grotesque coarse voice, he flicked the long whip out, between them.

Long shallow furrows remained in the sand after flipping it twice, the second it's full length of eight feet, and slowly retrieving it without speaking. Taunting the boy. The obviously inebriated man plainly enjoying his cruel amusement.

"Oh lord!! It's Ben Stroughby, and he's liquored up for a fare the well," Abner said to himself, looking at the figure standing spread legged in the dust, withdrawing his whip a third time.

No one with the exception of Jimmy D., paid much mind to the sheathed knife strapped to Ben Stroughby's side with the wide leather belt. But, from just inside the doorway with the two newly completed hats still in hand, Jimmy D. took great notice. The bullwhip, soon to be cutting deep into the flesh of Jojo's back, seemed not to bother Jimmy D. as much as the large bone handled knife. Still peering from the shadows, he could not void from his mind, the picture of cold steel slicing through Nigger John's gut, like a ripe melon. Eventually Polly took notice of Jimmy D. no longer concealed by shadow, but in the center of the open doorway. Curious as to his purpose she walked over, reaching him just as the air exploded with a loud crack. The sound, not unlike a rifle shot echoed off the buildings lining both sides of the street.

"My word! Whut's happening out there?" she asked, after having jumped at the explosion.

Dust, from the first crack of the whip, was being carried away by the wind, as the echo's died away. The barrel chested man whirled the long leather whip above his head once again, as if limbering it. Then "Kaaa powww," and more dust and echoes.

"Get there boy," he said, pointing toward the rear wheel of the Nash wagon, as the working end of the whip left it's mark in the sand, after being pulled back once again.

"Pa...I..."

"Now boy yo' jus' gonna make it worse, yo' know it's my re-sponsibility ta learn yo' lessons, being yo' pa an' all," he said gruffly, his body swaying as he spoke.

"Ben! There's no call for this," Abner said from the porch, nervously wringing his hands in his apron. "Why is it necessary to whip the boy like this?" he said, walking toward them, yet not leaving the porch.

"Ain't none ah yo' concern storekeeper, but I'm gonna say anyway. I sent'm in this mornin' to fetch me ah gallon of corn liquor an' ah quart ah' coal oil, well, he turned it all 'round, brought me ah quart ah liquor in place," the agitated intoxicated man argued, running his words together. "So Mista Abner Holder yo' bes' butt out. This here is ah family matter, ain't no never mind ta y'all." Ben Stroughby's harsh warning tone was meant for all those present, and not just the storekeeper.

Now the trembling boy was on his knees, his chest pressed against the wagon wheel, his hands tightly gripping its wide iron rim. The muscles in his arms twitched as he waited for the first agonizing bite from the whip bringing blood and pain. It came quickly. Ben worked the whip so rapidly the action was barley visible, it's tip splitting the back of Jojo's shirt, then repeating the action kaaa poww kaa poww. The back of the trembling boys shirt was expertly sliced away, blood stained remnants mixed with dust, and carried away by the wind. At first, the presence of so little blood appearing on the boys back and shoulder indicated his cuts might be shallow, demonstrating Ben Stroughby was more than a fair hand with his whip. And it was very clear that in his hands, it was indeed an extremely lethal tool. Slowly and deliberately he tossed the rawhide back once again stretching its full length in the dirt. This time he fully intended drawing more blood and screams, from the kneeling quivering Jojo. Ben's arm flashed forward, but the expected failed to materialize.

"Huh! Whut tha hell!" he yelled in astonishment, as his arm shot forward, his hand empty of the deadly whip.

Turning, the wide-shouldered man saw James' boot planted firmly on the end of the whip. Anger blanketed the big mans face, his eyes seemed to take on a red tinge and saliva secreted from the corner of his clinched lips.

"Whut cause yo' got hornin' in stranger? How yo' called?" he angrily demanded, clinching his fist seeing James unmoving on his whip.

"Names Nash, James Nash… I reckon I jus' don' take kindly ta seein' ah boy get hisself whupped in tha street lak ah cur dog,"

"Oh my God!" Polly said trying to get past Jimmy D., but he gently held her back, asking Betsey Holder to keep her there.

He moved from the building to the street next to Luke, not knowing what else to do. Looking at Jimmy D. Luke only shook his head, only the anxious youth wasn't sure what that meant, but he had confidence in his father and uncle. Yet unable to erase from his mind what Jojo had said about his pa, and his skill with the knife he carried. Sensing danger for James Tater growled from under the wagon. Showing teeth with the warning.

"Tie thet dog, Jimmy D," Luke said, not taking his eyes from the two men.

As he did so, Jimmy D. heard the inflamed voice of Ben Stroughby behind him.

"Well now, Mista. James Nash, it 'pears to me, thet yo' ma ne-glected yo' upbringin', ah tad. Mayhap she lef' yo' ah little short on manners. Ain't proper fo' folks ta buy inta other folks business, special it personal an' all. So reckon I'll learn yo' fust', then I c'n take care ah my business with tha boy here." Still slurring his words, his big fist clinched tightly at his side

Carelessly James underestimated the speed of the big man, mistakenly he had considered the brawny Ben Stroughby to be clumsy. But instead, Ben proved the opposite, demonstrating unbelievable agility by jumping for the whip. Quick as a cat he retrieved his whip from the ground, and was whipping it in the air once again. Unbuckling his pistol belt, James tossed it over to Luke, the extra weight would only slow his movements, and that he couldn't afford, especially after seeing the swiftness of his opponent. At first James was bent on the idea of first trying to calm Ben by talking to him, "I know yo' tha boy's pa an' all, but I cain' set back an' let yo' thrash'm. Special with thet cow whip," James said, pointing a finger toward the rawhide weapon, in the hand of the angry man.

"Well now, I ad-mire thet kin' ah sand in ah man mister. I purly do. So I'm givin' yo' ah chance ta back out peaceable lak. Mayhap get up on tha porch with tha women folk, or under tha wagon with thet ker." Expertly cracking the whip in the air as a final warning.

"I 'ppreciate tha ad-vice, but they is somethin' my ma did learn me, an' thet is ah man ought to do what he thinks is right, even if he has ta pay ah stiff price."

The sound of the exploding whip signaled the end of the dangerous badinage. In the background, James could hear Polly's distant cry amid the echoes. He dared not take his eyes from Ben, nor did he notice that other towns' people had taken to the street. Dozens or so men, the women and children were compelled to remain indoors. Hearing Polly and Kara Sue's cries, Luke instructed Jimmy D. to get them back and keep them quiet. There was no help for James now, he was compelled to follow through with what he had started. Alone, that was the way it had to be.

After another crack of the whip it took only a second, for the blood to appear from the slice in James' shoulder, instantly coating a portion of shirt and upper arm. The injured James was successful in dodging the next attempt, by moving his upper torso and keeping his feet in place, the whip cutting the air and barely touching his ear. By watching his attackers arm, James mentally calculated and precisely timed his next move. His action came as a total surprise to his attacker, and the tactic accomplished exactly what it had intended. His hands seemly as quick as the other mans whip, James snatched his hat from his head and threw it square into the face of Ben Stroughby, rendering him momentarily off guard.

In that instant the prey became the attacker. With Ben caught off balance, James was on him, strength for strength; with the barrel chested Ben once again having the advantage over his antagonist. But even with the strength and speed of Ben, James the smaller man, felt he held the advantage of quickness of body and mind. Once again James disarmed Ben by grabbing the whip pulling it free, and tossing it toward Luke. Then almost instantly feeling the mans heavily muscled arms, squeezing his upper body in a bear hug. Painfully James gasped for air, as he suffered the stink of Ben's foul alcohol smelling breath. His attempt, to push his opponents' face away from his own and break the painful hold failed.

Stars flashed in his tightly closed eyes, and pain hammered his head and constricted lungs. Unable to fight with his arms penned tightly against his own body by Ben's strong arms and grip. In desperation James slammed his forehead into his attacker's face only inches from his own with great force, shattering the big mans nose.

"Ugh!" A loud grunt came from the injured Ben and blood gushed from his disfigured nose mashed to one side and he staggered backward, falling to the ground in a sitting position. James was amazed that the grunt was the only sound that came from the wounded man, especially after seeing his damaged bloody face. But knowing now that he was in a fight to the finish, it had gone too far, and James knew that one of them would not walk from the street. He no longer heard Polly and Kara Sue's cries from inside the store.

"Damn," was all Ben Stroughby said, before wipping a sleeve across his bloody lower face. "Yo got more'n yo' share ah sand right 'nough. Yeah suh, I purly do admire it," he said shaking his head, causing more blood to flow.

The bleeding and badly injured man staggered to his feet, trying to focus on James through watering eyes. But he was far from being vanquished. Throwing a quick glance at Luke, James shook his head as if saying what else would be required of him to stop the attack from his very determined adversary. Something flashed in the corner of his eye that quickly draw his attention back toward the reeling Ben, and a fight for his own life. The blade of the long menacing knife now held now in Ben Stroughby's hand created the flash. It continued flashing as he moved the knife slowly side to side in a hypnotizing fashion. Assuming a crouching stance with arms and legs spread, James prepared himself as best he could for the renewed attack.

"Well now yo' aim ta make ah good fight of it. It lak I say before I ad-mire thet in ah man, I purly do. But this ain't much of ah place ta be dying," he snarled, spitting blood that had dripped into his mouth from his nose. His eyes were wilder than ever.

The muscular man wasted no more time talking, and he moved slowly for James, while continuing to wave the extended knife back and fourth between. Unwilling to wait for the onslaught, James once again became the attacker, and it would require brain over brawn and weapon. Squatting slowly all the while keeping his eyes on the advancing Ben, he scooped a handful of loose sand. The instant Ben came within effective range, James threw the sand directly into his already fluid filled eyes. Without delay, James took full advantage of his attacker's temporary blindness and went for him, with both hands he grabbed Ben's thick wrist and hand that held the knife. And once again, realizing his strength was no match compared to the knife wielding man as Ben's free arm closed around his neck. Fearing the force might snap his neck; he acted out in pure desperation.

Somehow James spun them both around as though, engaging in some deadly form of dance. Both men tumbled to the ground, with James beneath the big man, his back landing hard against the earth. A loud "aghh ughh" sound escaped from one or both, the onlookers could not distinguish which. Feeling a deep burning in his lungs and gut, James felt himself sliding away, unable to breath, especially with the added weight covering him. Yet; somehow being aware of the warm liquid that covered his chest and stomach. In his new world his brain seemed to retain some ability for thought, but was scarce of light, only flashing lights of assorted colors. The only sound in his world of fading light was distant wailing, moaning and thumping. The thumping he thought to be his own heart.

To the horrified Luke it seemed forever before Ben drew himself to his knees, and hovered over the unmoving James. Forcing his massive body up Ben slowly stood, his arms dangling loosely at his sides, his front covered in blood. Straightening his sagging legs he faced the prone wide-eyed lifeless James, covered in blood. Screams of shock echoed from inside the store James never heard them, but Ben did and turned toward the screams, a twisted smile formed on bloody face. Luke started for the standing man, fair or not he was compelled to take up the fight and finish it. He pulled up after taking only a couple of steps toward Ben, then stopped as if frozen in place. Just as determined was Ben Stroughby, that someone else must die.

The bloody Ben Stroughby, his frozen contorted smile, turned and faced Luke head on and started for him. He attempted to speak to Luke and his curled lips moved, but instead of words a stream of scarlet liquid gushed from his mouth. With a slow and deliberate move he dropped the deadly knife, and moved his hands over an undetected deep gash at his rib cage. Additional blood spurted from between his thick fingers and he looked over towered his son, positioned on one knee next to the wheel of the wagon, where his punishment was to be. A crimson puddle formed in the sand around his boots, he staggered backward a couple of steps, then slowly sank to his knees, his smile stretched thin across his face. Jojo opened his eyes wide, staring at the blood and sand caked knife after seeing it drop into the dirt, then elevated his tear stained face toward that of his smiling father. A strange look covered his face and the smile formed tighter.

Still on his knees where he had dropped, with his arms held out in an awkward position as if needed for balance, his words were garbled, discernable. "I ad-mire yo'sand, James Nash, I purely do. Yo' got some hard bark on yo'." He was not looking at James as he spoke, but at the sad eyes of his son. "Boy yo' pay min' ta ah hard man. Grow tall an' strong lak this man, James Nash…Boy, I, I always did." Pinkish bubbles blew from his bloody twisted mouth, while still looking at his son through wide glazed over eyes. He fell face down into the dirt. His unseen eyes remained wide, without finishing his last words to his son. He was dead.

As the others watched in horror, Jojo crawled for the knife, grasping it by its deerbone handle, and staring at the broad back of his father, and then toward James still clutching his chest and trying to suck air. Luke seeing Jojo with the knife ran toward his dazed brother, who by now had negotiated a sitting position. But as Luke might have suspected, the boy harbored no thoughts of retaliation, he had already determined that all fault was his father, now stretched out face down in his own blood, in the street of Honey Tree. But he felt very much alone, and he crawled over to his father and lay a trembling hand on his back. Saying nothing, just silently crying his body jerking clutching his fathers' knife.

"Whut happened?" Shaking his head to eliminate the cobwebs, and rubbing a hand across his bloody chest, another over his bare head, the bewildered James could not understand what had happened.

"Ain't zackly sho', happened so fas', but it looks ta be, Stroughby got ah mortal wound by fallin' on his own knife," Luke explained.

Polly with Kara Sue in tow ran for her husband crying his name and dropping down next to him, as did Kara Sue.

"Oh James, yo' gave us such ah fright. I declare yo' Nash boys are tha hard-head'st I ever run on to," Polly said, pushing his hair from his eyes.

While everyone gathered around James, muddled but standing, only Abner Holder noticed the weeping Jojo next to his fathers' body. Walking over, he laid a hand on the boy's back but quickly removed it realizing the cuts, first thought to be minor were not, several were quiet deep. The storekeeper wiped the blood on his hand from the wounds on his apron, before gently placing the dry hand on the boys head. A tear rolled from the corner of one eye, he wiped it away. So touched was he by the boy on his knees in the street, one hand on his dead father, the other grasping the knife that had caused him them both to be there.

"Reckon I'll be bound ta ask fo' tha loan ah Jerico, tote my pa home an' bury him proper, lak I done fo' Nigger John," Jojo said sorrowfully, looking up with swollen red eyes. His earlier tears dried

He knew his father's gelding Banjo, was corralled behind their shack just south of town but, he wanted to get his father out of the street as soon as possible.

"Sure, son, but you ought to let Miz Betsey look to those cuts first, one looks to be quite deep," he suggested.

"Mayhap later if yo' please suh, ain't fit ta leave pa layin' in tha street dead an' all, special them dogs 'roun'," he answered. "But I'll look to'm after," he promised.

"Well, son, there's no need of you asking, about the mule I mean. I'll get my gloves and a shovel, be proud to give you a hand." Abner Holder considered that enlisting himself to the undertaking, was the very least he should do.

"I be obliged fo' yo' offer Mista Abner, but I got ah ol' shovel at tha shack, handle's cracked but, it'll hold up jus' fin' fo' diggin'.

"'Sides pa wired up tha split handle, he's, er, wuz real handy fo' fixin' an' tha lak. But, I still be beholdin' fo' tha animal iffin thet be alright."

"All right, son, I'll fetch ol' Jerico, and you can do what you think best," Abner agreed.

As he walked away, he noticed Jimmy D. watching them. And earlier before all this happened, he took notice of the two boys together, and felt they had developed a quick friendship, as young people are so prone to do. He motioned Jimmy D. over out of hearing range of Jojo.

"I'm going to fetch my mule so's the boy can bury his pa," he said in a low voice, meant only for Jimmy D. "He's bound to do it alone, and refused any help from me. But, he might agree for your help if you are of a mind, and it's agreeable with your folks," Abner quietly suggested, looking into Jimmy D's eyes for an early answer.

"Gosh, almighty, 'course I'd be real proud ta he'p, iffin he allow it an' all."

"Well then, I'll be back directly."

His mother reluctant at first, but after a quick but convincing argument from his father, it was agreed Jimmy D. walked slowly over to his woeful friend, a little doubtful as to what he should say. Concerns for what the sorrowful boy might feel toward him after seeing his pa killed, especially by his own father, especially in such an awful way. Even though his pa wasn't split like a ripe melon, he was just as dead. He had not the slightest idea how Jojo might feel.

"Jojo, I'm plumb sorrowful 'bout yo' pa bein' kilt an' all, special it my pa whut done tha killin'," he lamented, dropping down on both knees, enabling himself to look more directly into Jojo's sad eyes.

"Ain't layin' no blame Jimmy D. 'special on yo' pa," he declared, looking down once again.

"It wuz thet ol' grapefruit wine what Mista. Del Smith an' his brother Joe Bob always making over ta tha livery," he said pointing a bloody finger from handling the knife, at he barn across the way. "Well Mista Joe Bob anyways now, 'cause Mista Del got hisself kilt too by them injins," he corrected his statement. "Thet ol' wine, it wuz tha same whut kilt Nigger John, tha very same. Put tha devil in'm I reckon," he said, wiping a ragged sleeve across his dripping nose, and jabbing the blade of the knife into the sand, for no other reason that Jimmy D. could tell, except cleaning the blade of dried blood. "My pa, he weren't no bad man. He wuz jus'sick an' all in tha head, on ah count ah whut happened ta my ma an' all. Same as it happened ta Miz Mary, Mista Del's wife in there," he reasoned to his friend, still unwilling to look up.

"My ma weren't scalped though, they jus' done them awful thangs, then kilt her," he added wiping away a tear before finally looking up. "Pa said them injins had to, on 'count my ma wouldn't be no slave. After Thet's when my pa took ta thet hooch, he took ta fightin' with Nigger John most every day. Till ol' John got hisself knifed by my pa, jus' lak he wuz gonna do ta yo' pa. No, suh, it weren't no fault ah yo' pa's. No, suh, it weren't," he repeated. "It's thet grapefruit wine, jus' lak I say," he expounded.

Continuing to stab the ground as he talked Jimmy D. listened and watched. "Reckon I could clean up thet knife fo' yo', iffin yo' aim on keepin' it," Jimmy D. offered, not knowing what else to do.

"Reckon." That was all he said before handing the blood-coated knife to Jimmy D.

Jojo failed, even with the help of Jimmy D. to roll his father over, so as to remove the belt holding the pistol and knife sheath, they couldn't budge the heavy body. Luke noticed the effort and grabbed James by a shirtsleeve and pointed toward the two. Walking quickly over they eased the two boys' aside.

"Boy, I'm powerful sorry 'bout yo' pa. I weren't aiming on killin'm. Jus' tryin' ta stop his usin' thet whip on yo'," James explained as he gently held the boy by the shoulders, and peering into his dry eyes.

"Ain't placin' no blame, suh, it were injuns an' liquor what kilt my pa," he said to James, as he told Jimmy D. but with far less detail.

"Well," James said quietly, before retrieving his hat from the ground, and accepting the fact that the boy truly placed no blame.

The storekeeper returned leading his brown mule and a large piece of canvas folded across the mules back, along with a coil of hemp rope. James and Luke rolled the still warm body over, unbuckled the wide brown belt from Ben's waist, handing it to Jojo. The two brothers with Abner's assistance rolled and tied Ben's heavy body in the covering mummy style. Grunting from the strain, the three hefted the bulky weight across the back of the mule.

Abner went back to his store returning with a new shovel, which he lashed to the mules' load, working together digging the hole, the two young boys could complete the burial and return well before dark. Just before they were ready to leave, Jimmy D handed Jojo the cleaned knife, sheath, and holstered pistol. The belt still wet from its scrubbing. Jojo took the already buckled belt much to large for his waist, and hung it over his shoulder and across his chest

"Reckon y'all be ah needin' this ta read over tha boy's Pa." Polly sadly handed a Bible to her son, its black cover worn from time and use. It was the very same Bible that had been used to read over her dead son Matthew. "An' if tha boy cain' read, yo' do it, son."

"Jojo c'n read, Mamma."

Together the two young boys walked south down the dirt street and out of town, Jimmy D. carrying the bible in one hand, and the lead rope in the other, with Jojo walking next to Jerico, a hand resting on the canvas covering of his father. They appeared not to be talking as they disappeared from view. Tater, standing at Luke's feet had also been watching them leave, and began a low whimper, especially now that he could no longer see them. Luke looked down seeing the dog standing stiff and gazing toward the spot where he had last seen them.

"Well, Tater, go find Jimmy D."

The dog took off, sounding a couple of yelps signaling Jimmy D. that he was following, stopping twice, first to sniff the bloody sand as he passed, then the mules tracks before running full speed out of sight. A sudden chilling wind blew down the length of the street, carrying with it new sand, covering the tracks of the boys and the animals. The earlier onlookers took cover in the store escaping the blowing sand, giving Abner a chance to relate the story of Ben Stroughby leading up to his death in the street.

Hardly a dozen words were spoken between the boys, even after they reached the Stroughby shack. With Jojo using the shovel that had been repaired by his father, they went about the business of digging the grave. Still silent and with the same shovel, Jojo pounded the marker into the sand, at the head of the fresh mound. The cross-had been crudely constructed from two weathered boards they had found leaning against the shack. Jimmy D. made no mention of his thought, of painting a name on the boards after they were nailed together. Instead, he smoothed the mound of gray earth, taking the time to remove a couple of leaves that had fallen on its surface. Being busy, Jimmy D. paid little mind to his companion. Even as Jojo stood by the nameless marker with his mothers opened bible and start reading in a slow deliberate low voice, did he take full notice.

"Fo' yet a li'll while, an' tha wicked shall not be: thou shalt diligently consider his place, an' it shall not be. Tha Lord shall laugh at him: fo' he seeth thet his day is coming. Tha wicked have drawn out tha sword, an' have bent their bows, ta cast down tha poor an' tha needy, an' ta slay such as ta be upright conversation." Jojo's read with difficulty because of his trembling hands.

To his sudden horror, Jimmy D. remembered he had not removed his hat, and quickly snatched it from his head, he hadn't expected Jojo to start reading from the bible. He thought maybe that Jojo would have said something first. That's what he would have done, say something first, give a warning. Not just start reading from his ma's bible.

"Their sword shall enter inta their own heart, an' their bows shall be broken. Fo' tha arms of tha wicked shall be broken, but tha Lord upholdeth the righteous." With that Jojo ended the reading and simply closed the bible, and gently patted its worn cover.

At first Jimmy D. considered Jojo should have given him notice that he was about to read. But then reversed his silent criticism, thinking possibly that he would not have been able to read, after just seeing his father stabbed to death in the street. If his metal should ever to be tested in such a way, he could only prey that his courage equal that of his new friend.

"I'm obliged fo' yo' he'p Jimmy D. an' ta yo' ma fo' tha loan ah tha good book," he said as he returned the bible to his friend.

"Thet alright glad ta he'p. An' them wuz right good words yo' read over yo' pa," Jimmy D. said, returning his hat to his head, after accepting the bible.

Without further conversation, Jojo turned and walked toward the back of the shack and saddled his father's small black pony, as Jimmy D. watched from a squatting position next to the grave. He didn't know quite what to think of his new friend, and he still could only doubt that he could react in such a brave manner, if it had been his own father, they had just covered with black dirt.

"Thet ah right smart lookin' pony, It one ah them Florida ponies, ain't it?"

"Yeah, he's ah good'n, ah Marsh Tackie. They called thet 'cause they so good in Florida swamp's, where regular horses ain't. Nigger John said they ah throw back from the early Spanish horses," he said, passing the reins to Jimmy D. as he walked up.

"Hol'm fo' me, I got ta fetch me 'nother shirt from tha house."

Jimmy D. patted the thick chest of the black gelding, and let the animal smell his hand so as to remember his scent. It was plain the little horse was well muscled and strong, with a sleek black coat, giving him an appearance of being almost blue. Jojo returned from the shack wearing a different shirt, an improvement over the one cut up by the bullwhip. Also on his head and pulled almost to his eyes was a wide brimmed hat of leather.

"Reckon we bes' get back," he stated, throwing a deer hide jacket over his horses neck before mounting.

The two rode back, Jojo on his pony and Jimmy D. astride Abner Holder's mule with Tater trotting behind, toward town and the others in the store.

CHAPTER SIX

"I don' reckon there's any law here 'bouts," James said with more certainty than as a matter of a question.

"No, suh, the nearest thing to law we have around here is the army, the garrison over at Fort King, commanded by a young officer, Lieutenant Brady. Then there's a sheriff over at Palatka, east of here on the St. Johns. As you know the army is not of a mind to get involved in civilian affairs. Besides, I suppose they have their hands full with this Indian business for the time being," the storekeeper opined.

"Reckon yo' be right 'bout the army, but, ah thing lak this ort ta be let known, 'special it be ah murder an' all," James said.

"No, it wuz ah accident, ah accident pure an' simple," Polly defended.

"That's a fact, James," Abner agreed, looking at each one, they shook their heads affirmatively ratifying the statements.

"If you like I could write a statement giving the particulars of the incident and you could sign it, and all the town folk who saw what happened could sign," Abner stated.

It was agreed, and the storekeeper went to a desk in the back of the store for paper and a pencil to write the statement. At the store counter, the three men set about forming the statement.

"Miz Holder, before all the excitement I wuz aimin' to make a purchase of a goodly supply ah coffee, an' mayhap a purty ribbon or two for me an' Kara Sue," Polly said as she and Kara Sue admired an assortment of colored ribbon.

"I'm pleased to make a sale of the ribbon, as you can see we have a small amount on hand, but as for the coffee I'm afraid I can't. Our order was being brought in by Mista Smith with our other goods, lord rest them both," Betsy Holder said, speaking of the woman as if she were also dead, then glancing quickly over at Mary Smith.

The unfortunate pathetic woman sat numbly rocking near the warm Ben Franklin stove, a large irregulr shaped splotch of red showing on a white bandage under the front of her bonnet, as was a small spot on the bandage across her nose. An occasional quiet moan birthed by either mental or physical pain or both could be heard as she stared blankly at the stove.

"But, maybe you could get enough sweet potato coffee from Anna Cade, to get you through until you make Fort King," Betsy said recovering from he temporary distraction by Mary Smith.

"Sweet p'tater coffee? Why mercy me I ain't never heard ah such," Polly said, almost doubtfully.

She started to ask about Anna Cade, but the concept of sweet potato coffee over shadowed any questions she might invoke concerning its producer, at least for the time being. Polly didn't have to inquire further about the sweet potato coffee; the look on her face was enough.

"Well it's a poor substitute for coffee, and I can't say there is any similarity to real coffee at all. I've heard that some crackers make a brew from parched acorns in hard times; I suspect that sweet potato is more suitable than that. Anna produces it by first parching the potatoes, then grinding them," Betsy explained briefly. "Anna Cade has a small place a little south of the Stroughby place. She's a widow and schoolteacher by trade. I'll wager she's unlike any widow or school teacher you may have met in the past, stays out there all alone, except for when Jojo stops by to lend a hand in exchange for his reading and mathematics lessons, she went on. Nice little place, even time to plant flowers. I've been a little concerned about her, with all this Indian trouble. Abner was planning on riding out there today along with Joe Bob over at the livery. Jojo helps her round up wild cows in winter to pen for fertilizing her potato patch every spring. She grows an ample supply of potatoes enough for the whole community, wonderful potatoes, there's some in the basket there," she declared.

"Bless me they are fin' lookin'," Polly agreed.

Having drafted the statement along with two additional copies describing the death of Ben Stroughby, Abner passed them to James and Luke for approval.

"I 'llow thet purty much sez what happened," James said, glancing at Luke for agreement.

"Yep, reckon thet's how it wuz 'right 'nough," Luke consented.

"Thet boy, Jojo, he got kin here 'bouts?" James inquired, after Luke had read the document, and accepted it.

"Nearest relative is a sister over at Fort King, named Lila. She ran off with a horse soldier, a sergeant McCall, not a bad sort, actually quiet upstanding, word is they're married now, according to the boy," Abner said answering James.

"Yo' allow he might hanker ta go there? Somebody ta look after him an' all. If he's of ah min' me an' mine would be proud ta see he gets there. 'Special it on account ah me, he," James ended his communication on that, and started anew. "Well I'll jus' see ta it thet's all." A softer voice, as he looked out the front window into the street.

"Well we can approach the boy about it when he gets back, as for now I best get over to the livery and get Joe Bob's signature as a witness. I noticed Lonnie Tucker on the street with Joe Bob when all this took place, he can make his mark," Abner said, picking up the deposition and copies.

"Ya'll come along if you like, if we don't get it now they will be too drunk later. Lonnie will just make his mark, but Joe Bob will have to be sober enough to write his signature, if it's not already too late." Abner said following them out the door.

"Who's thet?" Luke asked seeing the woman standing in front of a small-dilapidated shanty, drinking from a tin cup and watching them.

"That's the widow Callahan, Liz Callahan." Saying no more about her just kept walking as if he wished she hadn't been out there.

"Well mayhap she saw what happened, iffin them ol' boy's too drunk," James stated.

"I've no doubt she did, but her signature would not be suitable on a somewhat legal document, especially one given to the commander at Fort King

Luke gave his brother a funny look before asking, "Why in tha world not."

"Well, boys, she's the town's sporting woman and well known by the soldiers here ahbouts, everyone at the fort to be sure," he explained. "It's a shame though, she's an educated woman, and a good woman all things considered. Her husband was an officer with General Harney when they got themselves ambushed, sixty men massacred south of Fort King a couple of years back," he elaborated, making sure not to look at the woman.

"It's not been easy for her, with the town women folk not talking to her. She couldn't hold up to hard labor, she was from a quality Virginia family, that disapproved of her marriage to any officer who wasn't West Point," he went on. "She's tried sewing first but failed, just not enough business. She eventually turned to her present line of work. It's a real shame," the storekeeper said sincerely.

"Yeah, it is."

Both Luke and James acknowledged the long brown-haired woman by touching the brim of their hats as they passed. Abner considered doing the same but declined the opportunity to do so, just kind of bobbed his head slightly. The handsome middle-aged woman smiled slightly as they passed.

The three entered the front of the livery barn passing through, and out the back door, toward a low-burning fire in a circle where the ground had been raked clean. Smoke from the fire drifted through, and out the door they had entered, leaving the interior hazy. Perched on down-turned kegs on the opposite side of the low flames, sat the two men they sought. Each man with his half-empty jar of pinkish colored liquid, both continued staring into the embers, as they were approached.

"Well storekeeper whut brings yo' out ah yo' li'll money makin' cave?" the apparent older and one-legged man asked in a friendly way, without looking up, instead spitting a brown stream into the fire. The wet gob popped and sizzled upon hitting the hot coals.

"Yeah, yo' run out an' stock ta count?" the other asked, both laughing at the intended humor, and causing the fire to sizzle, as they both spit into the glowing chunks of burning wood together.

"Yo' the feller whut done ol' Ben in," the on-legged man mentioned through brownish-stained gray whiskers covering a toothless mouth, and pointed his long lumpy forked stick, substituting as a crutch toward James.

"This here is James Nash, and his brother Luke. Boys this is Joe Bob Smith, and Lonnie Tucker there." Pointing out the one-legged man to be Lonnie.

"You men witnessed the confrontation between Ben and Mista. Nash, so we've come to ask you to sign or make your mark on a deposition I've drawn up, for the commander at Fort King," Abner explained their business, coming quickly to the point.

"Ol' Ben Stroughby wuz one hell of ah injun fighter, I ort ta know. I fit' with'm more'n once. Tried ta save my leg when tha pizen set in from ah injin arror, but couldn't get it done proper. Thet's how I got this," the long-bearded Lonnie said, shaking the dirty rag padded stick, and spitting in the fire. "Took this leg off hisself, with thet very knife yo' kilt'm with, saved my life too. Least ways thet whut tha doc at tha fort said." Spitting. Sizzle. A small amount not leaving his lips, and dripped down on his whiskers.

"Now I sez, Ben wuz ah good frien' ah mine too, even though he ain't took nary ah leg ah mine." Joe Bob gave them a squinting stare before pushing his long stringy black hair from his face, before speaking again. Spitting at the fire, and watching the ball of juice bounce and boil… "An' me an' ol' Lonnie here're wuz havin' ah drink ta his memory." Joe Bob held up his jar as if studying the quantity remaining then gulped from it.

"Hit were ah fair an' square scrap. We both seen it plain. Sho' as ah bear shits in tha woods," Lonnie acknowledged. "I'll touch tha paper an' make my mark on it."

"Ol' Lonnie there, he's right as rain, it were ah gentleman's fight. Yo' ah hard case, Mista Nash. Special yo' kilt'm with his own knife lak yo' done. With my own eyes, I seed him split Nigger John complete, lak ah ripe melon. An' I ain't never thunk thet I'd ever see any man could take ol' John lak he done. I'll sign thet ah. Thet ah demolition, er, whut ever yo' call it. Whut thet mean anyways storekeeper?"

"Deposition, it means sworn testimony," Abner explained.

"Yeah, thet, I'll sign on it," Joe Bob agreed, spitting.

"Joe Bob's sayin' gospel 'bout Ben guttin' Nigger John, I wuz there too. Pushed his guts back in, an' tried ta tie his hat over ta hol'm in, but John wuz already dead. Yeah suh, when it come ta knife fightin', ol Ben did shine more'n mos'." Lonnie spoke as if he was describing skinning a catfish. "Yo' ah firs' rate killer Mista Nash. Yo'. One ah them assassin jus' lak in them dime books my brother use' ta read me, 'fo' he got his-self kilt by injins three days back. Yo' ol' boys care fo' ah drink?" Lonnie asked, holding out his wide mouth jar with very little of the pink liquid left in it. "Me an' Joe Bob pro-duced it our ownselves, right from grapefruits," he proudly boasted.

"Naw, reckon not, boys, obliged though. We bes' get ready ta move on," James said.

Joe Bob pushed the ragged floppy brim of his hat back from his eyes, after taking the sheets supported by a heavy large book, that Abner had brought for just such a purpose. Spitting once more into the fire and taking the pencil, he closed one eye cocked his head, touched the short pencil tip to his tongue, and printed out his name with some difficulty. Progress delayed only by his audible identification of each letter before marking it on the papers during the procedure.

"Thar she be," he said proudly, before passing the book, papers and pencil back to Abner, who handed it to Lonnie.

Lonnie duplicated exactly the ceremony of his chum, first spitting, pushing up his hat, focusing on the paper with on eye, taking more time than his associate, even though he could not read a word. He poked out his brown tongue and moistened the pencil tip, then scratched his X on the copies beneath his printed name as instructed.

"Thar's yo' paper, yo' demolition er whut ever tag it wuz yo' said. An' it all legal lak. Jus' lak thangs orta be done. Ain't thet right Joe Bob?" Lonnie asked, just before spitting into the fire, taking great pride in being involved in the legal system.

Joe Bob could not have agreed more puffing his chest both shooting twin streams of brown spittle, which met directly in the center of the small fire. In effect putting the official seal on the document.

"Well, boys, we best get on, and we appreciate what y'all have done," Abner said.

"Thanks, boys."

They walked away listening to the conversation between Joe Bob and Lonnie. Apparently there was an additional civic responsibility requiring their prompt attention. And their discussion over the matter grew even more audible.

"I ain't got no ide. It wern't me whut put thet paint and brush up las' time."

"Hit were yo' to, same as tha time befo' thet."

"I declare I got ta be re-sponsible fo' eveathang 'round here."

"We cain' afford ta be ah buyin' new paint eva time thet sign needs changin' on ah-count ah somebody ah movin' or dyin'."

"An' don' fo'get we got two signs ta ree-do. Both ends ah town lak yo' 'most fo'got befo',"

"They jus' ain't no end ta our chargeable jobs, is they?"

"Naw reckon not, it's got so's a man ain't got time ta do proper cogitatin' an' ree-laxin' no mo'. I sho' hope ain't nobody else gets theyself kilt soon, lak as not we gonna run out ah paint, an' cain' get resupplied, on 'count ah tha injin' on tha prod," Joe Bob lamented.

"'Sides Abner Holder ort ta be changin' them signs, he's better at sums then we are. 'Sides he ain't got ta use his fangers when he calculates."

"Yeah sposen mayhap five citizens gets theyself kilt at once, lak as not we might make ah grave mis-take in our calculatin' an' paint tha sign wrong?"

"Right as rain, Lonnie, lak as not they's laws coverin' such. 'Spect we bes' check with Abner fo' we wind up in thet St. Augustine jail fo' falsifyin' legal signs."

Postponing their departure momentarily James, Luke and Abner chuckled after hearing the last of the dejected conversation and the sizzling fire, before stepping out the front door of the smoky barn.

The widow, no longer standing in front of her thrown together hovel was inside because a wonderful aroma of frying bacon drifted out as they passed her opened window. Each man developed his own reminder of an empty stomach after picking up the scent of the side meat sizzling in the skillet along with the aroma of coffee boiling.

"Dad gum if thet don' smell good," Luke exclaimed.

"Yes, I hope the women folk have started something for dinner," Abner said.

After hearing the yelp of a dog they turned seeing the boys returning from their gloomy task. It was needless for Jimmy D. astride Jerico to guide the animal, because the lumbering mule headed straight for the rear of the store. Jojo held a loose grip on the reins of the spirited black pony, allowing it to lift its head snorting at the smells of other animals from the livery barn. Setting relaxed and straight in the saddle it was plain the boy was an accomplished rider.

With very little encouragement Jojo accepted the dinner invitation from the Holders' and Nashs', but only after they accepted his offer of the leather back, as his allotment to the meal. Consenting that the turtle did in fact still belong to Jojo, Jimmy D. decided it really didn't matter as they were sharing.

"Come on, Jimmy D., les' go an' clean thet ol' turtle fo' yo' mamma ta fry up," Jojo said as he ran a hand in his pocket feeling for his Barlow folding knife.

"It's settled then, we can fry up some ham to have with it," Betsy suggested.

The turtle along with ham, a large bowl of greens, plus sweet potatoes and a skillet of corn bread made a filling meal, with the scraps for Bakon and Tater

As was decided that after eating James and Abner approached Jojo concerning his future, particularly his going as far as Fort King with them and locating his sister.

"Cain' rightly leave Honey Tree right now," was the first response from Jojo as he looked out into the street scratching his head, pondering the idea.

"I don't understand," Abner said looking at Jojo, a little bewildered more by his tone, than the answer.

Any thoughts on leaving seemed to be serious problems for Jojo, presenting them the obligation of helping him remedy the situation.

"Well, suh. It's jus' thet. Sometimes ah man gets hisself obligated, then he's bound ta get clear of it befo' he c'n do somethin' else," he explained sincerely if only a little confusing.

"I can't argue with that, Jojo, and you're more than welcome to stay here in Honey Tree with me and Miz Betsy if that's what you're of a mind to do," Abner stated, still a little befuddled by the boy's statement.

"Naw suh it ain't thet, its jus' thet my Barlow ain't cleared off them account books. I calculate I'm owein' forty-two cents, an' I 'spect pa lef' some on them books too," he declared. "Pa always said it aint fittin' ah man run off bein' indebted. Said thet's tha same as stealin'. Ain't thet right?" he asked looking at the storekeeper for conformation on something he knew to be right. "Ain't it right, Mista Nash, ain't what I'm sayin' true?" the boy asked the question this time looking directly at Luke, the storekeeper not answering promptly enough.

"Well. Yeah, some is I reckon," Luke answered almost confused by the convincing argument from the perverse boy, confirming a portion of his statement. "But it ain't lak yo' slippin' out ah town in dark lak ah fox from ah chicken coop. I mean yo' come ta Mista Holder, fo' arrangement 'bout yo' obligation," Luke explained, as the boy listened intently.

Listening to the conversation Jimmy D. butted in, "'Course, yo' c'n. An' them two hats yo' made, my ma already said she'd buy'm. An' maybe give yo' ten cents fo' each one instead ah fo' both."

Jojo considered Jimmy D's words, as a strong reinforcement for their argument, that he leave with them, adding only a minor modification. "Cain' get ten cents fo' each, no suh, they always been five. Thet's my fair price," the resolute Jojo stated.

"Ten cents it is, and I'll deduct that from your account leaving a balance of thirty-two cents. You being an honest sort, I'll trust you to send me the balance when you are able," Abner said sticking out his hand, finalizing the arrangement.

It was agreed after stipulating, he be allowed to carry his own weight that he would travel with them as far as Fort King to be reunited with his sister.

"Yo' any kind ah hand at workin' cows, boy?"

"Yeah, suh, Mista Nash, some anyways, I been he'pin' Miz Anna pen up over ta her place. I reckon I'll do. An' I got ah fus' rate pony too" he answered with pride.

"Thet's good. An' call me Luke, yo' an' Jimmy D. mount up an' start them cows toward town, an' strap thet pistol an' knife 'round yo' waist."

The holstered pistol and knife that had belonged to his father was tied to his saddle, and there was no question in Luke's' mind, as to Jojo's ability to use them if needed, in defense of himself or others. His aptitude far preceded his young years, and what ever else Ben Stroughby might have been or done, he certainly had schooled his son well in the art of surviving.

"Yeah, suh, I'll strap'r on Mista…ah…. Luke," Jojo yelled as he swung into the saddle.

The boys trotted their mounts toward the waiting cows on the outskirts of town near the honey tree. There they stopped while Jojo with his knife modified his belt, by boring an additional hole and cutting off the excess, after which they along with Tater went about their work. After taking their places on the wagon, Polly and Kara Sue said their farewells to the Holders. Mounted James and Luke persuaded the emasculated sluggish animals forward. With clanking chains and squeaking leather the large spoked wheels began rolling south once again.

Polly turned toward Betsey Holder just as the wagon moved, "Lak we said, we'll stop in on Miz Cade an' see to it she's alright, 'sides we need ta try out thet sweet patater coffee ah hern."

Bakon grunted as she made a shallow plow mark with her snout through the dark spot in the sandy street, where Ben Stroughby had briefly lay, leaving one of the few visible signs the Nash family had been in Honey Tree. Even after the cattle had been pushed through following the wagon, the spot remained between the deep tracks left by the wagon wheels. Already familiar with the stain Tater trotted past not bothering to investigate, the dog seemed pleased at being on the move and chasing the hesitant cows once again.

"Thet dog ah yourn ain't much fo' lookin' at, but, he sho' do shine when it comes ta workin' them cows, don' he?" Jojo said as he moved his pony about.

"Yeah, Papa sez he's worth three men when it come to workin' stock," Jimmy D. bragged.

"Goodbye, ma'am," Jojo said to the widow Callahan, touching his hat as they rode slowly past.

"Goodbye, Jojo, you take good care of yourself now. You hear?" she called out waving a hand in the air. "And you too, boy," she added not knowing Jimmy D's name.

"Yes'm an' yo' too, ma'am, thank yo', ma'am," Jimmy D answered; touching his hat brim again as they walked their horses past the polite pretty lady.

Side by side they slowly rode off pushing the unwilling cows ahead, with Tater circling and prompting the cows steady movement, with occasional but abrupt low bark. In this manner they soon reached the Stroughby place, and

Jojo reined up as if taking advantage of time for one last visit at the grave, but instead turned his horse toward the shack.

"Yo' c'n keep movin iffin yo' want, I jus' 'membered somethin'," he said dismounting near the opened sagging door.

As suggested Jimmy D. continued on, turning in his saddle watching Jojo enter the shack before facing front once again. Very quickly though the two were riding next to each other again behind the small herd.

"What yo' fetch from yo' place?" Jimmy D. asked curiously, seemly compelled to find out what his friend had retrieved from the shack.

"Ah book."

"Ah book? What sort?"

"Ah story book 'bout a whale. Ah big white whale named Moby Dick," he explained in brief. "Ain't my book though, belongs ta Miz Anna, I aim ta return it."

"Thet a queer name. Thet tha name ah thet whale or tha book?"

"Both, but I ain't had no chance ta read it. Ain't had no candle ta read by of late. An pa ain't allowed no readin' in daytime, sezs more useful thangs ta be done."

"Ain't thet ah caution? Ah book 'bout ah white whale. Reckon it ah true story?" Jimmy D. had an instant interest in the book, and would like to hear more about it.

"Don' know it true or not, Miz Anna ain't said when she let me hold it. Said most folks ain't takin' ta it much, but they will some day. Tha day'll come it'll be ah real classic, Miz Anna sez."

"Ah classic? Whut's thet?"

"Miz Anna sez thet ah creation of enduring value," he explained confidently.

"Ah whut? What in tha world do thet mean?" Suddenly Jimmy D. cultivated a greater fascination for the book. The first book he had ever seen that was a creation of enduring value or what ever it was Jojo had said.

"Lak Miz Anna sez folks start readin' it an' lak it, they'll take ta it. Lak maybe even in school an' such," he expounded to the inquisitive Jimmy D, the best he knew how, about Moby Dick and what a classic meant.

"Dang! Thet do beat all. Ah classic, an' yo' got one. C'n I see it?"

Jojo retrieved the subject of the boy's attention from his leather war bag and held it up for Jimmy D. to view.

"Dang it new, ain't it? I declare I ain't never seen no classic before. Shucks I ain't never heard ah such," he confessed. "Most new, only Miz Anna done read it. But it lak I say, it ain't min'," he repeated.

Hours later Jojo knew they were nearing the Cade place, and he felt it best that he move up and tell James and Luke, maybe even accompany one of them in. This way he would be available to handle the introductions once there. More than an hour remained before sundown and according to Jojo it wasn't far now, still, it wouldn't do to ride in on the widow in darkness. To Luke's way of thinking, that was apt to produce a dreadful fright for a woman alone like she was, and James was in full agreement. It was decided that they should hurry along for the next few minutes making good use of what light remained. A symphony of sounds encircled them as if nature itself was welcoming the travelers in with the approaching dusk. Bawling cows with an occasional bark from Tater in concert with a great horned owl and other birds, made the orchestra, supported by a multitude of insects.

Suddenly, as if taking their direction from a phantom conductor all the sounds of the forest, even the cows quieted. It was some time after the unnerving explosion and its echoes fell silent, did the night sounds see fit to commence once again. The twin blast that had disrupted nature's modest opus, seemed close, causing Luke to reign up, as did Jojo, riding next to him. Listening a moment for following shots, they heard none.

"Thet wuz Miz Anna's double barrel!!" Jojo exclaimed, and dug his heels into the sides of his mount without further explanation.

The sleek pony jumped forward and was almost at full speed before Luke realized the boy had gone. Kicking Red, Luke pursued the speeding mount down the trail, not the way he wanted it, but it was too late to change the situation. Trouble could be ahead, and the boy could wind up square in the middle of it, and the widow was probably already in it from the sound of the shots.

As it were, Jojo had more savvy than Luke had expected, because he had stopped at the edge of the small clearing, that surrounded the widows small cabin. Bringing his horse next to Jojo who was hunched low over in his saddle, Luke joined in observing the area from the cover of the trees.

"See anythang?"

"Naw, suh, an' thet's whut's plaguein' me. Don' hear Banjo," he said continuing to study the house, engulfed now in the shadows of several large oaks.

"Banjo?"

"Yeah, suh, Banjo's her dog an' ah dern good dog too. He got tha wind on us an' he shor ta know we about by now. But he ain't let on," Jojo explained, concern masking his face.

"Yo' sho' thet were her gun?"

"Yeah, suh, it were hern, right 'nough," the boy answered not taking his eyes from the cabin.

"Well then, we bes' find out whut it wuz about," Luke said.

"C'n yo' cover me with yo' long gun whilst I go in?" Luke asked the question feeling the boy was capable, but expecting an answer just the same.

"C'n, but I fancy my hand gun, case I have to go in shootin'."

Luke felt a sense of admiration for the boy, so young, yet; conduct becoming a man. And if the boy had any fear he certainly didn't display any, with his dark eyes barely visible under the wide brim of his hat.

"Yo' keep low, boy," Luke said drawing his own pistol, and walking his horse slowly from the trees toward the cabin.

Stopping his horse near the front porch he dismounted slowly, keeping his eyes scanning looking for movement, always to his front. He would have to depend on the boy to cover his rear. And worse yet the light had given in to the dusk.

"Thet's far enough, stranger, you can drop that hog-leg and stand easy. State your name and business. Do it now, mister!!" Now there was urgency to her tone.

The female voice came from behind the cabin, at least he thought so the cabin was too dark to be sure, and he was distressed at being caught in the open. And by a woman no less, refusing to expose her self. Then he really felt stupid when seeing a glint from the barrel of the gun poking out from the darkness beneath the house, after a second warning, "Mister, I don't want to say it again!"

"Don't mean yo' no harm, ma'am," Luke said, after slowly lowering his pistol to the ground, keeping his eye on the twin barrels. "I'm Luke Nash, an' we heard yo' scatter gun. Come ah runnin' 'case ah trouble."

"We?"

"Yes'm, me an' tha boy, Jojo Stroughby, he's holdin' in tha brush yonder near the trail," Luke explained. "Take care with thet scattergun, ma'am."

"Jojo! Jojo's with you?" Still concealed in the deep shadows under the house. "Jojo, are you out there? Come on in!"

Luke's imagination wouldn't allow him to conjure a picture of the mysterious woman, only a disagreeable picture of the widow Pucket back in Agusta pervaded his mind. And he could not imagine her crawling around under a house with a scatter gun. Even though he was still somewhat put out with himself for being caught, he snickered to himself at such a picture. The widow Pucket tipped the scales at a very heavy one hundred and ninety five pounds, all five foot two inches of her fat self. For the life of him he couldn't picture her burrowing under a house like a gopher turtle under a pine stump. Jojo rode up as Luke was yet attempting to invoke an image of the dumpy Augusta widow stuck under a house. And stuck she would be if she was to ever get under one.

"It's me, Miz Anna," dismounting and speaking at the same time.

"Come on out, ma'am, I'll take yo' firearm." Luke carefully reached for the muzzle of the shotgun, fearing it might accidentally fire hitting the boy or himself.

Taking both of her hands Jojo effortlessly pulled her from concealment, after she had released the weapon. Even in the barely adequate moonlight, her face smudged with dirt, Luke could plainly see that comparing this woman to the widow Pucket would be like comparing a Rhode Island Red to an eagle.

"Jojo! What in the sam hill are you doing roaming around in these woods after dark? Are you trying to get yourself shot? Does your pa know you're out here?"

Firing a barrage of questions at the boy, while ignoring Luke for the moment as if he were not there. Stopping the inquisition only long enough to brush dirt from her clothes while waiting for answers from the Jojo. Even in the stingy light Luke could not help but notice how the slightest movement, caused her auburn hair to be lightly brushed with highlights, framing her pretty tanned face. As her spirit seemed to be unbound but never out of control.

"No need ta fret, Miz Anna, my pa's dead." Removing his hat and stating matter-of- factly, watching the brushing process and knowing he had said only enough to bring additional questions.

"What!! Ben's dead?" First looking at Jojo, then turning her gaze toward Luke, knowing that he must somehow have been involved.

"This here's Luke Nash, Miz Anna. It was his brother James that kilt Pa."

Luke quickly snatched his hat off upon hearing Jojo's awkward introduction.

"What happened?" Looking at Luke as she asked the question.

"Like tha boy sez, ma'am, I'm Luke Nash," reaching out a hand.

Almost reluctant to do so she took his hand and shook it keeping her eyes on his, and letting him know that she still expected an explanation.

"Tha boy's pa wuz aimin' ta use his bull whip on'm in tha street, an' my brother James stepped in. It got out ah hand."

She looked intently at Jojo, without comment.

"It's true, Miz Anna, yo' know how pa's been of late, special him liquored up an' all," Jojo butted in.

"Pa pulled his knife after Mista James took his whip away. He done cut my shirt near off with thet whip, but ain't cut me up much. Would have though," Jojo said describing the incident, briefly.

"That's tha short of it, ma'am. Like tha boy sez, they fought fo' tha knife an' fell in tha street. Tha boy's pa wound up with his own knife stuck in his chest. He died quick," Luke added.

"It ah pure fac', Miz Anna," Jojo said supporting Luke's statement.

"Well, Jojo I'm awful sorry to hear about your papa. But I know as well as anyone how Ben Stroughby could get, especially when he's drinking. It's tragic, but it appears to have been a fair fight," she said wrapping an arm about the boy's shoulders.

"It wuz, Miz Anna. An' I reckon it wuz good Mista James took it up. Pa wuz meaner then usual. He would've cut tha hide right off me proper."

"Mista James and Luke sez, I c'n go as far as Fort King with'm, ta be with my sister whut got married off ta thet soldier."

"Thet's right, ma'am, we agreed ta look after tha boy, an' get him ta his kin."

Feeling his face become warm Luke embarrassingly realized he was staring at Anna, a rare individual. This petite woman before him in the dim light stood as so few women could, beautiful and lady-like in such manly apparel. Her buckskin britches and shirt on such a woman, he could not have imagined such a thing. Not even the Indian women he had seen wore britches. But there was no confusing Anna Cade for anything other than a well-figured female, very pleasing to the eye, but somehow not delicate. She was almost Indian-like with her dark complexion, and splendid, confident manner.

"Luke, I'm Anna Cade," flashing a smile reaching and shaking Luke's hand once again, with confidence this time.

"Yes, ma'am, tha boy here told me 'bout yo'. He sez yo' never miss with this scattergun," he said, passing the long double-barreled gun back to her.

"We heard them shots, thet's why we come ah runnin'. Knowed it wuz yo' shotgun," Jojo said.

"Knew," she said, not bothering to correct the rest of his statement. "And it was indeed my gun," she answered.

"Yes'm knew." Replacing the word "knowed" he had used earlier.

"I shot a fine mess of coots down at the river." Explaining the shots, after correcting the boy's grammar. "Lucky you folks came by. I killed far more than needed, they were pretty well bunched. So if y'all haven't had supper and of a mind, they're still down there ready for cleaning," pointing in the direction of the dead birds.

"Yes'm be right proud. I declare I ain't had no coots in ah coons age." Oftentimes Anna would not always correct Jojo's grammar, it was far to arduous, and this was one of those times, realizing he grew more careless about his speech when excited.

Not even cognizant that she had let him slide, Jojo volunteered with enthusiasm, and enlisted Luke's help in cleaning the black migrating chicken-like birds, pulling him along by an arm. The eager boy had a craving for the gizzards and livers soon to be cut from the birds, and fried crisp. Luke thought that he might linger for a few minutes, using the excuse of introducing his family to Anna, but on second thought decided that she would take care of it alone. And why not? She seemed quite capable of doing just about anything else, without assistance. Jojo continued tugging at Luke's arm leading him toward the river, stopping after a few steps.

"Miz Anna, where's Banjo? I ain't seen him," he asked as he picked up two of the long sappy pine roots for burning torches.

"Oh Jojo.... I.... Well I must tell you. Banjo is no longer with us,"

"It were ah gator wern't it?"

"It was a gator." This time correcting his accidental bad grammar.

"Yes'm." Quickly acknowledging the correction, but wanting to hear what happened to Banjo.

"And yes, it happened yesterday early. We were crossing at the ford, and Banjo was already out of the water. I was near the edge when the alligator came for me from the cattails, Banjo jumped between us." Her voice tone changed, more downcast.

"Reckon it wuz thet ol' she gator, tha one with them infants," he lamented.

"It was, and it happened so quickly that there was nothing to be done."

"Ort ta kill every gator on tha river. Tha whole dang state." Anger in his voice.

"No, Jojo. We can't blame that animal she was only looking out for her young, just as any mother would have done."

"Well... dang thet ol' gator no how." Turning once again toward the river, shoulders hunched a bit.

The saddened boy would have loved to have shot the alligator, but he well knew it would have upset Anna. He considered Anna to be the smartest person that he had ever known, maybe in the whole world even, but sometimes she had awful queer ideas about such things. Like not wanting to kill the alligator that had eaten Banjo. Both his father and Nigger John, had schooled him about not killing for the pure joy of it, but it seemed to him that when an alligator takes your dog. "Well, seems ta me, thet 'llows yo' jus' cause fo' killing thet ol' gator." Thinking outloud, as he and Luke continued the task of skinning the small but fat water birds, throwing the waste into the river for the very alligator he wanted to kill. And remembering Anna's warning of throwing the carcasses far enough out to keep the alligators at a safe distance. With their chore completed, they returned with the cleaned birds, hearing the call from James.

"Hello the house!!"

"Ride in Mister Nash!! Y'all come on in," Her voice was strong and cheerful, as she called out her invitation in the cool air, standing in the light of the two-pine knot torches that Jojo had lit and stuck in the ground.

As Luke expected, the widow managed the introductions with ease. James and Polly, as Luke had been earlier, were pleasantly surprised by the young widow, and very quickly grew comfortable around her. Her manner of honest independence and strength drew them to her, for she seemed not to be hampered by any judgements others might have. To them it was refreshing to meet someone so different. Buckskins and all, they all became fast friends.

Supper was especially enjoyable, the coots were foreign to their Georgia diet, and they found the strong gamy flavor tasty when fried crispy brown, along with the grits, thick brown gravy and corn bread. A more than fitting meal.

"I declare, Miz Anna, I ain't never had better chuck," Luke said after wiping his tin plate clean with a small chunk of corn bread, popping it into his mouth, then washing it all down with a big swallow of sweet pertater coffee.

"Well there's plenty left for those still hungry. This wild country seems to make a body hungry. Hungry for life as well as food."

"Reckon I'll jus' have one or two more ah them gizzards." Jojo had kept his eye on the last two gizzards in the bowl, but was reluctant to mention them until he felt no one else wanted them.

"You have a very pleasant and happy family. I envy you." Making conversation, as she Polly and Kara Sue cleaned up, while the men took a final check of the animals. Kara Sue saw to it that Tater and Bakon as usual shared the table scraps.

"Why, thet's kind ah yo' ta say, Anna, I reckon we got ah lot ta be thankful fo'."

"Polly, I would like to ask something of you." Her unsure sounding tone seemed out of character.

"'Course, ask away," Polly responded, passing the wet pan to Kara Sue for drying.

"I realize you must think me bold as winter coming on, but…I'm thinking that I would like to travel south with you folks, that is if y'all will permit me to do so."

"Well my goodness ah 'course yo' c'n, but whut ah bout yo' place here…Yo' home?"

"That's just it. It's just a place, and even though my late husband and I built it together, and it is a fine house. But it's no longer home, he's gone and I'm alone to look after it. I." A disconsolate mask replacing her before blithe face.

"I reckon I know how yo' must feel. I don' know whut I would do if, if." She was unable to complete the statement. "Well yo' come on with us, as far as yo' want too." Pulling Anna to her in a firm hug.

"I have very little capital to finance my way. But I would be more than willing to tutor Kara Sue and the boys while traveling. I was a school teacher here and have a great number of books." The cheerfulness returning to her face.

"Now girl, who said anything about financing? But the youngun's could benefit from some extrie schoolin'. Don' know 'bout tha boy, but I 'llow them other two'll be plumb proud." Stepping back and grasping both of Anna's hands, and presenting a welcoming smile of her own.

"Good. And so will Jojo. He has shown to be an exceptional student, always hungry to learn."

"Of course, I understand you will have to consult with your husband and Luke."

"Consult? No. We'll jus' march right out there an' tell'm both."

The rest of the family could not have been more agreeable about the news. Each one entertaining their own reasons for having Ann Cade join them. Luke and James being grateful for an extra gun. Luke having first hand knowledge of just how clever she was and how capable that gun could be. Another woman to talk to suited Polly and Kara Sue just fine. Other reasons occupied the minds of Jojo and Jimmy D, such as reading Moby Dick.

"When can we start our lessons?" After seeing the three large boxes of books the boys had loaded into Anna's wagon, Kara Sue couldn't wait for school to begin.

"Hol' on, girl. There will be plenty ah time fo' thet once we get on tha trail. 'Sides we got ta get some sleep tonight." Was the answer for the slightly disappointed girl, from her mother. Sleep did not come easy for any of them, after all the excitement, but it finally did.

With the approaching light of morning, Jojo took Jimmy D. to the cow pen. "Naw they ain't Miz Anna's cows, them animals carryin' ol' Jacob Summerlin's ear mark an' bran'." Answering an earlier question from Jimmy D, as the two boys walked in the pre-dawn mist. "Got ah big spread south where y'all bound, richest man in tha state I 'llow. Folks say he keeps more'n five thousand Spanish gold pieces in ah box right in tha middle ah his bedroom floor.

"He ever get robbed?"

"Once. Tried anyhow. But Jacob's cow hunters caught'm. Jacob hung'm from ah barn rafter. Jacob Summerlin's as raw-boned as them animals. I seen him once myself." No further explanation from Jojo followed on the hanging of the gold thief as they neared the pen, some distance behind the house. That was one habit of Jojo's that bothered Jimmy D, but he suffered in silence.

"Thet bull an' even them cows, they small lak, but they look right ornery." Was Jimmy D's first comment, after pointing out the smallish red bull with it's long curving horns spreading over five feet. "Reckon thet bull will fight Bovie?"

"Yeah, suh, he will. They are even meaner than thy look. Thet li'l Spanish bull will kill yo' steer if he gets tha chance. He'll kill all yo' animals. He'll kill yo' mamma an' all tha women folk, children and babies too." Pointing out facts about the bull that Jimmy D. didn't want to hear. At the same time magnifying the truth somewhat about the rangy animal, and suddenly sounding as if he were not a youngster himself.

"I'll put ah mini ball right between thet devil's eyes too. Thet ort ta stop'm proper lak," Presenting a solution to the problem of protecting women folk and animals in a defiant tone.

"Right as rain." Jojo's point was taken, and he knew his friend could and would do what may be required in this harsh land. The quick lesson left both boys smiling once Jimmy D. had determined what had taken place. The young teacher went on to explain that the animals were strays that had wondered from one of the long drives north. Further describing how he and Anna had confined them over a month ago, for the purpose of fertilizing her sweet potato patch. For settlers, it had been a long-standing habit of rounding up strays for just such a purpose. Anna knew that Jacob Summerlin's' cow hunters would pick them up on their way back south. But now instead, they would add the beeves to their small herd, and drive them south to their rightful owner. As was his practice, Summerlin would offer a reward of a gold doubloon, or a couple head of cows for the effort of returning the stock. Before leaving, Anna wrote a note explaining her absence, and with Jojo's assistance tacked it to the front door of the cabin with her revolver. He read the note to himself before turning away.

To all my friends, and any pilgrims who might pass this way,

There are no locks, so you may enter this humble home. Should you see anything that you are in need of, it is yours for the taking. I ask only that you be Christian in the taking, and consider all those who may follow, as their needs may be greater than your own. I leave this place without debt. If mistaken in this belief, it is do to a failing memory with no larceny of the heart intended. In any case if I'm wrong, and you have reason for contacting me, you may do so by post or other means. I will be located with or near the Nash family, south of the PEACE RIVER.

P.S. We have five head of Summerlin stock with us.

God bless and keep you, Anna Cade

Turning back before pulling away Anna afforded herself one last obscure look through the mist at her former home. She would not look back again. If they made it at all it would be the start of a new life. But that was the big question. Would they make it? Being perhaps two weeks from Fort King, they expected to run into an army patrol at any time and get information on their chances. Now James was even more grateful for the

lumbering oxen, because of the addition of the Summerlin cattle to their herd. Driving the more than half wild range animals would be far more difficult, and nothing like the domestic animals they had been trailing. But with Jojo being an extra hand plus his experience of working cows, after three days settled to the trail once again, plus Tater keeping the little steer under control. The little train with its addition of friends and animals continued its way south, encountering no sign of other travelers, Indians or even the army. Anna believed as did Acre Foot Johnson the trapper who found Smiths burned body and wagon. After leaving the distraught Mrs. Smith at Honey Tree, had stopped by Anna's, for the purpose of warning her of the trouble. His impression was that a small group of liquored up renegades that had probably split off from a larger group, and Luke and James held the same thought. But having heard nothing from the military, they had no way of knowing just how dangerous a problem they faced. They must keep watchful and ready. More exact information would certainly be available once reaching the fort, in less than two weeks.

CHAPTER SEVEN

The Thomases were pleased with the progress they had made since leaving the Nash family at the Oklawaha River. Randle's opinion coincided with that of his wife's, the mules had done a more than adequate job, and they hoped the Nash's were equally as satisfied. More than once the subject had passed between them, as they made their way westward toward Tallahassee and their new home.

"I declare I'm weary, and I seem to have worked up a mad craving for food. Do you suppose that we might stop for a while?" Caroline posed the question after contemplating some crisply fried bacon, a skillet of Uncle Caesar's corn bread and a hot cup of coffee. Believing a short rest in the warming sun would quickly revive her energy, she pulled back her bonnet, exposing her delicate beautiful creamy skin to the suns rays. This she would not allow for an extended period, because in her judgment, the blowing wind had already dried her skin far beyond repair. But a tiny bit more color wouldn't do any harm.

"Whoa, mules! Yes I do suppose that a brief rest would be helpful," Pulling the mules to a stop in the trail. "Uncle Caesar, would you help Cork start a small fire and get a pot of coffee started? I'll look to the animals."

Cork jumped from the wagon before Uncle Caesar could speak and helped him out, supporting the old man as he limbered his shaking legs a moment.

"I'll fetch us some wood, bet I c'n get some good lighter from thet ol' stump over yonder." Still supporting the old man by his thin arm.

"Bet so boy, y'all fetch me some quick lak, I get us ah fire goin' fas'. Ah good cup ah coffee be real pleasurable, dat ah fac'." He gently pushed the boy in the direction of the pine stump in question.

"Randle I do believe I saw someone," her soft warm southern voice barely reaching him at the head of the mules, from her seat on the wagon.

114

"Where?" He set the bucket of water down, looked up at his wife, and moved beside the wagon where his rifle was kept.

"Up the trail there, the figure of a lone man I believe. But quickly he moved back into the shadows beside the trail." Pointing toward where she had seen the man, or was almost certain that she had.

"Probably an animal, deer maybe." Randle stood close to the side of the wagon, reaching for his weapon just in case.

Thunk, thud…The thud followed so close to the first it sounded as one. Caroline had been looking up the trail until she heard the unusual noise, still unsure if it had been one thud or two. Instinctively, she re-directed her attention toward the sound, and where her husband was standing. Randle looked up staring blankly at her through wide eyes; there was something outlandish taking place, even as she returned his stare. His usual dark complexion had turned white, instantly very white, like cotton. And wet, very much so. First taking notice of his blank eyes, gawking at nothing at all, and they didn't appear dark anymore. And how could she not see the queer way his arms moved, twisting, turning, and clawing at his back. Then, it was this thing with his mouth. Open. Close. Open. Close. No sound. None. Slowly… slowly…ever so slowly… Seconds into minutes, very long minutes. Why must things always move so slow, almost stopping, when such dreadfully quarrelsome matters besiege one?

But that would be of little matter to Caroline Thomas. No, because she had her own methods of copping with disagreeable matters. She just folded her arms, stamped her foot.

"What was the word papa had always used to describe it?" she thought. "Divest? Yes, that was it divest."

She would divest herself of the antagonist, and simply send them away. Something's were more difficult than others, she had to concede that. For instance, she had to admit she saw his tacit mouth, open… close…over and over. But the knife? No she would not see it. Not clearly anyway. She could admit to seeing a portion of its blade only. The shinny portion. A very thin strip of the blade, the working edge, as Big Tug always called it, when cleaning catfish back in Carolina, when she was small. The rest of the knife? No. Not at all. Nor did she record any mental note of the dark hand holding the knife. And you can be sure no memory of the one that grabbed her husband's hair, pulling his head back, slowly, forcing his blank eyes toward the bright blue Florida sky. Yes. Yes. Yes. She admitted the other. The thing about seeing his head move, just not the hand. The gleaming thin edge sliding smoothly and ever so slowly under his beautiful black hair? Yes of course, silly, she saw the shaft protruding from his chest, penning him to the wagon, she was looking directly at it. And then there was the saucer sized red spot left on his head after that, filling slowly with blood. Even slower now. His head falls forward, spilling blood on her shoe.

"Randle for haven sakes why must you continue moving your mouth in such an obscene fashion?" She actually could not see his mouth now, because his face was down, but knew it to be working. She just knew it.

"Well I must leave here. I will return to Carolina. My husband too, you ask? Of course, even though he has upset me. His mouth, and that business with the blood.

"You must think me mad to ask. We will go back to Orangeburg, and return only after my husband's color has returned and thing are more agreeable. What will Mamma think, when I tell her how Randle spilled a saucer of blood on my shoe? My prettiest. She will not believe a word of it. "Caroline I declare, you do have a way about you." That's what she would say.

Even though I plainly have the proof on my shoe, my very prettiest. Papa will though. He always did. Like when little Mary June, my special colored playmate for so long at the big house, took sick with spring fever. I was young then. Papa even called the white doctor, instead of the mule doctor for her.

"Nothing can be done, maybe two days," the doctor said.

Well I went away the very day that she took sick. Of course I wanted to stay and help her get well, but I had already made other arrangements. Papa knew. I had already promised the Indians that I had read about in the territory, that I would visit them, and I did. My dear friend little black Mary June, she was already dead and in the ground by the time I had returned.

"Well, little Miss Caroline, how was your trip to the territory?" she remembered her father asking. "How we did miss you so." Then he said to me, "You must go and hug Mammy and Uncle Caesar." He never mentioned Mary June at all.

"Fold my arms? Of course I did. Stamp my foot? Why yes…I think…I meant too. I tried."

She bent ever so low. Better to see the slow working mouth. Open. Close, and so on. She thought to touch it with her finger. No! "Bite this old stick." Poking at the open mouth. "I dare you. Double dare. No, triple dare you to bite this little old stick, you silly thing you." Poking. Everything foggy. There was not one clear thing left in her world.

"Miz Caroline! Miz Caroline!" She could hear the call plainly, she would swear to it. "Chil' yo' quit persterin' thet ol' catfish, an' get back over here next to ol' Mammy. An' yo' without yo' bonnet. If yo' gets ah finger stuck by thet catfish Uncle Caesar got ta run yo' all tha way home fo' soaking yo' han' in some Epsom Salts water. An' mayhap smear some lard on them li'l burnt cheeks too. He be mighty vexed. An' yo' Papa get Big Tug ta whip tha hide right off me, and Uncle Caesar too, fo' lettin' yo' get injured."

"Mammy, you must stop your teasing. You know very well that Papa does not whip his Negras. Won't allow it." Dear dear Papa. "Uncle Caesar loves me, and he would run all the way to Richmond where Mamma and Papa went last year, if that would stop my hurt." Dear dear Uncle Caesar I love him too. Why, every day he brought my pony to the big house for me to ride. Always a hand on my back should I fall, another holding the reins. And Papa's foxhounds playing, making my pony shy. Slow... everything so slow...

"Get from here! Get Whisky. An' yo' too Bugle! Make Miz Caroline's pony shy lak thet, I'll take me ah stick ta yo' good." Slow, very slow. So unclear.

"Uncle Caesar, you must stop teasing. You know Papa does not allow whipping his animals. Especially Whisky, his favorite. Dear Whisky."

"I know Chil'. Loves'm my own-self."

Wait... Wait. I declare, I must be mad. Whiskey, Papa's favorite foxhound has long since been dead. I know. I was there at Papa's knee when Big Tug brought him home draped in his massive black arms. I was eight, and Big Tug was only ten years older. But he was so big and strong. A Mandingo, Papa said.

"I foun' ol' bugle fo' yo' Massa Brax. He dead. Split from gut ta gizzard. Why he run thet ol' hog inta thet swamp lak he done? Thet ol' boar straight from Hades, Massa Brax." Slow... Slow... "I done run all tha way from deep swamp wid'm. Mayhap Mammy c'n stitch'm. But too late. He done gone, Massa."

"Yes, I'm afraid he's gone. You and Uncle Caesar bury him on the hill. Then go to the blacksmith shop and forge a marker from iron. Uncle Caesar can show you the letters." Papa reached into his pocket and took out two five-dollar gold pieces handed one to each of them. Slow, Slow. Big Tug was weeping. I was there. I cried. So did Papa and Uncle Caesar.

Papa told him, "Tomorrow Big Tug, you go see Mista John McDonald over at Green Hill. That bitch hound of his ought to have her puppy's weaned by now. Whisky is their daddy you know. Get us one. And train it just like you did Whisky." Everything is moving so, so, slowly. Why must it be?

Oh I do declare! Big Tug has long since been dead. Actually a year after Whisky died. Dear Big Tug. Why must things be so confound? I know I was there. Not when it happened, but just hearing Papa discuss it. Mamma asked Papa to stop talking of it.

"It's not proper conversation at the breakfast table, Mr. Claiborne," she protested. So slowly. Ever so slowly these thoughts filled her embroiled mind.

Papa stopped. All he said after that was. He was "glad he had not taken the three thousand dollar offer from Mr. John McDonald over at Green Hill for Big Tug last year." Even if he had known Big Tug was going to get his head pinched off in the sugar cane press latter. He would never have sold Big Tug everyone knew that. I cried. So did mamma and papa. Dear dear Big Tug. All dead, I Suppose I am too. Wait... Wait... Why does it all have to be so confusing, so foggy. I will, as Papa always said about me, "divest myself from you." Fold my arms. Stamp my foot. "I am not mad. I know they all have long since passed away." Oh no. But not Uncle Caesar. I saw him yesterday. "No wait! This very morning I saw him. Oh, Randle, please! Why must you work your mouth so, like a dying catfish? And why did we leave Orangeburg so suddenly? Your color has yet to return. And all this mischief is still about. Very annoying. Very annoying indeed."

Caroline attempted to stomp her foot. But she could not. As hard as she tried she was unable, and she could not fold her arms either, not even move them. She opened her eyes. But only slightly, and intended only for a short duration. He stood between her spread bare pale legs. Big strong and naked to the waist. Just like Big Tug was, a Mandingo. Papa would know if he were here. With the small keg high over his head he allowed the brown liquid to gush freely over his smooth face, chest and belly, making his black skin shine. His outrageously slow movement irritated Caroline, not to mention that it was Randle's bourbon keg the big Negro was being so wasteful with. Closing her eyes once more, then hearing screaming, yelling, and laughter. Which one of the emotional expressions came from her, she had no idea; it was all so confusing.

Feeling herself being pulled up by the front of her dress, she squeezed her eyes tight. Tighter yet, and feeling the front of her dress being completely torn away. Then there was more hideous loud laughter as the remainder of her clothes was ripped away pulled in every direction. Absolutely no cover now. None. Tried folding her arms again, but she could not.

"Oh dear Papa, you always said that I could go away, but I can't." No idea if she was speaking or thinking those words. No matter.

Continuous screams exploded from deep in her lungs, but still she was unaware of it. Hundreds more shrieking cries escaped her throat and as she was again on her back on the ground. No stomping, no crossing arms. Impossible. There were too many strong hands holding her. And the pain. She could no longer ignore the pain, as she had the other things before. Ignore the cutting edge of the knife for instance or the hand that had used it.

Things were not the same now, especially after being taken by so many, but having no true idea of their number or hours. But remembering being rolled over on her stomach. Pain like she had never known. Screams... Screams... Caroline wanted Mammy. She cried for the soothing cornstarch powder that Mammy had always put on her. Between her legs when she chaffed and burned red for some cause. Or the stewed prunes when she cried to Mammy when her little round bottom hurt, as it now did. Only much, much, much worse. "Please Uncle Caesar, take me to Richmond." Moaning.... Moaning....

But Uncle Caesar would not take her to Richmond. Could not ever. Earlier a short muscular Indian brought the old man down, whooping wildly as he swung his heavy club in the air. Uncle Caesar grunted as the painted faced savage reached down and grasped a handful of his thinning gray hair, then let it go. Dropping the club and even before it hit the ground, he pulled a knife and sliced it across the back of one of the old mans legs, near the ankle. The same knife, with the very shinny edge, the working edge. Uncle Caesar's lean body twitched and jerked, the blow was effective but not meant to kill him. Low moans developed from somewhere deep in his throat. And a coating of blood covered the back of his gray hair and his lower leg. The only movement now was the fingers on one of his hands clawing into the dirt, and a slight jerking from the cut leg, quivering lips continued moaning.

Cork saw what happened to Uncle Caesar, nothing to be done. And unlike how Caroline saw things, it was full speed and violent. He tried running for Caroline's screams but was stopped. The small boy's strength was no match for that of his interceptor. Quickly and easily, yet unhurt, he was tied to the wagon wheel. Soon even his screaming stopped, his throat no longer functioning. His wrists bloody from fighting the rawhide restraints, some dripping from the spokes of the wheel.

Bewailed screams mixed with stimulated whoops filled the air as Caroline was stripped and abused. Terrified and unable to see what was happening on the opposite side of the wagon, unable to make audible sounds, he silently sobbed. His restraints cutting into his skin each time his small body jerked. Through tear glazed eyes he could detect no further movement from poor

Uncle Caesar. Still low moans barely audible in spite of the disorder from the other side of the wagon. Soon not even that, from the old man. It became almost quiet. Caroline ceased shrieking, in its stead emitting a constant soft lamented cry. In spite of a leather strip around his neck securing his head, he twisted and looked at Randle Thomas. He could not bring himself to do so again. Somehow he dozed, not knowing for how long. From Cork's view the voice rattled him to a state of partial alertness.

Speaking slowly, deeply, and in English. No Indian could speak like that.

"Well de lawd do wurks in mysterious ways. Don' he? He done give me ah woman, ah real quality one wid red hair at dat."

"I be called Two Ghosts," the black man said, kicking the seemingly lifeless naked woman in the side with his moccasin foot, before drinking from the keg once again. The kick bringing a barely low grunt. It mattered not if she heard she would hear and feel much for a long time. He wanted her again, now. Swallowing large gulps, the excess streaming down his black sweaty face. His villainous companions could no longer. They were sleeping or passed out drunk and exhausted from taking the woman earlier. Two Ghosts laughed loudly as he kicked several of the Indians awake, forcing them up. Then back to Caroline, no longer lifeless, screaming, as he knelt forcing her cramped legs apart. In their language, Two Ghosts gruffly ordered the three weary, bored Indians to help. Easily, he could have taken her alone, but he enjoyed tyrannizing, them as well as his red haired captive. Two held her; the third, with strong hands forced her face to the earth, she was at their mercy, and they offered none. To struggle further would have meant strangulation. Later the three rolled her over on her belly, and continued their violation of her, after Two Ghosts had exhausted himself.

Cork tried to block the screams from his ears. He failed, and cried to himself again. Would there be no end to her torment? It was a helpless situation, he could only wait until they were killed, and for Miz Caroline he considered it would be a blessing. Finally Cork thought he had succeeded in thwarting the shrill screams, from his mind. But, it was not through the power of concentration that the screams ceased. Two Ghosts and his three companions had simply grown weary of assaulting and tormenting the pathetic woman. The Indians after many turns with her preferred the brandy. Squatting next to her, it took less energy to poke her naked body with sticks, as they swilled the strong brew. A mixture of sobs and whimpering replaced the wailing, as her body jerked with each sharp thrust of the sticks. This brought hideous drunken laughter from her tormentors. It mattered little to Caroline that the others were still sleeping and that, only Two Ghosts and the three had amused themselves again. To her disappointment they had not killed her, she would be good for many hours, days, months, of amusement, depending on just how strong she was.

"Boy de white folks whup yo' much?" Cork didn't look up. He didn't have to, he recognized the voice as the one calling himself Two Ghosts, and now standing in front of him.

"Well?" From the surly voice, it was clear Two Ghosts expected an answer. Cork was unsure of how to answer. It wasn't like talking to a white man, but just as dangerous, maybe more to be sure.

"Some." Giving an answer, he hoped would allow him more time for thought.

Whack! The answer brought a quick response. A large hand across his mouth, knocking his head back against the wheel, bringing blood from his lip.

"Well den dey ain't whupped yo' 'nough, 'cause yo' ain't 'speckfull lak. Mayhap I take ah whup ta yo' myself. Now yo' answer proper lak."

"Yas, suh, dey whup me real good, massea suh." This time he answered using his field hand dialect. "I be plum' stupid Nigger, mayhap needs whuppin', Massa."

"Dat, right, an yo' get hidded real good n yo' don't pay min' ta what I say. Yo' my Nigger now. Dat white woman, what use ta be yo' mistus, she my slabe now too, jus' lak yo' is."

"Dat right be proud ta be yo' Nigger now, 'stead dat ol' white trash woman whut use ta beat me."

"Now yo' 'spectful lak, an' yo' tries runnin', dem Godless chilren over dar day catch yo'. Dey kin track ah lizard 'cross ah dry rock. Yo' minfull, boy?"

"Yas suh, Massa suh. I be min'ful."

"Dat ol' Nigger dar, he yo' daddy?"

"Naw, suh, Massa, he jus' ah ol no count Nigger lak me. Ain't my daddy,"

"He ain't dead, boy. But will be least ways come dark, he be bear meat." Laughter.

Cork was beginning to understand just what he and Miz Caroline were up against. What Two Ghosts had said about the Indian's tracking ability, he believed. Physically, he certainly was no match; he would have to continue his deception. He couldn't see Miz Caroline, and could not know her condition. But, he was sure it would take some time before any thoughts of escape were possible. There was hope as long as they were alive.

Two Ghosts called to the Indians in their tongue. Two of the Indians, each grabbing a foot, dragged Caroline while still on her back over to the wagon. Had it not been for her sobbing, Cork would have believed her dead. Shocked by her appearance, as dark bruises were already beginning to show. Blood oozed from tiny puncture wounds over most of her body from the sticks. Badly swollen her face barely recognizable. Hair matted with twigs and filth, all plastered flat to her head. Once more, Two Ghosts shouted a command, and one of them jumped into the wagon and came out with a wool blanket, cutting a slit in its center with his knife. Caroline was pulled to a sitting position, and the blanket placed over her, with her head through the slit, poncho style.

The mules had been unhitched, one loaded with supplies taken from the wagon, Caroline was thrown belly down across the back of the other. Leaving her untied was no kindness; it was just that Two Ghosts knew that her condition rendered her incapable of walking. She would be kept alive, as he and the Indians would amuse themselves later. With only hand signals given by Two Ghosts, the Indians left in two different directions. The half dozen in the group that split off, being led by an Indian called Iron Bull. The one who had knocked Uncle Caesar to the ground, and cut his leg. Another Cork recognized as the young Indian, who had stopped him. Tying him to the wagon wheel unhurt. He remembered the Indian's slight limp.

"Grab thet animal boy, an' foller us, an' yo' fall back, I take my knife an' skin yo' an make ah possible sack out'n yo' hide."

"Yas, suh, Massa." Obediently grabbing the lead rope, pulling the mule after him. "Ain't fallin' back, Massa. I be ah strong Nigger, suh."

They left, Cork looked back at Uncle Caesar, and tears streaked his small face. Still unable to look at Randle Thomas, yet: dangling limply on the side of the wagon, with flies swarming in and around his gaping mouth. What Caroline had thought a saucer, was no longer dripping blood.

A chilling rain began falling, no doubt increasing their misery, however, Two Ghosts seemed pleased as it would aid in covering their tracks. Cork somehow determined they were moving south. Maybe southwest, but unsure, the mist masking the suns location. Hours passed, yet he had no idea how many, only that he was tired and his captors had no intention of rest. To the confused boy, time and direction meant little, especially direction, as any opportunity for escape appeared limited. In the rain he felt escape possible for himself, but he couldn't leave Miz Caroline. Darkness was coming fast especially with the rain, and night was an ally of their captors. Fright and confusion was weighing heavy upon him, and he had no idea how he might save Miz Caroline.

Earlier he had wondered why Two Ghosts had not burned the wagon. Now he knew, the absence of smoke afforded them more time for evasion. But, as to why a portion of his confederates had departed separately, he couldn't grasp. Then it hit him, tracks in different directions, made trailing more difficult. Two Ghosts knew well what he was doing, he was smart, however Cork felt that their only chance for survival was his own thinking. He would have to keep his mind clear and out think their captors. Miz Caroline was way past using hers he felt sure of that, at least for now. He moved his position from in front of the mule, to beside the animals side, yet still able to guide the slow walking mule.

"Miz Caroline, Miz Caroline, it's me, Cork." Keeping his voice low. "Miz Caroline, it's Cork, can yo' hear me?" He dared not speak any louder for fear that Two Ghosts or one of the others might hear.

Caroline, balanced on the mule's back leaning over its neck, gave no responsive sign or sound in return, to the desperate boy. He couldn't tell if she was alive or not. The thought hit him that she might be dead, yet he dare not cogitate on such a possibility. Fear almost overwhelmed the young boy, robbing him of clear thought. Suddenly feeling exhausted, from the hours of walking at the rapid pace, and wondering how much longer he could continue. Suddenly Two Ghosts stopped, holding up one hand, indicating the rest should do the same. In the darkness he barely saw the signal, walking closer to Two Ghosts than he was comfortable with before stopping, holding back the mule. Two Ghosts must have heard something in the darkness. As for himself he had heard nothing, except maybe frogs and crickets.

"Hoo, hoo, hooa," came the call of an owl, from somewhere in the night.

Cork had heard the bird, and was quick to identify it. But, he could not locate the direction from which it came. "Hoo, hoooo." That came from Two Ghosts, cupping his hands over his mouth, imitating the earlier owl call.

He looked back at Cork, held out one arm, and motioned for him to get down, squatting low himself. Cork knelt on one knee, keeping his eyes on the black figure to his front thinking maybe that he had heard a slight noise, the snapping of a twig perhaps. But he was unsure with the light rain falling against the fronds of the many cabbage palms about them. Staring intently into the darkness caused his eyes to water, he blinked attempting to see anything at all. He focused his attention on Two Ghosts then saw a figure step silently from the darkness and squat next to Negro leader.

Cork heard neither noise nor conversation from the Indians. Once again, they started moving single file in the darkness. Cork recognized the silhouette, as the one with the limp. The young Indian stepped aside and allowed Cork and the mule to pass, taking up a position behind. Traveling once again in a direction thought by Cork to be southwest. but still unsure.

But just like the time, what difference did it make their direction of travel? For the next two hours they walked in water, at times reaching Cork's waist. The boy feared the water might get deeper, as the cold penetrated his body. The unknown was a fearsome thing, and he wanted to die, as he believed Miz Caroline had already. Yet after more thought, the fear of death grew, and became greater than the unknown. His body shook, from cold or fear. What matter? They continued moving fast, even faster for the past hour, as the water became less deep. Two Ghosts knew exactly where he was leading them, and Cork felt his captors had been to this place before, many times perhaps. The Indian following Cork and the mule gave a slap to the mules rump, causing it to climb out of the water and onto solid ground.

Barely keeping his footing, as the animal drug him onto the bank. Relieved to be out of the water, even though his body continued shaking in the cold damp air. But, at least he might have a chance to dry out, especially since the rain had stopped. He moved close to the mule hopeful that he might draw on the heat escaping from the animal. At first he thought it his imagination, and listened more closely. It was not imaginary. Miz Caroline had indeed made a sound. She wasn't dead after all. Perhaps being bumped about as the mule ascended the bank had revived her.

"Miz Caroline, Miz Caroline, it's me Cork. C'n yo' hear me talking?"

A low grunting moan, a hand weakly moved. But just barely

"It gonna be alright, I'll get us loose somehow. Yo' gonna be alright." Trying to sound confident. Whispering words he felt likely, to be untrue.

Yet he was hopeful that she at least believed them. The Indians began talking amongst themselves for the first time. Then flames. Wherever they were, the Indians must feel secure by starting a fire. One of the Indians after an apparent order from Two Ghosts, came over and pulled Caroline from the mule, and drug her over next to the fire. Laying still on the ground the blanket, barely covering her otherwise naked bruised body

Setting on a wet log in the darkness Cork watched, knowing better than to approach the fire without being invited. Shivering out of the firelight, he watched them cut up what appeared to be a large snake. To Cork, they appeared almost festive, and for the first time in a long while he felt hunger. The aroma of the small chunks of meat searing on sticks over the flames reached him. He watched as the apparent younger one, offered Caroline a portion of half cooked meat. She ignored it, as if not understanding. The Indian called Iron Bull, slapped the meat from the younger Indian's hand. Anger and irritation was apparent in the in Iron Bull's voice, as he spoke to the Indian. The rest, including Two Ghosts laughed. Later one of them tossed a small chunk over to him, bringing additional laughter as he scooped it off the ground and quickly devoured it.

Even though exhausted, sleep seemed impossible as he sat on the log, rocking to and fro. His misery was born from the awful cold, gnawing hunger and fear. Unable to watch them any longer he faced the ground at his feet. His eyes widened as something interrupted the rays of light from the fire. A shadow appeared where his eyes focused, causing him to freeze his rocking. He heard no noise to warn him of anyone near. Too frightened to look up he continued staring at his own feet, bracing for a possible blow that never came. In its stead a hand appeared offering a sizeable chunk of meat. The Indian tendering him the food was the young one, the same who had made the offer to Miz Caroline by the fire. His gaze moved quickly over the standing Indian, but not his eyes. He cautiously reached for the meat. Tough with an unfamiliar flavor, not very tasty, yet he ate quickly still not looking up. Still grateful after remembering the snake he had seen them cut up earlier. He would have eaten more had it been offered, and feeling he should thank the Indian, but did not.

"Our leader Two Ghosts the black one, and you are of the same skin." Making the comment in English.

Cork glanced up saying nothing, too astonished to answer, even if he had known what to say. Astounded not only by the kindness offered by the heathen, but that he communicated in English.

"Two Ghosts says you are like the sick cub, that the she bear kills because of its weakness. Is it so?" Another strange thing to say thought Cork; and appearing to expect some answer to the charge.

"No. I ain't no bear cub. No animal, I am a human boy. An' I'll be ah man someday," he answered with courage and irritation, at being called an animal. "Maybe someday I will kill Two Ghosts lak yo' say. Tha bear kills her sick cub." Expecting to be struck for the statement but was not.

"Ha, maybe you are right. I think you are not a sick cub. A young panther maybe. Already you have the claws and heart of the big cat."

Lightly grabbing a handful of the boy's kinky hair forcing Cork's face toward his own. Smiling down at the confused boy. Without saying anything further, the Indian turned and walked toward the others, stopping after taking only a few steps.

"I am called Jumper Three Toes." A second thought before leaving the puzzled boy, and joining the others. Cork wondered if the limp was only temporary, as he watched Jumper Three Toes walk away. Quickly switching his thoughts from the Indian back to himself and Miz Caroline. How much longer the two of them might survive, and would he live to become a grown panther and carry out his threat? Miz Caroline certainly could not last much longer without food. But understanding why she would not be hungry, after her torment. Most of the remaining darkness was spent with the Indian's amusing them selves at her expense, yet she cried no more, as if lacking enough life for further crying. Surely, soon they would grow weary and just kill them both, and be done with it. Through the darkness he noticed, the young Indian did not participate in the evil sport of the others.

Instead, simply moving off to the side out of the firelight, his back against a tree, covering him self with a skin. Now that the rain had ceased and the wind lay low, mournful call of wolves could be heard in the stillness. Softly Cork cried, ashamed that that was all he was capable of. Realizing that he could do nothing else his crying continued, still quietly. Not wanting his captors to hear.

Barely awake, still sobbing as the evil activity around the fire ceased, Cork fretted over Miz Caroline, uncertain of her state. She remained quiet. Asleep perhaps? He prayed. She might enjoy peace even if only temporary, as long as her tormentors were the same. Her being dead was not an option Cork wanted to accept, and hated thinking of it. But at least her perpetuating terror would be terminated. Sleep eventually overcame the weary boy, at least a hazy state similar to sleep. His thoughts muddled in guilt, not wanting Miz Caroline to die and leave him alone. Hunched over on the log, he drifted to another place. The last thing his hearing picked up before he drifted, was the sound of rolling surf, clearly floating through the still darkness.

A yelping animal sound disturbed his semi slumber. With tired red eyes, he searched for the sound. The picture was unclear at first, hindered by the low thick mist. Iron Bull was kicking something, he couldn't see what. He could guess the target of the painful kicks from the cruel Indian. The yelping was coming from Caroline, on the ground rolled up in a blanket. As always, Iron Bull's harsh treatment of the woman drew laughter from the others. Cork noticed some of the Indians missing, Two Ghosts being one that he didn't see, plus a couple of the others.

Jumper, however, was still sitting with his back to the cabbage palm, the skin over his shoulders. After one more kick Iron Bull walked a short distance away from the rest apparently to relieve himself, laughing as he did so. Once again the sound of a rolling surf, that had preceded him into his dark hole of sleep, found his ears. It was no dream, he now knew that they were in a swamp near the ocean. Any other time the sound might be relaxing, but certainly not now.

A loud grunting almost rumbling sound vibrated the air. Cork had never before heard such a noise, it was fearful. Jumper, as if sensing the boy's fear, came toward him, stopping and bending down, where the fire had been burning the night before. Cork curiously watched as Jumper with his knife, cut a chunk from the blackened unidentifiable form.

Hope that Jumper might bring a portion for him, whatever it might be. A pang of guilt came over him, as he realized he had not wished any for Miz Caroline. Jumper had indeed intended the meat for the hungry boy, first knawing a piece off for himself. Cork shook his head refusing to take the offering, instead pointed in the direction of Caroline still curled on the ground.

"The woman will not eat," he explained, still holding out the burned meat.

The famished boy took the meat, and promptly pulled a mouthful with strong teeth.

"Do you know that sound little panther?"

"No, it's fearsome though." His mouth was full of the tough chewy meat, still warm from the coals. The meat was unidentifiable to Cork and full of grease, yet tasty enough.

"Alligator, a big bull." Looking directly into the boy's eyes.

"Ah gator?"

"Yes, as many as the trees. That is why Iron Bull will not tie you or the woman. If you run, you run only to the gators."

Cork made no comment, but caught the part about Miz Caroline being left untied; plus what had been mentioned about the alligators.

"Why do you care for the woman? Two Ghosts said she owned you like a dog. Beat you. My people have taken many slaves, beat them too, but they never like us. Now she is a slave to Two Ghosts." Speaking as if it didn't matter to him about the woman. "Two Ghosts said you must be crazy like a dog with a bug in his ear. To like the one who owns and beats you."

"Thet's not true, I jus' lied ta Two Ghosts. I'm free, or wuz."

"Why do yo' run with tha laks ah them? Yo' ain't tha same, not mean an' all." Feeling a degree of comfort in talking to Jumper. "An you don' look lak them."

"I am no Seminole. I am Cherokee. Most of my people are gone now, killed by the white soldiers or taken away, to a place the white leader called

Arkansas. Or to a place they call Oklahoma Territory, far from here. To become tame, the white men say. Some of us would not go. We hide in a place far to the south, the river of grass and the big water. The whites cannot find us there, Two Ghosts leads us to kill the whites and steal their property, even their women and slaves like you."

"I ain't no slave!" Now feeling anger.

"Two winters ago I watched from hiding, I saw one of your color put chains on my father with fire and hammer. My father and mother were old with white hair, and they take them away with my sister, and many others. They take them to this Arkansas. My father made my sister and me run away to join the others in hiding below the big water. But my sister was hurt and could not run."

"Yo run an' lef' yo' family?"

"It was not what I wanted. My father said if I did not, he would say to the spirits that I was without honor, like the big black birds that eat what others will not. And the spirits would not let me be with them in the world of the spirits." Jumper explained with sadness.

"Yo' say it wuz ah colored man what chained'm?"

"It was the dark one they called Nigger. He worked for the white man called Mickler. This Mickler does not wear a soldier shirt with shinny button as the others from the Great White Father. Chief Billy Bowlegs our chief has talked with the soldier chief from a place called Washington. They all wear shirts with shinny buttons, this I have seen too. Mickler never wear such a shirt. But makes war on my people for money, and the soldiers protect him."

"Yo' mean he gets paid to ketch yo' people?"

"Yes, it is so." Jumper reached into a small pouch strapped over his shoulder, bringing out a folded, wrinkled paper. "Two Ghosts cannot say what it means. But a white man told him what the tracks say, before Two Ghosts killed him."

REWARD
$500.00 for warriors, $250.00 for women, $100.00 for children
Must be taken to nearest military post
Reduced reward if dead.

Cork read the faded paper aloud, realizing what Jumper said was true. He could only shake his head as he refolded the paper returning it to Jumper.

"This is why yo' hate all whites, an' will not he'p Miz Caroline."

"I cannot help the woman. And I do not hate all whites. I like the white man who talks the words from the black book about your God, and taught me to speak the white man's words," he explained. "I do not hate all Niggers. I think I like you, but not the one who works for Mickler. Do you like all whites?"

"Naw. But tha ones thet I wuz with thet yo' killed wuz my family, an' Miz Caroline is all I have. I lak her. And I don' lak all Indians lak Iron Bull, an' thet Nigger called Two Ghosts," he declared, finding him self somewhat in agreement with Jumper.

"I hate the one called Mickler the most because he captures my people, and takes them away in chains to the soldier's house, called Fort Myers. Always hiding we follow, and saw them put my people on the big boat. The women and little ones cry. Now we have only a small war maybe can get my father, my mother and sister back. But, I'm not sure I can find this far place Arkansas, or Oklahoma. Even Two Ghosts can not find it." Looking out into the mist and shaking his head slowly, then asked, "Do you know this place?"

"No, but the woman will know, she c'n tell yo'." Cork thought quickly of a plan. He was not happy about deceiving Jumper, but it might keep Miz Caroline alive, and afford her better treatment at the hands of the others. At best it might give them more time to consider a plan of escape.

"Why wuz they ah war with yo' people anyway?"

"Soldiers came to the Okeechobee to make the marks on paper. They draw pictures of the rivers and the trails, I can not remember what this paper is called."

"Maps?"

"Yes, that is the paper. Some of the soldiers got sick on whiskey. Mad like the bear that can not reach the honey, and runs in circles. They chopped down most of the Banana trees belonging to Chief Billy Bowlegs. The trees were many, and like children to Chief Billy. Chief Billy had three slaves of your skin picking the fruit, and the soldiers killed them when they tried to protect the trees. Chief Billy and some warriors killed the white soldiers who had done this thing. More soldiers came to fight us. We could not get enough powder and bullets to fight them all; they were like the trees and the alligators. That is why we fight the big war that is no more. The one with dark skin hammered chains on Chief Billy Bowlegs too, this I saw from hiding. Because I promised my father, I had to run like the fox from the wolf." Jumper displayed a look of disgust.

"Running' don' make yo' no coward," Cork proclaimed, having had his own thoughts of running. "'Sides whut cause yo' got ta kill us? We ain't never done yo' harm, an' we ain't soldiers or tha lak. Mista Thomas, tha one y'all stuck ta that wagon ain't got no soldier shirt, with shinny buttons."

"It was Two Ghosts, he wanted the woman with the hair of fire, he hates all with such hair because Mickler has the same hair of fire. Two Ghosts was made angry because the other wagon taken at the Oklawaha had none with red hair. The people suffered much because of it."

Cork froze when hearing from the Indian, of another attack. He didn't want to think of Kara Sue or Miz Polly suffering as Miz Caroline was. They had all been kind to his family, and helped them cross the river. He was compelled to ask if any were still alive

"The young girl and the woman are they still alive?" Not sure if he actually wanted to know the answer.

"The woman from the wagon was used as this one. Iron Bull scalped her after cutting her nose off, but she was left alive. Her man was tied to the wagon and burned alive. Two Ghosts and Iron Bull did not want to keep the woman because she was not good to the eyes as this one, and not young, how do you say, ah?" He could not remember the word needed.

"Ugly yo' mean?" Cork supplied the unknown word, shuttering at the picture in his mind. But he had not considered Miz Polly as being ugly, nor was Kara Sue.

"Yes, that is the word," Jumper agreed.

"Whut about the little girl and the other men?" He continued his questioning about the welfare of the remaining Nash family members, yet apprehensive about what he might be told

"The ones I talk of. They are not the same as the ones you talk of. It is a different wagon. The ones you talk of, Two Ghosts says we will take later. He has sent warriors to watch them always. They have many guns, so we wait for more warriors, then they will die, but not the woman and girl with yellow hair," he explained. "Many warriors will die for the woman and girl, and the guns, maybe I will join the dead." To Cork, Jumper did not seem sad at the thought of dying.

"Why does Two Ghosts want them so bad? Yo' said he hates all the whites with red hair," Cork said. "Thet woman an' girl got yellow hair, yo' said yo'self," Cork argued.

"This is true. But Two Ghosts wants the yellow-haired woman to keep. And Iron Bull will trade the young one to his sister's son, John Tiger for a wife. John Tiger once had a woman with yellow hair, but she was not good to look at and not strong, and could not carry enough wood. The squaws beat her much with sticks, and she went to the spirit world to soon."

To Cork, Jumper spoke of the unfortunate woman as he had heard Uncle Caesar speak about a chicken-stealing dog once.

"The two that you talk of are young and strong. They are your friends maybe uh?" he asks.

"Yeah they my frien's an' they got lots ah guns, maybe Two Ghosts and the others cannot take them, at leas' not alive. Maybe Two Ghosts and Iron Bull will, as yo' say go to the spirit world."

"Maybe you are right Little Panther." Jumper did not want to talk further and got up and returned to the others. Leaving Cork to mull over what had been said, and hoping that the Indians believing Caroline's knowledge of Arkansas might keep her alive a little longer. He refused to consider if that wish was for her or his own fear of being left alone.

CHAPTER EIGHT

Normally the old black-and-white hound in its pursuit of a meager meal, its ribs rippling under sagging dirty skin, would have drawn scant attention in the street of Honey Tree. So it was, the merchant paid it his normal regard while glancing out his storefront window, as the scrawny animal sniffed and dug into the dark spot where Ben's body had briefly lain. It was not until the stranger entered the picture and dismounted did his interest peak. Especially after seeing the outsider lightly kick at the dog, causing the mangy cur to retreat, but only a short distance away. And even as the defiant dog growled and flashed his long yellow teeth, the stranger yielded little thought to the animal. To Abner Holder, that in it self was an attention builder, ignoring an angry dog like that. Still watching the storekeeper experienced an increase of anxiety. Not because of the snarling dog, but because of the actions of the man. Especially after seeing him dig into the sand with the toe of his boot. Then by the time the stranger knelt, and stuck his finger into the sand where he and the dog had dug, Abner Holder couldn't tear himself away from the window. Mesmerized he watched as the mysterious man lift the finger to his nose, then to the tip of his protruding tongue. Still kneeling, he slowly looked around as if looking for something or someone.

"Betsy! Betsy, come over here." The storekeeper normally calm appeared agitated and secretive at the same time. Calling out to his wife almost in a whisper, but in a tone indicating a state of emergency. But at the same time fearing that someone else might overhear especially the man in the street.

"My goodness, Mista Holder, what's come over you?"

Betsy walked over to the front window, where her husband was standing, wiping her pale smooth hands on her apron for no reason.

"Look!"

Noticing his nodding head, she looked through the window toward the street, as the man stood and began walking slowly toward the store, leading his horse.

"Who is he?"

"I don't know, I've never laid eyes on him before. But he must have some of the same blood as that mangy hound out there." He backed away from the window and gently pulled her back with him, without explaining.

"My goodness, Mista Holder. Why would you say something like that?" she asked about his bazaar statement, it being so unlike him.

Betsy couldn't understand all the intrigue. After all he wasn't the first stranger to pass through Honey Tree, and hopefully he wouldn't be the last. But after Abner explained how the stranger had investigated the dried blood spot in the sand, did she agree it was queer behavior. She resisted with the help of her husband pulling her arm from returning to the window.

The thin wiry, slightly rumpled stranger stopped and seemed to be reading the sign indicating the business as Holders', before hitching his horse and entering. Inspite of his appearance, he possessed the good manners to stamp his boots leaving the sand outside. Deliberately glancing around the interior of the store with penetrating eyes, before entering completely.

"Ma'am." Touching the edge of his hat and nodding toward Betsey.

It was apparent that he had taken notice of the woman setting in the rocker by the stove, her two loose, white rag bandages, staring through glassed over eyes. The narrow one wrapped across her face covering her nose, the other on top of her head, both showing red stains. How she nervously clutched the blanket over her shoulders with shaking hands. And even though he made no comment, they somehow knew by his eyes, that he had taken it all in. Quickly he turned his gaze from her and back toward the storekeeper, as the woman began to moan quietly.

"Yo' be Holder by chance?" A suspicious tone that Abner didn't care for, especially after watching him in the street.

His attire was that of most other Florida cow hunters, topped with wide brimmed leather hat, homespun shirt and canvas britches held in place by suspenders, yet somehow, he was different. Abner first noticed how he wore his holstered bone handled Patterson Colt revolver on his right hip; a bit low, and not appearing to be strictly for snakes and the like. All cow hunters carried a side arm, not always the latest model as the strangers, and usually on the opposite side requiring a cross draw for use; and usually with little requirement for speed, only accuracy.

"Not by chance suh, by birth." Abner extended his hand, which the stranger ignored. He didn't bother mentioning the fact that he was the proprietor; he knew the man had read the sign outside and only introduced Betsey. The stranger nodded his head once more but did not speak to her a second time. Instead the dangerous looking man scanned the inside of the store once again with cold gray eyes. Not at the injured woman however, even as she screamed out, as she tended to do on occasion. Always keeping his arms low to his side, Abner noticed that especially.

"Uh, well, yes, suh. And what can I get you, suh?" the storekeeper asked, returning his hand to his side and glancing quickly toward his wife with a raised eyebrow.

"Reckon yo' got makin's fo' tradin'?" the slow speaking stranger asked, his slow drawl being from somewhere other than Florida or Georgia.

Appearing as if he were not in the habit of asking twice, and expected some response after tobacco was first mentioned, and he had not gotten it quick enough. Betsey noticed that.

"Well my goodness, Mista Holder, get the customer his tobacco, like he wants."

"Oh, sure we have plenty. I'll get it, but only one brand though, our supplies got waylaid." Abner mentioned nothing more about the onslaught.

"Reckon thet wuz yo' supply wagon I come on burned out on tha ol' Spanish Trail, ah mile east of tha Oklawaha ah couple ah days back." A statement, not a question, as he continued staring at the merchant.

"Yes, that's the one. A large sum of money up in smoke." A hint of disgust from the ever frugal storekeeper. "But then the loss of life is much greater, poor Mista Smith was killed, his remains were brought in, and well…. His missus there." Abner realized his mentioning the monetary loss first, must have sounded heartless to the newcomer, and felt a need to somehow redeem himself. And at first was briefly disappointed that, the man had not given him that chance.

"Yeah," was all the man said, feeling the storekeeper really was truly saddened more by the death, and the dreadful treatment the woman must have experienced, than the loss of his goods.

"Reckon I might bargain ah cup ah thet coffee, ma'am? Ain't had ah drop fo' ah spell, no fire an' all." Gentler tones now, leaving to Abner to believe that, he need not explain his earlier statement. "No. smokes neither. My makin's got soaked crossin' tha river. But then ah man would be ah fool lightin' up jus' anywhere."

No reason for him mentioning that, it was plain this man was experienced in surviving any situation.

"Why I suppose you must think us ill mannered, please help yourself." Betsy motioned toward the pot on the warm stove and the cup on the table nearby.

"Y'all had any other excitement 'round here? Other than tha injin trouble, thet is." Speaking as he poured his coffee, then glancing over at Mary Smith rocking slowly back and forth, moaning once again, the bloodstains on her bandages appearing larger.

"Ah…no, no, we haven't." Taken aback by the question, Abner looked at Betsy once more with a raised eyebrow. "Well that is if you don't count Granny Story loosing her rooster to a bob cat, a couple of nights back." Abner attempted to inject humor; yet feeling somewhat disconcerted over the stranger's question.

"Are you a peace officer?"

"Naw ain't law. Whut reason yo' got askin'?" The stranger sensed anxiety in Abner's question.

"Oh! No reason. No reason at all. It's just that I can't recall ever seeing you before." The nervous merchant pulled a white hanky from his pocket wiped his face, before returning it to his pocket, in a rumpled ball.

"Be obliged yo' lay me out ah box ah forty four cartridges with my makin's, with all this injin scare an' all. I'm obliged fo' tha' coffee ma'am. Bes' be movin' on now."

Touching his hat once again toward Betsy and looking toward the Mrs. Smith realizing addressing her was fruitless. The gold doubloon that he tossed on the counter was not unusual, as most big cowmen paid off their help in the Spanish coin, the tender exchanged by Cuba, for the cattle shipments received from Florida.

"Your goods total three dollars and ten cents." Abner quickly calculated, pulling a small metal box from underneath the counter.

Abner was inclined to ask the stranger where he was from or where he was bound, and maybe even his name, but didn't. Only counted out and handed him his change, in greenbacks and coin. As the untalkative stranger was walking out the door, Abner noticed for the first time his footwear, pointed toed boots. The type worn by westerners, not the round toed brogans that cracker cowmen wore. They were listed in his catalogs, but he had never had an occasion to stock any. He also wore spurs, seldom used by cow hunters. Betsy and Abner held their positions until they were certain he had left the porch. Then they immediately beat it to the window from where they had observed him earlier in the street. But to their astonishment the stranger did not mount and ride away. Instead with long slow strides, which to Abner didn't seem natural for a man, not to be considered tall. He led his horse toward the livery stable across the street.

"I sure hope Joe Bob, and Lonnie aren't too liquored up, and run their mouths about things they shouldn't be talking about, especially to a stranger." Abner spoke quietly.

"Pray so."

The mysterious man spent little time at the livery, maybe ten minutes if that. Abner and Betsey stayed at the window watching for the short duration, for them it seemed a long time. He looked both ways down the street, then stepped out into the sunlight, pulled his hat snuggly on his head, and slowly mounted. Another thing Abner made note of was the saddle; he had missed it earlier. It was a Spanish or western type with a horn not used by Florida cow hunters. The whip was however, and he was well mounted on a Marsh Tackie stud. Abner somehow felt the man had a purpose. Maybe the newcomer was following the Nash family. He felt that.

"My God, I hope not," speaking outloud, and watching until the rider and horse disappeared from his view, before heading for the livery.

The black pony after galloping out of town walked easy now, his rider sat straight as he followed the tracks left in the sand. The trail was leading to his old friend Ben Stroughby's shack not far ahead. Like, as not Ben would be drunk he thought, but he would visit for a while anyway. From the trail, the crude wooden cross jammed into the fresh mound of dirt, caught his experienced eye. A slight touch on the reins guided his horse over where he dismounted for a closer inspection. Standing at the head of the mound he glanced slowly around, as if some habit had forced it. He made a mental note of the tracks around the grave, before taking the shovel that the boys' had left, and digging into the loose sand.

"Damn, it's Ben!" After pulling back the canvas covering, shocked at the ashen face of his dead friend.

The attempt at closing Ben's twisted mouth failed and he gave up, after hearing bones snap and his mouth was still contorted. Instead began investigating further by pulling more of the crude shroud away.

"A knife ta tha gut shor' as hell. Ain't thet ah caution?" After seeing Ben's dried blood, coated shirt. "I ain't ever seen tha man thet could take Ben Stroughby one on one drunk or sober. Not head on. Ben yo' an' me beat ah lotta brush together, but I reckon yo' finally made yo' las' one. Ah pure caution," the puzzled man said out loud.

The cautious investigator looked about once again, before getting to his feet, rolled a cigarette with sure callused fingers. Lit it, and smoked while staring into the grave. "I'll be damn," he said, before returning the grave to its original state, after tossing the short still lit butt into the hole. "Ol' Ben had queer ways right 'nough, special after whut happened to his wife an' all, but he wuz one hell of ah man in his day." Talking as if someone was with them. Ben had a boy he remembered, but he couldn't calculate what the boys age might be now, and if the boy might have been responsible for some of the tracks. He led his horse behind the shack checking the stable, discovering Ben's mare missing. Ben would never have gotten rid of that horse he was sure of it. "I'll find out whut happened ta yo' boy Ben, thet's fo' sho'."

Shaking his head in amazement he mounted and rode south, following the wagon tracks. Seated well in the saddle he pulled his hat down tight on his head, almost to his ears and pressed his mount into a steady lope. The stud responded obediently after a light touch of the spurs. Confident the tough little stallion could maintain the pace until dark, he soon reached the Cade cabin. With the slightest command the barely sweating horse came easily to a stop. The horse snorted and stamped his feet wanting to run some more, as his rider peered at the cabin from cover. Seeing no sign of life not even smoke from a cook fire, he walked his mount toward the cabin. Cautiously he surveyed the area even turning in his saddle and checking to his rear before dismounting. He rubbed the horse's nose, while watching the animal's ears for any movement, a sure sign that the horse might sense danger. Before reading the note on the door, he removed his tobacco pouch, and rolled another smoke.

"Danged if thet don't beat all," mumbling as he read the message. "Cade, Cade." Mulling the name over in his mind. "I knowed ah Cade sometime back, ah Lieutenant in the army. Dead now though. Got hisself kilt in thet ambush of General Jessup's brigade near thet little settlement of Orlando. Maybe..." Looking about.

"Lock stock and barrel, took out fo' the Peace River." Still thinking out loud. "I ain't never seen tha lak of it,"somewhat louder. Shaking his head and removing his drooping hat exposing a shock of thick brown hair in need of cutting. After scratching the side of his head he replaced his hat and looked around somewhat perplexed. But more resolved than ever.

"No, suh, I ain't never." Adjusting the cinch on his saddle before mounting, and allowing the stallion to gallop without command, as if knowing what was expected of him. He pulled his leather hat tight on his head, lean agile and relaxed in the saddle, horse and rider moved as one, closing the distance. By good dusk he would catch them. Well prepared for what could lay ahead and what might be required of him, in getting answers about Ben and his son. Allowing his dead friend to rest, and ease his own mind. He galloped on following the clear and easy trail, while those he pursued were beginning to make camp.

"Pull tha wagons up on thet high ground there, it looks lak ah likely spot." Luke shouted, looking around.

Jimmy D. guided the sluggish animals over where Luke had indicated a grassy area near the clear running stream; the other borders lined with scrub oak and thick palmetto. Anna turned her one horse cart parallel to the larger wagon, forming a degree of security. Kara Sue was out and on the ground running toward her before she pulled the rig to a complete stop. There was adequate space to bring the stock in close near the water. Everyone was excited about stopping early allowing ample time for relaxing after the stock was taken care of, and supper out of the way. How wonderful. Such a pretty place Luke had chosen. The December weather had taken a pleasant turn, sunny and warm, one would almost think of spring.

"Luke this place has the look of being rich with squirrels." Anna called out as Luke and Jimmy D. passed, driving the two oxen toward the stream.

"I 'spect yo' right 'bout thet. Yo' aimin' ta get us ah mess fo' supper?"

"Sure, I see no reason not, as long as you agree to a fire tonight."

"I'd be plum' proud ta sink my teeth into ah mess ah squirrels an' gravy," he answered. "James an' I agree that a fire would be alright. Bes' take them two half grown boys with yo' though, lak as not ya gonna need help totin' yo kill, and take thet ol' sorry dog too."

In the back of his mind they still had to be cautious, even being this close to Fort King, and agreeing to a cook fire. The woman back in Honey Tree, her head wrapped in bandages was still in their thoughts. There was more than one occasion where disaster had followed negligence, and he and James would try hard not to allow it happen to them. Trouble could strike like a rattler in this untamed land; and they had already experienced examples of that. Only a short time had passed before the echo of Anna's shotgun could be heard, then another shot, this time it was Jimmy D, firing Polly's smaller gauge gun. From the sound, James calculated they would not be far from camp. His assessment was correct; the hunters had reached the western boundary of the huge oak grove, not a half-mile. Anna was right on the money too, because the area was teeming with fat squirrel.

Those back in the camp heard a few more shots, then a long period of silence. Polly was bothered by the extended silence, but gave no indication to the others. Her concern was unfounded however, because without notice the hunters broke from concealment at the edge of camp. No ratification of their success would be necessary, for Jimmy D's shoulders were draped with the proof. Almost two dozen plump gray squirrels, tails tied together filled any need to ask. As a bonus, Jojo carried his coat stuffed full of poke greens, that had been picked from the bank of a nearby creek. The dark green elongated leaves would be a delicious accomplishment for the meal. Poke greens being unfamiliar to the Georgian diet it was necessary for Anna to explain the quirks of cooking them.

"There's a trick to cooking poke, it's necessary to change the water a couple of times during cooking."

"Why?" Kara Sue inquired.

"Well, it's because they are poisonous. Not deadly, but sickly, and it must be washed out during cleaning. And these red stems must be pulled off," she explained, demonstrating.

Kara Sue at first, had doubts about eating the once poisonous greens, but after tasting them cooked with bacon she agreed it was worth taking a chance of dying over. They all agreed. Especially when sopping up the pot liquid with a piece of hoecake.

"Reckon I crave ah 'nother dipper ah thet gravy, on my sweet-per-tater," Jojo said, reaching for the long handled ladle.

"I declare Jojo yo' gonna bust ah seam, yo' keep eattin' lak' thet," Kara Sue teased.

"Miz Anna, reckon yo' might read thet book yo' gave ta Jojo? The one 'bout thet whale?" Jimmy D asked, spooning in a last bit of greens into his mouth, while awaiting the answer.

"Now, Jimmy D, y'all let Miz Anna be 'bout thet story, I declare y'all been at her 'bout thet since she joined up with us. I 'spect Miz Anna's ah might tuckered, special her doin' all thet squirrel huntin' an' all," Polly admonished.

Secretly, Polly hoped Anna would consent to supplying entertainment for the evening. It was all Jimmy D, Kara Sue and Jojo could talk about lately.

"By gosh, Jimmy D. I think that's an excellent idea. I would be pleased to do so."

With thoughts of Miz Anna reading Moby Dick on their minds, the supper clean up was accomplished in record time. The animals hobbled by the stream, they made ready for the evening's pleasure. The crickets and frogs among the cattails, seemed in direct competition with the night birds. Each was trying to outdo the others in the still dusk. Those more agreeable sounds soon was disrupted by the roar of a bull alligator, from his muddy den nearby, warning intruders that he was not to be bothered. The price extracted for ignoring such a warning would be severe. Jimmy D. struck a match and put it to the wick of a lantern, making ready as the rest took a comfortable place forming a semicircle facing Anna. Kara Sue leaned back against Bakon's round belly, with Taters head resting on her lap. Adults with a cup of coffee completed the picture, as Anna began reading.

"But what takes thee a-whaling? I want to know that before I think of shipping ye." Anna read, giving her voice a touch of gravel, and looking up before turning page seventy-eight. "Well, sir, I want to see what whaling is. I want to see the world," changing her voice to indicate that of a young boy.

"Want to see what whaling is eh? Have ye clapped eyes on Captain Ahab, sir?"

"Who is Captain Ahab, sir?" she continued switching her voice.

"Aye aye, I thought so. Captain Ahab is captain of the ship."

" I am mistaken then. I thought I was speaking to the captain himself."

"Thou are speaking to Captain Pegleg. That's who ye are speaking to young man," she read in as deep a voice as she could muster, making eye contact with as many of her audience as possible.

Suddenly standing up and growling low, Tater stared out into the darkness, not barking. Anna ceased reading as James gave an unspoken signal to Luke, after dousing the lantern. Without speaking Luke kicked sand over the flames and directed Jojo and Jimmy D. to take cover in the shadows on the opposite side of the wagon, with instructions to watch their backs. The women armed themselves and took refuge in the darkness under the wagon. James moved to a clump of palmettos nearby.

They knew from Tater's warning that something or someone was out in the darkness, what and how many was the question. They waited but they didn't have to wait long.

"Hello, tha camp."

To James the voice appeared to have come from several directions at once. He couldn't see a thing. Nor could any of the others it was far too dark. Who ever he or they were, they definitely had the advantage, as it was obvious that the camp had been watched from the darkness before the call. At least there had been no shots fired, and no one had been hurt so far, but the intruders were holding the good hand of cards, and they could only wait until they were dealt.

"Hello tha' camp. Seen yo' fire, an' smelled yo' coffee. Mayhap I c'n come in?" The location of the caller was still unknown. Only concealed in the dark shadows somewhere in the scrub.

James was positive that the man had relocated himself, because the second call seemed to have came from further to their left. He also knew that Luke was aware of the man's tactics, but would not attempt to move on the crafty caller. They would wait, believing that to be their best hope, even if it took until daybreak.

"Lak I say I seen yo' fire, an I been pushin' hard all day. An' I jus' lookin' fo' ah friendly cup ah coffee. Cold air done reached my bones. Stove me up ah might," the persistent man repeated his request for coffee.

"Mayhap. How many yo' be?" James returned the call, all the while his eyes circling the darkness for movement.

"Be ah-lone," the answer came in a slow deep drawl, still hidden.

"Move in easy, be proud ta see some hands, Mista." James pointed his rifle in the direction of the unseen voice, along with the warning.

The invited stranger walked his mount up to the edge the fire, making his hands visible as instructed. Looking around slowly and deliberately after stopping his horse, using only a low voice command. James surmised the man to be maybe ten years older than his own age. But clearly more than capable, by the way he wore his gun and sat his horse, while studying his surroundings.

"Be obliged yo' tell them two young'ns not ta get heavy with them fingers. Ain't aimin' ta get myself shot, 'special it a couple ah scairt boys." His hands still high as he continued searching around for Luke, yet hidden.

"Well now, mista, I reckon it don' much matter who done tha shootin after ah feller already been shot," James answered, his rifle aimed at the strangers belly and moving nearer the fire himself. "An' I reckon it ain't real smart fo' ah feller ta be travelin' alone, special with all tha trouble we been hearin'." Not bothering to caution the boys as the stranger had requested.

"Yo right as rain mista. How yo' called?"

"'Spect yo' might 'llow me ta ask all tha questions. Who yo' be? An' whut's yo' business with us?"

"Mista, mind if I drop my hands? I ain't fool 'nough ta kick up trouble, special with all them guns on me." His voice deep and slow. Still cautious.

"Yeah, I reckon yo' c'n drop'm, but yo' move real easy," James cautioned.

"Name's Moon. August Moon. An' I be bound fo' tha same place y'all be, south, tha Peace River. Thet is yo' be tha Nash Family, lak I reckon. " The stranger partly answered the question about his business. The answer shocked James, leaving many more unanswered questions.

"Mista tha way yo' carryin' thet side arm, it 'pears yo' one ah them pistolairos. Are yo'?" James inquired after noticing his low-slung holster.

"I've killed men, mostly Indians an' Mexicans. An' some whites thet needed killin'."

The dangerous looking stranger gave no indication of his awareness of Luke quietly moving in behind, until he spoke.

"Mista, I don' reckon yo' ta be ah back shooter."

"Jus' how tha hell yo' be knowin' who we are mista? Yo' be tha law?" The question came from Luke who like James, was not the least bit surprised over the man capabilities.

"Naw, suh, ain't no law. But they seem ta be ah powerful interest in who's law 'round here." He gave no explanation for the comment. "Use ta be law sometime back, but no more. I be ah cow hunter fo' ah big outfit, Mista John Overstreet, Peace River Valley. We jus' finished ah drive up ta Jacksonville. Mos' ah tha hands took ah paddle wheeler back down tha St. Johns River ta Palatka. Me, I don' hold with boats, done thet once. Got sick. Off my feed fo' ah week, prefer ridin' now. Y'all got reason fo' fearin' tha law?" The question appeared as an afterthought. But wasn't. It was clear; the stranger was more interested in acquiring information than giving out any.

"Naw, reckon not. No cause fo' frettin' any law. Go ahead Mista clim'down an'grab yo'self ah cup an' pour, it's still hot. Y'all come on in; I reckon Mista Moon means us no mischief."

Anna lit the lantern, as Polly chunked a few pieces of wood on the hot coals, causing sparks to rise as the developing flames cast additional light on the stranger's sun creased face, lightly covered with brown stubble. He appeared to young for the few streaks of gray that highlighted his long hair hiding his ears and back of his neck.

"Never said how it is yo' come ta know who we are an'where we be bound." Luke was still a little uneasy with the stranger.

"Seen thet note thet Miz Cade there, lef' on her door, when she took up with y'all. Reckon thet be yo', ma'am." Turning cold cautious eyes on Anna.

Anna was surprised to say the least over his identification of her. "Mista Moon, would you kindly explain how it is you know me,"

"Them injin moccasins, ma'am." Nodding toward her feet after sipping coffee.

142

"Noticed they showed up after yo' joined with this outfit. Jus' curious thet way I reckon." He set down without being invited. His eyes less cold now, and his voice more friendly

"Reckon yo' are at thet," Luke said, glancing at James, yet untrusting. But admiring the stranger's uncanny art of observation.

"'Nother thang I'm right curious ahbout. I come on ah fresh grave this mornin' an' it causin' me ah great deal of puzzlement. 'Pears the unfortunate man met his de-mise with ah knife."

"Now, mista, it 'pears yo' takin' ah boundless interest in thet unfortunate man. Yo' acquainted with him, wuz yo?" With more than a trace of suspicion returning to Luke's voice. Just when thinking he might take to the mysterious stranger.

"Yeah, suh, I knowed Ben, we busted brush together scoutin' fo' tha army sometime back." Looking directly into Luke's eyes. Blowing across the top of his tin cup, then slurping.

Jojo, about to take a sip from his own cup, quickly retracted it and stared at the visitor. He could not recall ever seeing Mister Moon before, but that didn't mean anything. Nigger John had been the only friend of his father's that he had known. Mostly because all the times his father had been scouting, he had been left with his sister. That is until she ran off with that army corporal and got married. After that he had been pretty much on his own, with Miz Anna looking out for him some. Very few visitors came, especially after his father took to drink. Except Nigger John. Often Jojo had wished Nigger John had stayed away too, had he done so he might yet be alive.

"It lak I said I'm ah real curious sort. An' ah picture of anybody takin' Ben Stroughby out in ah fair scrap is ah hard pill fo' me ta swaller. Special with ah blade." Looking over at Luke again, now setting next to James on a log across the firelight.

"Well, Mista Moon, I be James Nash an' this here is my brother Luke an' thet's my wife Polly." James didn't bother introducing Anna, as Mista Moon already knew her. The stranger touched the brim of his hat toward Polly, then Anna. Quickly returning his attention back to James. "An' it wuz me whut kilt Ben Stroughby. An' them two young'ns there burried'm," he said, pointing toward the boys, "Yo' right. He wuz ah hard man right 'nough, hard as I ever run on. But he wuz bad drinkin' an' I reckon I had luck all on my side. 'Cause he fell on his own knife in tha scrap an' thet's whut kilt'm. I never had no knife when we faced off."

"Thet tha way of it, boy?" Turning his gaze toward Jojo, confirming he also knew him as being the dead man's son.

Jojo glanced at James before answering the question. James nodded his approval for Jojo to answer, showing the boy a thin smile, telling him it was all right, without speaking.

"Thet's tha way of it, suh, it lak Mista James said, accident kinda lak. My pa wuz gonna hide me good with his whip," Jojo added. "An' yo' knowin' my pa lak yo' say, yo' knowin' he wuz more than ah fair hand with his whip. Near ta cut my shirt off me before Mista James took it up."

"Yeah, boy, I 'member how good yo' paw wuz. Reckon thet's tha way of it then. I'm sorrowful 'bout whut happened boy." The sadness actually did show in his eyes as he looked at Jojo, shaking his head slowly. Satisfied now about the death of his friend, and knowing the boy was safe. He appeared more relaxed and in a talkative mood, and inclined to visit and enjoy the fire and company.

"Thet hound, he any 'count?" The inquiry came as if any discussion of Ben Stroughby's death had never come up. "Thet kind of ah queer pig ain't it, tha way he act jus' lak ah dog?" he asked a second question as if it really didn't matter to him about the dog's value. Then started talking about Ben once again.

"Well, I reckon tha boy bein' with y'all an all, shows it wuz square, an' ol' Ben wuz as hard as they come. Him an' me joined up with Captain Jacob Mickler in fifty-four, to capture Billy Bowlegs. I 'llow we chased thet varmint over every square foot ah swamp 'round tha big water. Thet ol' chief wuz real slick." Continuing the conversation on Ben Stroughby. This time, however to talk about Ben, not ask questions. "We quit Mickler though, discovered he wuz jus' ah low down scalp hunter. Cain' abide thet kin' ah behavior." Without further explanation, he stopped talking and drank the last from his cup.

"Thought Bowlegs wuz caught?" James remembered reading that somewhere.

"Wuz. But only after we quiet Mickler, an' wuz workin' with tha army. Ma'am, reckon I might beg borrow or steal 'nother cup ah thet coffee?"

"I declare yo' shore c'n, an' don' have to do nothin' but ask. We done with supper, but we got some hoecakes lef' if yo' care ta have any."

"Be proud, ma'am, mayhap yo' got some sorghum ta top 'em off with." His once suspicious cold eyes now displaying a glint of contentment.

"Kara Sue fetch Mista Moon ah plate ah them cakes an' thet crock ah' syrup."

August took the plate containing the half dozen-cornmeal cakes and

144

covered them completely with a thick layer of dark sweet syrup, adding a generous amount to his coffee.

"He wuz caught right 'nough, an' shipped off to Arkansas with most of them Seminoles. Some never did get caught don' know how many though, or who be they leader. They too far back in them everglades fo' tha army ta get at. Thet wuz proper chuck ma'am." Wiping a sleeve across his mouth, then reaching for the cloth pouch containing his tobacco. "But, I reckon, how many an' whoever they is, whut's doing this mischief will be caught soon." Licking the thin paper and sealing in the tobacco, then putting a burning stick to it, lighting it. Tossing the burning stick back into the fire.

"August, yo said yo' wuz once a law man."

"Yeah, suh, I wuz. Weren't much more 'en ah button myself, little more'n these boys here." Looking at James after taking another deep draw on the perfectly rolled cigarette. He continued. "Me an' ah frien' I growed up with, Joe Lee Kendall along with ah bunch other Texican boys joined up with Captain J.D. Patterson's Texas Rangers. We rode tha Brazos country runnin' down the apach' Didn't ketch many though, but did dis-courage'm from raidin' tha small ranches so much." he admitted.

"Joined tha army in forty-seven. Wound up with General Winfield Scott in forty-eight, an' landed at Vera Cruz by boat. Joe Lee wuz kilt, I took ah mini ball in tha leg, at Churubusco. Got me shipped home. Healed up, went back ta tha rangers, with my younger brother. Lak I say, them Apach' lak these Seminoles, never wuz able ta get'm all, some run off into Mexico. But we got some ah their leaders, but they'll still kick up again though. Injuns do thet from time to time. Thet's whut we got now in Florida, they come out 'en them swamps, steal an' kill, then run back."

All thoughts of *Moby Dick* and Anna's reading, disappeared like smoke in a high wind. They all wanted to hear August Moon continue his tales; even James and Luke found themselves listening intently. They both had had their run ins with the Cherokee as youngsters, but nothing compared to the Apache or the invasion of Mexico. August needed no special inducement to continue, just keep the coffee hot, and allow him time to roll a smoke now and again. The once thought to be restrained Texas born August Moon, was a gifted storyteller. The bright fire yielded, as red and white embers replaced the flaming larger chunks of oak. They all felt a little more secure, especially since August Moon was there, with an extra gun.

"Well I reckon I been jawin' fo' quite ah spell now, an' it time I turned in," August said, throwing a short butt into the coals.

Polly agreed about the time and rose to her feet moved toward James. Jimmy D. and Jojo was the last to make any effort, they lingered a few more minutes watching August prepare his sleeping spot. With his large knife he quickly cut an armful of nearby palmetto fans, and spread them at the base of a substantial live oak away from the dying fire. Over the silver blue green fronds he placed his canvas ground cover and threw his worn saddle down as a pillow his approximate body length from the tree. The preparation for his safe comfortable night's repose was done quickly and efficiently. He removed his holster with pistol and placed it next to his saddle, before shedding his boots leaving his socks. In the dim light, Jimmy D. and Jojo continued watching as August lay down placing his hat over his blanket covered feet against the tree. Covering the rest of his body including his head with the same worn dark wool blanket.

"How come he sleeps lak thet? With his feet agin' thet tree an' all. An' puttin' his hat over his feet lak he done?" The inquisitive Jimmy D asked his friend, as he pulled his own blanket up to his chin.

"It on ah-count ah bushwhackers or injuns an' tha lak."

"Bushwhackers?"

"Yeah, my pa sez ah bushwhacker lak as not'll shoot thet hat thankin' it's his head. Say that ah body prefers bein' shot in tha foot instead ah his head." Jojo whispered tugging at his own blanket, after using his hat to cover his bootless feet, as August had done.

Before falling asleep, Jimmy D. calculated that without a tree, it didn't matter much which direction his head pointed. He did however throw his hat over his feet, wondering how painful it would be, to be shot in the foot. Maybe even to having your big toe shot clean off by a bushwhacker. As a final act of safety he attempted to flatten his feet as flat to the ground as possible. Causing both feet to cramp beneath his hat and blanket. The big bull alligator bellowed another warning from the swamp, causing Jojo to think of something he would share with Jimmy D.

"Jimmy D?"

"Yeah?" Moving his feet, easing the cramping.

"C'n yo' keep ah secret?"

"Reckon. Whut kin' ah secret?"

"It 'bout ah dream I always have. 'Bout ah big ol' gator after me." Whispering. Not wanting anyone else to hear about his dream.

"One lak thet big 'n out there in tha swamp, whut keeps blowin'? He get yo'?"

"Don' know I always wake up jus' before he clamps them big jaws ah his'n down on me."

"Jojo."

"Yeah."

"Yo' ever seen ah whippoorwill?" Jimmy D. wanted to talk about something else; he didn't want to hear anymore talk about alligators with clamping jaws. He shuttered, forgetting about his cramping feet.

"Yeah, I have," he answered with a small amount of pride. "But, them birds'r hard ta get up on. They tricky as ah back house rat."

"I know they are. How is it yo' got up on one?"

"Nigger John learned me. Yo' gotta cover up complete with palmetter fans, or mayhap a big pile ah moss. Stay real still, an' when one lands in ah big pine close by, an' starts his callin', yo' c'n see'm," Jojo explained.

"Dern! I shor' would lak ta try thet." Peering over his blanket at his feet, checking on his hat.

"I'll learn yo', jus' lak Nigger John learned me."

Both boys fell asleep thinking hazily on whippoorwills and Moby Dick. Their hats shoved snugly down over their feet. Believing what Miz Anna had said about Moby Dick being a classic someday, a work of enduring quality or something like that. That means it would be around a long time, Anna could not have agreed more. And Jojo would teach him how to see a whippoorwill; things would be real good. Soon neither boy was aware of the sounds of the night birds, crocking frogs from the creek, or even the alligator.

CHAPTER NINE

The chirping of the day birds helped usher in the transition of the dawn to daylight, sending away the bellowing of the alligator and call from a lone wolf. The hundreds of spindly tall cypress trees, covering the eastern side of the great swamp failed to block the determined rays from the rising sun. They were however; assisted in the effort by a heavy mist that prevented the shafts of light from reaching the black water. Where succeeding, they cast a yellow orange haze across the surface of the cool water.

First Jimmy D. moved his toes, then both feet before uncovering his head from under the wool blanket to the cool dawn. Sometime during the night, he had dreamed a bandit had shot through his hat and took a big toe right off. He felt no pain as he slowly pulled the blanket from his bare feet. Squinting he stared into the thick fog and inventoried his toes feeling relief. To be sure, he recounted before watching his mamma and Miz Anna throw wood on the fire.

"Ain't no bandit or bushwhacker shot off nary one toe." Smiling to himself, he nudged Jojo awake, before slipping his healthy feet with toes intact into his cool boots.

"Come on, Jojo, we gotta check tha stock, lak as not thet ol' gator done drug one off las' night," he said excitedly.

After his dream, Jimmy D. was much more excited about being intact than about checking for any losses the alligator might have inflicted during the darkness. But it had to be done.

"Well alright slow down Jimmy D. ain't nothin' we c'n do iffin thet ol' gator did ketch one ah them cows. I shore ain't goin' out in thet water ta fetch 'em back, an I 'llow yo' won't neither."

"No suh, not me neither, I ain't cravin' no run in with no bull gator, not today. An' I bet even August Moon ain't gettin' in thet swamp." The aroma of boiling coffee reached the boys.

A quick nose count confirmed that none of the stock had wondered, and to the disappointment of the hungry alligator, none had entered the water. Had any of the grazing beasts done the latter, they surely would have been subtracted from the numbers moving south. Soon the boys followed the agreeable smell of frying bacon and boiling coffee, after promising Tater they would return soon with something for him. Over breakfast, it was agreed that August Moon would stay and travel to the Peace with them. They expected the days travel to be comfortable, as there was no hint of foul weather, with the sun now well above the trees, bringing with it full light and a gentle breeze. Even with this, James, Luke and August could not allow themselves or the others to become slack. Still a full day out of Fort King, danger could be waiting at every turn of the trail.

Soon the wheels were churning deep into the white sugar sand, a pleasant replacement for the black muck of the low saw grass terrain they had left behind. Thick clumps of thorny stalked palmetto reflecting the blue sky spotted the immense fields of deep green-brown grass. A hawk, its white head reflecting the sun, glided low through the tall straight pine standing above the shorter scrub oak. Soon the panicked cry of a rabbit could be heard from nearby brush. Further along the trail they scattered a large flock of turkey. Polly ignored the death cry from the rabbit, instead focusing on a fawn still with its spots, in the tall grass off the trail. Not completely hidden by the palmettos, the doe watched her young one, ready to signal danger if necessary. Beautiful. This was the way Polly had dreamed Florida to be. Not the picture painted by Homer Dew, back in Troopville Georgia; deadly swamp vapors, Indians, bandits, and rattlesnakes. She was compelled to look back for her daughter. She smiled; Kara Sue had discovered another doodlebug in the sand.

"Reckon I might get us some supper," Luke said turning his horse off the trail after seeing the birds fly off westward, through the piney woods.

"C'n I go, Luke?"

"Sure, Jojo, come on."

"Ya'll pay mind," James warned, as he returned his brother's wave.

Within the hour the two returned with a couple of plump gobblers tied to Jojo's saddle. They knew they would arrive at Fort King well before dark, and fried turkey would be an extra special supper. In her mind, Kara Sue could taste the leg off one of the birds already, as she walked next to Bakon.

"This was a perfect place for doodlebugs," she thought out loud, searching the sandy soil for the shallow holes. She caught a slight whiff of smoke in the air as she trailed behind the wagon, confining herself between the tracks, having earlier learned a hard but valuable lesson.

Jimmy D. reined his horse in, and stopped the oxen when they saw the cabin, and the source of the smoke. A small shack, roughly constructed of cypress logs, and a thatched roof of palm fronds. The shanty was built right on the ground, an indication that it had no floor other than dirt. Only a dingy clothe material hung over each of the two visible open windows. A thin stream of smoke drifted from the dilapidated stick and mud chimney, with no hint of cooking odors.

The crude hovel gave the appearance of sinking into the deep gray sand, considered to be the yard, with the only plants being a small collard patch off to one side in dire need of tending. Holes in the dwarfish pale green leaves left clear testimony, that bugs had collected their share first. A skinny milk cow with one short horn and ribs showing was trying to push through the rail fence and munch what remained of the withering plants. As the wagons stopped a man appeared in the doorway. A mob of ragged barefoot children of assorted age scurried around him and into the front yard. It was difficult to access their numbers as smaller ones stayed inside and peeked around the gaunt partially balding, bearded man. Others shot for an outside corner of the shack, peering around with large dark sunken eyes. While the rest stood with a hand shielding the sun from their dirty faces, and runny noses.

"How do, pilgrims," the little man mumbled through an almost toothless tightly drawn mouth under his scraggly coal black beard. However the greeting seemed friendly and sincere.

"How do, mista? We be tha Nash family, thet's my ma, Miz Polly Nash."

The man politely nodded his head toward Polly after Jimmy D's introduction, then shot a burnt umber ball of spittle into the white sand between his bare feet, then with a dirty toe pushed a thin covering of sand over the damp spot. The act probably more a matter of manners, not hygiene.

"I be Jesse Bill Books, an' thet be my ol' woman Ivey there," he said, pointing a lean finger toward the only window in the front of the cabin. The sad looking figure appearing in the opening somewhat resembled Jesse Bill, without the facial hair. The same blank stare through similar dark sad, sunken eyes. In place of his thinning black hair, hers was a thick gray pulled back and tightly tied forming a ball in the rear of her head.

She made no comment only nodding her head once. She too carried an obvious pinch of powdered tobacco between a sunburned cheek and pale gum.

"Be proud ta in-vite y'all in ta noon with us, but our chuck been ah might skimpy an' all, ain't hardly got 'nough fo' this bunch ah hungry young'ns." Jesse Bill Books apologized. Truly embarrassed over his inability to be gracious toward the travelers. A humble attitude to be sure, which hinted the Books' as being perhaps not always prosperous, but far from paltry, as they now appeared.

"Oh, thet's fine, mista. Books don' be ah frettin'. We ain't hungry ah-tall, on account ah thet big meal we had this mornin'." Polly regretted the part about the meal, after the fact.

"Thet be alright then. We craved us ah mess ah collards, but they so pore, 'cause ah tha bugs got in'm so bad. Been ah real plague on ah-count ah tha warm winter an' all," the pitiable Jesse Bill said, automatically acquitting himself for their lack of fresh greens.

"Thet's too bad. I'm James Nash, an' this here's my brother Luke. August Moon there," James said as they rode up.

Jesse Bill acknowledged each with a nod, before speaking. "Fac', tha young'ns went an' got us ah mess of poke salat, down by tha creek, an' tha ol' woman worked us up ah big pan ah pone ta go with it. Used up tha las' of our meal though, an' had ta cook them greens without any side meat." He spit after lamenting the lack of side meat available for the wild greens, in his low voice

From the window his wife nodded her head in agreement. One of the smaller children worked up enough courage to move next to the old man, hugging one of his legs with her skinny well-tanned arms. It was a distressing picture presented to the travelers. He acknowledged the child with a gentle pat on the head. Her stringy hair pulled high from her head after sticking to the palm of his hand; then releasing and falling back to it's disorderly fashion on her little head. He spit, pushing sand over the spot once more.

The canvas breeches worn by Jesse Bill Books were far too large, and lacked suspenders to keep them up. In their stead a length of hemp rope knotted tightly around his thin body, served the purpose. The big-legged trousers were ragged at the bottom. Not the result of wear, but had been imperfectly altered, and absent of proper hemming. A bony knee could be seen through a split in the rough material.

"Yo' folks new here ain't yo'?"

The question was asked through tight lips as if not wanting to spill any of the flavorful substance contained in his mouth. He failed however, in the attempt, as a thin stream of the gold brown liquid dripped over his whiskers. With a badly frayed sleeve of his dirty shirt he wiped it away.

James wasn't sure exactly how to answer the question. Did he mean, new to this particular area near Fort King, the state, the south, or what?

"Yeah," came a simple one-word answer.

By now Anna had descended from her wagon, and stood next to August, Jojo and Kara Sue and was introduced to Mr Books and his wife yet in the window.

"My ad-vice ta ya'll is ta go back to where y'all come from. This ain't no fit place ta live. We lost four young'ns since we been here, two this year alone, one jus' las' month from a snakebite, down at tha creek tryin' ta git some poke greens. Moccasin bit her right on tha butt, she wuz gone before tha other young'ns got her back home," he lamented. "Tha other took fever, they all buried back ah tha house, along with 'nother'n what died two year ago. Which 'n were it, Ivey?" he asked his wife, forgetting which of his children had died from fever, or which had been snake bitten.

"Hit were Cassie Rose."

The woman spoke for the first time, and it was unclear whether Cassie Rose had been the snake bitten child, or the one who had died from fever, or the one two years ago. Anna did a simple calculation that totaled three children dead, remembering that Jesse Bill had mentioned losing four. She did not mention it. To Polly it mattered not. She shook with a chill at the thought of how close Kara Sue had come to snakebite. Sadness overcame her as she looked at the window and Mrs. Books. Then back at the others.

"We wuz aimin' ta save 'nough eggs fo' breakfast come tomarrie, but them ol' hens done let up layin'. 'Ceptin mayhap one or two eggs ah day," he added, pointing toward a half dozen hens of assorted colors, scratching in the sand, that had surely been scratched out long ago.

Just then the hens scattered clucking in protest as a big hound came around the corner of the shack holding a large brown rat in his mouth. A poor excuse of a dog to be sure, his thin frame loosely covered by a coat showing patches of red dry red skin, where the hair had fallen out. Jesse Bill quickly glanced at the hound, then continued speaking.

"Hit were Buster's doin's, they don' lay no more. He went out thar, an' banged on tha tin roof ah tha coop with ah pine knot. Nigh ta scare them hens ta death. An thet ol' rooster ain't been actin' right since." After spitting, he pointed toward a big black rooster wandering in small circles and head low, his beak plowing a shallow furrow in the sand. "Ain't natural fo' ah chicken ta act lak thet, least thet I ever knowed."

"Hit weren't zackly Buster's fault. He were only tryin' ta get ah weasel out'en tha coop. Thet varmints done kilt one ah them hens tha night before."

Ivey Books spoke a second time, defending her son's action of banging on the roof of the coop.

"An' on top ah tha queer ways he's ah actin' there an' all, he's took up crowin' at noon time 'stead ah mornin' time lak ah rooster ort ta." Jesse Bill plainly ignored Ivies' defense of Buster, as he pointed toward the disconcerted rooster.

Buster, the apparent older of the brood stood shirtless with his head down in shame. The skinny boy showed a full shock of black hair shabbily cut pointing in every direction, as he churned a bare toe in the sand. They all looked at Buster, then at the coop out back. A ramshackle affair barely supported on cypress stilts, standing few feet off the ground. Were it not for the big pine tree to its rear for additional relief, it surely would have fallen over on its own, with little or no help from Busters.

"We plannin' on pullin' stakes an' head back ta Alabamie, we done been here nigh on ta eight year now. Ain't thet right, ol' woman?"

She didn't answer her husband.

"Buster got us ah possum tha other night though, kilt'm out back behind tha privy with ah hoe. Near ta chop his head right off. Hit wuz ah big fat'n tha ol' woman cooked it up real good with tha las' of our sweet pertaters. Thet wuz right smart eatin'," the little man said, spitting and covering.

"Yep," the untalkative woman said supporting her husbands' words, about their plans of returning to Alabama, or about Buster killing the fat opossum behind the privy or both.

With all the talk about the opossum and how it was killed, Buster now was able to lift his head, no longer feeling shame. Now he stood tall, feet spread looking up, with his thumbs hooked in the bib of his warn and too short overalls.

"Thet pig, she ah pet, ain't she?" Jesse Bill asked, seemingly unable to resist in asking, after noticing the way Bakon and Tater reacted towards each other.

"Yeah, she jus' lak ah dog, names Bakon," Jimmy D replied.

"I declare yo' hear thet Ivey thet ah pet pig an' thanks she ah dog, names Bakon. I declare if thet ain't ah caution," the unkempt man.

"Cain' yet though, not since thet ol' mule up an' died ah month or two back," he said sadly, once again back on the subject of returning to Alabama.

"It's always ah bad thang ta lose such ah animal," August added, considering the man's dilemma.

They all assumed that Jesse Bill had changed the subject of pulling stakes and the conversation would lead to other things. But after the quick comment about the pig, the subject again returned to leaving, and his plans to acquire another mule just for that purpose. Everyone shook their heads in agreement, not knowing what else to do or say about the dilemma that the family now found themselves. James had seen similar families in Georgia, but none quite so bad off. Maybe the Bookses should return to Alabama, for a new start. Polly wondered what she herself might do, should they find themselves in a similar predicament. What would it take to make them surrender to this wild land, and march back to Georgia a beaten family? Just as the Bookses were being forced back to Alabama.

"We cain' pull stakes till late spring though, on 'count ah Capt'n Whidden's mule I been dicker'n fo'. He 'greed ta trade thet ol' mule fer my labor, pickin' oranges from his grove, me an' tha woman an' whut young'n c'n pick," he explained, with a hint of elevated spirits over his plan for gaining a mule.

"He got ah couple of slaves ah pickin' but, they ain't able ta keep up," he added.

"Well, Mista Books, trying ta grow anything in this sand would lick jus' about any man," James said, making ah effort to lift the beaten man further from his low.

"Pure fac', an' it good yo' got ah plan fo' acquirin' ah mule ta leave. This soil be hard pressed ta grow weeds," Luke added.

"Oh hit will grow oranges right enough an' good too, but I ain't no orange grower. But it ain't jus' thet. Hit ah lot ah thangs, y'all see whut I mean soon 'nough. They's thangs out there what eat ya. Gator got one ah my young'ns right off, tha firs' week we set foot on tha' place, snake got 'nother," mentioning once again the snake casualty.

"Oh my word!" Anna exclaimed. "That's terrible!" she said. Making special note of the statement about the alligator victim and the forth child lost. She looked at the other nine remaining children of assorted ages at least that's how many there were in view. Three or four of the youngest did not appear well, judging by their protruding stomachs, and they all seemed to be suffering from some disease, which caused their teeth and gums to be beet-red. And by Mr. Books' own admission, it certainly was not from over eating.

"An if it ain't them thangs what get yo', mayhap it injuns, if yo' don' starve firs', lak we ah doin' rat now." August noticed the bewailing man failed to spit.

"I reckon thet be true 'nough." August pushed his big hat back from his eyes. He had seen many families like this before here and Texas, plus many more in Mexico. And he well knew that, sometimes a man can get so far down there's no getting up. Books appeared on the edge of having reached that point, being permanently broken. Like many a good stallion broken, instead of being trained well, he hoped not. Although it seemed the door to any kind of future in this land was closed tight for Jessie Bill Books and his family. But in the past August had also seen many good men, accept death rather than give up their pride. Jessie Bill was still alive.

Jesse Bill continued the conversation on their present problems. "Shore is, some soldiers come by two day ago say injuns on tha sneak, an' done kilt some folks. Thet's why we wuz holt up in tha cabin lak we wuz. But it seem lak now, hit wuz jus' ah small bunch causin' a ruckus. If I had me some shot and powder, I'd go an' get myself ah look-see. 'Sides thet, all them young'ns come down with a fretful case ah belly worms."

Books' eyes displayed some fight left in him, especially when he mentioned scouting for Indians, but quickly reverted back as he returned to the problem of his broods belly worms.

"Tha ol' woman been dosin'm with poke berries, thet whut thet ol' Nigger mammy over ta tha Whidden place say ta do 'bout belly worms. Say she done treated more'n two or three dozen young'ns, an' some be white folks too. Don' know it workin' or not yet, jus' set ta tryin' it. But it sho' do make teeth red don' it?"

"So that's what's causing their red teeth, thank God." Anna had been thinking all along that some dreaded unknown disease had come on them.

It was difficult at times to hold a conversation with Jesse Bill, because one minute he was discussing Indians, and the very next breath it would be his young'ns belly worms and their treatment.

"Allow thet true ''nough, but ya'll still pay mind, we seen some ah their devil work already," August warned.

The warning pertained only about the Indians. He hadn't the slightest idea as to whether pokeberries would be a suitable treatment for belly worms, however the Negroes usually had knowledge of such remedies. But he would have to agree about the red mouths, he had noticed it just as the others had, but none wanted to mention it.

"Aim to, but I sho' am put out ah mite, thet them chicken shut down layin' an all. Wuz cravin' some eggs fo' Christmas breakfast tomarrie, we got ah tad ah grits lef', but nary ah egg on tha place." The sad look returned to Jessie Bill's eyes once again after mentioning their lack of eggs. And he changed the subject as if not wanting any further discussion on Indians, alligator and snakes or the like. But the lak of eggs seemed equally perturbing to him.

"Mamma, it's Christmas tomorrow." Kara Sue was beside herself with excitement.

"I declare it is. It plum skipped my mind 'bout Christmas an' all," with an implication of excitement in her own voice.

Luke dismounted saying nothing as he unhitched one of the turkeys from his saddle, handing the large bird to Books. Jesse Bill was stunned, completely taken aback by the generous gesture, and for a moment found himself unable to speak.

"Merry Christmas." Luke stepped back smiling at the astonished man.

"Yes, Merry Christmas. Kara Sue, how about looking in my wagon and fetching a sack of that corn meal," Anna said.

"Why I declare ah big ol' gobbler! Ain't had one in ah spell, since we run out ah shot an' powder. Buster there he ah first rate hunter, c'n track ah hawk in flight."

For the first time Buster smiled, and scratched a big toe in the sand, then looked down as if determining what his toe was doing.

"I 'llow we would've starved ta death long time ago, if it wern't fo' him bein' such ah good thrower."

Buster's big toe dug deeper and his smile grew wider, as his father continued boasting on his ability to kill small game with a rock.

"Jimmy D. pull out ah basket ah them sweet taters, fo' Mista. Books, an' oh yeah, ah piece ah thet side meat an' ah sack ah coffee too." Polly was suddenly and fully into the Christmas spirit.

"Sweet Baby Jesus, it ah Christmas miracle! We ain't had ah speck ah real coffee since August, when our supply run out. Tha young'ns been scratchin' up acorns fo' me ta parch an' grind up, hit's tolerable, but hit ah fer piece from regular. Hit ah sight bitter fo' mos' folks," Ivey Books mentioned, no longer in the window, but standing beside her husband. She took the sack of meal from Kara Sue, as Jimmy D. placed the basket of sweet potatoes and other groceries at her feet.

"Polly, I reckon we got extrie pickled pigs' feet?"

"I'll get them, Papa," Kara Sue returned with the crock of pigs' feet.

"Praise be, I ain't never seen tha lak ah such a fin' folks. I reckon this be 'bout tha bes' Christmas we ever had. Ain't it, Ivey?"

"Peers so, Mista Books," Ivey confessed with a glint in her eye.

"We be thankin' ya'll kindly fo' all them fixins'. Hit been ah long dry spell since my young'ns had such ah meal. Reckon me an' Buster might take ah notion ta cut us as swamp cabbage tomarrie to go with thet turkey an' sweet taters." Jesse Bill feeling a bit of provocation for self help.

"Mercy thet would be fin' an' I c'n make us ah nice stuffin' fo' thet ol' gobbler," Ivey added, as the smaller children gleefully danced around.

Jessie Bill placed the turkey on top of the basket of sweet potatoes for cleaning later. He must remember to caution Buster about removing all the pinfeathers, when cleaning it. Ivey had fussed the last time the boy had cleaned a chicken because; he had failed to remove some of the pinfeathers.

"Meanness, go fetch ah sack ah them oranges, what Mista Whidden give us fo' these fin' folks. Thet be our Christmas present fo' them," Jesse Bill instructed.

One of the smaller boys standing next to Jesse Bill scampered away into the shack. He returned shortly dragging a sack of fruit too large for him to carry, as he flashed a row of red teeth. Ivey explained that Meanness was not the child's real name, that it was just a nickname that his father had given him. His given name being, Jesse Bill Jr.

"Mista. Books we cain' approve takin' none ah yo' fruit." Polly felt uncomfortable taking anything in exchange from an apparently starving family.

"'Course yo' c'n 'count ah we got more'n we can eat. Mista. Whidden gives us plenty every week. Lak as not we wind up throwin'm ta them chickens," Ivey insisted.

"Then we be thankin' yo', they look lak right tasty fruit."

"Well, folks, I reckon we bes' get movin', aim ta make tha fort well befo' dark." James reached a hand for Jesse Bill's giving a firm shake.

Polly and Anna took both Ivies lean hands feeling their roughness, as they passed Christmas greetings to each other.

As the wagons rolled away, one of the children exited the shack with an old but well-kept fiddle and handed it to Ivey, another handed a banjo, to Jesse Bill. As Luke, August, and Jojo moved the cattle past, they failed to notice that Buster had pulled a harmonica from the pocket of his worn jeans. Jimmy D. took his place beside the oxen, while Tater circled slowly; there was no need for barking. The cows by now were in the habit of following the big steer. Already on the trail, they were unable to see Jesse Bill preparing his little band for making music by patting a bare foot in the sand. And after acquiring the proper rhythm, Ivey joined in with her fiddle, and Buster added lively notes from his harp, his own foot patting the sand. The enjoyable concert could be heard over the sounds of the animals and the copper bell of the steer, as the caravan moved away for Fort King.

With a hand August blocked his eyes from the sun, trying to determine its location in the clear blue December sky, around noon by his calculations. Luke looked over at August smiling as they heard the old black rooster crow loudly right on time and plainly over the music.

Jimmy looked back at his mother and asked, "Mamma, whut's thet song they playing?"

"Thet's 'Tha Rose of Alabamie,' boy." Polly smiled at her son enjoying the music.

They could clearly hear Ivey singing the words of the song, blending perfectly with the instruments.

"It real purty. I reckon thet's my favorite song in tha whole world," he quickly judged, having heard the song for the very first time.

CHAPTER TEN

As usual Luke decided to ride out ahead, even though they were aware they couldn't be more than a half-day from Fort King, and the danger had decreased considerably. Mostly to locate a suitable campsite, with ample grass for the stock close to the fort. For a change Anna had asked to ride along, and August agreeing to handle her wagon. Within a matter of a couple of hours after seeing constant fresh sign and the smell of smoke drifting across the thick palmettos, they met their first human since the Books family. Thanks to a covey of quail scattering from a palmetto thicket, drawing their attention in that direction, they saw the rider before he was aware of them.

The rider had come out from a side trail onto the main trail, intended on traveling the same direction as they. Well mounted on a large white stallion he pulled up after seeing Luke and Anna, turning his mount better to face them.

"How do pilgrim, ma'am." The tall neatly dressed man appeared friendly enough in greeting them, touching his hat brim as he addressed Anna.

"Howdy, mista. We ain't bandits or tha lak." Luke thought it best to say that after seeing his hand move slowly closer to a white handled pistol stuck in his belt. He had missed seeing it earlier because of the long white coat the man wore.

"No, I reckon not." Returning his hand to the rein.

"Luke Nash is tha name, an' this here is Miz Anna Cade. We be bound fo' Fort King, an' reckon it cain' be far, we got family coming' up."

"Aisa Tucker, suh, and your' right as rain it's not far, maybe twelve miles. Heading for Ocala myself."

"Ocala?" Anna spoke; she had never heard the name before.

"Yes'm, that's the town near tha fort. Building fast now, a hardware store, post office, and a courthouse. The latest construction being a Methodist church and a whore, eh, ugh. I mean ah boardin' house." The man stuttered

159

the final part of his statement describing the new town, being more than a little embarrassed.

At first Luke wondered why August had not mentioned the town of Ocala in their earlier discussion about Fort King before, then realized Mister Tucker had just explained that it was a new town.

"Like I say, I'm on my way there now. I had a visit from sheriff Howse last week; and he's saying I'm to bring this boy in as security for a debt of eighty-one dollars, I owe at Mista Coles' general store."

They failed to notice the young light-skinned Negro boy until the man spoke of him. The boy, approximately ten years old was hidden behind him on the horse, peered around at them.

"This boy is called Lord Wellington."

"Lord Wellington! My goodness what a crackerjack name," Anna exclaimed.

"Yes it is first rate. But it was not my doing. It was my brother who gave him his name. He used to belong to my brother along with this horse."

Because they seemed genuinely interested, Mister Tucker went on to explain how his brother, then an army captain at Fort King, had acquired the boy and the horse in a game of chance at the boarding house in Ocala. The previous owner of the boy, a riverboat gambler, called High Spades Jack from Jacksonville, had been caught cheating, and shots were fired. Mister Tucker related; how his brother had caught a round in his side, and that his own well placed shot hit the gambler right between the eyes.

Mister McLeod, the owner of the establishment along with other witness declared the fight a fair one, and the gambler positively dead, and the looser. The self appointed judge McLeod, also declared Captain John Tucker the new owner of the slave boy and the horse hitched outside. The young captain at first unsure about taking the boy, but opined leaving the boy, would only result in further maltreatment by others, as was the habit of the deceased gambler. Remembering, and disapproving of how the gambler had required the boy to set on the floor at his feet, and fetch drinks, food, or anything else being desired. Captain John Tucker was a West Point officer and compassionate man, and quickly grew fond of the boy.

Further explaining how the boy was never given a name, for if so the boy was unaware of any. "Always called boy or little Nigger and the like. So my brother named him Lord Wellington, after the British Duke and victor over Napoleon, who he studied at the point. As it stands now, that is his legal name," Mister Tucker explained.

Mister Tucker had never been ashamed to relate how his brother had taken the boy in, caring for him and commencing his education. Always quick to declare how bright the boy was.

"What an amazing story, Mista Tucker! And yes, truly a wonderful name for such a handsome youngster." She smiled at the boy. The slight Wellington saw her smile and returned one of his own.

"I agree, Miz Anna, but I may be forced to change it. Lots of folks don't think it is proper, and unlike my late brother I do not wish a confrontation over tha matter." No further elaboration.

"Well, I certainly hope that is not forced upon you, Mista Tucker."

"Yo' said late brother Mista Tucker?" Luke gave the man a questioning look as they continued slowly riding toward Ocala.

"Yes, suh. My brother caught ah arrow in tha spine a year ago. He held on at the fort infirmary for a few weeks, but finally died after the poison set in," he explained with a sad slow voice. "Before passing he sent for me. Had me swear to take Wellington and care for him, and complete the boy's education as best I could. I agreed of course, as my wife is a former schoolteacher from Carolina, and she's taken charge of the boy's education. I also promised that Wellington would be freed when he is able to take care of himself."

"But yo' said yo' got ta put ta boy up as security for a debt."

"True, Mista Nash. I have a hunch that it's all about John Reardon, owner of a warehouse and dock over on the Silver River, at the springs where the steamers come in. He's been plaguing me to break my oath and sell Wellington for quite ah spell now. Up to now, I have always been able to refuse. I'm sure it is his intention to work Wellington at his warehouse, but the youngster is far to small for such physical labor. I refuse to sell the boy for any reason. But if I am forced to give the boy up, Coles will sell him to Reardon, for a considerable profit. He's just a special boy, and my wife is very fond of him. I suppose I am too." Reaching back over his shoulder and touching the boy on the top of his head affectionately.

"John McIver McIntosh is the judge in Ocala and a fair man. I hope he will let me keep the boy, or mortgage my land instead. I will be able to pay the debt after my fruit gets picked this winter."

"Yo' ah fruit grower?" Luke asked.

"Yes suh, I have over one hundred acres of the finest trees in Florida, China Oranges. Have y'all ever eaten a China Orange?"

"No suh, not knowin'"

He took one from a small bag tied to his saddle. With his knife he expertly slit the rind from top to bottom in four equal parts quickly and effortlessly stripping away the bright orange peel. Passing the peeled fruit to Anna, then doing the same for everyone including himself, the second one for the boy.

"I declare Mista Tucker you are so right, this is very sweet and juicy. It has a most agreeable taste," Anna agreed.

"Thank you, ma'am." As they ate the fruit, Mister Tucker continued, "I tried putting this horse up too, but Reardon would not agree to that either. He knows he can sell Wellington very easily for a great deal." Mister Tucker lamented his dilemma, as they rode along eating the shared oranges.

"That's ah fin' animal, Mista Tucker. What breed of horse is it?"

"It is Arabian Mista Nash, there are a very few of them in this country." The man patted the horses' neck as he explained. "It is sure the gambler had a good eye for horse flesh. This horse is the fastest horse in the state. I believe that. There are many that would disagree on his speed. He is not much for hunting cows however; the little Florida ponies like yours is more suited for that Miz Anna," he explained. "And I wouldn't argue thet your mare might be faster for a long run, their endurance is astounding," he declared.

"You are right, Mista Tucker, but I do hope that things go well for you and Wellington." Anna shuttered at the thought of Mister Tucker losing the boy. With the slight Wellington being forced to labor on the docks at Silver Springs.

"Me too. Judge McIntosh is a good man. A Christian man," he added.

"This area is a prime spot for my family to hol' up for tonight, an' from tha tracks we must not be far from town," Luke said, looking around.

"Yes, suh, it's prime, and you're only three miles or so," Mister Tucker explained.

"Well then I suppose maybe we should go back an' fetch the res' of my family, an' get'm here 'fo' dark. It has been a pleasure talkin' ta yo' Mista Tucker, an' I sho' hope thangs work out fo' yo' 'n' tha boy," Luke commented, extending a hand.

"The pleasure has been all mine, suh, and do not forget there is to be a Christmas frolic in town tomorrow afternoon," he answered, taking Luke's hand firmly.

"I suppose we will see you in town then. And good day to you Lord Wellington."

"Thank you, ma'am, and a capital day to you both," the youngster responded in perfect cavalier fashion.

It was clear that Mister Tucker's wife was teaching Lord Wellington very well.

Anna and Luke both raised eyebrows, smiling before riding away. Cantering their mounts for the next half-hour, until they sighted the wagons.

They couldn't wait to tell the others about Ocala, Mister Tucker and Lord Wellington. It seemed little time had passed before reaching the spot chosen by Luke and Anna for their camp sight. Agreed by all, that they would have been hard pressed for locating a better one. Everyone including the animals was in need of rest, while agreeing that, they were close enough to Fort King for an early arrival the next morning. Polly located the wagon under a large oak; with green grass and good water close by. The temperature dropped not cold only cooler than they had experienced previously as dusk drew closer.

With tomorrow being Christmas and so close to the fort, they felt relaxed, but not as cheerful as they might have been under other circumstances. Polly, Anna and Kara Sue could not bring themselves to muster much excitement over the frolic that Mister Tucker had mentioned. Surely there would be music, dancing and many new faces. Most thoughts of merriment dwindled when remembering their purpose for stopping at Fort King. Although the evening fire yielded comfort from the cooler night air, it produced little in the way of lifting any dampened spirits. With a final check on the stock, an early turn in was decided upon.

"Reckon they ain't much cause fo' beddin' with our feet ta thet tree tonight, Jimmy D?" Jojo asked rhetorically before pulling his wool blanket under to his chin.

"Naw, ain't no cause ta put our hat on our feet neither."

For the next hour the two boys discussed what they thought life might be like at an army fort and new town. Wondering whether there might be other boys Jojo's age, and if his sister might require him attend school. And would there be a better market for the hats he had made and sold in Honey Tree or even skins from animals he could trap. They had no idea.

"Reckon they ain't no time lef' fo' me ta he'p yo' see ah whippoorwill now, Jimmy D."

"Reckon not." A detectable melancholy in his short answer.

They spoke no more after adjusting their blankets a final time, and remembering to pull the canvas over their blankets. It was at least a comfortable evening, but not a single whippoorwill called to help deliver sleep. August remained by the dying embers drinking the last of the cooling coffee as the others fell asleep. Soon the light that reflected from his dark shadowed face faded and disappeared and a light drizzle began, yet he sat. Only pulling a blanket over his shoulders.

"Jojo! Jojo! Look!" Jimmy D. excitedly shook Jojo's shoulder even before the dull sun afforded enough light to see clearly.

"Huh, whut is it? Whut's happened?" The drowsy boy rolled over facing his friend, and throwing off his damp canvas covering.

"Look!" Jojo followed Jimmy D's pointing finger toward the nearby figure, with his back against the tree, only his face showing from under a poncho in the dim light.

"Dang! Thet's Buster! Buster Books," Jojo exclaimed, his unbelieving eyes bulging.

"Hi," was all that Buster said to the startled and now very wide-awake boys.

"Buster Books, whut in tha worl' yo' ah doin' here?" Jimmy D. asked the calm Buster, his hair trimmed and sporting a clean shirt and britches, but still shoeless.

"An' where's yo' ma an' pa an' all them other young'ns?" Jojo asked.

"Heck they at Ocala by now, I 'spect."

"Ain't thet ah caution. Y'all must've walked all night long, " Jojo opined.

"Did. Under ah tarp. Bunched up tighter'n chickens in ah hailstorm. An' I be mighty proud y'all agreed ta tote my goods fo' me in y'all's wagon," he stated about their earlier agreement by Jimmy D. to transport his hides into town for him, and deliver them to the hardware store. "Cain't say I would've made it with all them hides."

Buster explained how it was his pa's idea to go into Ocala for the Christmas doings. But his mamma insisted that the turkey given them would have to be cooked first. Then describing how they had cooked the turkey first by digging a hole behind the house, and building a hot fire in it. Wrapping the bird in layers of wet burlap, placing it in the hole after first covering the coals with green palm fronds, then more fronds over the bird. Jojo and Jimmy D. eyed each other as Buster told how they covered the whole works with sand and let the turkey cook.

"Pa wuz agin it, worryin' 'bout cookin' thet bird, but ounce ma set her min' they ain't no changin' it. Ma sez it ain't proper manners lak, ta go ta ah frolic an' not take ah nourishment."

"Well I declare, les' look ta tha stock an' get us ah bite ta eat. Yo' mus' be real hongry walkin' all night lak yo' done," Jimmy D. said, getting to his feet.

"Thet ah pure fac' I been smelling thet cooked bird all night, whilst me an' pa spelled each other totin' it. Pa borrowed Mistta Whidden's mule ta tote tha li'll'ns."

To say that the rest of the family was surprised when Buster was presented for breakfast would be an understatement. August was the only exception among them; for he had watched the boy find his way through the dark camp, as the remainder of the Books family, mule included passed quietly down the road. Under the tarp in the darkness, to August they resembled a huge moving haystack. It was after that, that August smiled, and then slept. The boy flashed a big smile, a tinge of red still on his teeth from the pokeberries, as he took the plate from Kara Sue. Glancing at each other with raised brows, Polly and Anna smiled as the famished boy dug into the plate of grits and fried side meat with great enthusiasm; both shaking their heads mulling the same question. How did the Books family get here so quickly, and how did Buster get in the middle of their camp undetected? They didn't bother asking the boy though, instead letting him eat, and feeling Buster Books wouldn't consider it much of a feat at all. There was one thing they felt sure of, and that was, the Books family might have been down but they would not be held there. August felt the same, just before he snoozed. Kara Sue gently shook him, and handed him coffee.

The Nash clan along with Buster Books was well on the trail by the time the sun exhibited it potential and burned its way through the cool dampness, promising a bright and merry Christmas day. The wagons rolled especially easy now, on the hard packed road, the wheels and animals barley leaving any trace. The broken shell covering the roadway must have been hauled all the way from the gulf coast. Surely at the expense of the military only they would have gone to the trouble.

The taller of the buildings, a two story unpainted wood structure came into view, just as the ox drawn wagon topped a low rise. Others could be seen including walls of the small fort as the wagon reached the peak. The fort itself was typical, small maybe eighty feet square, of mostly cypress log construction.

Ocala, the new settlement had developed into quite a busy town. Close enough to the fort for security, but not so close as to cause trouble for either the army or the town. Luke along with Jojo and Tater, held the small herd in a field suitable for grazing, water supplied by a small lake. A forest of pine, clusters of huge spreading oak and cabbage palm surrounded the village. As far as they could see to the next hill, crops of all sorts were abundant. Unlike the homestead where Jesse Bill Books was trying to scratch out a meager existence for his family, this area was lush and green. The black soil was not sucked dry by the greedy palmetto. In those palmetto-infested areas, which covered a great deal of Florida, most other small plant life was practically non-existent. Even after clearing the land of the wicked roots that grew longer than a mans body. It was understandable how a man could feel worn and defeated, as was Jesse Bill Books.

165

This area was different anyone could see that. Large fields were cut out of the tall forest, planted with corn, beans, peanuts, cotton and the like. Jimmy D. guided the team of oxen onto the main street of the small community. The little town was thriving, but had not grown to the extent that it appeared crowded. The crowd was mostly made up of people from the surrounding woods. Anna, Polly and Kara Sue waved and spoke to the folks coming out of the stores, the greetings were returned.

"What a wonderful and friendly little community," Anna remarked.

"Look, Anna! There's Mista Jesse Bill an' Miz Ivey with all them young'ns, an' they all cleaned up!" Kara Sue exclaimed, pointing past the building that had first appeared from the rise. Anna driving her smaller wagon behind the lead wagon, past the unpainted two-story structure, with the sign indicating.

THE OCALA HOUSE
WHISKEY AND WINES
BEAUTIFUL YOUNG LADIES

Another smaller sign pointed out that hot baths could be enjoyed for a ten-cent charge. Laughter and music could be heard from inside.

"Mamma, hear thet? It's Christmas music."

"Yeah, I hear honey, its real purty too."

"Well, I guess me an' Jojo bes' get over ta tha post an' see if'n we c'n take care ah that business we come here fo'." James stopped his mount near the wagon and waited for the somber Jojo, moving slowly in their direction. Once again remembering their main reason for coming to Fort King. Displaying a forlorn look, Anna and Kara Sue joined them. Even the merry making next door could not erase their sadness, as reality covered them like a trite wool blanket. None including James dared to look at the others for fear of revealing their own sorrow and causing the woefulness to expand; Polly was the first to interrupt the silence of the disconsolate family.

"Jojo, yo' come back an' say yo' proper good-byes. Yo' hear me now?"

"Yes'm," he said nothing else. Turning his pony slumping in the saddle, he and James rode toward the fort.

"We be lookin' fo' someone, ah young lady," James said to the apparent older of the two young-armed sentinels at the opened gate.

"Sergeant Lauderhill! Tha gentleman's lookin' fo' somebody. A young lady," the dark soldier called out, without looking around.

"Yeah, suh." A burly, whiskered sergeant with faded yellow chevrons stopped in front of James and Jojo. Removing a large chaw of tobacco from his cheek, tossing it behind him, and knocking dust from his worn, but clean blue tunic. Making himself more military, before speaking again.

"How might I be of service, suh?"

"Names Nash an' this here is Jojo Stroughby an' like I say we be looking fo' ah young woman, this boy's sister." He swung a loose arm toward Jojo as he spoke. "Her name be Lila, used ta be Stroughby. I'm told she married ah soldier, ah corporal name ah Cline."

"Yeah Cline. But he ain't no corporal no more. He's been made ah lieutenant now, an, ah, dern good officer," the seasoned soldier replied.

"They here ah-bouts?"

"Naw, suh," he answered politely.

"Lieutenant Cline lef' with Capt'n Brook's detail, escortin' captured injuns. They lef' Yankee Town over on tha Gulf fo' Galveston, Texas maybe two months past," Lauderhill explained.

"How 'bout my sister?"

"She went too son bein' ah officers wife an all. 'Long with Capt'n Brooks wife, an' ah sergeant's lady." Answering Jojo's inquiry, the sergeant looked sad, mirroring the boy's expression.

"They comin' back?" James asked, pushing his hat back.

"Knowin' tha army it hard ta say, but least ways not anytime soon son. They bound fer Fort Smith Arkansas, ta help guard ta nations. Thet's where them injuns is relocated on ah reservation."

"Well, I reckon thet's tha way of it boy. Yo' wantin' ta stick, yo' welcome ta travel on south ta tha Peace with us. Ain't knowin' whut we gonna fin' when we get there."

"Be proud. It'll be ah sight more'n whut I got now. Reckon ain't no sense ta be ah stayin' here, seein' my sister's not comin' back an' all. An' ain't cravin ta go back ta Honey Tree, ain't nothin' there fo' me either. Y'all kin' ah lak my family now." A sense of silent deliverance overcame Jojo. Not emotional however, and he couldn't wait to share the news with the others.

"Good then, les' go tell the others," James said slapping Jojo on his shoulder.

"By tha way, Sergeant, how's tha injun trouble south?"

"Bad, suh. But cain' say fo' sho' jus' how bad yet; tha way it looks, it ah sizable bunch involved in raidin' an' killin'. Got two jailed over at St. Augustine, they ad-mitted being part ah tha bunch thet killed ah feller named Smith, an' violated his woman real bad. Burned his wagonload ah supplies east ah tha Oklawaha River. Got word this very mornin' 'nother wagon got hit. Name ah Thomas. Don't know many details yet thought."

"Thomas! Man ah woman an' two Negro's? Ol' man an' ah boy?"

"Could be. But only found ah dead white man, don' know 'bout any others. Lak I say we ain't got all tha word. Y'all know them?"

"Met'm on tha trail south. They wuz bound fo' Tallahassee. No sign ah tha woman and young colored boy an' ah ol' colored man?"

"Lak I say, jus' tha one dead, wuz foun' so far. If there wuz ah woman with ah boy an' ol' man, they could be captives. Will get tha word out. Them two injins whut got caught won't tell how many wuz raidin'. 'Spect they hung by now, so cain' ask 'bout no captives. Injuns funny thet ah way. They know they gonna hang, they wont talk."

Sergeant Lauderhill failed to mention any word of Mrs. Smith, probably because of the boy and the two young soldiers within earshot. James didn't bother saying anything of their seeing Mary Smith in Honey Tree, or the condition she had been found, by Acrefoot Johnson. It was certain that the army was in possession of that information already.

"Well, Sergeant, be thankin' yo' for yo' information, we bes' get on back ta our folks. We'll be movin' on early morn'," James explained turning his mount.

"Where yo' folks bound?"

"South, all tha way ta tha Peace River."

"Well yo' folks mind now. Like I say. We don' know how many ah them troublesome injuns they is. Mos' ah tha trouble is south yet; I ain't aimin' ta alarm yo' but, mayhap ain't nobody lef' alive south ah tha Peace by now."

"Hope yo' wrong there, we travel cautious, thank yo' suh, an' Merry Christmas ta all yo' soldier boys."

"Thank yo', Mista Nash, an' tha same back ta yo' suh. By tha way they's ah Christmas frolics in town tonight, be lookin' fo' yo' folks if yo' ah min'. Be plenty ah good eats," the sergeant called as they rode away.

Mixed emotions washed around in James' mind as he rode for the others. The news concerning Jojo would be welcomed. But the unfortunate information about the Thomas' would not be easily accepted. Especially with the fate of Caroline, Cork and Uncle Caesar being in question. Jojo certainly was disappointed he had not found his sister as they had expected, realizing he actually missed her. And there was after all the news concerning their father's death, and he wondered if somehow, she might discover the information in some other way.

"Well we done our bes' boy, mayhap Miz Anna will agree to help yo' write ah letter ta her. Thet sergeant allowed she would be at Fort Smith Arkansas. Then yo' c'n 'splain whut happened ta yo' pa."

"Reckon thet will do fine, mista. James, reckon it ortta be done lak yo sayin'," Jojo agreed, convincing himself further, that that was the only solution available to him. He wondered however, if he should include all the details of their fathers' death. The part about the whip and all, or just say that he had died. Miz Anna would know best about such things; he would write the letter based on her suggestions.

"We kinda lak family now boy, mayhap it c'n be jus' James an' Luke. Respectfulness ta tha womenfolk an all though."

"Yeah, suh."

After another check of the stock, Jimmy D. Luke and August joined the others in town, waiting on the porch of the hardware store, for James and Jojo's return. With all the Christmas doings going on they still felt downcast, even the Books' couldn't draw them away from each other. The problem, of which news should be disclosed first, caused James to appear as he really was. Confused.

"James?" Polly had noticed something in his eyes. Concern maybe.

"It looks lak we gonna be stuck with this young'n fo' ah while." Reaching over and playfully roughing up Jojo's head, almost knocking the boys hat off and unseating him from his saddle at the same time.

"What!" Anna was very excited over the news, as the rest would be.

"My sister an' her husband done lef fo' Fort Smith Arkansas. He's been made ah lieutenant now, an' Mista Ja, ah, James said I c'n stay with y'all."

"Thet true, Papa? Jojo goin' ta tha Peace River with us?"

"True 'nough boy. We all goin' together, ah family now."

"Now jus' hol' on here," Polly stated.

"Huh!" James looked hard at his wife. "Whut yo' mean, Polly?" Puzzled at the reaction from Polly.

"Well, whut I mean is we ain't ah goin' ta no Peace River or no place else. That is, till we done enjoyed ourselves at this Christmas doin's."

James allowed the youngsters to leave, before breaking the dreadful news of the Thomas' to Polly and Luke.

"Oh James. The army cain' tell yo' no more news on whut happened? My God, them pore dear people." Polly made no effort to disguise her dismal feelings.

"No, Polly. Except, they only found Mista Thomas' body. No sign ah Caroline or tha boy or Uncle Caesar."

The welcoming from the town residents was earnest, the music delightful and food abundant, yet; Polly's disposition remained dull. She tried being otherwise with even the new about Jojo failing in bringing relief for her low feelings. What truly plagued Polly, was what she hadn't heard. Knowing only that two of the Indians had been caught; but not knowing how many may be involved in all the mischief. And surly no way of knowing what could happen next. A truly worrisome situation for Polly and Anna, knowing tomorrow night they would be miles from the security of a fort. Equally troubling to Luke, James and August, but they didn't let on. Armed only with the good news about Jojo, the youngsters had no problem enjoying festivities. Agreeing it to be the best Christmas ever and it was just beginning. Anna had insisted over Polly's objection that she give them each a silver dollar, plus a China orange, in a scrap of white cloth. Each small bundle topped off with a small red bow produced from a length of ribbon purchased at the store. Mister Tucker received his own special Christmas gift. He was given a year's extension on his debt, allowing him to keep Wellington. Another gift, of a silver dollar with a handful of dried peaches instead of an orange, was made for Wellington.

"It is a true kindness of you folks, considering Wellington and all. It's something we are not used to." Wellington put his gift in Mister Tucker's saddle pocket to open at home latter.

"We been tol' yo' stallion is gonna race today."

"He is indeed, Luke. He's to run against one of those tough little Florida marsh ponies. I understand that little mare he's to run against has never lost a race," Mister Tucker explained.

"You said yourself how fast those ponies are, and your still willing to challenge one?" Anna asked.

"I'm gambling on the distance being our advantage, Miz Anna. On a long run my stallion would probably lose, but it's only a quarter mile. I believe that my horse with his longer striding gait will carry the day," Mister Tucker said it with confidence.

"I believe yo' right, Mista Tucker, I aim ta place ah small bet on him myself."

"Me too," James added.

"Why James Nash! If Miz Penny ever got word ah yo' two ah gambling, she would come down here an' take a stick to tha both ah yo'."

"But I sho' do hope yo' win Mista. Tucker." Thinking about the race helped to lift Polly's spirit. Especially with James and Luke placing bets, she had never seen them wager before.

"Well, folks, I hope I don't let y'all down, and good luck to us all. The race will start in about an hour."

The Nash youngsters and Wellington, latter joined by Buster Books roamed the street from one end to the other sampling the food, especially the pies, cookies and other deserts. Buster with the red tinge worn from his teeth was especially happy, after recieving eighteen dollars for the hides that had been transported into town for him. They were also aware of the race, and knew it was time when the music stopped. Buster had not mentioned it to his friends, but he had placed a ten-dollar bet on Mr. Tucker's stallion, declaring himself a fair judge of horses. Everyone picked a spot for watching. The population of the little town had suddenly increased, including many soldiers from the fort. The mayor appointed himself the starter. The time had come.

To everyone's astonishment, Mister Tucker had removed his saddle, knowing the riddance of weight, would be an added edge considering the short distance. The white stallion appeared extremely fidgety, his coat already soaked from sweat even before the competition began. As if he knew what was expected of him. However, his opponent, the little dun colored mare appeared relaxed. She was a tough well-muscled pony, leaving little doubt she could run. James and Luke began feeling a little uneasy, after hearing most of the money was bet against Mister Tucker's stallion. The young undersized rider, maybe sixteen sat calmly in the saddle, gently patting the pony's neck. It was apparent that he had done this many times before today.

"Boy, you look to be a likely horse man. Can you ride bareback? Really ride?" Mister Tucker was looking directly at Jojo.

"Reckon I could ride ah whirlwind iffin yo' could catch it, suh," Jojo answered

"Would you be willing to ride this stallion?"

"Willin', an' will if yo' approve, suh."

"I approve." Mister Tucker handed Jojo the reins. "All you have to do is hold on and let him run, guide him around the flag. He'll do the rest."

The confidant Jojo took the reins and bound onto the jittery stallion's back with only a "Yeah suh."

"Ready, boys? When I give the signal y'all go. Yo' run out toward thet big oak yonder where we got thet white flag, circle tha tree an' come back here to this line." The plump red face mayor pointed to the shallow trench raked across the width of the dirt street. Understand?" Making sure both young riders understood his instructions.

Both boys nodded. The smaller pony leaped forward, running full stride even before the echoes from the pistol shot died away, kicking up clouds of dust as she made for the end of the street. The stallion was prancing and turning sideways as the pistol fired. By the time Jojo regained control of his mount, the pony was some thirty yards ahead, and had already turned in the direction of the oak in the far field. The quick little mare was already halfway to the oak by the time the stallion passed the last building.

Leaning low against the stallion's neck Jojo was still some thirty yards behind when the mare reached the oak. The equally able rider slowed the pony as she reached the tree. Jojo rode the stallion into the thick cloud of dust kicked up by the little pony. Horses and riders became temporarily hidden in dust and out of view. The cavalry-trained stallion planted his front legs in the sand and pivoted his rear end, circling the tree much faster than did the ponies slower pace around the tree. Less than ten yards now separated the two speeding horses, both exiting the cloud. The smaller horse still leading.

The white stallion appeared without a rider as Jojo lay low behind it's out stretched neck, lightly slapping the horses flank, encouraging him to run harder. The eager stallion did what was demanded, closing the distance with his longer strides. With both horses reaching the first buildings, the mare was slightly leading. Loud whoops, yells and cheering erupted from the spectators as the speeding horses raced for the finish. With less than fifteen feet to the line the big white stallion pulled even. In all the yelling and confusion it appeared the contest should be declared a tie. But the judge who was eyeing it more closely declared the stallion's nose crossed over first, as the two thundered past all the way to the other end of the small town.

"Thet wuz ah little close fo' comfort, thought sho' I los' my money," James said. "Yo' do know ah mite 'bout horses, Mista Tucker," he added.

"As you say, it was a little too close for comfort," Mister Tucker proclaimed. "And you are correct again, suh, I know horses, my family was in the horse breeding business in Carolina."

Wellington and the other boys walked the stallion cooling him down slowly. Later brushing him well before feeding him a quart of grain, putting him in a stall at the livery. The rest of the evening was spent talking about the race, and congratulating Jojo on his ride, listening to the music and watching the dancing into the late afternoon. The sun was dropping low, but not yet lost from sight, that would take another forty-five minutes. The Nash family, Mister Tucker and Wellington, along with the Books clan, left the small town of Ocala. Mister Tucker was anxious to get home. Buster had won enough from his wager to buy the Whidden mule and buy seed for spring planting, plus enough left for extras like repairing their broken wagon. Jesse Bill had made an agreement, that his whole family would help Mister Tucker pick his fruit for a small wage. And with the mule and wagon it was agreed that Buster could haul the fruit along with his hides, to Sanford or St. Augustine for shipment north. He had not mentioned it to his family, that, August had given him an address of a boot maker in Texas who would buy all his alligator hides. They could be shipped from Yankee Town on the Gulf coast.

"Y'all welcome ta stay tha night at our camp if yo' ah mind, Mista Books, yo' too, Mista Tucker." James extended the invitation after reaching camp.

"Be obliged ta yo' Mista Nash, but, we bes' get on home, be there by good light," Jesse Bill stated. "No time fo' jawin', but ta say, we mighty prideful ta know y'all, an' owin' yo' fo' yo' he'p."

"No cause ta speak on it, Mista Books, but yo' stay alert till all this injun business is done," James stated, then looked at Mister Tucker.

"Me too. Me and the boy here can't wait to tell the news to the missus. She will be pleased to find out that I won enough to pay off our debt, and I am not about to tell her how close it was. But the news of our business arrangements with Mista Books and his family will be welcomed."

They said their goodbye walked away in the darkness. Part of the Books children on the borrowed mule soon to be their own property, and the rest of the children on the back of Mister Tucker's horse. The white stud led by Wellington was the last to disappear into the shadows. August went with the boys to check on the stock and feed Tater and Bakon before turning in. He fell asleep quickly thinking of how the Books family had come to Ocala under a tarp, and no doubt troubled by circumstance. Now going home, unrestricted by any need of the tarp, and plans for lifting themselves, and rebuilding their dignity. Mister Tucker and Wellington's life, had, in the same night improved. Young Lord Wellington in the future would become a free man of color. The Nash family had made new friends. And unless because of some unwritten page in history, should never see them again. But always remembered and thought of.

"James yo' ort not ta have spent yo' hard earned money on purties fo' me," Polly lightly chastised her husband over the cloth goods he had bought her, for the sewing of a new frock. Luke had done the same for Anna. August was deeply touched by the pouch of tobacco he had gotten. In his whole life until now, he had never gotten a Christmas present before.

"It's fo' Christmas." James explained the small gift. They were up and gone by good light, passing through Ocala on their way south. Quiet now, only a barking dog.

Polly took advantage of time earlier, to scratch out a letter for posting at from the new post office in town. She posted it as they passed through heading south.

Day after Christmas
Fort King, Florida

Our very dear folks,
We made Fort King with no trouble to speak of. Give up our old milk cow cause she could not keep up. Give her to a old colored man and his wife before we got to Troopville. James said that was better than leave her for injins. Met a couple at the Oklawaha River and James and Luke helped them cross the river. They had 2 free darkies with them a old man and a boy of 10. They were bound for Tallahassee. We made Ft. King and spent christmas day and had a good Christmas party. We saw a good horse race that wuz won by our friend Mr Tucker. The weather is very tolerable and warm. We are all in good health and are doing fine. We had some trouble at a little town named Honey Tree where a boy named Jojo about Jimmy Ds age took up with us. He come to Fort King with us cause his pa is dead. After that a young woman named Anna said she wanted to go to the Peace with us. James said it was all right. Ain't seen no injins or bandits yet. But August Moon a cow hunter from the Peace River sez that you don't see injins till it is to late. August throwed in with us too and is going all the way to the Peace with us too. At Fort King and a new little town called Ocala we could not find the boys sister so he stays with us. We wuz told by the army that the folks we helped at the Oklawaha got kilt by injins. That is all for now I will rite more when we run on to another post office which should be a settlement named Orlando. August said the old army trail runs right to there.

Love always,
Polly

CHAPTER ELEVEN

Polly conveniently left out some facts in her letter. Especially that the death of Jojo's father was brought about at the hand's of James. And that James and Luke both had placed bets on the race. The trail from Fort King to Orlando was indeed a good one, well used and clean of most overgrowth. August mentioned the reason, was because it was the main trail for cattle drives up from the Kissimmee and the Peace River prairies. Most cowmen used this trail pushing their large herds north toward Jacksonville and as far as Savannah. The lush green grass with its clear running water around the tiny hamlet of Orlando served as bedding down site.

With the episode between Kara Sue and the snake forgotten, or at least not dwelt on at any length, she was allowed to walk behind the wagon once again. Three days out of Fort King all were feeling a little more secure, and some relief that they were getting closer to home. Even with the slow gait of the oxen, August declared they should reach Orlando within four days.

"James!" Polly called out to her husband, who was now in the habit of riding along beside the ox team directing them.

"Yeah I see'm, Polly."

"Kara Sue clim' in tha back, quick now yo' hear," Polly shouted.

"Yes'm," Kara Sue answered and did as she was asked.

August stared intently at the two riders who had suddenly appeared on the trail some distance to their front. James stopped the oxen as he and August reined their mounts from their slow walk. The two were rough looking and appeared to have been on the trail for some time, with their whiskered faces and dirty clothes, yet well armed with pistols and long guns. However they were well mounted on two typical Florida ponies, and appeared to be in no hurry.

"Look ta be ah couple ah cow-hunters," August said. "Don't see nobody else with'm, least ways not yet," he added.

175

"Howdy, pilgrims!" one called out yet some distance away.

"Howdy, boys!" James returned the greeting.

"Them two don't 'pears ta mean us no harm," James said, but still cautious as they drew closer.

"Wait, yo' right as rain. I calculate I know one ah them," August declared. "I do, thet ol' boy on thet red horse is High Pockets Raulerson, an' he use ta ride fo' ol' Jim Knight's spread down on the Myakka prairie, fair size outfit too." August rode close enough to notice they both had bullwhips coiled and tied to their saddles.

"High Pockets!" Now close enough, for a clear look at the mans face, showing a bulging tanned cheek

"August Moon? Thet sho' 'nough yo', boy?" the man he called High Pockets spoke, before spitting a brown stream of tobacco juice off to the side.

"Yeah, it's me," August answered, as they both reached out to shake hands.

"Dad gum August, everybody down on tha Peace calculated yo' ta be dead. Thought mayhap injins or assassins or tha lak done kilt yo'. 'Special since yo' ain't come back from tha las' drive."

"Well, now I might look dead, but I ain't. Naw I jus' hooked up with some pilgrims jus' south ah Honey Tree. This here is James Nash, them his folks back there." August pointed a thumb at James next to him.

"Proud Mista Nash, I be Harley Raulerson, most folks jus' call me High Pockets. August yo' 'member Little Willie Harold, don' yo'? High Pockets asked pointing to his young companion.

"Little Willie? Sho' I do. Yo' Buck's kid brother ain't yo'?"

"Yeah suh, wuz anyways till thet ol' Spanish bull from hell kilt'm." Little Willie spoke slowly. His eyes remained bright, even as he mentioned his brother's unfortunate death.

"It looks ta be yo' goin' ta be ah sight bigger'n yo' brother when yo' full growed," August said to the lanky youngster, whose tanned face displayed only a hint of whiskers.

"Ah yeah, well, Little Willie got tha makin's ta be ah first rate cowman, jus' lak his brother use ta be. An' I believe he c'n mammy up calves better already." High Pockets slapped the boy's back as he bragged on him. "Mista. Nash y'all got any beef stock or tha lak with yo'?" High Pockets asked.

"Some ah few head. Why do yo' inquire?"

"Well, suh, we pushin' a considerable herd, me an' Willie jus' workin' out front. Nigh ta twelve hundred head, rank and wild as a son ah tha devil hisself."

"Whose beef is it?" August carefully placed tobacco in his paper for rolling as they talked.

"Jim Knight, I'm tha big auger fo' his outfit now, after Buck got hisself kilt. We pushin'm ta St. Augustine." Slicing a hand through the air toward St. Augustine as the crow flies, and describing his job of foreman in typical cowman fashion.

"How far back?" August inquired.

"Mayhap seven ta eight miles, jus' south ah tha Big Econlahatchee ford," High Pocket answered. "Aim ta cross'm before dark, an' push ta Fort Christmas tomarrer or tha next." High Pockets removed his hat and wiped his forehead on his frayed shirtsleeve.

"Then we got time. We can move up ta tha Big Econ an' hol' up on this side," August said. "It'll be nigh on ta dark by then," he added.

"Thet suit yo', James?" August realized after the fact that he should explain just incase James was unsure of what his concerns were.

"Sho it is. I reckon it ain't good ta be on this trail an' run head on inta ah thousand head ah wild stuff," he answered, without an explanation from August. Adding, "Crossin' tha Econ in tha mornin' will be plenty good."

"Good. Me an' Little Willie'll ride back an' try ta hol'm up south ah tha river till y'all all set, if need be." High Pockets doubted if that would be necessary. Believing ample time was available for securing the Nash animals.

At James' suggestion August joined High Pockets and Little Willie riding back toward the herd to locate a suitable campsite at the river.

"Me an' August going up quick lak an cut saplin's fo' ah small pen to hol' our stock. Lak as not they'll run with them wild cows iffin we don'. Sho cain take no chances."

"Yo' want me ta go with yo', James?"

"Naw no need Luke, calculate yo' might stay with Polly ta keep thangs movin'. Special these slow oxen, me an' August c'n handle tha pen, won't take much. 'Lak as not them two cowmen will lend ah hand 'till their herd makes tha river, they 'pear ta be ah real decent pair," he added, as he pulled two axes from the rear of the wagon, plus a coil of rope.

James noticed a look of concern on Polly's face as he returned to the front of the wagon to say goodbye.

"Gal ain't no cause fo' frettin', we jus' takin' pre-cautions thet's all. See yo' in ah couple ah hours. Luke will handle them slow animals, Jojo and Jimmy D. c'n handle tha cows." Having stated that, James wheeled his horse and disappeared down the trail.

As James had predicted, High Pockets and Little Willie volunteered themselves in the construction of the small corral, from the ample supply of young cypress trees. Little Willie and James wielded the axes for the fence rails, while High Pockets and August lashed them to standing trees. The corral site chosen was about one hundred yards off the trail, and constructed by the men within an hour, with ample time to spare for August to roll a smoke. A procedure unnecessary for High Pockets because as always, he had a considerable wad of tobacco stored within the confines of his jaw. Soon after the wagons rolled down the trail toward them. James had the women move the wagons in close to pen separating it from the trail with instruction for Jimmy D. and Jojo to move the cows inside the pen and securing the crude gate behind them.

"Boys this here is my wife Polly, an' thet's Anna Cade there." James smiled introducing the women. "An' this here is High Pockets an' tha boy there is Little Willie. Ol' frien's ah August.

"Pleased ta make yo' acquaintance, ladies." Unexpectedly, High Pockets was very polite, quickly removing the wad of tobacco from his mouth and tossing it away behind him, then snatching off his hat.

"Proud ladies." Little Willie also quickly removed his soft leather wide brimmed hat.

Polly with Anna's help quickly had a hot fire from the generous supply of pine knots, Kara Sue had gathered after her introduction. Soon a welcomed aroma of boiling coffee and beans with smoked hammocks drifted through the trees. Very soon the meal was ready.

"Ma'am, ah feller sho would have ah hard time passin' on ah cup ah thet hot coffee," Little Willie suggested.

"Well Little Willie, ain't no need fo' ah feller ta even try such." Polly passed him a cup, then filled it with black coffee.

Anna poured coffee for High Pockets then offered milk and sugar, only August accepted.

"Boys James an' Luke here gonna be takin' over the Hendry place south ah tha Peace." August spooned in a mouthful of beans, after speaking.

"Thet ah fac? Ol' Major J. T. Hendry had ah likely place goin'. One time had neigh ta five thousand head, done right good fo' hisself," Little Willie said before gulping coffee.

"What happened?" Anna asked, as she approached High Pockets to fill his cup again, from the large pot.

"Injins ma'am, same as most always ma'am. They hit'm one day 'bout noon when his wife wuz makin' dinner. All his hands wuz out markin' springers an' ain't knowed nothin' wuz goin' on. Thet lef' tha major with only ah man slave ta he'p fight 'long with his wife an' ah girl slave with her. Burnt tha main house with her in it, her an' her girl fightin' too." High Pocket blowing across the top of his cup each time before drinking, during his explanation.

"Sweet Baby Jesus." Polly's eyes declared her anxiety. "Thet's jus' awful," she added.

"Yeah hit were. Tha major an' thet ol' slave ah his'n fought hard from tha barn bes' they could, he wuz ah real fightin' man. They kilt six ah tha varmints before tha res' lit out. Thet young slave girl whut wuz in tha house with his wife got out somehow an' run fo' he'p. Sez Miz Hendry made her go.

"I believe she did too. Tha Hendrys set great store by the slaves. But she ain't made it in time fo' savin' Miz Hendry," Little Willie added, apparently just as familiar with the story as his companion.

"Oh my it all sounds so terrible," Anna said.

"Yes'm it were, tha Major took it real hard, her screamin' tha whole time an' all, an him ain't able ta he'p'r." Somberness covered his tan whiskered face as he talked. "Folks say his min' never got right after thet, an' I reckon it so." High Pockets sadly related.

"Wern't no way fo' him ta he'p her. He took ah arrow in ah lag an' ah mini ball in his side. His slave lost ah arm later from his wound. Thet girl is hired out, workin' in tha whore, ah, ah, as ah cleanin' girl." Little Willie suddenly realizing that, ladies were present.

"Yeah thet's got ta be real hard on ah man. Losing his wife lak thet an' all, my brother los' his wife ta injins back in Georgia." James rescued Little Willie, knowing he meant no harm.

"How is tha injin problem now?" Luke glanced at James as he asked.

"Some bad right now, but cain' say how bad it gonna stay. Some trappers say they seen big sign south of tha Okeechobee, but they ain't doin' great harm yet, an' don't know how many. An' tha army say ain't no cause ta go in after'm. 'Sides the army's pullin' out." The tone in High Pockets' voice exhibited his displeasure with the army's policy.

"James they ain't no house on tha place." Polly lamented her thought of no shelter, as if she hadn't heard the part about Indians, or even the army leaving. She studied James' eyes waiting for an explanation, then High Pockets for conformation of her statement. "Whut we gonna live in?" Feeling a response from either to slow.

"Oh no ma'am, thet ain't so. Me an' tha boys an' even Little Willie here, an' lots ah other folks too, come ta he'p build tha Major a new place. 'Course it ain't nothin' lak tha one whut got burnt up, but it's passable," High Pockets quickly understanding her concern, hoped his comment would ease her mind.

"Now yo' see there Polly, they is ah house ready an' no cause fo' frettin'." James also attempted to satisfy his apprehensive wives concern over living quarters.

Polly harbored little doubt of High Pockets and his companions being competent cowhands, but she was left unconvinced of what carpentry skills they might possess. She could only hope that a carpenter or two might have been among the, "lots ah other folks," mentioned in his statement. Plus the plain fact was that what passable meant to him, and her understanding of it, might no doubt be entirely different. Especially remembering, a considerable amount of his living arrangements was spent sharing a spot under a pine tree with fleas and rattlesnakes. Her thought was interrupted by a single shot, and then others fired quickly followed barely audible shouting. The startled Polly dropped her cup, and looked at James. Eyes showing fright, she quickly scanned around for Kara Sue, locating her near the wagon sharing a piece of cornbread with Bakon and Tater.

"Gunshots!" she exclaimed excitedly, before jumping to her feet with the intentions of racing for her daughter.

"No, ma'am, don' be ah frettin' them ain't no gun shots. Them's whip cracks from our boys. Sendin' me ah signal they gettin' close ta tha river. Mayhap ah half mile away now."

"They awful loud."

"Yes'm, sometimes yo' c'n hear'm three or four miles when yo' got tha wind. It ah handy way ah talkin'," he added. "We 'ppreciate y'alls kindness ma'am, but me an' Little Willie bes' be gettin' on," High Pockets said, getting to his feet and handing his empty cup to Polly.

Little Willie did the same. Touching his hat brim, "Thank'e, ma'am. Thet wuz mighty fine chuck, ma'am," he added.

"Yo' an' yo' boys welcome ta eat supper with us if yo' ah min' to." James looked at Polly after realizing he should have gotten his wife's approval before extending an invitation for super supper. Especially not knowing the number.

"Sho, be proud ta have y'all," Polly added, realizing her husbands dilemma, and certainly not minding at all.

"Proud ah tha invite, ma'am," High Pockets answered. "But we got ah grub wagon, be arrivin' real soon, if yo' ah min' ta make arrangements, with our cook, y'all join us fo' chuck."

After first tightening up their chinch straps, the two cowmen mounted and rode across the river toward the sound of the whips, already the faint bawling of the cows reaching them. Just as High Pockets had predicted the grub wagon pulled by two mules came around a turn on the far side of the shallow swift running river. The small covered wagon pulled by four mules barely slowed after reaching waters edge. Instead making every effort to keep the animals moving fast, they entered the water. It was obvious the driver was very familiar with this crossing, and handling animals. Quickly the wagon splashed across, the rapid water barely reaching past the bellies of the mules.

As if not even seeing anyone watching from the opposite bank, the driver cracked a long whip several times over the heads of the mules, pressing them up the steep incline of the opposite bank. The driver resisting any intention of slowing the wagon, until reaching the onlookers standing near the fire. Then vigorously pulling the reins and expertly turning the wagon's direction; bringing it to a quick and full stop, loudly yelling out a command.

"Hol' up there yo' lop eared no count glue pots. Else I'll have me ah fin' swamp steak fo' supper," the large driver yelled, shoving the brake forward with a heavy leg.

"Howdy folks! Tha names Maude Olive Donner, an' my frien' jus' call me Maudie fo' short. An' I'm real proud iffin they don't call me worse." The big woman made her introduction emphatically. Laughing afterward sounding a high-pitched cackle. "An' y'all join us fo' grub, an' I ain't takin' no fo' no answer."

It was a shock to all except August, that the driver of the grub wagon would be a woman. He had been on drives and spring branding's with Maudie Donner before, and knew her to be as raw and rank as she looked. He also knew as everyone within a week's ride of the Peace, that a more kindly soul was not to be found.

"Well, Maudie, I'm called James Nash, an' this here's my wife Polly an' Anna Cade an' my brother Luke there. An' if I wuz ah betttin' sort, I'd say yo' already acquainted with August Moon," he said, pointing toward August. "An' we be proud ta join y'all fo' grub," he answered, after Polly shook her head affirming.

"Good, an yo' would win yo'self ah sho' fire bet Mista James Nash. How yo' been gettin' on August?" Her well tanned faced flashed a smile under the broad brim of her straw hat. A thin leather string from the hat disappeared under a copious double chin, and seemed without function, with the hat crammed down tightly to her unseen ears.

"Fair ta middlin', Maudie." August returned her smile. And seemed to be truly happy to see her again.

"Young'ns I'll give yo' two bits fo' seein' ta my mules." She was looking at Jojo and Jimmy D., still standing with their mouths open. "An ah nother iffin yo' feed'm some ah thet grain in tha back ah my wagon, an' rub tha wet off'm with ah hand full ah grass gentle lak. My animals require ah lot ah love an' attention."

"Be proud Ma'am no cause fo' payment though. Ain't thet right Jimmy D.?" Jojo took the leather straps from Maudie's heavy rough hands.

"Fac', ma'am," Jimmy D. answered, grabbing the lead mule.

The boys walked them over near the pen before un-harnessing them. Looking back the whole time as large woman climbed from the wagon seat to the ground. Maudie ran a large callused hand into a side pocket of her loose overalls, retrieving a small round can of snuff. Popping the cap she put a couple of generous pinches of the reddish brown powder into her mouth, forcing it behind her lower lip with her tongue. Even though her full face displayed long years of rough outdoor life, there was also a placid confidence in her dark eyes. A kindness in her face, contravened the long mincing forty four pistol strapped high on her expansive waist. While the frayed cuffs of her faded yet somewhat clean red paisley shirt, demonstrated her resolve toward hard work.

Maudie's vigorous actions and lively conversation camouflaged her over sixty years, even as thick gray hair from under her hat hid her ears.

"Them two got tha makin' fo' likely hands," she mentioned as she watched Jimmy D. and Jojo hobble her mules. "Polly yo' got any butter milk?" Asking without waiting for comment about the two boys.

"Why yes, we got plenty, good an' fresh too."

"Whut's yo' name, little gal?" Somehow Kara Sue had been eliminated from earlier introductions.

"Kara Sue, ma'am." Unsure if she like the big woman or not, yet; answering her question respectfully.

"Well now ain't yo' jus' as purty as ah speckle-d-pup. An' I'll wager yo' c'n lift my Dutch oven from my wagon fo' me. August Moon! Yo' must fancy yo'self one ah them deb-u-tantes at ah Nawleans co-tillions or tha lak. Or yo' would've done got yo'self ah rope ta fetch us some frying meat." Maudie was even louder yet as she snarled at August, maybe teasing, maybe not. Only August would know.

"Ain't thankin' such. I jus' fancy hearing yo' caterwaulin'. It pleasures me more'n riches. Come on boys, afore thet ol' woman splits ah gut."

"Whut yo' aimin' ta do August, steal one ah them cows?" Luke was puzzled when August got a short length of rope from Maudie's wagon.

"Naw, ain't stealing nothin'. Jus' gonna foller tha cowman's code."

"Cowman's code? Whut tha heck is thet?" James was just as perplexed as Luke.

"Well boys, its lak this. Them cows is dumber than ah mule, an' by tha time half gets 'cross tha river, them cowhands ain't gonna be able ta prevent'm from bunchin' up. Then panic sets in. Some gonna drift downstream inta deeper water, an' one or two ain't gonna make this bank, least ways not alive. So it's jus' natural an' bes' fo' folks ta get'em 'stead ah tha gators," he explained, while preparing his rope as they made their way downstream for any of the unfortunate animals.

At first like Kara Sue, Anna and Polly disapproved of the harsh manner in which Maudie took over. But they had to admit she accomplished things. Suddenly after lifting the heavy black iron cooker from Kara Sue's straining arms, Maudie stopped.

"Girls y'all jus' gotta forgive my hard ways an' all; it jus' thet I been workin' tha trail too long, with ah rough bunch ah cowhands. It's all I know. My pa always allowed it on ah count my mamma birthed me in tha middle of ah injin attack. Happened whilst we wuz makin' our way down the Old Woodpecker Trail in north Florida ta get here. So y'all jus' give ol' Maudie ah hand an' pay no min.' ta my ornery ways, special yo' purty girl." She wrapped her large arms gently around Kara Sue.

"Be proud ta he'p, Maudie, jus' say whut," Polly answered, as she watched August with rope in his hand, followed by Luke and James. They disappeared into the thick trees bordering the edge of the narrow river

"Yo' c'n get ah couple ah dozen sweet taters from my wagon an' mayhap throw in ah half dozen extrie an' bury'm in them coals. We need thet extrie coffee pot too, an' I'll mix up ah big batch ah biscuits. Boys yo' bes' be puttin' yo' dog in ah wagon an' put ah rope on'm. Them cow dogs they got will kill'm. An' thet pig too."

"What are we going to do for meat?" Polly asked, placing sweet potatoes in the coals, as Jimmy D. and Jojo secured Tater and Bakon in the wagon, as Maudie had suggested.

"Thet's easy, girl, August gonna take care ah thet shortly. He'll be bringin' us ah hind quarter directly. Less'n he got too much rough wore off him from all his travelin' 'bout an' easy livin'." Another high-pitched laugh over her own joke.

As she worked her dough, the big woman expounded the unwritten code to Polly as August had explained it to the men. That anytime settlers or towns people received word of an approaching drive, they would travel for miles and gather at the known river crossings, waiting. Just as Maudie had predicted, within twenty minutes James and Luke appeared with a hindquarter swinging from a pole. Maudie didn't say, but she knew that August was still at the river cutting the back strap from the animal. Anna being familiar with the code finished the explaining, because Maudie turned her attention toward instructing James where to lay the meat, before grabbing a sharp knife.

"August Moon where's my back-strap?" Seeing August return empty handed.

"Aint got it."

"I c'n see thet plain 'nough."

August explained his failure to bring the tender meat, instead leaving it for two skinny boys along with an equally skinny dog appearing at the river from nowhere. After a minimal greeting and permission from August, they collected the remaining quarter plus the unfortunate animal's liver, and the portion of meat in question. Seeming barely able, the two slender youths quickly had the large chunk of meat secured to a stout pole, with the liver and strap tied in a cotton sack.

"Me an' my brother beholdin' fo' yo' kindness, mister, but we got ah long ways ta go," the taller one stated.

"Don' mention it boys, but y'all be quick now, 'cause thet meat gonna be drawin' bears and wolves an' tha lak," he cautioned, seeing that each carried only a knife.

After slicing off a good size chunk and tossing it to the dog, they lifted the heavy burden to their bony shoulders and staggered away. August watched for a moment until the two barefoot lads disappeared into the thick brush, followed by the hound having already wolfed down his portion of meat with little chewing. The long legged black and white dog, sniffing at the drops of blood left behind on the ground from the dripping meat, was also lost to the tall palmettos. On the far bank August saw a man and woman with a little girl pulling another drowned cow to the bank, he turned and walked away feeling they had things under control. The smell of smoke from a half dozen fires drifted through the pine and cabbage trees, along with the aroma of cooking meat.

Little Willie and a few of the cowhands came in to eat after the herd had crossed and moved up the trail to an open grassy field a mile away. The others with their dogs would stay with the herd until the cows settled. Each cowman heaped his plate high with thick rare steaks, sweet potatoes and a biscuit, then washing it all down with black coffee.

"Maudie yo' got 'nough ah them cat head biscuits fo' us ta take some with us?"

"Sho do, Little Willie, put ah few in yo' pocket we got plenty."

Before leaving the fire each placed a couple of biscuits in his pocket for later. Saying their thanks and goodbye, they rode off to spell their companions. The last of the cow hunters having eaten, they prepared sacks of scraps for their hungry dogs, and thanked the Nash family for the hospitality. Like the others they took extra biscuits and joined the other men, taking turns with the help of the dogs guarding the stock.

Indications of their fire reflected from the trees separating the two camps and could be witnessed by the three women remaining up hours after the others had retired. They completed the task of cutting the remainder of the meat into long thin strips, draping them on green sticks over the fire. By daylight the meat would be dried of juice, for the boys to "slap in ah biscuit or two fo' eattin' on tha go." Polly felt very tired and she thought of how tired Maudie must be, as she glance over to see the rough talking woman crawl under her wagon. She felt admiration for the cook and was now more understanding of her rough ways, she did indeed have a soft heart. A cry from a lone wolf not far away, was the last sound Polly remembered before being overcome by sleep. The night as usual was far to short especially for the cow hunters, Maudie had their grub ready before sunup and the wagon, men and herd were gone. The sound of bawling cows and cracking whips could no longer be heard, before the sun burned away the dew.

Friday
Big Econ River

Our Dear Family,
We are at a river named the Big Econlahatchee where we run into a cattle drive at the river. There was over 1000 head of cows that crossed. They are going to St. Augustine. We met all the cowhunters and the cook they was all nice folks. Their cook was a real rough woman but real nice. I started riteing this letter after we crossed. The trail is good and will take us to a town named Orlando in two days. I will stop for now.

It is Sunday morning and we have reached Orlando it is a small town but growing. It was named after a young soldier kilt by the injins. James said we can take time here for going to church because they have two here. From here we go south to Fort Blaunt it is not a army fort. August said a man named Reading Blount and his 12 sons and some slaves built it. We can be there in 2 or 3 more days. August said 3 or 4 days after that we should reach the Peace River and home. We cannot wait to be in a house. One cowhunter said the house was burntdown by injins but they built a new one. I will rite when we get there. We are all fine. It looks like a rain building.

With all our love,
Polly

CHAPTER TWELVE

Polly decided to write later and explain the cowman's code, and tell more about the little town of Orlando and the church service. Also she intended to write about a marvel they discovered in a hardware store in Orlando.

"Ain't this ah pure wonderment?" Polly could only shake her head at the new invention by a man named Mason. After all who would have thought that anyone would make a glass jar designed so you could actually screw a lid on it. James agreed that they would buy two dozen of the jars lids included, and also an instruction booklet for using the jars for preserving foods of all types. Anna and Polly were as excited about the Mason Jars as they were about being only days away from the Peace River and home. They carefully packed the jars and organized plans for supper that night. Sleep came easier for them all that night.

Her forecast concerning the weather in the hastily written letter to Miz Penny proved to be correct, as the rain started early the very next day and continued even as they pulled into the already opened gates of the crude fort well after dark. The chore of opening the gate was assigned to a lone man. As the travelers pulled closer in the darkness, he appeared to be a young boy. The upper portion of his tall body covered with a skin as a torrent of water poured from the brim of his hat. The drenched boy offered no greeting, other than the motioning of a long swinging arm appeared invitation enough for them to proceed forward. August knew that the lone figure was a son of Captain Blount's but could not identify which, and also declined conversation in the downpour. Instead guided the oxen in a river of mud stopping in front of a large two-story building forming one wall of the log fort. The wagon's wheels sank into the slick dark muck almost reaching the axles of the wagons and the knees of the animals.

The huge hatless figure appearing in the opened doorway, almost blocked out the light from behind him; barely admitting enough for Polly to read the sign over the door. "BLOUNTS TRADING POST," the shadowed sign declared in faded black paint on cracked cedar boards. Captain Reading Blount proved to be as callous as the land he wished to harness, and as lasting as the weathered sign he stood under. But like many newcomers to this harsh land, his hardened ways took a back seat to a true un-hostile nature. With a loud deep voice he invited the pilgrims in to dry and warm themselves by the pot bellied stove, even before recognizing one as his friend August.

"August Moon! Folks hereabouts allowed yo' ta be dead, mayhap kilt by injins'r assassins or tha lak," he declared after the invitation, and realizing who he had invited in.

"Naw, suh, Capt'n, I'm still kickin', folks been tryin' ta kill me off fo' sometime now; I been travelin' with tha Nash family here, an' they fin' comp'ny," he explained, before completing proper introductions of both families.

"We lef' ah few head ah cattle in yo' north field, yo' 'llow they will be alright?"

"Yeah, I don' reckon even tha wolves gonna be out on ah night lak this, an' I reckon they ain't in-clined ta wonder with all thet grass. They'll jus' stand with their asses toward tha wind, till daylight," he vulgarly declared. "'Scuse my talk ladies." Expressing regret for his vulgarity before turning his attention toward James. "Where y'all bound, Mista Nash," he asked as one of his six boys set down a large pot of coffee, and two others brought enough cups to pass around.

"We takin' over tha Hendry place south ah tha Peace."

"Thet ah fac?" the bearded gray-haired man appeared to be quite surprised. Then opined on the subject. "Yeah it plum' sorrowful whut happened ta J. T. Hendry, he wuz ah proud man. But them injins took tha starch right out ah him. Mayhap not even ah place there now." Stopping only long enough to puff his pipe, before being interrupted by August.

"Yeah sho' is. We run onta High Pockets pushin' ah herd at tha Big Econ, he sez they con-structed 'nother house, an' tha army's pullin' out. Thet ah fac'?" Thet mean tha injin troubles lak ta be settled?" he inquired further, before his first question was satisfied.

"In ah pigs ass it is." Came a quick statement.

All unsure which question the crude statement answered. Polly and Anna almost choked on their coffee, covered their mouths, preventing it spewing out over the table, Kara Sue made a sound resembling a stepped on cat.

"Ah pardon, ma'am, ma'am an' litt'l miss." Apologizing more formally. "Me an' my boys gettin' rough as pine bark since they mamma passed. Lawd res' her soul. She wuz ah real Christian woman, an' did not hold with profanity, card playin' an' dancin' an' tha lak. An' we ain't use' ta bein' 'roun' quality." A sheepish look masked his rough upper face.

"Thet's quiet all right, Capt'n," Polly responded, sipping her hot coffee.

"But it lak I wuz tryin' ta say, it ain't over 'cause tha army's pullin' up stakes. It jus' thet, whut's lef' ah them got orders not ta patrol south ah tha Peace, an' thet's where them varmints is workin' out of. I wuz tol' thet by Lieutenant Hardy hisself, he's tha officer in charge ah 'em horse soldiers. Ain't but two companies of troops lef', ta cover all tha land from tha Peace River ta Fort Pierce on tha coast." he lamented.

"Why jus' two weeks back them brazen sons ah bitches kilt two ah my Niggers an' neigh kilt 'nother, whut wuz out pullin' turnips. Clubbed'm down not ah hundred yards from my gate!!" he proclaimed, seemingly to have forgotten his crude language in his anger. "Stabbed tha boy 'bout tha age ah them two in tha back." Nodding toward Jimmy D. and Jojo. "He'll be on his feet in ah few more days, an' I aim tha give him freedom papers fo' his courage in fightin' them heathens off with ah axe lak he done. My boy Josh there fired at'm with ah scattergun. Run'm off, five or six ah 'em Josh calculated."

"An' yo' 'llow they 'scaped south ah tha Peace?"

"Don' 'llow, Luke, know so, they vanished quick as ah fart in ah whirl wind. Pardon ladies," he apologized again, glancing at the Polly and Anna for some sign of forgiveness for his words before continuing on with his story.

Both Polly and Anna smiled slightly, indicating their desire to forgive his crudeness.

"We tracked'm with dogs fo' ah full day, but los'm in thet long swamp thet tha Dempsey Cruse Trail follers, an' runs stright ta tha Peace River ford at east ah tha Hendry place, yo' place now." He shot a warning glance toward Polly.

Polly's eyes widened as she gave her husband a disturbing stare, saying nothing only squeezing his arm tightly. He patted her hand, attempting to calm her fear. His effort failed, and he knew it. This was not the news they had wanted or expected.

"Thet bunch kilt ah defenseless ol' man an' ah Negress, an' cut up my boy over ah sack ah turnips, ah hoe an' ah axe an' mostly 'cause tha boy re-fused ta run off with'm!" he exclaimed. "They run south, right 'nough, an' I wager they still movin' far pass tha Okeechobee."

"How many yo' calculate is in tha whole bunch," James asked.

"Cain' say fo' true'. But I wuz there when Chief Billy Bowlegs wuz took four months past, an' he sez they wuz less than two dozen braves, he ain't said 'bout tha women an' young'ns. Jus' don' know," he repeated his uncertainty. "Ol' Chief Billy could talk American good when he took ah notion, an' lie too, good as any white man. Injins don' normal lie," he stated. "'Nother thang he said wuz, thet every white south ah tha Peace would be kilt an' burned out. Heard it plain from his on devilish mouth."

"Reckon them injins got 'nough lef' in thet bunch ta do thet?"

"Already done thet, James. Major Hendry wuz one ah tha first, then three or four after him." He failed to mention if the reference was the original house or new structure built by High Pockets and his companions. "Ain't but two families still south ah tha Peace River as we speak right now. One's thet ol' widow Rice an' them two half wit growed up twin boys ah hern. They got ah shack down on Crazy Woman Creek whut runs inta tha Okeechobee," he explained. "An' thet ol' sea Captain Kormac McBean, he ain't zackly ah family though. He lives 'lone west ah yo' place. Jus' him an' his monkey an' a bunch ah queer animals an' tha lak." He puffed his pipe and shook his large head slowly back and forth.

As they continued to talk, a woman appearing to be Spanish brought out a large basket of cornbread and biscuits, and placed it in the center of the long table. Another son of their host carried an oversized pot of venison stew, placing it next to the basket. Another boy brought in a stack of tin plates and spoons.

"How is it that they were not burned out with the others," Anna asked, as Polly and Kara Sue passed out plates of food and refilled their cups.

"Well Ol' Bowlegs tol' me he led ah raid hisself on tha Widow Rice, ten nights before he wuz caught by tha army." Said when they got there, thet ol' woman an' them two boys, Roelon an' Raelon wuz hunkered down 'roun' ah burned out pine stump. Fust thought mayhap they wuz preyin'. But thet ain't whut they wuz up ta."

"Whut wuz they doin'?"

"Well young'n," looking at Jimmy D, "Billy said thet they wuz ah ant nest in thet ol' stump. Said them three wuz ah eattin' them bull ants jus' lak they wuz hard sugar candy." He answered then shoved a heaping spoon of stew into his mouth, and packed it further with a large bite of cornbread.

"My goodness! Yo' mean they wuz starvin' ta death?"

August grinned at Polly's question being aware of the story and knew it to be true.

"Starvin my ass! Uh pardon ladies. Naw ma'am. Between tha two ah them boys, they ain't got brains 'nough ta poke ah thumb up they ass with both hands, but they good. Ah ah umm, pardon me ladies fo' my words. Whut I mean ta say is they real good hunters. No cause fo' doin' without," he opined, wiping his mouth on his sleeve. "'Sides tha one named Raelon tol' me latter thet they jus' plum' lak eatin' them ants. Done it since they wuz young'ns still shittin' yeller. Uhh pardon my words ladies. It lak I say we ain't use' ta quality.

"Don' fret, Captain," Polly said about his vulgarity, doing her best not to smile.

"Yeah well, Billy bein' chief an' all, he ain't 'llowed no harm ta come to'm. Ta his way ah thankin' they had tha spirits ah dead bears in'm, 'cause bears craves them ants too." He explained before another spoon of stew.

"Ain't such!!" Luke was astonished that the Indians would see it that way.

"Thet ain't tha whole of it. Chief Billy not only prevented any harm come to'm, he kept them fed."

"Aint so!"

"Yeah, suh, it's so James. One ah them boys got tha notion ta nail ah board on ah tree by tha shack. An' if they wanted pork or gator meat, they would draw a pig or gator on thet board with ah burned stick. Them boys claim they never saw nobody, but, whutever they drawed on thet board, would be laid out under thet tree come dark. Why the whole bunch wuz gettin' fatter'n pigs an' ain't had ta walk no further than thet tree fo' all tha grub they c'n eat."

"That is an amazing story. Truly amazing. Eating ants."

"Yes'm, an' gospel too Miz Anna. But they could jus' as well been rat turds."

"Whut!!"

That came out as if the captain could not have prevented it. The women having almost choked as he continued with his story without bothering to ask for any pardons. It was too late anyway he calculated.

"Story is Roelon ate ah rat...uh, a rat droppin'. But said he wern't recommendin' it fo' nobody else." Reading Blount took a bite of stew, as if he were talking about eattin' boiled peanuts the whole time. "Said them turds aint got ah crunchy texture lak them ant's." This time for some reason, it never occurred to him to beg a pardon. "Mammer, thet whut they call tha ol' woman, laid it on ta tha fac' thet, them turds wuz too fresh. Any rate, I ain't recommendin' them either."

That did it, Polly and Anna was left with no desire for continuing with the meal. Not taking another bite. Appetite vanished. Suddenly, Polly wanted the conversation directed toward matters other than the Rice families' experimental eating habits.

"Then they are still there?" She thought of a quick question.

The captain answered without further thought of rat turds. "Wuz Miz Polly, after Billy wuz caught ah month ago anyways. Don' know now. Ain't seen hide nor hair ah them boys fo; nigh on ah month now. Thet bunch whut kilt my Niggers mayhap done kilt them too." Reading Blount was also a straight talking man.

"How 'bout thet other one, thet sea captain, yo' spoke 'bout?"

"Tell yo' plain Luke, thet's 'nother strange one, Chief Billy spared him too, on ah count ah thet litt'l monkey whut wears thet litt'l red hat."

"Monkey with ah red hat?"

"Yeah, suh. I calculate they ain't too many white folks in these parts ever seen a real monkey, let alone ah injin seein' one, special it wearin' ah red hat. I ain't never seen one myself till thet one," he confessed. "Billy figered thet monkey wuz some kin' ah spirit too, but ain't knowed whut kin'. Ain't thet ah caution, how injins with clubs will attack ah full troop ah well armed soldiers, but ain't havin' no truck with ah monkey tha size of ah dried cow turd," he said. "'Scuse me, ladies." Like before, he didn't wait for his pardon before continuing.

"Word is now, since Billy got hisself caught though, they got ah new leader, ah 'scaped slave." The captain continued without glancing at the two women. "An' it stands 'cause my boy say he could swear thet one ah them he shot at were ah Nigger. An' tha boy whut got cut up say so too."

"Ah Nigger?"

"Yeah suh, thet whut they sayin'. Them injins been tellin', when he wuz born he grabbed ah knife his ma had, an' his mammy nigh had ta break his fingers ta get it loose so's ta wash'm." He paused talking long enough to shake his head, then continued. "They believe thet make him some sort ah spirit warrior. Ah war leader. I declare them injins set great store in spirits."

Polly shuddered openly at the thought of such a birth, and the captain took notice.

"Pardon my vulgar talk ladies, I reckon them ain't proper words fo' ah supper table an' all." Once again finding it necessary to ask for another pardon, after ignoring the many others.

As before, Polly was left knowing that, there were an unknown number of rampaging savages. And according to Captain Blount, they were operating south of the Peace River, with free rein preying on any whites at will.

Especially considering that they very well could be the only whites left on the far side of the river. Yet, she still nodded her forgiveness, as did Anna. It was becoming habitual now.

"Well, Captain Blount, me an' mine'r obliged fo' yo invite fo' stayin' tha night, an' tha fine chuck an' all. But we bes' turn in iffin yo' don' mine', an' jus' point tha way." James got to his feet, as did the captain and the others.

"'Course, Josh yo' show these fine folks tha rooms upstairs. An' lak always breakfast will be ready by six, iffin y'all ah mine fo' it."

"We 'ppreciate yo' kindness, Captain, an' we'll be right proud ta join y'all fo' breakfast," Polly answered, as they followed the lanky boy upstairs

Well before any thought of sun, the wagons passed through the fort gate, Polly feared making any further predictions concerning the weather. Even though the rain had let up some it was still misting, as the animals labored moving the wagons in the deep muddy trail, that was to lead them to the Peace River. To Polly, it wasn't the final warning from Captain Blount as he and his boys waved goodbye from the gate that lingered in the back of her mind. It was the story he had related of the threat from the captured Indian, Chief Billy Bowlegs. That, no whites would be left living, or property standing south of the Peace River. Now, the structure that High Pockets and his friends had built seemed less significant if no one survived to live in it. She shuddered openly at the thought.

On second thought the Captain's words of, "Keep yo' heads down and yo' powder dry," was indeed sound advice, for failing to do so might very well guarantee a tragic conclusion to the Bowlegs pledge. They had high hopes that once reaching The Peace River Valley, all this Indian business would have been settled once and for all. But the very idea that treachery was perpetrated within sight of the walls of Captain Blount's fortress; and that the renegade Indians were being led by an escaped slave; was discouraging news indeed. Equally unwanted, as the black slick muck blanketing the trail; the one being followed, guiding them toward their new home. Homer Dew, the old soldier from Troopville wasn't so far wrong, and at this moment he and Polly were in complete agreement, "It ain't fit fo' white men, only rattle snakes and injins." Oh how she pined for them to be once again, back in the safety of their old Georgia home!

However; the disheartened Polly dared not allow her secret feelings to show, especially to her husband or children, even to the point of suggesting Kara Sue keep Anna company for a while. For some time Polly failed to realize that the rain had stopped, and only until she noticed the sun striking the back of James' shirt did she regard it. Almost instantly the warm rays from the tardy sun afforded new light to her anxious disposition. James, as if reading her mind and feeling her lifted spirits over the sun, turned in the saddle, smiling, she returned the smile with one of her own. The sun and smiles failed to totally eliminate the thoughts of Indians and other dangers from her mind, it did however transfer them somewhere in the back of her mind. For the first time they could see dark dots, thousands of them far on the distant horizon, as the sun lit up the bright green river of saw grass.

"August, look!" Polly said pointing, as August moved his horse up next to the wagon.

"Is thet?" She didn't complete her question; he knew what she was asking.

"Yes, ma'am, it's cows," he answered, before she had completed her question.

"Lord have mercy," she said. "James!"

"Yeah, I see'm, Polly."

"James, I 'llow if we don' stop, we c'n make tha river by dark," August suggested.

"Yo' sayin' we cross in dark?"

"It could depend on if all this rain we jus' come out of brung thet water up much. It mayhap ain't even reached thet far south, if so we c'n stay put on this side 'till sunup," he explained. "Either way we as good as home," he added.

"Yo here thet, Polly? We home. An' I reckon if push comes ta shove, we c'n leave tha stock an' wagon this side an' cross over with jus' tha horses, an' enough grub fo' supper," James said.

Polly had mixed emotions about finally reaching their new home, there no doubt would be new and additional dangers on the far side of the river. Dangers somehow different from those encountered on the trail, yet she could not get a clear picture. But what of those dangers? All those awful stories bore her a punishing imagination as a clairvoyant gift that she failed to understand, yet created fear. Calculating they were within four or five hours from the river, Luke and August decided to gallop for the river, for the purpose of gathering information concerning their night arrangements. The uneasiness Polly felt earlier revisited as she watched Luke and August ride away. The bright sun earlier that lifted her was once again losing its battle of holding her spirits. Especially being aware that within three hours, darkness would call the sun completely away, like the river drew Luke and August.

Watching the sinking sun James determined they would not make the river anytime soon sent Jojo ahead to locate a suitable campsite. Quickly accomplishing his chore within an hour's search. Jojo chose a hardwood hammock near the trail, with an ample supply of firewood. The small dry parcel of land was well elevated and carpeted from the years of falling oak leaves. With barely enough remaining light, he quietly scouted the area for sign. There was no question of what made the sounds as he carefully peered from behind the cover of a large oak. He eased his pistol from its holster judging the nearest target to be an easy shot, even with his handgun. And if his aim were true, it would require only one, but be prepared just incase another would be necessary. The loud explosion immediately followed the metallic sound of the hammer being pulled back, then a high pitched squealing from the pig as she jumped high in the air.

Jojo's attention was diverted from the squealing shoat before it hit the ground toward the direction of a noise from his right. An enormous boar, huge and ugly with its head down, his dripping snout raking the ground, throwing leaves over his humped back was on top of him. The screaming animal was running full speed even before Jojo saw him. With no time for aiming Jojo fired. Quickly fired again, both shots as true as that fired at the sow. The striking rounds failed to stop the fierce boar, only making it more determined in its attack. Attempting to evade the charging animal Jojo dodged behind the tree. His attempt was not accomplished totally; one of its two six-inch long curled tusks from the animal's wildly swing head caught his leg, throwing him in the air. His pistol flew from his hand as he landed hard on his back on the ground.

Out of the corner of his eye Jojo could see the cloud of leaves and dirt flying about the huge black animal as it spun sharply to renew its attack, easier now that his victim was down. The demon like swine pawed into the ground throwing leaves and dirt high into the air with its nose, tormenting his prey. For and instant Jojo took his eyes from the flashing yellow stained tusks and burning red eyes, to grasp the pistol he had brushed with his hand. The foul smell of the animal's breath was in his face as he pointed and fired accuracy was unnecessary with the fierce boar on top of him. He felt himself being thrown into the air once again, this time more harshly, as a warm liquid spread over a portion of his upper body. Feeling no pain but aware blood soaking his now ragged clothes. There was no time for thought only survival. This time however, he managed to hold onto his revolver.

The forth blast deafened him and the muzzles flame burned his bare wet chest, and he no longer heard the shrill screams from the angry animal. Panic overcame him, as he became aware of the course wire-like black hair scrubbing his naked upper body. Somehow he had the sense to roll his limp weakened body over, but the determined boar failed to continue its attack or even move. And for the first time since the attack started Jojo was afforded time for lucid thought. He forced himself to his knees; his ringing ears detected a faint gurgling sound, instead of the grotesque screams from the wild hog. Large red bubbles came from the boar's mouth as it attempted to suck air into its lungs. He felt his own body relax after realizing for the first time that the boar was dying, and he couldn't help but watch as the animal resisted death to no avail. Jojo's body quivered as he contemplated such a death as the boar might have dealt him. Being killed by Indians would surely be preferred; at least an Indian would not eat him. Regaining his feet, he knew how lucky he was, at least one of his shots had penetrated the huge boars heart and damaged a lung. His father had taught him years ago to aim at the nose of a charging animal, but in this case he had fired blindly, there was no time for aiming. The fortunate boy felt pain for the first time as he watched the last bubble form from the globe of blood from the boar's nose, then pop as its side rose and fell for the last time. The fiendish animal had lost its battle for life.

Jojo had lost track of time since he had entered the hammock, but more importantly he had lost blood. How much he couldn't tell, only that he felt very weak. With a shaking hand he felt the wounds in his side and chest. Involuntarily his body recoiled, he quickly pulled his hand from the open wound in his side, causing more blood to flow.

"Lordy I'm cut clean ta my ribs." Looking down at his bloody chest for the first time.

His legs almost buckled yet; he maintained his balance with the assistance of a nearby cabbage tree, as additional pain racked his brain. He noticed his right leg also had a deep gash with only the blood hiding the bone under the ripped flesh. Determined, he must resist his on death and not die next to the animal he had just dispatched. Somehow he had to make it to his horse for his canteen, but it wasn't clear how far it might be or which direction.

"Hold on, just' hold on." He spoke quietly, talking to him-self. "Yeah thet's tha way, ain't far either, maybe ah hundert yards."

With the numerous trees for support, he slowly and painfully made his way to where his pony stood.

"Ho boy, easy now, ain't no cause fo' being scairt." In a calm voice. "Yo' jus' ah smellin' blood from thet ol' dead boar on me. Ain't no cause fo' fear,"

The pony snorted as he reached for the reins to rub its nose, to further calm him.

After settling the pony, Jojo untied his canteen and removed his neckerchief soaking it with water. Black and red spots blinded him for an instant when the wet rag made contact with the bloody wound in his chest. The dead log he sat on began spinning; he grabbed it and held tight with his free hand until the spinning ceased.

"Got ta get help 'for I bleed plum' ta death right here in this swamp."

Now just barely able to think, he drew his pony near and secured the horse's long reins over its neck, preventing them from being dragged.

"Yo' gotta get back ta tha wagon boy, an' fast." He slapped the reins across the pony's rump. "Go now! Go!" Almost to weak to shout, close to falling from the log once again, with strained eyes he watched the horse run from the hammock and onto the trail.

"Go." Very faintly, he tried to yell. But could not, to weak.

Feeling himself growing weaker by the minute, he vowed to fight for life, and hoped he would fair better than the wild boar now lying in its own blood. With darkness about him Jojo felt panic, and was forced to clear his mind of fearful thought. He allowed himself to slide from his seat on the log to the ground. By applying pressure with the wet bandana he was able to control the bleeding from his chest, but blood continued to drain freely from the deep gashes in his side and leg. With his belt he fashioned a tourniquet and applied it snugly to his leg, it, it worked. Almost fainting again as he placed his other hand over his side wound, pressing down. Alone in the darkening shadows of the hammock he dreamed he walked away, following the light before him. He lost consciousness.

"James! Thet's Midnight, Jojo's pony comin' with ah empty saddle!" Polly pointed toward the galloping black horse in the scant moonlight.

"Yeah it is. I'll fetch Tater and see to it. Y'all stay on tha trail, and come quick as yo' c'n," Turning his horse around for Tater, he called out instruction for Jimmy D. to ignore the cattle and move up with the wagons. "Stay alert boy, don' know whut sort ah trouble we in."

"Yo' fin' thet, boy! Yo' hear me, James Nash?" Polly yelled as James rode away in the darkness with the dog following.

"I will, Polly. Now don' y'all fret. I'll fin'm." She barely heard him.

"It lak papa said. Y'all don' fret," Jimmy D. said to his mother, as she hugged Kara Sue crying loudly.

"Thet's right, honey, no cause fo' it. Yo' ah knowin' Jojo's capable ah takin' care ah hisself better'n mos'." Calming her daughter, holding her tight.

Anna secured Midnight to rear of her wagon, as Jimmy D. urged the oxen forward as fast as possible. Fighting his irritation at the sluggish animals, knowing they would resist any attempt to coerce more speed. Like the others he felt helpless. The return of a riderless horse was seldom-good news.

Alone in the darkness of the dense hammock Jojo fought to maintain at least partial alertness, with only light from a half moon permitting to trespass the thick trees. It was only adrenaline that stimulated his keenness of sight, allowing him to distinguish the figures in the shadows. By moving his eyeballs in a circular motion as his father had taught him for night vision, he was able to pick out two. Moving slowly at first they disappeared in the darker shadows of the oak maybe thirty yards away. He lost them. He raised his pistol, only to lower it after losing them in the darkness. Feeling too weak to hold it longer. Panic returned as his sight blurred, which he resisted by blinking several times, it failed to help. Closing his eyes he listened for noises other than the familiar night sounds of the hammock. He heard none, and determined whoever they were; they were certainly not careless. Wondering how long before the intruders found him.

From instinct he attempted to yell out, but the hand was pressed to tightly over his mouth and his strength had waned from his blood loss. Another strong hand grabbed his pistol and wrenched it from his hand. And even though he was weak and barely able to move his will to live was still strong, yet; his attempt to kick failed. Having no idea how many held him and realizing further resistance was futile, he ceased struggling.

"Hold on, boy. Easy, boy. Easy now. It's me, Luke an' August."

"Luke?" The startled boy asked as if he couldn't believe what was happening, and maybe dreaming.

"Yeah, boy, me an' August." Luke assured the frightened lad. "We heard shots, figured it come from this hammock, come ta 'vestigate. How come yo' ta be out here alone? Whut happened?"

"James sent me ta locate ah site, reckonin' y'all ain't gonna get back in time. Just before dark I kilt us ah shoat fo' supper. An' out ah nowhere ah boar come at me. Got me too. Wern't real smart I reckon, could be he done kilt me," he added.

"Naw he ain't kilt yo' by ah long shot, an' no cause fo' bein' hard on yo'self, boy. Bad though, wern't able ta get on. But I sent midnight back," he explained.

"Lordy, I 'spect yo' pony done made his way back by now. They gonna be right upset," Luke lamented.

August scraped up a pile dried of leaves and struck a match to it as he spoke. "Luke, reckon I bes' head in thet direction, an' let'em know tha boy's hurt some, but gonna live. But jus' take some mendin'," August suggested.

"Yeah, an' mayhap yo' c'n have Anna bring up her rig and fetch some bandages." Luke found some wood and placed it on the burning leaves. In the dim light, they discovered Jojo wounds to be worse than they first thought.

August met James after riding less than a half mile, walking their mounts long enough for August to explain the situation then rode hard for the wagons. Quickly Anna gathered the necessary material for Jojo's injuries, and with August as a guide, before long she was treating the boy's wounds. Because of the denseness of the trees, they were forced to leave the wagons near the trail. While Anna and Luke looked after Jojo, August located and butchered the pig. It wasn't long before Polly was frying tender strips of meat from the shoat while sweet potatoes cooked in the hot coals. Gently Jojo was moved up to the wagon.

"Ain't likely yo' gonna have ah good nights sleep son, but yo' strong an' gonna heal up right quick, mayhap ah week."

"It don' hurt much, Aunt Polly," Jojo grunted as he was helped into the back of the wagon. "Be right proud ta have me some ah thet pig though," he suggested, smelling the cooking meat.

"I would say, if you are able to eat after what you just experienced, your going to heal real quick," Anna said smiling at the boy.

"Yes'm." He ate, especially enjoying the meat. Then was asleep.

With the excitement over Jojo, Luke had little time for mentioning what he and August had discovered at the Peace, or even if they had reached it. But now with the injured boy resting comfortably in the wagon, time was available for discussing particulars. For Polly and Anna, one of the more important questions was the condition of their new home.

"Well, ladies, it's ah right tolerable place, it got ah good tin roof an' all. Yes ma'am it'll do jus' fin'," Luke answered.

"Now Luke Nash yo' idea ah whut's tolerable is ah sight different from whut ourn is, an' yo' well know it," Polly lightly chastised him, with Anna in agreement.

"Thet ah pure fac', Polly. It gospel. It ah fin' place, August there, he'll tell yo' hisself."

"Who August Moon? Him whut's happy sleeping under ah pine with his hat over his feet!"

Anna laughed with amusement at Polly's statement as she poured another cup of coffee for August and herself.

"I declare Luke's telling it true. Now we ain't ah sayin' it ain't in need. But, it'll do jus' fine'," August argued, blowing across the top of his cup before drinking.

"Is it close ta tha river Uncle Luke?"

"Sho is girl. I 'llow Jimmy D. or Jojo when he gets on his feet c'n chunk ah rock from tha front porch right inta tha Peace River."

"Fac' if it's ever been tol' young'n," August declared. "An' y'all c'n see fo' yo'self 'fo' tha dew dries tomarrer, place only five miles from this very spot."

"Speaking of Jojo, I best check on him," Anna suggested.

After looking in, she reached and gently pulled the blanket up over the sleeping boys chest. Afterward she leaned down toward Jimmy D. setting at the rear of the wagon, playfully but quietly mashed the top of his hat down on his head, almost to his ears.

"Come on over by the fire, son, he's doing fine," she instructed, pulling at his arm to help him along. The two of them returned to the fire. "That boy is as tough as whip leather. He's sound asleep."

They turned in falling asleep easily, to the pleasant sounds of crickets and whippoorwills, drifting on the cool night air covering the hammock. Before falling asleep Polly shuddered thinking of what might have been, then rolled over closer to James and realized the day had finished quiet agreeable after all. Jojo would mend well, and they were home, almost. He was thankful that so far God had been with them; now he must pray that God would be with them on the far side of the Peace River.

CHAPTER THIRTEEN

"Look darlin'." James stopped the oxen and pointed ahead, after an hour of travel

Polly stood in the wagon shading her eyes from the bright glow of a rising sun. The prediction August had made the night before proved out, the sun had already dried the dew. Still standing, she pushed her bonnet back for a full view.

"Glory be! Yo' see it chil'?"

"Thet's it, ain't it mamma? Thet's tha Peace River." Her small hands resting on her mother's shoulders as she stood on the seat behind her mother. "It looks jus' lak ah silver ribbon laid out, an' runnin' all tha way ta tha sky yonder." Kara Sue like always had her own way of description.

"Thet it does chil', thet it does."

For the first time Polly looked around in all directions, while still standing in the wagon. Green, everything was green except what wasn't sky, as far as the eye could see. Even the hammock some four miles back, where the boar had attacked Jojo. Named Jojo's Hammock by Jimmy D, was a mass of darker green against a blue sky. A sky bluer than she had ever seen, or even thought possible. To Polly's eyes, there seemed to be nothing between the two colors, other than the silver reflecting off the rivers smooth surface in the distance. And for a moment she remembered the words of Homer Dew, back in Troopville. Surly he could not have seen this place. This was their home. Nothing like the place he described with such distaste.

Her thoughts of Homer Dew were disrupted when Kara Sue pointed out the hundreds of birds, that her mother had somehow failed to see, between them and the river. Some pink, some gray, and most white of assorted sizes, all about them.

"We're home Miz Nash." James looked back at his wife with pride, as he stood in the stirrups, allowing himself a better view.

"Yeah we are husband. James does tha place have ah stove?" she asked as a second thought.

"'Course it got ah stove. August said."

"Then we'll have supper in our own house tonight," she declared, as James started the animals again, and she took one last glance at the river before taking her seat.

Once reaching the river's edge, Jojo insisted on riding his pony across, instead of being transported in the back of the wagon. And with the help of Jimmy D., who saddled Midnight and assisted him in mounting, he did exactly that, over the objection of Anna and Polly.

"Boy lak as not yo' gonna bust open them wounds an' start bleedin' agin." Polly's protest was to no avail.

"Tha boys fit 'nough ta ride Polly. 'Sides if he bust'm lak yo' say, jus' patch'm up again." James understood the boy's feelings. Besides he promised to keep an eye on him.

James urged the slothful animals into the water after Jojo's pony entered, and it was clear that the river had receded since Luke and August had crossed the evening before. Luke and Jimmy D. along with August rode up determined not to be left behind. Anna eagerly drove her wagon in following Polly. Both banks had been graded years ago making the chore less burdensome on the animals; and the water reaching just past the bellies of the oxen half way across. Loud whoops could be heard from the men as they ran their horses up the bank, soon followed by the wagons. Anxious to inspect the house, Polly and Anna jumped down and hurried inside. The men on the other hand intended on inspecting the barn. Kara Sue joined the men and ran ahead for the doorway of a small addition attached to the side of the barn.

"Young'n don' go in there!" August yelled, causing her to stop, before pulling back the canvas covering hanging over the doorway.

"Why August?" Kara Sue was prepared to pull back the canvas.

"Let me check it fus'."

Gently pulling the curtain back August peered into the shadowed room. Slowly drawing his pistol and fired once, before stepping inside. Kara Sue was horrified upon seeing him come back out grasping a large diamond back rattlesnake by its tail.

"Thet's why litt'l gal, there ain't no floor in there, an' sometimes them snake go in fer rats an' such." Explaining before tossing the snake aside. Bakon would eat it latter.

"Whut happened!!!" Polly called from the porch, with Anna.

"Nothin', no cause fo' frettin'," James yelled back.

"Don' worry girl, we gonna floor it quick lak, they's boards in tha barn fo' such," Her father explained.

After supper James explained to Polly about the commotion earlier at the barn, which brought about another reevaluation of Homer Dew's assessment of Florida. But it passed quickly and her thoughts returned to improving their home. Time south of the Peace moved as quickly as the healing of Jojo wounds. Days passed into weeks, then into months. Each day brought longer hours and harder work. The hard work was no stranger to the Nash family, or those who joined them. Improvements were made on the house, and the promised floor to the room adjoining the barn, made an excellent bunkhouse. Crops were barely in before spring arrived pushing out the last of the already mild days of Florida's winter.

The arrival of spring as expected brought rains, forcing unexpected adjustment, especially from Polly and Kara Sue. Thick swarms of mosquitoes the likes of which they could not imagine descended upon them after each rain; and on more than one occasion forcing them from their work in the fields even before sundown. The horrifying stories of how at times, they would become so thick as to suffocate the cattle was easily believable, yet; their work progressed. And along with the plague of mosquito's the spring brought another visitor, but in this case a more pleasant one.

The former sea captain Kormac McBean along with his monkey showed up at their front door, to the delight of the youngsters.

"Just a neighborly visit," he said. But before leaving, he and James had dickered over an additional twenty head of cow for the Nash herd. It was more than agreeable to the captain, that Jimmy D. and Jojo would give him three weeks labor around his place in payment. Luke also assisted him with carpentry work on his house. McBean's visit answered at least one question; the renegades had not killed him. As far as the widow Rice and her boys, McBean had not a clue. And it was plain that if he had no news of them, no one would. James and Luke's were anxious to round up the additional cows they had acquired from the eccentric McBean. But August urged them to hold off awhile. August in the mean time spent many hours and days away from the ranch scouting for sign of the renegade band of Indians. Using the pretext of locating the best cows as his reason for being absent. Keeping his true reason from the women, and uncovering little evidence of intruders. Spotting footprints in the mud occasionally, but no proof they might be Indians. Doubting not a minute that the Indians were aware of them. Once while out he made use of a practice learned from the Indians, and with a favorable wind, set fire to the saw grass prairie between their place and McBean's. Within two weeks the grass re-sprouted with high tender green shoots. The renewed savanna drew countless head of cattle, deer and other game.

It was now time August declared, to capture and re-brand the cows bartered from McBean. James and Luke decided on what would be the Nash brand, it consisted of two short, slightly crooked parallel lines over the capital letter N. The two bent lines represented the banks of the Peace River over the N for the Nash clan.

"Whut do yo' think ah thet, Polly?"

They all granted approval of the brand, but Polly advised them on not making use of it within the next few days. It was close to Easter, and she and Anna planned a trip to town for supplies and maybe material for making a new dress for Kara Sue. There was church to attend for Easter service soon. A trip to Tater Bluff would be necessary to have the blacksmith fashion the branding iron. It was agreed not all would go for the dress material and branding iron; there was too much work. Luke and JoJo along with Anna and Kara Sue, would make the trip. The others were forced to agree to wait for Easter Sunday to arrive, before they would make their visit to Tater Bluff.

The next day however, the four were enjoying a wonderful spring day in Tater Bluff, as Kara Sue skipped past the bundled squatting figure taking little notice. Allowing herself only a quick sideward glance intent on passing, on her way to the dry goods store. She wanted to inspect all the cloth goods before Anna got there; while Luke land JoJo visited the blacksmith. But instead she suddenly stopped, turning her head after doing so. She would grant herself a second look at the small figure before moving on. In doing so she couldn't help but notice the rusted chain dangling from the wooden cross bar of the hitching rail. It captured her attention so; she turned completely around staring intently.

The figure seemed to be a young person, not much larger than she was. Only the hands were visible, the rest hidden from view by a ragged coat and hat, both much too large. The unmoving slim hands were that of a Negro, and there was no way for Kara Sue to determine whether they were the hands of a boy or girl. Nor could she tell because of the long coat, as to whether the young Negro was secured to the post by the chain. Curiosity forced her to step closer for a full-blown look at the apparently chained figure. But, even after doing so, still couldn't tell much. A slave? Sure, it no doubt had to be a young slave. She had never been so close to a slave before, and moved closer yet.

Taking it upon her self to bend low, trying to gain a better look into the face of the small figure.

It was to no avail. The big hat kept the downward face hidden from view of the prying girl. But Kara Sue refused to let it go however, and was determined to get a better look at the slave.

"Hey there." She spoke quietly, moving to a spot, now directly in front of the hunched over little figure.

The mysterious form failed to move, not even a skinny black finger, and Kara Sue spent no time for pondering her next move for solving the puzzle.

"Hey there!" Louder the second time, looking for reaction.

It worked; the head raised exposing a small black face in the shadow of the brim of the hat. At first Kara Sue said nothing; she couldn't, only able to stumble backward almost falling, just barely able to retain her balance.

"Li'll girlie, yo' bes' get 'way from thet boy. He mos' mean as ah rattler an' twise as fas'." The high-pitched voice came from inside the doorway of the saloon that the hitching post serviced, and caused Kara Sue to look that way.

"But…. But thet," she stuttered pointing a shaking finger toward the squatting figure, confused and shocked.

Kara Sue retreated only far enough to regain some composure, but continued to point toward the sweaty small black face while looking toward the voice in the doorway. The squeaky voice had come from a dirty little man, who by now had walked to the edge of the covered porch. Confusion continued to envelop her, and she considered it must be some sort of a bad dream. What else could explain why Cork would be chained to a horse rail in Tater Bluff, when he was supposed to be dead? Everyone knew that the Indians, had killed him along with Uncle Caesar and The Thomas' while on their way to Tallahassee. Or at least taken captive. If the latter, why would the Indians have turned him loose?

Quickly Kara Sue turned her eyes from the ugly little man, too frightened to stare at him any longer. His skinny rough and darkly tanned face was dirty and unshaven. Under his facial hair could be seen numerous red knots. His ears, why they didn't even look like ears. The left, somewhat resembling a large multi colored mushroom after a week of hard rain. The other, like a half-eaten Georgia peach stuck to the right side of his head. Just hanging all dried looking. Like his face, his hands were dirty and covered with an equal number of large red knots. One eye was almost swollen shut, causing his other to appear bugged out, as he look at her.

"It lak I done tol' yo' gal, get yo'self on down tha street an' go play. Else I'll unhook thet chain an' turn thet Nigger loose on yo'. He powerful mean an' lak as not he bite one ah yo' skinny littl' fingers right off." The ugly man warned in his high squeaky toned voice, at the same time pointing a dirty finger toward her.

"Naw suh. He ain't no danger, least not ta me, an' I 'llow ta nobody," Kara Sue argued with as much respect as she could muster.

"Raelon! Raelon!" The ragged little man called out, refusing to take his gaze off the defiant little pigtailed girl, even for a moment.

"Whut?" The loud inquiry came from a deep voice, from inside the dark saloon.

"They's ah gal young'n out here, what's takin' ah powerful shine in our Nigger."

"Well, run'r off. Thet is, Less'n she got tha funds ta make ah dicker'n' purchase." The unseen mans comment was followed by laughter from others inside.

"Yo' cain' sell'm. Thet's Cork an' I know him, an' he ain't no slave." She informed them dauntlessly.

"Gal I ain't aimin' ta argie with no sassy young'n. Now yo' get, lak I say. Or I might take ah notion ta switch yo' good an' proper, lak yo' ma orta' do," he warned her in a hateful way.

Kara Sue looked into Cork's eyes; unsure about what to do next, still totally befuddled by what was happening. Why in the world would Cork be chained to a hitching rail in Tater Bluff? Especially after they thought he was dead. And how could this skinny, bumpy faced ugly little man, along with the unseen voice inside be under the impression that they owned him? Cork was as free as she was; as free as any of them, because she had seen his papers indicating such back on the trail. With his own hands he had taken the document from his possible box, and shone it to her plain as day, Jimmy D. saw the paper too.

"No! Kara Sue, go fetch yo' pa, it ain't no use." Cork spoke quietly not wanting his captor to hear him.

"Raelon! Yo' bes' get out here." The scrawny man shouted again, this time sounding alarmed. He commenced a jittery dance, brushing his stringy dirty, long brown hair back from his distorted face, as if not knowing what else to do.

"I declare Roelon, if yo' ain't ah caution. Yo' act lak yo' scairt of ah li'll gal. She totin' a firearm is she?" The unseen voice chided, bringing additional laughter.

Kara Sue could tell the one called Raelon was on his way out. She stared at the swinging doors waiting.

"Well boys, reckon I bes' get on out thar. 'Pears lak my brother fixin' ta get hisself shot or mayhap cut up by ah gal young'n. Mus' be ah real dangerous assassin or tha lak." Laughing he walked toward the front door of the saloon. "An I'm plum' short ah funds fo' ah proper buryin'. 'Sides ma'll be real put out an' all, I 'llow if thet little fart Roelon get hisself cut up by ah gal young'n."

Raelon's comments were followed by a round of joyous laughter from others inside, and by the sound of heavy tramping boot steps on the plank floor, they were all on their way out, to see for themselves.

"Go fetch yo' pa Kara Sue, hurry! Hurry!" Cork didn't bother whispering this time.

Kara Sue took a step backward, again looking at Roelon. His mouth was wide open as if going to speak, but not knowing what to say. Yellowish brown stained teeth displayed under his swollen upper lip, and a black hole in front where a tooth had once been, creating an almost comical appearance. But, the confused girl found little to be amused about at the time. After glancing at Cork once more, she turned and scampered back in the direction she had come.

"I'll go fetch Uncle Luke." She called back assuring the boy. Deciding it prudent not to wait on the one called Raelon to show himself. What good would follow that? She ran faster kicking up dust in the street, taking the longest strides that her short legs would allow.

"Thar yo' are Roelon, yo' jus' got ta stand yo' ground when it comes ta li'll gals lak thet." The bigger man mocked Roelon producing laughter from him and friends, after seeing Kara Sue run off down the street.

"Kara Sue! What in the world is wrong, child?" Anna struck out an arm to stop the swift-moving girl.

The action almost toppled them both. Kara Sue hadn't even noticed Anna, as she was so intent on reaching Luke at the livery barn. Anna glanced toward the small group of men on the porch, and couldn't imagine what they might have done to or said to frighten her so.

"Kara Sue what is it?" Anna asked again, after getting her under control.

"It's Cork!" She shouted out, pointing toward the saloon.

"Cork?" Anna had heard that name before, but could not remember where.

"Yes'm, Cork, tha colored boy we tol' yo 'bout. Thet family we met on tha trail, an' he'ped them cross tha river. Tha Thomas'. An' he's 'sposed ta be

207

dead with'm. But, thet ugly little man got 'm chained ta thet hitching' rail yonder." She explained pointing toward the group of men in front of the saloon, once again.

"Are you sure, girl?"

"Yes'm, I am. I know Cork anywhere. An' he knows me too. He tol' me ta fetch my pa, he's in trouble right 'nough an' he's scairt too. So I was runnin ta fetch Uncle Luke."

"Well then let's go get Luke, he'll get to the bottom of it."

"There's Uncle Luke now," the determined girl said pointing in the direction of the livery.

"Uncle Luke! Uncle Luke! We need yo' help quick!"

Luke couldn't imagine what all the excitement was about; glancing up as Kara Sue pulled free of Anna and scampered in his direction. In a million years he could never have guessed what the emotionally charged child was so eager to tell him. He looked at Anna knowing something was amiss by her quickened stride as she made her way toward them. The excited girl almost ran past him too, with Anna right behind, he reached out and snared a thin arm.

"Hold on, girl, where yo' headin' in such dispatch? Whut's got yo' so worked up? Put me ta mind of ah sow runnin' ahead of ah ketch dog."

"Yo' 'member Cork?" Yo' 'member?" She tried talking and catching her breathe at the same time.

"Shore. But slow down. He wuz thet little colored boy with tha Thomas'. But whut's thet got ta do with yo' takin' on so?"

"It's them men over yonder Uncle Luke, they got Cork chained ta thet horse rail!" Anger in her voice as she pointed toward the saloon, still trying to fully gather her breath.

"Cork chained? Yo' certain girl?" Thought he wuz dead, or captive. He looked over toward the men, then a questioned look at Anna.

Anna understood the look. "She said he asked her to get help, the boy is shackled for sure. I saw that much."

"Come on, Uncle Luke! We got ta get him loose!" Kara Sue attempted pulling Luke in that direction.

From inside the livery barn, Jojo heard the noise, joining them with a puzzled look on his face, but said nothing. Knowing Luke would deal with it.

"Now hold on, girl, we'll do what we have to." Luke cautioned, but it's got ta be done right. The three walked for the sheriff's office.

"Anna would yo' check an' see mayhap the sheriff's in." They stood in front of the small-unpainted structure, a sign indicating the sheriff's office.

Anna quickly came out followed by the tall slim man; Sheriff Mizell, referred to by almost everyone as Bones. Hardly an imposing man and it was difficult to determine his age at first glance. Long premature graying hair hung unkempt from under his floppy hat, framing his unshaved weathered, suntanned face. Dark gray suspenders held his baggy pants up around a long thin waist. The metal star signifying him as sheriff hung heavy, tugging on the front of his homespun shirt. When his arms moved, his bony wrist stuck out from his frazzled worn, a little too short, shirtsleeves. The long forty-four revolver, its bone handle showing from its holster seemed out of place on Bones, leaving the impression that, its weight might topple him. His absents of hips allowed the worn brown belt and holster to drape low, as if it all might slip from his waist to the ground. It could be that the red rag hanging from his back pocket prevented that from happening.

But appearances weren't everything. Bones Mizell held the respect of any and all, who had ever met him; and all others who had only heard his history from stories. The long pistol had been used for killing in the past, and Bones was more than prepared to do so at anytime, should the need arise. Now however, it was mostly used to club down a quarrelsome cowhunter on a rowdy Saturday night in Tater Bluff.

"Whut's doin', Luke? Miz Anna here sez they's ah ruckus brewin', somethin' 'bout ah Nigger slave boy?" Wiping a faded sleeve across his tanned face. Habit, he didn't appear to be sweating.

"Well thet's jus' it, Bones. Thet boy ain't no slave, 'cause me an' mine know him. An' I say, he ain't no slave naw suh. Kara Sue sez he talked to her, 'bout gettin' he'p, sez ah man got 'm chained up yonder."

"Then les' see whut it's all 'bout." Bones walked with long lanky strides toward the saloon.

"Dang nab it! I should ah knowed." A hushed tone, almost to him self, as they drew closer to the saloon and the small mob on the porch.

"Whut?"

"Them's tha Rice boys. Yo' be knowin' 'em?"

"No suh, ain't had tha pleasure. But I heard Captain Reading Blount mention thet name before. Said they live down on Crazy Woman Creek, whut runs all tha way to tha Okeechobee. It's plain as day tha injins ain't kilt'm, like tha captain calculated."

"Naw tha injins ain't kilt'm. An if them two's mixed up in this, it goin' ta take ah spell ta get it cleared up. An' believe yo' me it ain't gonna be no pleasure," Bones warned.

"Whut do yo' mean by thet?" Luke looked into the sheriff's dark squinting eyes as they continued walking with the girls following. He noticed for the first time the sheriff had sweat on his brow. The air was cool.

"Yo' calculate trouble?" Thinking of Kara Sue and Anna's welfare. Jojo would lend a hand if it came to it. Then there was the boy too.

"Naw, reckon it won't come ta nothin' harmful, but it sho' gonna get ah might plexin,'" he stated knowing what Luke meant by the question.

Bones just didn't know exactly how to explain the Rice boys, as they were generally referred, because Roelon and Raelon Rice were quite unique. Not mean, but by birth just hard headed as a pine knots. Once they had their minds set, you would be hard pressed to change it. And Bones had an idea that this was one of those situations. Without saying so, he secretly hoped that Luke could prove his statement about the boy being a free Negro.

"Thet big'n, be Raelon an' tha littlest be Roelon, an' they twins if yo' c'n believe thet." Bones acted as if he wanted to turn around, but continued walking.

"Them two! They twins? One's two feet taller than tha other'n! But they both uglier than hell though. Look lak they both been drawed through ah knot hole back'ards," Luke added, not realizing he was gawking with his mouth open.

To Luke's way of thinking, the two couldn't even pass for brothers, let alone twins. Some would argue that they wouldn't pass for human beings.

"Yeah suh thet's true on all counts," Bones said. "When they wuz born, ol' Doc Jones he's dead now. But he wrote'm up in some kin' ah medical journal, said they wuz freaks thet put ah considerable strain on nature," he further explained. "Roelon's proud ah tha fac' thet, he gets his runtiness from his mammer's side ah tha family, she's ah tiny woman right 'nough," the sheriff stated. "An' damn nigh as ugly as them two boys. But I declare I ain't never seen'm with knots all over'm lak thet." The sheriff was puzzled by their appearance; even more unpleasing to look at than usual.

"I'll be dogged, I ain't never seen tha lak of it." Luke had difficulty closing his mouth.

Anna and Kara Sue still following and close enough to hear, could hardly believe what the sheriff had said either. It was stated for the truth. It must be.

The Rice Twins were well known around the Peace River Valley, but it came as no surprise to Bones that, Luke had not acquainted himself with them. Because they seldom came to town, spending the majority of their time hunting and trapping and the like in the swamps. And they were forced to work harder, especially since Billy Bowlegs capture. It appeared this time that, they had trapped themselves a different kind of prey, with thoughts of gaining some reward for a captured runaway. The twins had not ventured more than twenty miles in any direction from the shack where they were born, on the western edge of the Okeechobee, except once. When one day they decided on making a trip to Punta Rassa on the gulf coast. The venture was undertaken for absolutely no reason at all, except to say that they had been someplace, other than Tater Bluff.

That decision changed their lives forever, because Punta Rassa was where they first laid eyes on Captain Kormac McBean. The old rough and salty sea captain intrigued the two from the very moment he disembarked the big sailing ship from Cuba. Actually they became mindful of the cargo even before they caught sight of McBean. The meeting took place over four years past, and their interest in the captain remains strong, maybe stronger. By some divine guidance, the old captain was bound in the same direction as the Rice twins. As it happened there was a shortage of conveyances forcing him to dicker with the Rice boys for use of their rig. He could have gotten use of their old wagon for nothing, but agreed on one Spanish doubloon as an acceptable price. The captain a generous man had been willing to go higher, three, maybe even four doubloon for wagon and driver, not to mention loading and unloading. But the boys agreed to the very liberal terms, because of the unusual freight.

The sudden and lasting interest by Roelon Rice was the monkey, he had never seen one before, and the captain had one. He nor Raelon had never seen a picture of a monkey before, let alone a live monkey. Heck they were even taken with the monkeys' name "Geechee." And once Roelon overcame his apprehensiveness of the animal biting him with its tiny teeth they became fast friends. Along with the catchy name, Roelon was especially fond of the little red hat, with the small white feather stuck in the band. To Roelon the hat somewhat resembled a small red lard bucket. The focus of Roelon's interest, set cocked on Geechee's little brown head, secured by a string. Much better than his own hat especially, with the white feather and different from any hat he had ever seen before. At first a tiny bit of mortification plagued his mind over the red hat. Roelon had never considered, one day meeting an animal wearing a better hat than his own. Status envy.

His ill will if any, toward the monkey altered however; after Geechee handed him a small chunk of coconut meat taken from a small bag secured to his waist by a tiny leather belt. Deciding soon, he would acquire a hat like

Geechee's white feather and all. It was already on his mind to see if Mister Biggers, the owner of the dry-goods store, might order a lard bucket that would fit his head. Mr. Biggers could even keep the lard. Scratching up enough red paint would not be too difficult. Raelon on the other hand was taken with the monkeys red britches and little black belt, and decided that he would save enough hide to fashion a belt just like the one Geechee wore. And maybe a small bag like Geechee's, to carry fishhooks and the like.

The monkey and other cargo hauled that day would cause the difficulty for sheriff Bones Mizell on this day. Everyone acquainted with the Rice twins was aware of the annoying method they had acquired since, in communicating. Especially Roelon who felt the need to describe things in detail, and could only do so, if comparing his subject of conversation with something that belonged to Captain McBean. Along with a moral sense of duty to name exactly where the captain had acquired the comparable property. For this he was compelled to rely on Raelon's gifted memory, his own always failed, during his attempt at communicating the parallel item.

As far as Bones was concerned he expected his patience, if not destroyed, would be worn thin, because of their bazaar method of conversation. Not to mention how Luke might react, knowing his lack of previous dealings with the Rice boys. At any rate, that was not sufficient reason to postpone his lawful duty.

"Whut kin' ah fuss yo' boys creatin' here?" The inquiry was directed toward the larger twin, Raelon.

It probably wasn't the ideal question, but he had to start somewhere, and aware he would have to start with Raelon.

"Hit wern't us, hit were thet litt'l yaller haired gal thar." Raelon disputed the accusation right off the bat, pointing a dirty-welted finger toward Kara Sue.

"Yeah she come up here making ah big ta do over our Nigger thar. She took ta fussin' more'n thet big ol' bird ah Capt'n Kormac's did, when thet coon got after it." Roelon blurted out their defense. "Whut kin' ah bird is thet, Raelon?" Asking his brother for identification of the bird.

"Hit ah Macaw." Raelon's steel-trap mind came into play.

"Thet's right ah Macaw. Where he get it?" Roelon asked.

"From Brazil." Raelon named the homeland of the large colorful bird, as if reading it from a page in a book.

Bones glanced at Luke for his reaction. Luke had just gotten his first sample of what Bones would like to have explained about the Rice twins, but lacked the know-how. Confusion was plain on Luke's face as he studied the two strange men. Having never seen such down right repulsive looking men anywhere before, he made no comment... Disbelief...Wide-eyed staring...

"Forget thet damned bird ah McBean's where'd yo' get thet, boy? An' why yo' got 'm chained up lak thet?" Aiming the question at either of the two

"He's ah runaway, an' he right mean. Maybe even ah killer. Ain't no law 'bout chainin' ah Nigger," Roelon defended their rights. "Is they?" Asking his brother.

"Naw they ain't. Folks got rights." Came a quick answer.

"Thet young'n, ah danger yo' say?"

"Yeah, suh he is. Look at whut he done ta us, near ta kilt us both." Raelon spoke, extending his thick neck, better displaying his traumatized face.

Bones couldn't disagree at least from the appearance of the two. Both Raelon's eyes swollen badly, one almost shut completely. An ear puffed up so, it resembled a large red cotton ball. The red swollen knots covering his face and hands, were to numerous for counting, as was his brother.

"Yo' ah sayin' thet boy done all thet ta y'all?" The sheriff looked on in amazement at the small figure chained to the hitching post. The boy looked up. His black dry face showing traces of tear streaks.

"Sho did. Some of hit we got tryin' ta ketch'm though. Look at our clothes, tha way they tore up an' all. I 'llow thet boy's quick as thet big ol snake whut Capt'n McBean got ta guard his treasure. Whut kin' ah snake is thet?"

"Hit ah Cobra." Like always the confident answer came swiftly.

"Thet right ah cobra. Where'd he get thet ol' guard snake?" Roelon shuddered. His voice squeaked even more, picturing the big snake. It's puffed up head, swaying and hissing.

"Madras India." Raelon answered with full assurance. Slightly irritated his brother had not remembered where the snake had come from. Sometimes he felt his brother was a bit lazy; and just not wanting to think, and making him do all the thinking. It was draining.

Luke shook his head in amazed confusion. Turning and looking at Jojo, then Anna and Kara Sue. Having no idea what to make of the two brothers. As ugly as they were they didn't appear dangerous and even less like twins, with Raelon at least a foot and a half taller than his brother, and at least seventy-five pounds heavier.

"Shucks it ain't likely we would've ketched him ah tall, 'ceptin' we got'm cornered at Duck-Bill Lake an' he seen thet big ol' gator in tha water an' cain' go no more," the smaller brother explained through swollen lips.

"We would've been ah heap sight better off if we'd jus' let thet gator eat 'm too. We shore would be ah lot more fit right now," Raelon testified. "An' lak as not our clothes wouldn't be raggedy lak this. Mammer's gonna be ah might vexed. Havin' ta stitch'm up." Raelon exhibited a badly scratched up muscular arm. The sleeve completely torn away… Missing… His arm, once having been protected from the sun by a long sleeve, now a profusion of red bumps and cuts on once pale skin, now naked, and sunburned.

"It were ah heap ah doin' fo' us ta put them chains on thet boy. Mos' ah this damage wuz done then," Roelon lamented, pointing a shaky finger toward his knotty blotched and swollen red face. "An' looky at my head where I got hit with ah green pinecone." Bringing up the same damaged hand, barely touching the lump between his eyes ever so tenderly with a fingertip. Dried blood covered the cut on the lump; one of many on or about his head.

"Now, boys, I'm sad 'bout y'all being so beat up an' all, but I purly would be proud ta know jus' how all thet come 'bout, special yo' saying yo' had tha boy chained an' all." Bones inquired. Suppressing a laugh, looking at Luke, also trying to avoid laughing.

"An' I be proud ta 'splain too. We wuz plumb tuckered, chasin'm an' all. We stopped ta res' under ah big tree lak tha one in Capt'n Kormac McBean's yard. Whut kin ah tree is it?"

"Hit ah big ol' hickory tree," Raelon answered. "An' they grow mos' everywhere," adding the second answer before asked, but confident it would have been.

"Thet right, ah big hickory tree. An hit were ah nut from thet ol' tree whut he chunked." Roelon attempted to raise his arm to simulate a throwing motion. Winced.

"Thet whut done this," Raelon declared, lifting his own swollen red finger toward his nearly ravaged face, and pointing out a different knot.

"Are y'all ah sayin' this boy done beat y'all up thet ah way with ah hickory nut?" Bones questioned, unconvinced. But it was apparent that something or someone had beaten them up quite badly. There was no doubt. The proof coated them.

"Yeah, suh, thet's ah pure fac'. Hit were ah hickory nut right 'nough. Thet boy tricky as thet little monkey ah Capt'n Kormac's. Whut kin' ah monkey is it?" Roelon asked scratching his head, without lifting his dirty ragged hat. Wincing once again.

"It ah spider monkey, an' he got it from Panama." Raelon answered again before the question came up, smiling proudly through swollen lips. Because of the pain, his smile faded quickly.

Luke was straining hard for patience. But was not at all confident he could continue to do so. Especially seeing Cork in chains. A thousand questions swirled in his mind, as he struggled to hold them and allow the sheriff to handle the situation. All the while finding the whole thing almost amusing. Bones was right on the money about one thing, the Rice boys were in a world all their own. Deciding he must hold back a little longer, and allow the sheriff do his duty.

"Hit were mostly Raelon's fault, he wuz 'sposed ta be guardin' tha boy, 'special he bein' so dangerous an' all." Roelon placed full blame on his bigger brother. Looking up at him with one eye. The accusation made through barely moving lips. They both were speaking that way now.

"Reckon I got ta own up. Hit were my job. But, I reckon I wuz too tuckered." Raelon confessed. Hanging his head. "But I woke up jus' in time ta see him chunk thet big ol' hickory nut. I ain't ah knowin' he hit thet hornets nest, an' knocked it down right on Roelon, till I heared'm ah screamin' lak he done." Raelon weakly defend himself. In his heart, he knew there was no defense, and that they both were paying dearly for his laxity.

Roelon accepted his brother's confession and weak defense, moving his head affirmatively... Winced, before speaking. "Thet's rat, an' then thet boy took ta runnin', chains an' all rat through them palmetters higher then yo' head.

"Naw, suh, he ain't run none. He ain't run nary ah bit. He were ah hoppin'." Raelon disputed his brother's description of what the boy was actually doing.

"Thet rat I 'member now. He wuz hoppin' jus' lak thet litt'l three-legged pony whut Capt'n Kormac's got over ta his place. Whut kin' ah pony is it?"

"Hit ah Shetland. An' he got hit from County Cork Ireland." Raelon quickly shot back. Supplying an additional satisfactory answer, plus saving time by naming its homeland. "An' Roelon's right as rain about tha way he hops. Now I had time ta think on it, thet Nigger wuz ah hoppin' jus' lak thet pony. I ain't never seen tha lak of it," Raelon added.

"Betwixt them bees ah bitin' on us. An' them palmetters ah cuttin' on us, he dern near hopped right away an' 'scaped. But them chain's got hung up on ah palmetter root too high fo' him ta jump. Thet's when Raelon here grabbed holt, an' hung on."

"Now boys I hate ta be tha one thet rains on yo' cook fire, but I reckon yo' gonna have ta turn tha boy loose. Lest ways goin' by whut Mista Nash an tha girl here sayin'."

"Tha hell yo' say Bones Mizell… Uh, I mean sheriff." Quickly ratifying his verbalism, sounding more respectful. "Who's ta say he talkin' true? Mayhap he jus' figurin' ah way ta keep this boy fo' his own self. I 'llow this boy bring seven or eight hundert dollars in Jacksonville, even though he cain' talk ah word, an' dangerous lak he is." Raelon presented the strong argument. One he felt the sheriff couldn't counter. He was close to being right.

Luke, instead of speaking out, whispered something in the sheriff's ear, then turned and whispered something to Kara Sue. The girl smiled before turning, and scampering away.

"Boys… I reckon I gotta arrest y'all legal lak."

"A-rrest!!! Sheriff yo' cain' a-rrest folks fo' ketchin' ah run-away Nigger. Thet ain't legal lak." Roelon protested loudly. "Can he?"

"Naw suh, ain't no such law agin ketchin' Niggers. Decent folks got rights." Raelon's statement carried with it, a small hint of uncertainty.

"Ain't throwin' y'all in tha stockade fo' ketchin' ah Nigger, it fo' stealin'"

"Stealin'!!! Stealin' whut?"

"Capt'n Kormac McBean complained y'all took his mule and wagon without per-mission. Thet's obtainin' befo' tha fac', dishonestly after tha fac' an' snatchery between tha fac'." Bones hastily make up legal sounding grounds for arresting them. Official sounding. "An' this tha fus time I seen y'all since his complaint," he explained.

"Thet right, Raelon?"

"Reckon. I ain't never herd ah no snatchery before, after or between tha fac' but it do sound serious." Raelon answered, uncertain of what punishment might fit such charges. "But thet wagon use ta be ourn." His argument failed to satisfy the sheriff.

It was true that they had only borrowed the mule and wagon. Captain McBean had loaned out the rig to the twins every spring, ever since he had purchased it from them. It was necessary so the boys could move their boat, for the purpose of hunting alligators. Captain Kormac McBean was as fond of alligator steaks as anyone in the state. So he had the first pick of a hide and a large quantity of meat, for the loan of his mule and wagon.

And he always made a practice of picking the largest hide, and a more than generous quantity of tender meat from the smaller alligators. The twins considered this unfair of Captain McBean but, because they had never come to any detailed agreement before hand, made no protest. But they could not believe he had accused them of stealing the wagon and mule however.

Admittedly, he wasn't at home when they had taken it; or in their minds borrowed it. It had only been in their possession a half day, so a charge of stealing they couldn't understand. Captain Kormac McBean was their best friend, actually they're only friend. Their day was not going well at all. First there was the argument over their captive colored boy; and now the threat of arrest over a serious charge of snatchery. They were unsure if it was before or after the fact. The sheriff hadn't made that clear. Just as they were prepared to protest further, Kara Sue rejoined the group along with Jojo leading a large gray ox, stopping in front of the group of men.

"Boy yo' familiar with this animal?" The sheriff pointed his finger at the animal in question.

Cork raised his head and peered at the big animal held by Kara Sue.

"Well, boy?" Bones asked gently prodding the boy for a response.

"Yas, suh, I know thet animal, he called Blue Nose, an' Mista Thomas dickered ah trade with Mista Luke an' Mista James. Mista Thomas gave up dis animal an' 'nother near as big fo' four mules." Cork answered the sheriff, still looking at the big gray ox.

"Dad burn! Yo' hear thet Raelon? Thet boy c'n talk all 'long. As good as thet litt'l black bird thet Capt'n McBean went all tha way ta Punta Rassa ta fetch, Whut kin' ah bird is it Raelon?" The astonished Roelon asked, after hearing the boy speak for the first time.

"It ah mynah-bird."

"Thet right. Where them birds come from?

"They come from India," Raelon named the starling like bird, and it's native land.

"Well thet settles it. I reckon yo' boys know Mista Nash is speaking true. Thet boy ain't no runaway, he's ah free Nigger. So I 'spect yo' ain't got no cause fer keeping tha boy chained up an' all."

"Mayhap we c'n turn'm loose, but we laid out fo' ex-penses, grub, smoked mullet an' tha lak. An' our clothes torn up lak they are, an' they almost new, ain't even two year ol'. Why I 'llow they won't hold up till full summer. All on 'count we tried ta save this boy's life,' Raelon lamented.

"Yeah, I reckon we got somethin' comin' fo' him puttin' them hornets on us an' all too. Could be we gonna need medical attention. Why we actual rescued thet boy. They's laws ' pro-tectin' innocent folks lak us," Roelon added, especially since he had gotten the worst of the bees.

"Will two dollars cover yo' ex-penses?" Luke reached in his pocket.

"Two dollars eh? Wall I don' know, we done ah heap ah sufferin' on account ah them bees. An' lak as not ah heap more, when Mammer sees whut them saw tooth palmetters done ta our new clothes. An' it all thet boy's fault too, on account ah him hoppin' off tha way he done." Roelon presented as strong a business deal as he could, while moving his lips as little as possible.

"'Nother dollar ta trade fo' ah purty fo' Mammer, she been cravin' ah store bought comb fo' her hair. Mayhap we c'n get'r ah store bought brush too. An' they's thread fo' sewin' an' all. Special tha prices thet Mista Bigger's got on his goods." Raelon countered, taking full advantage of his quick mind to make what he considered a hard bargain.

"Three dollars it is then. Yo' boys drive ah mighty hard bargain." Luke handed the coins to Raelon because it was his swollen hand that shot out first.

"This mean we ain't gonna be charged with snatchery after tha fac'?" he asked after slipping the money in his pocket.

"Naw yo' two boys done tha right thing, cooperatin' with tha law an' all; ain't gonna be no charges agin y'all."

"Well ah feller got ta be sharp, times bein' hard lak they is." Raelon was proud, he had bargained for another dollar, plus outwitted the sheriff by beating a snatchery charge. He had no intentions of spending time in jail. It was their season for hunting alligators.

"We ain't gonna be held accountable fo' whut this boy gonna do when we turn him loose, special since we done warned y'all, 'bout this boy bein' ah killer. If it were me I'd clear tha street of tha women an' children." Raelon cautiously unlocked the chain, jumping back, as if preparing himself for attack.

To the great surprise of the Rice twins, and their supporters from the saloon, the boy made no move to run or attack. Instead he simply stood and stretched his small frame, and walked over to the large gray ox held by his friend. A couple of tears fell from his dark eyes as he rubbed the animal's nose.

"I be thankin' yo' Mista Luke," he said, turning from the animal and facing Luke. "An' yo' too Kara Sue, I wuz in quiet ah fix." He stared at Jojo, not knowing who he was.

"It okay boy, les' go talk, an' fin' out how yo' come ta be in this fix. This here is friends ah ours, Miz Anna an' Jojo." Cork extended his hand; toward Anna and gently pumped it, then repeated the greeting with Jojo.Jojo, before Luke placed a hand on the boy's shoulder, turning him toward the livery stable.

Kara Sue and Jojo walked next to Cork holding the lead rope for the ox. They all made their way down the street and away from the saloon. Luke felt a small twinge deep in the pit of his stomach, knowing the story that the boy would recount about the rest of his family could not be a good one. He was not looking forward to hearing it, but knew that he must. The boys' eyes told him that he had had some awful experience, and he knew telling it would be hard on them all.

"Well I'm plum' proud ta get shut ah' thet boy, an' thet Luke Nash gonna fin' out when thet boy cuts an' runs off. Mayhap turns bees on'm or tha lak, he'll see right 'nough." Raelon fingered the coins in the pocket of his ragged britches, as he watched them walk away.

"Thet ah pure 'nough fac', an' I hope they search thet Nigger fo' hickory nuts an' other dangerous weapons an' tha lak," Roelon agreed, gently putting a finger to a large swollen red knot on the end of his nose. "Yeah, suh, we done warned'em. No cause fo' tha sheriff tha be talkin' no snatchery after tha fac' charge on us." They returned to the saloon, they had three dollars to spend, forgetting about any gift for Mammer.

CHAPTER FOURTEEN

At first Luke said nothing, only watching Cork for a moment setting on the bundle of hay. As badly as he wanted to get all the information from the boy, he knew Cork needed a little time, and he meant to allow it. Cork sat with his face in his hands. Luke could detect a slight shiver in the boy's slender form, even under the oversized tattered coat he had neglected to remove. Sheriff Mizell, the only other person in the livery with them, gave Cork a gentle tap on his shoulder looking at Luke as he did so. Cork looked up. Wiped his eyes with a ragged cuff of the dirty coat. Then as if remembering it wasn't his coat, he stood and removed it; and droped it to the ground at his bare feet as if shedding one burden, and preparing him self for another. Luke fought his eyes from tearing, deliberately not looking directly at anyone.

"Son, yo' up ta talkin'?" Bones asked after gathering his thoughts.

Cork once again took his place on the bundle of dry grass, "Yeah suh Capt'n, I reckon I am." Looking at Luke through wide, yet tired damp red eyes.

"C'n yo' tell us whut happened ta yo' family, an' how yo' come ta be chained ta ah horse rail by them two?

"'Spect so suh. They hit us tha day we lef' yo' folks, after y'all he'ped us cross thet Oklawaha River. Little after noontime I reckon. Miz Caroline say she hungry an' wanted ta stop fo' nourishment, we ain't had no chance ta fight Mista Luke."

"Injuns yo' mean?"

"Yas suh, Capt'n." Answering the sheriff's question without looking up.

"Everybody else kilt?"

"Jus' Mista Thomas dead when they took us away, Uncle Caesar hurt real bad, bad lick on tha head, but still 'live. Thet injun called Iron Bull, cut tha back ah his legs, here." Cork demonstrated, touching the back of his leg at the

220

ankle. "I seen him do it, po'Uncle Ceasar cain' walk after thet, jus' moan tha whole time. Thet Iron Bull mighty mean fo' doin' thet ta po' ol' Uncle Caesar. 'Spect he wuz dead by dark though." Shaking his head slowly side-to-side, not bothering to wipe the tears streaking down his cheeks.

"Tha same bunch wuz aimin' ta 'tack y'all. But Jumper say y'all got too many guns. Then 'nother white man joined up wit y'all, an' he say they need more he'p. I figured y'all gone too by now," the boy said staring with damp eyes.

"I reckon yo' right 'bout Uncle Caesar, he must' ah crawled off an' died. But yo' sayin' Miz Caroline wuz took with yo'? She still alive then." Luke presented a statement, thinking it should have been a question. "An who is this Jumper yo' mentioned." Luke realized he must allow Cork more time. Slow down.

"Don' know now. She in ah awful way Mista Luke, them injuns done some mighty mean thangs ta her. Jumper, he ah injin with'm, but he ain't lak them, he talk American. She try ta bite through her arm, make her bleed ta death, lak stickin' ah knife in ah pig's neck." Pulling a thin shaking finger across his wrist, indicating the location of her self inflicted wound.

The anguish displayed in Bones' face reflected that of his own, but he forced himself to speak. "My god how tha po' woman must be sufferin', ta try an' kill herself lak thet."

Luke spoke the words quietly; and Bones wasn't sure what he had said. In his mind Luke could picture a wolf chewing off his own paw, freeing itself from a trap. Stopped his body from shivering by erasing the vexatious picture, after hearing Cork speak.

"But them squaws caught her bitin' herself, an' they patched her up with moss ta stop tha bleedin', an tied her up. Iron Bull took ah pine knot an' busted out her front teeth so's she cain' bite herself no mo'." Cork began sobbing. He attempted wiping the tears away with the back of his shaking hand, but others followed, too many as his body jerked.

Luke turned away for a moment thinking he might throw up, his mind conjured a picture of what the boy in such elementary fashion, had just described. Cork used the palm of his hand to wipe at his wet face.

"How is it they ain't kilt yo'?" Bones asked the boy.

"It on ah -count ah Jumper tellin'm I c'n read an' all. Two Ghosts he keep me so's I c'n read them letters they steal from tha white folks. Special the soldiers, an' news papers too."

"Two Ghosts?"

"He tha leader. He ain't no injun though, he colored same as me. Say he 'scaped from Louisiana, an' mos' them injuns scairt ah him, cause he big an' strong," he explained. "Named Two Ghosts, cause he can be in two places at once," he added.

Cork related the same story that Captain Blount had told them earlier, of when the Negro was born, how he grabbed his mamma's broken butcher knife and refused to release it.

"They say he kinda lak ah spirit on ah'count of it," Cork explained. But I thank Iron Bull tha meanest of all ah them." Cork's eyes suddenly exhibited a change, and Luke took note. Hate perhaps.

"Yeah, seems I heard ol' Acre Foot Johnson an' Capt'n Blount make mention of ah Nigger leadin' ah bad bunch." Bones removed his hat, scratched his head, trying better to remember. He did. But said no more about it, it wasn't the time. Instead looked at Luke knowing that Luke admired the courage of the boy, and the still captive woman. While wondering at the same time if the woman might still be alive, after what he had just heard. Being aware of the fact that death probably was a better alternative, than the hell she was suffering, at least in his mind. But the will to live often breeds additional suffering; this could be one of those examples.

"Miz Caroline, yo' thank she still 'live?" Luke unsure of what answer he truly wanted from the boy.

"Yeah suh, least way's mayhap four days ago. But she's in ah awful bad way Mista Luke…" Shaking his head slowly, side to side, not looking up. "Jumper Three Toes say she cain' las' much longer though, I ain't knowed Jumpers las' name till jus' before I lit out. He short two ah his small toes on one foot. He showed me, say it 'count of ah snakebite when he ah boy lak me, an' he cut off his own toes. Cain' 'member which foot though." Seemingly a hint of guilt over his poor memory of which foot the toes had been amputated from.

"How is it yo' managed ta 'scape?" Luke handed the boy a large tin cup of fresh milk that Kara Sue had brought in and departed just as quickly.

"Jumper Three Toes," answering quickly, after taking a long drink from the cup.

Using Jumpers full name, feeling he owed it because of his help, and because of his failure in remembering which foot had the missing toes. After all if someone has enough sand to cut off two of his own toes, anytime he relates the story, he felt he should remember which foot the toes were cut from.

222

"This Jumper Three Toes sayin' Miz Caroline cain' las' much longer?"

"Yas suh he say 'cause Two Ghost gave Miz Caroline ta them squaws an' chil'ren. Make her tote firewood an' all. An' tha young'ns be whippin' her with sticks all tha time. I try ta he'p her but they wont 'low me. An' she cain' eat no more on 'count Iron Bull, knocking out her teeth lak he done."

"Boy, kin yo' say how many injuns they is in thet bunch? Growed up men." The sheriff making it clear he had no interest in the number of children.

"Mayhap two dozen, mayhap more growed men; two, three boys bigger 'en me, cain't say fo' sho'. 'Cause they come an' go all tha time, huntin' an' raidin', but I thank thet right. Theys mayhap a dozen squaws, an' I 'llow tha same number of youngun's." Rubbing his chin, calculating numbers in his head.

Bones gave Luke a concerned look. Both knowing it would be no easy task, going in, and expecting to rescue the woman. Those two or three young boys that Cork had mentioned would be as dangerous as the full-grown warriors. And to help defend their children, the squaws would put up some fight. They would kill the woman too if given the chance. As a matter of fact it was probably impossible. But, whatever they tried, they would have to try very soon. They knew Jumper Three Toes was correct in his assessment of Caroline's chance of surviving.

Cork reached down and pulled at the coat he had dropped on the ground. Feeling into a pocket he retrieved a piece of smoked mullet.

"Hol' on boy yo' cain' eat thet, it got dirt all over it." Luke restrained the boy's arm before the pungent piece of fish reached his lips.

"Dang Cork I should've knowed yo' ta be hungry. Jojo yo' Kara Sue run over an' see Miz Biggers at tha dry good store, an see she might have some proper nourishment fo' tha boy." Luke called out, knowing Kara Sue, Jojo and Anna waited just outside.

"An' fetch 'nother cup ah milk ta wash it down with," Bones said, passing the empty cup to her.

"I 'pollogize fo' not offerin' yo' vittles, reckon I wern't thankin' proper."

"No need Mista Luke, I been eatin' thet ol' smoked mulled fo' quite ah spell now, an' wuz real proud ta get it. But I be thankin' yo'." He tossed the black chunk of fish toward a hound lying on a pile of straw near the door. The seemingly sleeping long eared dog snapped up the portion of meat with the minimum of movement, then returned to his nap.

"Boy, c'n yo' say where them injuns kept yo' captive?" the sheriff asked as he continued watching the hound return to his original stretched out position near the door.

"Mayhap I c'n Capt'n. It wuz on ah island lak place, water real shaller though, mos' dry. Jumper tol' me ta foller tha river whut leads away from tha island, 'till I come ta tha black water. Then go north, sun always on my right hand in tha mornin'. He point tha way ta start, think I los' at fus', on ah 'count ah tha way thet ol' river do. It go one way then tha other so much." Moving his hand around trying to explain the wonderings of the narrow river.

"Yo' mean it zig zag?"

"Thet right Capt'n."

"Tha Devil's Crutch." Thinking out loud, picturing something in his mind.

"Huh?"

"Thet river, tha one tha boy talkin' on, it's called tha Devil's Crutch."

"Yo' know tha place?"

"Well…Know of it… Only tha injuns know it. It ah miracle, or blind luck this boy come out ah thar. Thet island they camped on called Skull Mound. Mayhap me an Acre Foot Johnson's brother Dooley, an' August Moon be tha only white men been thar, least way's an' come out. An' then tha boy here. Yeah suh, plum' miracle," he repeated. Even Dooley got hisself aet by ah gator after goin' back. All we found wuz one ah his legs, knowed it wuz Dooly's 'cause it growed crooked. Horse stomped him when he wuz ah young'n. Named thet creek after'm, an' we got ta cross it ta get where we goin'.

Luke could not have agreed more, about it being a miracle that Cork could have walked his way out of such a place, after Bones described the place as an alligator and snake infested hell, not mentioning panther and bear. It certainly appeared far worse than anything Luke and James had yet encountered.

Penetrating the miles of thick saw grass would be a more than a troublesome hindrance. Their target, a patch of high ground called Skull Mound, located squarely in the center of this enormous river of grass. It was easy to understand why the Indians had chosen such a place to hide. Infiltration into this area by a conventional army would be impossible.

Mounts would be of no use, infiltration would have to be on foot, because of the sometimes-deep mud, plus the saw grass with its razor edges would cut up man or beast. Besides the Indians, alligators and snakes, which Bones mentioned, would have to be dealt with. Could it even be accomplished? Perhaps, but it would take a bigger miracle and even more luck than Cork had experienced. Luke didn't even like the name of the place, and was wondering, but didn't ask why the hammock was so named.

"Boy whut kin' ah weapons yo' seein' them injuns got? Rifles, side arms an' tha lak?"

"They got plenty ah both," Cork said looking up at Luke as if warning him.

"Thet ain't good, No suh, ain't good at all, an' thet saw grass don't give no cover, 'special when looking down tha barrel of ah long gun," Bones added.

"Yeah, reckon thet true 'nough sheriff."

"Jumper Three Toes say they real short on powder an' shot though,"

"Thet ah fac'?" More a rhetorical question by Bones as he scratched his stubble covered chin.

They counted this a miracle already, a small one perhaps, but they would welcome any and all sent their way. An assault no matter the results would be quick, so the lack of shot and powder would be a tremendous advantage for the attackers, with surprise being more help than anything else.

"Yas suh, Jumper say they been usin' bow's ta get meat. Savin' whut shot an' powder they got lef' fo' ah raid Two Ghosts wuz plannin' on white folks ta get mo'. An' thet man Mista Acre Foot Johnson yo' say befo'. Jumper sez Two Ghosts is savin' shot ta kill him."

"Ta kill Acre Foot?"

"Yas suh, Jumper sez Two Ghosts 'fraid ah him on 'count he so big an' strong an' all. Say when he kills Mista Acre Foot Johnson then he be stronger. Two Ghosts plannin' ta do it soon when thet Mista Acre Foot bring tha mail fo' tha army from Fort Pierce."

"Now ain't thet ah caution," Bones said, almost amused.

"This Two Ghosts, he ain't so dumb, 'special he ah knowin' Acre Foot carry mail fo' tha army. Got ah contract. An' he got ah run next day or so from Fort Pierce ta Punta Rassa, clear 'cross tha state. I declare thet ah real caution." He repeated himself.

"Wonder yo' might be able ta tell us how thet camp's laid out?"

"Mayhap Mista Luke, las' I saw they was eight huts laid out lak this." Cork drew the locations of the huts into the sand with the tip of a finger. "They kinda lak make ah half moon tha way they set up an' all."

"Thet ah fac'?" The sheriff threw a surprised glance toward Luke. Luke shook his head in agreement. Cork was passing on valuable information, information that they would surely find useful, if they were to free Mrs. Thomas. And even if the captive was already dead as was suggested, they might rid the state of a few more treacherous bandits.

"Which one ah them huts they normal keep Miz Thomas in?"

"This'n," Cork pointed to a drawn square on the left side of his crude sketch.

"Tha huts made high off tha groun', lak this high." Holding his hand up approximately four feet from the ground.

"Regular Seminole cheekee, built fo' high water."

"Them squaws all sleep inside, but they make Miz Thomas sleep underneath with tha dogs," Cork explained

"Dogs!"

"Yas suh, Capt'n they got two. But one real ol' lak, nigh blind I reckon; but tha other'n he ah real mean dog. Jumper say Iron Bull aimin' ta kill thet ol' dog real soon fo' food fo' Miz Thomas. Them young injuns take tha other dog huntin' ever day, ketch hogs ta eat."

"If they go out every day, then maybe, jus' maybe thet houn' be gone when we make our move," Luke said, rubbing his chin with the back of his hand, as if deep in thought.

"Sho' will make thangs ah might easier ta get close. Them hunters sho ta start early Luke. Let's hope they go in ah different direction from where we commin' in."

"Mista. Luke,"

"Yeah, boy,"

"Miz Caroline cain' eat no dog, special no ol' dog, it tough an' all. She ain't got no teeth in front, on 'count ah Iron Bull knockin'm out tha way he done."

Luke hesitated before speaking. He wasn't completely sure just how to answer the boy. He wasn't even sure if, the words Cork had spoken were meant as a question or statement. Luke looked into the boy's face; his large dark eyes manifested a look expecting some remark from him. One thing was clear; Cork was worried about Caroline. And anguishing over her eating the dog, forced or not. And they new he had just cause for being concerned for her.

"Don' know boy, mayhap thet injun, thet Jumper Three Toes wuz jus' raggin' yo'. Mayhap they ain't really gonna kill thet ol' dog, 'cause Injuns jus' lak white folks set great store in they animals, special they brave an' all. I 'llow thet ol' dog caught many ah ornery boar hog, so it ain't likely they feed'm ta Miz Caroline."

"Thet ah fac' boy. Them injuns ad-mire courage in animal or man. Naw suh they ain't lakly ta kill thet ol' dog ta feed Miz Caroline. Lak as not they have some religious ceremony to honor him when he does die," the sheriff added.

"Mayhap suh. Come ta think, they do feed'm tha liver from them animals they kill. He got no more teeth than Miz Caroline got."

Luke and the sheriff saw fit to alleviate the boy's mind as best they could, his concern over Miz Caroline being fed the dog. Cork appeared to have accepted their explanations of the loyalty of the Indians toward their animals. The expression on Cork's face altered. Less strain seemed to be present. What a few moments ago, was a face of great anxiety. Now converted to exhaustion. He had experienced things that no one should, especially a child. Now he perceived a sense of a possible deliverance for Miz Caroline. The first of any such feelings, since shortly after leaving the Nash family back at the Oklawaha, seemingly years ago. It had been the Nash family who had assisted them in safely crossing the swift running water. Now in a time of deep trouble they meet once again.

Help was far too late for poor old Uncle Caesar and Mr Thomas. But perhaps for Miz Caroline there was a chance, even if slight. Saddened by knowing just how slight, even in his young years, but exhaustion prevented him from displaying it. The weary boy swayed atop the hay bundle, his lids drooped oppressively over his tired eyes. Luke caught Corks limber slim frame in his arms as the boy tilted forward, preventing him from falling to the ground. He carried the limp form, already in a somnolent state through the front door of the livery, laying him on a saddle blanket covering a bed of hay in the wagon. Cork would say no more this day, his slumber would continue until well after reaching the Nash homestead.

Bones retrieved a stub of a pencil from his vest pocket, wetting the pencil point with his tongue; he sketched a crude map, handing the rumpled piece of paper to Anna.

"Yo tell tha boys ta meet us there, August knows thet area real good," Bones said, pointing to an area on the hastily drawn map indicated by an X. "Me an' August scouted thet whole area fo' tha army tha las' time them injuns wuz on tha prod. Let'em know I'll be near thet eagles nest with our horses, mayhap two mile due north ah Johnson Creek, cain' miss thet big tree even in dead dark. Be 'spectin'm by midnight." He looked directly into Anna's eyes should she have a question. She had none.

"Tell 'em ta make haste, an' bring extrie powder an' shot an' mayhap some venison jerky, ah sack ah smoked fish. An' ta brin' two extrie slickers, fo' me an' tha boy here, looks lak ah storm brewin'," Luke said pointing a thumb toward Jojo, and looking toward the eastern sky.

"Luke, not the boys! You can't. Polly...." She stopped.

"Anna we're gonna need all tha guns we c'n muster, an I 'llow Jimmy D. an' Jojo c'n shoot better'n most men." It 'pears we gonna be facing mayhap two-dozen hostiles, on their ground. It ain't lak we got choices."

227

She reached out her hand; Luke took it, a slight squeeze. There was no need for speaking their feelings; their eyes said enough, a slight nervous smile from both. Turning from Luke, and giving Jojo a light kiss on his cheek. God be with you son. God be with you all. Her gut hurt awful as she walked away. What if she never saw him again? Any of them, she hated saying goodbye like this. Her eyes welled with water. She was afraid, so very afraid.

Luke, Bones and Jojo watched her drive away, Cork sleeping in the bed of the wagon. A team of horses was borrowed to pull the wagon in place of the slower moving oxen. If Caroline Thomas was to be helped, time was of the essence, and they all knew it. Luke felt confident that he James and August would be of the same mind, concerning what must be done. It had been discussed over and over after leaving Blount's Fort, especially since crossing the Peace. But never talked about in the presence of the women. It would be very unfavorable news for them, but the men had known it would be only a matter of time. Either they attack the Indians, or the Indians would eventually get around to attacking them. The first option was the best alternative for the Nash family, now that they knew where the Indians were, even if unsure of their number. With God on their side and a lot of luck, they should have the advantage of surprise. It would be needed, one, if they were to be successful, and two, keeping the price to be paid low for such a venture. Blood, the price is always paid in blood... But whose blood would be drawn?

Hours had passed since the men and Jimmy D had ridden away, yet, Polly still nervously paced the floor. She knew where the early evening spring sun would be on the western horizon, even before opening the door, but she looked anyway. Trying anything to rid her mind of what plagued her. Secretly wishing the faint pink and orange colors filling the sky might erase her tormenting fears. She was too anxious to even continuing looking for very long, and even if she had, there was no relief for her.

"Reckon we bes' pull tha window covers down, lak as not tha skeeters gonna try an take us off. Tha sun gonna be down directly, an' ain't no breeze ta keep'm down." She gently closed the door. Almost opening it to look once more, and wondering had she looked long enough before?

"Yes those pesky bugs have been awful since tha spring rains." Anna tugged at one of the kerosene soaked burlap curtains over the nearest window, bringing it down, blocking what little light was left to come in.

Polly turned slowly looking around wringing her hands in her apron, checking on the location of the sun through the burlap, as Anna pulled the remaining curtains.

"I jus' don' see why they had ta go off on they own, an' special ta take them two boys. I tell yo' Anna I got ah real torment," she lamented, still ringing her hands.

"I know Polly, I suppose they had little choice about that decision, with most of the able bodied men out on the cattle hunts. It's like Luke said they were up against time as well as the Indians. And remember you said yourself, if it were Kara Sue in the hands of those Indians, you would go yourself if need be."

"I know, I know an' God knows it's true." Looking over her shoulder toward her daughter, setting on a bench, Cork sleeping on a pallet on the floor nearby. If it were Kara Sue out there, she would go anywhere to rescue her.

Kara Sue had hardly moved from her bench, watching over him in case he should wake and want something. Occasionally she would shoo a buzzing mosquito from him with a palmetto fan. It frightened her thinking about what he had gone through. And even though Polly spoke otherwise, she knew her mother agreed on the men going. They had little choice, an attempt had to be made for rescuing Miz Caroline from the Indians.

"Here Polly have a cup of coffee," Anna said passing her a tin cup of warm black liquid.

Polly really didn't want more coffee she had consumed enough, they both had. But, they had no mind for anything else. Pacing the bare plank floor or rocking in the rocking chair, they passed the time between cups of the bitter brew.

"I think you are correct Polly, the boys should have delayed until more support could be summoned." Sounding as if she should have stopped them, and could have.

"Naw, not so. It would have been too late to he'p poor Miz Thomas, an' mayhap too late already, from whut tha boy said 'bout her treatment. No better'n ah animal. An' thet awful place, Skull Mound an' Devil's Crutch don' even sound fit fo' animals ta take shelter. Naw they wuz right as rain in goin' now." Looking again, only a flush of color remaining, the sun was completely gone. She started to say more about that awful sounding place or something about the sun. But didn't. Both were quiet for a few minutes as if there was nothing left to be said on the subject. Polly resisted the urge to lift the mosquito screen and look outside, once she reached the window. Instead she turned and walked back to the rocking chair, placing her cup of cold coffee on a nearby bench.

"Do you think he even notices that I'm on the place? Often I've wondered." Speaking out of the blue, as if she suddenly realizing they needed to talk, but on another subject.

Polly needed no explanation of Anna's simple question and comment, but she knew Anna required her opinion. "Anna I got ah notion thet Luke Nash notices everythin' 'bout yo. He'd have too, 'less he's blind as ah bat. An' he ain't. All them Nash's got eyes lak hawks. They jus' got ways ah seein' thangs, but not sayin," she added.

Polly's smile brought a slight smile from Anna, the first since she had left Luke and Jojo in the Tatter Bluff street, months ago seems like, instead of a day. But her smile was short lived however, she didn't like thinking what was on her mind, but she was unable to prevent it.

"I saw the death bird," she said matter-of-factly. I saw it plain as a morning sun. It flew from that tree right outside that window you're at. It circled the house and came back to the same tree." Speaking as if there should be no question about it; as if it were scientific proof of a coming death, and very soon.

"Why Anna Cade! I'm surprised, yo' ah talkin' lak thet. Jus' lak ah fiel' han' an' yo' bein' ah educated woman an' all. Yo' know thet ain't nothin' but colored folk tales, ain't no such thang as no death bird," she admonished.

"But."

"Ain't no butts 'bout it. What yo' saw wern't nothin' but ah plain ol' black crow plain an' simple. Why I declare they flyin' 'round tha place all tha time, them ol' black crows."

"Oh, I know, I guess I'm just not thinking clear anymore." Ashamed now that she had mentioned such a thing. She felt foolish.

"I 'pect thet's so, ain't neither one of us ah thankin' lak we got good sense. It's real hard, but them boys gonna be fin'." The night passed ever so slowly, with only Cork and Kara Sue achieving what could be called a sleep state.

Pulling the oilcloth back from the window. Gold and yellow reflected from the edges of the trees, the opposite side, while the side Polly was looking out at remained shadowed, in a purplish to dark-umber color. As dark as the unseen cover cloaking them, even as the sun's brilliants reached it's fullest. The clouds of mosquitoes thinned, taking their leave with the darkness. The rising sun teaming with a slight breeze caused their rout into the deep brush. Only to reappear with vengeance after the suns westerly movement would steal the light away once again. Polly refused to look directly at the tall pine, that Anna had mentioned the night before. The one where she had seen the crow; the sign of death. Polly along with Anna gazed out into the daylight. Eyes seeing but her mind registering little. Time would pass, but slowly.

CHAPTER FIFTEEN

Bones, along with Luke and Jojo, made the Little Bow River before dusk; and decided that they would not cross at the ford. That was the spot where the Devil's Crutch and the Little Bow River joined flowing west, making its way toward the Gulf.

"It's shallow right 'nough, an' them renegades know it too. This is where they jumped them soldiers ah General Harney's an wiped'm out, ah couple ah years back." Bones uttered the comment low, as he peered intently at the far bank of the Little Bow.

Opting instead, to move slowly east a few miles, to a location where the water was deeper but narrow, their fresh horses should have little trouble swimming the black still water. The sheriff knew that, August Moon was also aware of that, and would follow their lead and tracks. Jojo urged his black pony into the water first, as Luke and Bones covered his crossing. Bones was right, the water was deep and barely moving, and his Marsh Tackie was a strong swimmer. Luke crossed last, his big red stud crossing as easily as the others did. Jojo, his maturity exceeding his years, had already checked his revolver, making sure the powder was dry, as did the others after crossing.

The sun would soon be lost to the small scouting party, yet; dimly visible above the distant trees toward the west, where the Little Bow River disappeared into horizon. Within twenty minutes they would navigate by stars. Bones calculated that the location where the Rice brothers had picked up the boy was maybe six to eight miles from where they stood, and he chose to follow the higher ground straight south rather than the winding water. It would be easier on the horses than the muck along the river's edge and leave behind less obvious sign of their presents. This part of the expedition would be covered by a sea of deep thick saw grass, surrounding hundreds of small islands of hardwood and cabbage hammocks. Locating the one island that the

Indians occupied, and held Miz Caroline captive would demand skill and thought. Any water they encountered would vary in depth, from ankle to waist. Fairly certain that he knew which island harbored the Indians, from something the boy had said, Bones was certain he could take them there.

"A peanut like shape," was how Cork had described it. "Lots of giant oaks,"

But Bones knew the shape to resemble more a skull than a peanut, there the origin of the name. He and August along with a small detachment of soldiers had spent weeks there, during the last uprising. Knowing the hammock to be a higher elevation than other nearby islands, and would afford dryer ground for life. Being aware also of how difficult it would be on a captive, because they were used like animals to wade through the water hauling firewood from the other islands. The squaws went along to protect their slaves from the alligators and snakes, plus see to it that an ample supply of wood was gathered in one trip.

Bones looked up at the partially misty concealed moon, reined in his slow walking horse to a halt.

"Be lookin' ta leave tha horses soon at the end of this high ground, thet's where I'll turn back fo' tha others, maybe ah mile yet" August stated in a whisper, after listening for a minute.

"Yo' 'allow August c'n pick us up all right?"

"Yeah, he'll know we went south as the crow flies, 'sides I plan on runnin' on to'm before they get this far," Bones explained.

It was now full dark when Bones reined his horse again, dismounted without speaking; Luke and Jojo followed suite. Knowing Bones had something to say, they moved in close. Sufficient moonlight filtered through the trees for highlighting their faces, they backed deeper into the shadows of a clump of cabbage trees.

"I calculate thet we be gettin' mighty close to injins," Bones whispered, they could barely see his face now.

"How far?"

"Six miles, mayhap eight, due south. Cain' take tha horses no further though, we purty much at tha end ah cover, have ta hobble 'em here. Not many acorns fo' them ta eat an' get sick on. This is tha place I wuz lookin' fo'," Bones said.

"Place smell lak it been burned." Luke spoke quietly, but could not be sure in the dark.

"Has, lak as not them injins burnt it during tha winter," Bones answered.

"I ain't counted on thet, but thet's good, horses do good on tha new grass an' won't stray off."

The clouds would often hide the stars they had been navigating by making travel very slow if not unreliable, especially with the absence of the North Star; Bones was uneasy about that, especially since they were splitting up.

"Tha breeze comin' out ah that southwest. Reckon it'll stay thet way?"

"I 'spect it will Luke, least till well past sun up anyways."

"Thet breeze is all we got fo' guidin', if them stars get covered. Keep thet breeze in our right ear, we be movin' south close enough. Yo' understand boy?" Luke touched Jojo on a shoulder.

"Yeah, suh I'll keep it there 'case we get split up an' all," Jojo answered.

"Luke yo' gonna hit black water maybe two miles south, 'bout hundert yards 'cross, ain't deep though. Even with tha spring rains we got, I 'spect it be waist deep, thet be Johnson Creek, an' it one ah tha wors' places fo' gators in this whole land. Ain't nothin' wors' than gettin' in water at night, knowin' they be there too." Bones said, with a warning tone to his voice.

"Cain' skirt it?"

"Naw suh, it be to far an' take too long. Jus' cain' do it at night."

"Thet's where Dooley Johnson, Acre Foot's brother, got caught five year back. Tha only thang we found wuz his leg, Acre Foot buried it somewhere close. Sayin' ah crooked leg wern't 'nough fo' takin' back fo' ah proper buryin'. Reckon hogs done rooted it up by now." His thoughts seemed to have drifted in another direction for a moment. Then, quickly back on the business at hand. "But yo' boys stay close together, 'member them gators c'n see yo' even if yo' cain' see them. Ain't likely they bother yo', if yo' look big to'm in tha water." There wasn't much else he could tell them. He could not see them clear enough, but he could feel the expected tension. He felt his own pounding heart plain enough.

Jojo thought to himself, "Bones could have talked all night without telling that story about Acre Foot's brother." But he was right; they would have a better chance of getting across that water staying close together. Jojo knew that to be fact by hunting with Nigger John at night. A thousand years ago. At least now it felt that way.

"Ain't no cause ta fret Bones, me an' tha boy make it alright, we be jus' fin'."

"Ain't frettin' Luke. Ya'll get ta tha other side, an' get ta thet banana grove whut use ta belong ta ol' Chief Billy Bow Legs. Cain' miss it. Them soldiers only cut down a few, but they's plenty lef' fo' concealment."

"Ya'll hol' up on tha southwest edge ah them trees. I'll lead tha res' of tha boys there before daybreak."

"All right Bones. Me an' this boy, we'll be there."

"Sho' will sheriff," Jojo attested.

"Well I guess yo' bes' be about it then, I'll look ta tha horses."

"Right," Luke said reaching in the dark for the sheriff's hand and giving it a firm shake. Jojo barely seeing them in the dark did the same.

"Yo' take care, boy,"

"Will Bones," Jojo answered, being a little less formal than usual.

The two started walking south and after only a few yards, Bones could just barely see them, and called to them softly before they disappeared completely into the darkness.

"Luke."

"Yeah?" Came a whisper.

"Ya'll keep yo' head down an' yo powder dry, yo' hear?"

"Will do sheriff," Luke answered back just as quietly, not looking back in the darkness.

With Jojo trailing through the blackness, his hand on Luke's shoulder preventing their separation, they made their way through the thick damp darkness of the hammock. The night sounds from the swamp enveloping them, with a variety of unseen insects, joined by birds and animals. A panther's scream reached them faintly from the night somewhere to their rear, far back. Jojo surmised that, the cat had picked up the scent of Bones and the horses. The normally quiet hunter screaming out its anger at the human scent. Hopping it wasn't so; Jojo instead, wished it might run down a pig or young deer to feast on this night.

"There it is boy, jus' lak Bones said," After an hours walk, Luke pointed toward the ripples of light from the slight moon, reflecting off the still black water.

"Reckon thet's got ta be Johnson Creek right 'nough." Jojo spoke, Luke barely heard him.

Both were anxious over reaching and entering the water. Their anxiety was not borne, only because of the danger of what the water embraced under its surface. There was the open field of saw grass stretching from their curtain of cover in the hammock to the water's edge, which had to be crossed first. It afforded little in the way of concealment, forcing them to move slowly in a low crouch. By this method they moved to the water.

Luke put a hand on Jojo's shoulder applying some pressure, indicating they should set down. They did so, quietly and removed their boots. The purpose was not to keep them dry, it was far too late for that, they had already waded through water. Luke calculated that the water to be crossed would have a muddy bottom, and there was danger of their boots getting stuck in the mud and pulled off their feet. And then there was the danger of the water being deeper than Bones had suspected. That being the case, they might have to swim for the far bank, and it would be a sight easier without wearing boots. They both were experienced in the ways of the woods and not easily caught off guard.

The two slowly and cautiously made their way into the water, after tucking their revolvers and powder in their boots, and securing the boots together with a short length of rawhide, and draping them around their neck, hopefully keeping their pistols and powder dry. Their rifles would be held above the water. The splash they heard was probably nothing more than a raccoon snaring a bullfrog at the waters edge, but it caused them to stop and listen a few minutes longer. Only after feeling it safe to continue, then did they proceed further into the cool muddy water. Hoping the millions of croaking frogs would drown out any noises they slowly pushed through the tall thick cattails lining the bank, and into the open water. With Luke leading the way, Jojo hung onto the back of his coat, their feet sinking past ankle deep into the mud. Each trying to catch any sign of movement or noise from any direction, they kept their eyes moving side to side, staring into the dark night. Jojo would turn his head back to watch the rear as they moved through the, now waist deep water. Luke considered they might be half way across the water, and it didn't appear to be getting any deeper, but it was impossible to see the intended bank in the darkness.

Another loud splash off to their left was sudden, and the distance away was difficult to discern. Even though they both strained their eyes toward the direction of the noise they were unable to see anything. If there was any doubt at first what the noise was, what followed left none at all. The loud blowing, then deep rumble vibrated the still air.

"Gator!" Luke said as quietly as he could yet still allowing Jojo to hear.

"It ah gator right 'nough, ah big bull an' he's mighty close and put out 'cause we in his territory." Jojo strained his eyes in the darkness to no avail.

They tried moving with more haste, while at the same time being as stealthily as possible. What may be waiting for them on the far bank was yet unknown, but it might offer a better way of dying. As he trudged forward, a too clear picture of the alligator forced it's way into Jojo's mind. An evil scene of how it would, with the tremendous strength of its tail and legs force the upper half of its body out of the water, and then splash down hard onto the water's surface. The bellowing sound that followed could be heard for miles across the swamps at night, a warning for all to steer clear and avoid his territory. To disregard this warning as the two intruders were now doing could prove fatal. The alligator would be coming fast for them, and they knew it. An alligator attack was quick and violent, with no chance for escape once in its jaws. A year ago, Jojo had seen one catch a cow dog belonging to Rolle Dean. With Rolle on horseback, belly deep and cracking at the alligator with his whip, the dog was snatched away, as Rolle attempted to pull the dog over his saddle.

Suddenly the moon broke free of the clouds, allowing them to see the red glaring eyes, appearing as chunks of burning coal across the water's surface. A shallow wake trailed the monstrous wide head. It moved toward them, now close enough in the dim light, that Jojo could plainly see its teeth. Numerous yellowish teeth of various sizes protruding from its unopened corrugated upper and lower jaws. Judging from the width between its reflecting eyes, the alligator could reach fourteen feet in length. An alligator of such length would easily weigh in excess of a thousand pounds; nothing could escape its attack. Its present intended prey, now would have to move even quicker. Gambling that they were alone and no Indians about to hear any noise, they forced themselves through the water with greater speed. Knowing the only chance if any existed at all, would be to successfully reach the bank, which seemed unlikely gauging the alligator's speed. But they intended on trying.

Jojo expected death would visit at any moment, and being aware that his death might not be instant. Actual time for Jojo, appeared to be standing still, but the process of life whizzed through his anguished mind. The process of dying would not be quick, and surely would seem an eternity once the steel like jaws clamped on his body, its teeth sinking through, crushing bone, tearing flesh. Jojo continued forward, faster now, as the picture of the monster animal pulling him under the surface of the black water plagued him. Continued vision of mud and water being sucked into his lungs as he fought for air. Initially feeling no pain, while being rolled like a rag doll on the bottom. Then thre would be pain, unbearable pain. As his lungs burned, denied life giving cool air. The rest of his broken body would begin to feel the same fire, straight from the depths of hell. Parts torn from his body. Even before the fatal event, his mind tormented him further showing pictures of other alligators fighting for their share, churning the black and bloody water. Screams! The water plus his paralyzed vocal cords, would refuse granting permission for the actual sounds to pierce the night air. So far the only torment, was the picture's flashing in his mind. It was his perpetual dream plaguing him, demonstrating the full horror of what was to befall him in a matter of minutes. No seconds. That was the way of the alligator, and how nature intended their gluttonous and wicked feeding habits to be. Catfish would eventually feed on smaller bits of him drifting to the depths of the black water. That was the vivid concept of his dream, the one that had tormented him, causing him sleepless nights. The nightmare he had described to Jimmy D. on a starlit evening. How long ago?

Still Jojo had no intention of dying such a death, because he intended on cheating the alligator of his fun, if not his meal. With trembling fingers, he felt in his boot for his revolver. Would the pistol fire if he pulled the trigger at the very instant his head was forced under water? There seemed a total lack of time progression, as the boy planned to place the muzzle into his mouth. That was the only way he had of preventing the hideous death that was as sure to come as the sunrise. Firing the pistol with the muzzle under water should hopefully muffle the sound of the explosion and not compromise Luke's' location or their mission. He must do it now. He prepared to drop his rifle, enabling him to hold the pistol with both hands. No, not yet. Yes now! Shutting tight his eyes, he grasped the smooth handle of the forty-four pistol in his determined hand.

Jojo thought he heard Luke's voice. Something? "Jojo!! We made shallow water!" But it sounded more as a dream, and too distant for reality. Just a dream. In an instant his body flew forward, refusing to open his eyes, he attempted screaming, but he could not. He held his breath as his body flew through the air; the pistol slipped from his hand and fell back into the boot. No chance to fire it, or even put the muzzle in his mouth. In his dream, it was unclear as to whether the alligator had actually devoured him; it was always just a picture of what could be. A warning. He had always awakened from the nightmare in time. Even now it remained unclear and confusing. What was taking place? Something hammered his body, and he felt pain as he attempted to draw air where there was none. Finally air, at the same time forcing his eyes open, just as Luke landed next to him in the mud.

"What tha?"

"We made it boy! We made it! We're on land!" Hoping he had not declared it too loudly.

It was necessary for Jojo to replenish his lungs with oxygen before trying to speak once again, or even consider the thought. Only then did the faint understanding of Luke reaching back and grabbing his coat begin superseding the last horrid picture of the demon alligator.

"Dang! I sho' thought thet ol' gator had me fo' supper. Thought I wuz ah goner. Yo' mighty strong ta throw me lak yo' done, Luke." Deeply sucking in more air, just because he could.

"Could be boy, but it wuz 'bout tha only thang I could do," Luke said gathering himself, as he sat spread legged next to the surprised boy in the shallow water.

"Where'd thet ol' gator go?"

"Don' know fo' sho', he's still out there, but it ain't lakly he be comin up in this shallow water fo' us boy," Luke explained.

"Yeah, reckon he ain't thet hongry. But, I shor don' aim ta tempt 'em either," Jojo answered, getting to his feet.

After standing they saw the alligator's broad head surface, maybe fifteen feet away, but as Jojo had stated the reptile seemed reluctant to come closer. Instead it just stared at them; its large teeth protruding from the sides of it's closed jaws. The alligator appeared to have a perpetual smile on its face, as if thinking there would always be another time. The huge head sank in the black water and disappeared.

Suddenly, Luke remembered that there were other dangers to be addressed, because in their attempt to evade the alligator, he had no notion of the noise created. Reaching out he gently pushed Jojo back down, and visually explored the surrounding tall sawgrass until it blended into the darkness. They listened, hearing only crickets and croaking frogs, until a nighthawk screamed some distance away.

"We bes' check our weapons, then move on quick," Luke advised as he dropped to his knees into the cover of the sharp cutting grass.

Luke scoured the southern sky for the lone star they had been guiding on, finding it concealed by clouds, he raised his head higher feeling the gentle breeze on his face, his damp right ear felt a slight coolness.

"Thet way," he said pointing in the direction of what he believed to be due south.

"How far ta thet stand ah banana trees, what belonged ta thet injun chief?" Jojo whispered.

"Well by whut tha sheriff said, I calculate it ta be 'bout three mile,"

Cautiously the two moved south, barely feeling the mild breeze touching the right side of their faces. Soon, yet still some distance away, the darker outline of low trees stood out against the dark purple sky. Luke was sure that it was the banana grove Bones had mentioned as their temporary hideout. It was calculated by Luke to be midnight, and without speaking, they hunkered down next to each other well within the shadows of the tightly bunched trees. Many of the newly sprouted trees were much smaller than Luke had envisioned, but still offered more than ample wide green leaves for security from detection. Both were able to if not relax, at least rest, now that they were no longer moving.

"Boy, yo' pa ever learn yo' how ta kill ah dog?" Luke asked quietly, offering the boy an alternative for his apparent jitters, as they leaned back in the dark shadows.

"Whut? Kill ah dog? Yo' mean lak shoot'm in tha head or tha lak?" Strange question.

"Naw boy not shootin', thet is unless tha shootin' already started. Yo' throw a chunk ah this dried meat we got in our pockets to'm. Then ah nother. When he comes close, yo' take tha but ah yo' knife an' hit'm real hard right between tha eyes. Thet'll knock'm out, then yo' stab him in tha heart, between his ribs. He'll die quiet lak," Luke explained.

"Reckon yo' up tha thet Boy?"

"I'll do lak yo' say when it comes ta it," the confident boy declared.

Neither Luke nor Jojo made any further remarks about dispatching dogs, and there was nothing to do now but rest and wait until near daybreak. Just as quickly as they stopped moving, the mosquitoes came in force, causing them to cover the lower half of their faces with bandannas, leaving only their eyes exposed. Jojo was thankful he had spotted the stink vine they had rubbed on their exposed skin and clothes, it helped somewhat repel the insects. He refused to smear it on his face however, and would depend on the handkerchief and his shirt collar pulled high to deny the buzzing pests access to his neck and face. There was also an added benefit from the smelly plant. It might help prevent the dogs in the Indian camp from picking up their scent, as the Indians also took advantage of the natural mosquito repellent.

Time was passing ever so slowly while buzzing mosquitoes swirled around their ears, almost drowning out other sounds of the night. But the peacefulness other than the battle with the mosquitoes, and the awful odor assaulting their sense of smell, was short lived.

The call of a lone wolf sounded loudly... Near... The cry penetrated the night air and sent chills down Luke's' spine. Luke knew Jojo was also equally shocked by the unnerving cry as he was, but said nothing. As expected an answer came quickly, in the form of a mournful wail from somewhere further south, then a third, faintly from another location. Even the frogs and crickets ceased to communicate, as if allowing the wolf priority of the night. There was something queer about the wolf calls, Luke knew they seldom called to each other. Plus wolves usually kept themselves to higher ground. The calls ceased after the three and the stillness lingered for a while.

However the wait was short-lived when out of the darkness, a silent lone figure appeared in their front. The sinister shadow appeared to be floating as though his feet were not even touching the damp earth, as he moved in complete silence toward them. The ghost-like shadow stopped directly in front, they could almost reach out and touch him. Still silent with the same soft movement, he turned away and stopped again a short distance away.

In full view of their watching eyes stood a near naked muscular Indian, his bare skin glistening in the dim light. He turned again toward them. A frontal view of the savage produced an evil wide painted face with round black eyes, and a strong square jaw. He appeared to be looking directly at the two concealed witnesses in the shadows. Sensing something, maybe smelling, as an animal would do. With very little movement of his short almost bowed legs, his whole body turned away from them. Luke eased his hand over, slowly, touched Jojo's leg, signaling him there was nothing to fear. Jojo understood as they watched the Indian raise his hands cupping them around his mouth, producing the same wolf call that they had heard earlier. Jojo watched wide-eyed, as the savage's chest heaved with each gulp of air imitating the call once again. The Indian moved off into the darkness after his call had been answered by a similar cry from the south. Just as his arrival, the departure was soundless, leaving Luke and Jojo feeling that they might breath once again. Yet leaving them unsure as to whether the Indian had sensed something amiss.

Time passed without further incident after their encounter with the Indian, with daylight less than two hours away Bones showed. Moving as stealthily as did the Indian.

"How yo' boys holdin' up?" Asking quietly as he presented himself in the dim light

Both Luke and Jojo had seen movement, yet being unsure at first that it might not be another Indian. They were quite relived to discover that it was Bones, especially Luke. Concern was weighing heavily upon him after seeing the Indian, and not knowing whether James and the others were still among the living.

"We be fair ta middlin', seen one injin though ah-while back.

"Thet's good thet yo' saw him, instead ah tha other way around. I lef' tha others back yonder where we crossed tha creek. Jus' wanted ta locate y'all befo' I brung them up. I'll go back an' bring'm along."

240

"I'd be proud ta fetch'm up sheriff." Jojo enlisted himself, hoping for an opportunity to burn away some tension. Especially knowing he would not have to cross Johnson Creek alone.

"Well alright boy, reckon yo' c'n locate 'em right 'nough." Bones agreed, showing his confidence in the boy.

"C'n an' will." I'll give'm ah hootie owl call when I get near." Jojo walked away.

"Thet youngster's got plenty ah sand, an' he'll need every once of it before this night is finished." Bones watched Jojo until the darkness enveloped him completely.

"Thet injin y'all saw, reckon he tha one making them wolf calls?"

"Wuz fo' ah fac'. Dern if he aint done it right there," Luke declared, pointing to the spot where the savage had stood. "Thought mayhap he smelled us, but he had stink weed on him jus' lak us."

Bones explained how the Indians had made a mistake, he hoped, their first of many by demonstrating a false security by using the wolf calls.

"Any cracker knows wolves don' come this far south into the glades. They fancy higher ground. Lots ah big cats an' mayhap bears, but not wolves. Injins sho' ta be ah knowin' it. It shows they ain't worried none. Thet's tha part ah tha puzzle we ain't got. Why ain't they?" Not expecting an answer to his rhetorical question. "Jus' tha same it might make our job easier."

"Easier mayhap, but not easy," Luke stated. "Then again they might be too many ah them varmits fo' us ta handle," he lamented.

Jojo quietly made his way back to the others waiting at the creek, he had another reason for returning to the creek. Bringing the others forward was his primary mission, but he also had a more personal reason, another look at that alligator. Perhaps there would be enough light to allow a close look, and Jojo harbored little doubt that the alligator would be close by. Surely the alligator would have been curious enough to investigate what was in the water, when the others made their crossing.

"Derned ol' gator no how. I aim ta kill me ah gator one of these days, learn'm ta try an' catch me fo' his supper." Mumbling out loud, just before making his owl call.

In return he received a like call, discovering them at the same spot where he and Luke had crossed. As he approached the waiting group he spied the alligator floating on the surface of the creek, causing a shiver through him after seeing it's full length, fifteen feet if he was an inch.

"Pa thet's Jojo comin'. Howdy Jojo."

Jojo recognized the voice greeting him as Jimmy D's.

241

"Reckon thet big ol' gator ain't done took ah bite outten nary one ah y'all," Jojo stated quietly, but matter-a-factly, still staring at the alligator. Jojo could see the large yellowish teeth even from where he stood.

"Naw, he's ah big ornery cuss though," Jimmy D answered.

"Well boys we bes' get movin'. We burnin' dark," August said, pulling the boys gaze from the alligator.

"Jojo, reckon yo' c'n take us ta tha others?"

"Sho c'n, straight out pa."

James smiled, he was proud of the boys and it pleased him that Jojo took to calling him pa; yet, unaccustomed to it, but it always brought a smile. Polly was pleased that he addressed her as ma. Concern suddenly smothered James as he brought up the rear of the short formation. He began to doubt his decision on bringing the boys along, not that he harbored any uncertainty over their ability or courage. Only should anything happen to either one, he could never forgive himself, and worse, Polly would be even less forgiving. How would he live with that?

There was no delay, and soon Jojo recognized the familiar profile of the banana grove. He led them directly to Luke and the sheriff. The two men watched the line approach in the darkness, and gave a low owl hoot, and Jojo answered the familiar call. In the cover of the banana trees, the plan that Bones had devised, while waiting, was discussed. August agreed the plan to split and hit from two sides was a simple one. Bones along with Jojo and James would work their way around and come in from the opposite side. As most such plans its success depended on complete surprise. A good run of luck and the good lord being on their side wouldn't hurt according to Bones.

"Them dogs is gonna be a problem, least ways' one, tha boy said tha other ain't much 'count," Bones said. "They ort ta pick up tha smell ah tha dried fish, we totin', take they minds off everything else." For now the dog appeared to be their greatest problem. If the one dog gave them away, there was no chance at all for saving the woman, maybe not even themselves.

"I reckon I c'n take care ah thet dog, I got me ah mess ah smoked mullet, an I come in with the north group up wind. Thet Kerr mayhap be part wolf an' he'll smell thet fish ah mile away," August stated with confidence. "I seen my share ah them injin dogs, they mean an' smart. An' it'll take ta thet smoked fish right 'nough."

"Ain't likely he'll pick up our scent on account ah this stink weed we got smeared on us. We smell jus' as bad as them injins do." James spoke the last words about the dogs. No need for more.

"Boys we ain't gonna have no time to pick and choose our targets, but, when yo' see somethin' ta shoot, shoot fast and straight. An' remember them squaws an' young'ns are jus' as dangerous as them bucks," August cautioned.

The warning directed toward Jojo and Jimmy D, both nodding recognition of the warning. In the scant light James noticed Jimmy D's expression, hinting the boy was apprehensive about what lay ahead, and he knew Jojo felt the same. Even with his high confidence in the two, he was fearful for them. He looked directly into Luke's eyes, and wanted to ask Luke to help look after them both, but didn't. It would have made him appear foolish knowing such a request was un-called for. If it came to it, he knew Luke would give his life for any man present; and any man among them would do the same without hesitation. In the darkness they made a final check of their weapons without conversation. Their nerves were stretched, and they were reluctant to speak unnecessarily.

"Well boys I reckon it's time ta move. I calculate it ah good hour ta thet island, should be easy march before daybreak," August said.

"An' remember if we get surprised ourselves, we scatter an' make our way back 'cross Johnson Creek an' meet up there," Luke said.

Once again they moved south, single file with dispatch and stealth for the island, quickly reaching the shallow water encompassing the Indian camp. Bones held the group up in a small bayhead, where the ground was slightly elevated, a few cabbage trees of assorted sizes provided cover.

"Them injins is still in there, or least ways was las' night." Bones sniffed the air as the others gathered near.

"Yeah, I c'n smell smoke." James spoke, after facing into the wind.

"Them injins is tricky though. Been known ta build fires, decoy us in. Could be behind us right now. Got ta be more cautious."

"If what August said was true, why were they continuing on?" Jimmy D. was thinking it. He didn't ask, however.

"Yeah only thing it means is, we still got tha wind. 'Pears ta be pickin' up. Sho' hope it keeps blowin'." As he spoke, Luke faced into the wind and the direction of the island, where their fate would soon be decided.

Maybe that bit of luck that they needed was still with them as dark clouds had already formed in the west toward their objective. A tropical storm was building and they knew it would move with great speed, producing high punishing winds and a drenching rain. The raiders would profit by the noise and confusion that the storm would cause, plus prolong the needed darkness for a while longer.

"It'll come quick, and bring ah gully washer." James stared toward the black sky.

"Thet'll be good fo' our side. Rain will cause them fires ta smoke. An' them dogs jus' like humans, they'll want ta stay dry if'n they c'n." August whispered, thinking he might not have to lure the one dog out with the smoked mullet.

"Boys, I reckon it's time we lance this boil, ah get thet lady out ah her fix an' maybe get shut ah some varmints at tha same time. Ready Luke?"

"Ready as c'n be Bones," came a quick answer.

"Yo' an' tha boy ready August?"

"I 'llow we're ready as we will ever be, right Jojo?"

"Yeah, suh reckon so. See yo' Jimmy D." Jojo said as he turned to move away.

Jimmy D. motioned a nervous wave at Jojo. "See yo' pa."

"Yeah, boy see y'all in thet camp. Y'all keep yo' heads down an' yo' powder dry."

"We aim ta be real cautious, don't we boys?" Bones directed his rhetorical question for Jojo and Jimmy D. Also informing James, that he would look after Jimmy D. as best he could.

James suffered a noxious wrenching in his gut. He fought hard to ignore it by refusing a last glance at his son, before following Jojo away, with August leading. He wanted to, but feared if he did so, he might not leave the boy standing there. Two boys' should be home fishing or skipping flat rocks across the water. Mumble Peg with a jack knife. Not here, intent on killing.... Or be killed... God... James knew he must clear his mind of such thoughts, they had come too far for any of them to back down now. Caroline's torment at the hands of the Indians would come to an end this day. And James knew that only with the help of her God, would she be totally healed in body and spirit. As James crept along through the high grass, the pitiful woman back in Honey Tree slipped into his mind. It seemed a million years ago. God help her, God help us all. He forced himself to disregard such diversions, instead render his mind too the purpose at hand. More determined now.

"Boys might jus' as well set ah spell, it'll take them awhile to get positioned. I sho' hope thet storm is movin' as fast as it looks ta be. Yo' alright boy?" Bones leaned back against a tree trunk.

"Yeah suh. But, I sho' do crave ta get this over with." Jimmy D. duplicated Bones, by getting as comfortable as possible against a tree.

"It be fin' boy, by noon it'll all be over an' done with, an' we c'n get back ta tha house with Miz Caroline." Luke spoke matter-of-factly attempting to ease the nervous Jimmy D.

"Thet'll be real good Uncle Luke." The anxious boy stared toward the storm, and the direction the others had disappeared.

"'Member whut I said 'bout them rattlers in thet dry marsh boy, they thick as flea's on ah hounds back."

"Yeah suh, I aim to move real careful," Jimmy D. vowed as they sat close in the brush.

Jimmy D. was well acquainted on how to move through thick brush and deep grass. It was one of the first things they had to get used to upon their arrival in swampy Florida. It was Jojo who had taught him to move in brush, by lightly dragging his feet, all the-while moving quietly. The rattlesnakes were sensitive to vibrations and in most cases would try to avoid humans if possible. If evasion were not possible for the snake, it would at least coil and send a deadly warning, a hair-raising spine-chilling rattle. Jimmy D. looked up into the sky as the storm fell upon them, first feeling large single drops of rain peppering his face, then a blanket of wetness. Flashes of lightning painted the black sky, and reflected off his wet cheeks, and quickly disappeared back into the dark thunderous sky. The boy knew why Bones had reminded him of the snakes. The sounds of the storm would make it impossible to hear the deadly signal from the snakes surely to be encountered while crossing the marsh.

Jimmy D. differed from Bones, who welcomed the fast moving storm that beat down on the tall saw grass, like a giant flat paddle. The transitory bursts of light illuminated the river of grass and tall reeds as if in bright blue sunlight. Each burst forced the marchers to squat low in the grass, where the rattlesnakes were. Jimmy D. flinched, ducking his head from the thunderous claps and preceding voltaic charges. He didn't want to be hiding in a bay head or crossing a snake infested marsh, in a storm at night. Killing Indians wasn't high on his list of things to do either, even if he got across the sawgrass without being bitten; he wanted to be home. Suddenly the boy felt guilty and wondered if the others had similar thoughts, especially Jojo being his own age. No, he knew the others would not have such thoughts and he knew Jojo to be as brave as any. He vowed that he would be too. Dern the storm, dern the rattlesnakes and the Indians; Miz Caroline was in there, and he would be as big a man as any, doing his part to get her out.

"No suh I ain't feared ah no injins or snakes." Mumbling low. Closing his eyes from the bright flash.

"How's thet boy?" Luke thought he heard Jimmy D. speak to him.

"Boys reckon its time ta get on with it. God be with us all." Luke stood.

Without speaking, Jimmy D and Bones stood, Bones stepped from the cover of the cabbage trees, and into the rain and wind. Lightning flashed giving them a blue appearance, as they stooped low into the saw grass, Luke bringing up the rear. The howling wind forced the cold rain into their faces as they slowly made their way toward the island and what ever destiny God had chosen for each of them. With each streak of lightning they stopped, and Bones turned making sure he hadn't lost his two companions.

Hand signals now would be the only form of communication, as talking above the wind would be ill advised. Quickly the dry marsh under foot was beginning to hold water as they moved forward dragging their feet lightly. At least the snakes would move out of the rising water rapidly covering the marsh, and Jimmy D knew they would head toward higher ground.

Many would retreat to the island that the Indians now held, and the liberators were bound. Hopefully, along with the Indians the island would contain a number of half-tame hogs, to either eat the snakes or drive them away. Jimmy D. welcomed the fleeting image of Bakon rescuing Kara Sue by killing the rattlesnake on the trail. Quickly his thoughts returned to the task at hand, the Indians on the island. He, as the others, must now concentrate on freeing Miz Caroline. They continued forward freezing during each flash of lightning. The water in the once dry marsh, now was knee deep as Bones, Luke and Jimmy D. reached to the perimeter of Skull Island. The storm although dying down created the only sounds, causing Bones to ponder whether the Indians might have been aware of their coming, and had retreated ahead of them.

The band could have taken refuge on any one of the thousands of hardwood hammocks, scattered throughout the immense prairie. Bones rejected that idea rather quickly. In the first place, if their presence had been compromised, the Indians more than likely would have ambushed them. Especially if their numbers amounted to the dozen or so that the boy had reported to be in camp.

"I reckon them injins got to be holdin' up in them cheekees from the storm, jus' lak we would if we was them, ain't no cause fo' them feelin' any fear." Bones whispered into Luke's ear. Luke nodded his agreement.

"Yeah but it looks lak it due ta pass real quick now." Luke commented, noticing the wind gusting occasionally in lieu of blowing steady.

"And it ain't rainin' so hard now either," Jimmy D added, as he pushed the brim of his hat up a little.

The three knelt close together in the shadow of a clump of cabbage trees, as they determined that James and the others should be in position by now and prepared to move directly into the camp. But they had to hold where they were until they could be sure.

"If them others are in place and ready, August must've got thet dog. I ain't heard him make ah fuss," Luke said.

"Yo' right. We would've heard thet dog start up even in all tha wind ah blowin' lak it was," Bones suggested.

"Mayhap they gone,"

"Naw, they ain't gone. 'Member we smelled smoke from their fire before tha storm hit." Bones had already sorted that possibility out earlier.

"Be light in 'bout twenty minutes. Hope them boys gets tha show on tha road quick lak. Shor' don' cotton rushin' them injins in full light," Luke said.

He had no sooner completed his statement than they heard the first shot. Quickly followed by three additional shots, even before the men could gain their feet. Then too many for counting.

"Thet's it boys lets move in fast. Yo' shoot quick an' straight boy." Bones addressed the remark toward Jimmy D. as he slapped him on the back.

Jimmy D made no comment only nodded his head slightly. The three moved in the direction of the shots. No longer in single file with Bones taking a position on the left, Luke on the right, with Jimmy D between them about fifteen yards apart. To Jimmy D.'s left a loud shot exploded, then a shrill wild scream that seemed endless. Jimmy D had seen nothing at all, but knew the scream had not come from Bones. Determining it must have been Bones who fired the shot, hitting his mark. Another shot came from that direction, then more rapidly now. Jimmy D entertained the urge to look in that direction and investigate, but refrained from doing so, instead keeping his eyes frontal, scanning for movement. All the while attempting a steady pace toward the earlier shots, in the direction of his father and the others. Now Luke was firing.

In the varying shadows Jimmy D., his weapon still cold deemed it nearly impossible to distinguish anything no matter how hard he looked. Rapid gunfire followed by echoes of gunfire assaulted his ears. Seemly from every direction, leaving him confused. More shots came from the direction where he reckoned Luke to be. Two maybe three, then frightful animalistic screams of pain, as hot lead destroyed flesh. Foul odors of blood mixed with burned powder draped the damp dawn air. Suddenly to his front, a shadow moved in a low crouch toward him. Jimmy D. fired one round, stopping the dark figure in its tracks, the impact sending the figure back in the direction from which it came.

Jimmy D. lacked time for reflecting on his first kill, but the short high-pitched scream set him aback. Now the dark gray smoke from his own pistol and the blood it shed added to that of the others. Increasing obscene smells. Increasing gunfire. Cautiously the boy moved for the prone body, keeping his pistol ready just in case. Pulling at the blanket he rolled his target over, mostly to determine if he was indeed dead. Jimmy D was shocked to discover that he had shot an old squaw, and instantly turned away from the wide eyes that stared back at him. But, how was he to know? Besides didn't Bones or August say how they were just as dangerous as the bucks? He justified the killing to himself. Constant firing now, some had to be return fire from the Indians, he was sure of it, as he continued forward. Meanwhile Luke had reached the location of the three huts, but stopped before proceeding further across the small area of open ground. In the dim light he observed muzzle flashes from other weapons being fired. And from the cries knew that many of the Indians were either dead or wounded, but no knowledge of their own casualties if any. And he refused to think about it.

Relieved to observe Bones, Luke marveled at the speed his long slim legs churned as he traversed the open area. Covering Bones with his long gun, he quickly dispatched one Indian challenging the lanky sheriff. As Luke reloaded his rifle, Jimmy D. broke from the cover, running for Bones. Two screaming Indians emerged from the shadows intent on killing the scampering boy. Bones hearing the commotion behind him, whirled and fired, killing one. Jimmy D. fired, killing the second attacker. The excited boy scurried forward following Bones around the hut. After reloading, Luke ran after them, taking a path opposite theirs around the cheekee, then diving to the ground, when bullets whizzed by him.

After rolling over closer he heard a whimpering noise further under the hut, in the shadow. Quickly turning thinking it to be a wounded Indian, he prepared to fire. It was not an Indian however. At first, he was unsure of what it was, maybe a dog. Cautiously in the obscure light, he inched closer for a better look pulling away a portion of the filthy covering. Thinking his mind was misleading him, yet; feeling no threat he lowered his revolver. His stomach churned in tight knots as he repositioned himself for yet a better look at the bundled figure. The whining animal sounds continued, only softly.

Now after close inspection, he was stunned beyond belief. "My God! Caroline is thet yo' under there?" He called out while attempting to get a good look at the face of the crawling dark form.

Glancing around before sliding completely under the raised floor of the hut, the height allowed him to stay on his knees. Reaching out he attempted cutting the leather restraint around her neck, the other end secured to the huts corner post. The pathetic figure was on her hands and knees and whining like a kicked dog, and she attempted to move away, but was restrained by the cord from doing so. After his eyes adjusted to the dim light under the shelter, Luke moved forward for a better look at the disfigured and bruised face of the woman. He cut the leash. Knowing it had to be Caroline, even though he could not recognize her, and even tried resisting the notion that it was. Any similarity between the beautiful woman he had met on the trail and this almost animal like creature before him was impossible to discern. He fought puking. She jerked back when Luke lightly touched her shoulder after cutting the restraint, bringing additional animal sounds. She quickly turned away after seeing Luke's eyes.

"Yo' be fine now Caroline, they can't hurt yo' no more. I got ta go now and check on tha others, yo' stay right here." Luke started to crawl from under the hut, stopping short when he felt a tug on his shirtsleeve. First glancing down at the bony dirty fingers grasping his arm, then into the tortured woman's face, again she turned away as she pointed at his holstered handgun. "Uh, yeah, I reckon thet might be ah good idea." Pulling his pistol, he handed it to her.

The pistol almost fell from her weakened grip, but she held on as she changed to a sitting position, and pulled the revolver to her lap. She didn't jerk when Luke patted her shoulder a second time, instead began slowly rocking backward and forth. Luke removed his hand from the roughness of the ragged blanket covering her when she renewed her continuous low moaning. Turning for one last glance at the slow rocking figure before leaving, he realized he couldn't distinguish the color of her matted filthy hair.

"I'll be back directly ma'am, yo' stay put now."

After scanning the area, he quickly emerged from under the hut, and sprinted to the next shelter. Making a running dive underneath it, rolling to the far side as he hit the bed of pine needles, covering the ground, then rolled to his belly and realized he wasn't alone. The low growl caused him to point his rifle toward the sound and seeing the dog. The mangy animal made no move to attack, instead eased itself closer to the ground and continued growling, as it watched the intruder. After realizing this must be the old dog Cork had mentioned, and without any sudden moves, he slid out leaving the animal alone. There was fair light present, and the once heavy rain now was reduced to drizzle. With great relief, Luke caught his first sight of his brother since his departure with August and Jojo. Intending on making his way for James whom had just fired his pistol, and had taken cover behind a tree to reload. Luke had covered only half of the distance when he saw an Indian approach James from behind. Unaware of the Indian, James continued reloading his pistol.

Raising his long gun to his shoulder, Luke aimed and prepared to fire into the back of the Indian, but did not. Instead he hesitated, watching in amazement as the Indian stopped short and dropped to his knees. Realizing someone was behind him James whirled and brought his loaded revolver up. He didn't squeeze the trigger. Like his brother he only watched the Indian. Spreading his arms high the Indian began to chant, gazing skyward ignoring James. The startled man watched cautiously, his revolver still pointed at the chanting Indian. Luke lowered his rifle, looked around and started slowly toward them. As he closed the distance, he noticed the Indian seemed different from the others. While still on his knees and still chanting, Luke could tell he appeared taller, less stocky and muscular than the average Seminole. His shinning black hair was long; not short as the other males kept theirs. However he wore the traditional cloth band keeping the hair from his unpainted face.

"Brother." Luke spoke quietly to James as he stood next to the ever-chanting Indian.

"Howdy Luke," James returned the greeting as if they had just bumped into each other on a street in Tater Bluff, all the while watching the Indian.

"This one ain't no Seminole,"

"No, 'pears ta be Cherokee," James answered, quickly turning in the direction of a single gunshot.

"It seems ta be winding down, but reckon I bes' check on tha others," Luke said.

"Reckon so. I'll keep an eye on this one. He don' appear spoilin' fo' no fight though, he ain't even painted," James said.

"Tha woman, she's under thet hut yonder. My God James." He pointed, after first staring into his brother's eyes. "She's ahlive, but in ah real bad way."

Finally ceasing his chanting he stared at James with dark eyes, lowering his slim arms to his side, leaving James confident that the he represented no danger to anyone. Lowering his pistol he glanced quickly in the direction of Luke watching his brother move slowly and cautiously from tree to tree.

"The little panther brought you here."

Startled, James turned and faced him; puzzlement cloaked his face as he absorbed the words, spoken so matter-of-factly.

"Panther? Yo' mean Cork tha young colored boy, yeah he ain't here, but, he tol' us where y'all wuz camped, an' said tha white woman wuz ahlive. We come ta fetch her back," James stated his business.

"My heart is glad the little panther is safe, he has the heart of the big cat," the Indian said slowly in almost perfect English. "The young one has courage, but he had little chance to reach safety."

"Is thet the only reason yo' let tha boy go?" Thankin' he would die in this swamp?" James felt anger.

"No. I say two times, I am glad. I wanted the woman to go too. But she could not.

The woman is dead now," he added looking back toward the hut.

"My brother said she ain't dead, he saw her under thet hut yonder," James argued.

The Indian said nothing in response to James' statement about the white woman.

"Yo' not Seminole, an yo' speak mighty good English, how are yo' called?"

"I am called Jumper Three Toes. My friend the white giant taught me how to say your words good." he stated. "And a white man who carries the black book, with the words of your God taught me to read the words."

"Giant? Acre Foot? Acre Foot Johnson? Well I'll be damned," James said in astonishment.

"Yes, that is the one. Two Ghosts will try to kill Johnson, if he escaped from this place."

"Yeah thet's whut Cork tol' us. Thet won't be no easy chore fo' anybody, thet Acre Foot Johnson is ah lot ah man. Tha boy said fo' me not ta kill yo' if we wuz ta meet on account ah yo' he'pin' him an' try ta do fo' tha' woman." James said. I will think on his request," he added.

"I do not ask for my life. It is for the whites to decide. I will only ask safety for the women and little ones. We are few in numbers now. Maybe I am the only one left, if so it is good that I die like the others."

"We will decide later. Fus' I got ta check on tha woman," James said coolly, leery of trusting the Indian, as he motioned him to his feet.

Luke's scream reached them at the very moment Jumper stood.

"Jimmy D!!!!" Luke screamed once again as he looked in horror and raised his rifle to shoot the Indian that had jumped from the tree.

Jimmy D. whirled upon hearing his name called and fired just as the Indian's feet hit the ground, soundless in the leaves. The muscular half-naked Indian screamed and fired his revolver at the same time. The round from Jimmy D.'s pistol shattered the Indian's bare lower leg, the same instant the large caliber ball from the attacker's pistol made a thudding sound as it tore into Jimmy D's lower stomach. An involuntary scream erupted from the boy as the force lifted him from the ground, sending him back against the base of the tree. After his initial terrifying scream when leaping from the tree, the wounded Indian made no other sound.

A more than capable opponent and knowing someone was behind him, he quickly rolled over facing Luke and fired. Again his shot was accurate, and Luke was knocked hard to the ground. Seeing Luke fall without making a sound, and confident him rendered harmless, the warriors attention again turned toward Jimmy D. for another shot at him. After careful aim he fired, but the result of the hammer falling produced only the loud metallic click, his pistol misfired. Oblivious to any pain caused from the bloody bone protruding from the flesh of his leg, the savage cocked his weapon again. James watched in helpless horror as Jimmy D attempted to recover his own pistol, determined on shooting his attacker once again. But he was to late; the stocky Indian had gotten to one knee and balanced himself for another attempt at finishing the boy. So intent on killing Jimmy D. he failed to hear Luke running behind him. Luke's wound although serious, failed to keep him down, and he ran for the Indian, reaching him just as he aimed his pistol. The butt of Luke's empty rifle smashed into the back of the Indian's head, causing the shot to go harmlessly into the ground next to the wounded boy. The blow sent him face down to the ground unmoving.

Still ignoring his wound, Luke continued on for his injured nephew and knelt beside him. Severely wounded, the boy only grimaced in pain but said nothing when Luke loosened the belt and trousers to inspect his wound. Ashen faced, Luke almost turned away after discovering the seriousness of the injury. Adjusting his mind to the pain, Jimmy D. slowly lifted his shaking bloody hands and attempted to look at his stomach.

"Easy son don' move. We'll fix yo' up quick."

"Did yo' kill thet injin Uncle Luke?" the boy asked, his voice weak and cracking, staring at Luke through glazed wet eyes.

"Don' know boy. But I cracked his head good. Yo' jus' res' easy now, don' talk." Gently attempting to move Jimmy D's clutching hands again to observe the wound, at the same time trying to conceal his own pain and uneasiness. He failed to accomplish either; he was trembling too badly, and feeling faint.

James ran toward them after seeing what had happened, Jumper trailed him with his noticeable limping gait, and was beside James when he reached Luke and Jimmy D. With quivering hands James wiped tears from his eyes as he sat on the ground holding his son's head, and fought vomiting after seeing the small black hole running with blood where the ball entered, just below his navel. Again Jimmy D. recoiled in pain when his father moved him, feeling underneath for blood, there was none; the ball was still in his body. Through blurred eyes Jimmy D. recognized the helpless distressed look on his fathers face, as Luke placed a handkerchief over the hole to control the bleeding. His own tortured eyes reflected those of his brother's deep in torment, as they exchanged look

"It don' hurt much papa," Jimmy D. bravely uttered, trying to ease his father's anguish. The attempt from the courageous boy failed. "My legs aint straight." He seemed concerned over his bent legs, as he looked down at them. "C'n yo' strighten'm up fo' me?" I cain' feel nothin'. Thirsty though." His voice was very weak already.

In truth the wound actually was extremely painful, the large, soft lead ball had mushroomed and splintered, a fragment lodging in his spine. His lower body was already left dead; plus his gut was shredded. James turned white with fear, realizing that his son had no chance of surviving. His last minutes on earth would be filled with more pain than any man could stand. He was helpless. He forced himself to speak. "Cain' give yo' no water son..." He didn't explain that, it would only increase the already unbareable pain. He could not.

"Here son ah wet rag, I'll wet yo' lips." Luke gently placed the wet cloth to Jimmy D's pale drawn lips.

"Did yo' kill thet injin whut kilt me, Papa?" Asking the question a second time.

James looked over at the Indian on the ground, then at Luke. Luke shook his head indicating that the Indian was not dead.

"He ain't dead yet, he mus' have ah awful hard head from tha looks of it, broke tha stock right off my long gun. An' yo' ain't kilt either boy yo' gonna watch thet varmint hang," Luke answered.

After walking up with a frightened Indian girl, and realizing there was nothing to be done for the boy, August pulled the wounded Indian into a sitting position, by the hair, paying no mind to the badly injured leg. No one paid mind to the bloody rag that August had wrapped around his left hand, or the girl as she walked over to Jumper.

"This one's heart is as hard as his head, he is called Iron Bull. The one that claimed the white woman for his own." Jumper spoke, as sporadic shots yet could be heard.

"Naw boy he ain't dead yet. We gonna take'm back ta Fort Pierce an' let the army hang 'em." August repeated Luke's promise, clinching his mouth tight, staring at the wide square painted face of the Indian.

Soon Jojo and Bones, appeared, their pistols still smoking from the last shots fired. Along with them was a young terrified Indian girl. A quick glance at James' anguished face and sorrowful red eyes erased any need of inquiries, over the well being of his son.

James moved his head slowly from side to side, as tears streamed down his face. Jojo stared in disbelief at his mortally wounded brother lying on the ground. Anger welled up in him; he started moving toward Iron Bull, his pistol still in his hand.

"An' I bet yo' this red skin's tha one whut shot Jimmy D ain't yo'?" The boy spoke with hate, pointing his cocked revolver toward the unflinching Indian. He only grinned up at the angry Jojo.

Luke reached for Jojo's hand, gripping him firmly, until he eased the hammer of his pistol down, preventing it's firing.

"No cause fo' thet boy, it's lak my brother sez, we gonna take him ta Fort Pierce fo' ah hangin' an' all." Looking into the boy's teary red face, he was about to explain further to calm Jojo, but instead silently dropped to the ground.

"Damn! Luke's got ah wound!" Bones said after noticing the blood covering Luke's shirt.

Quickly Bones and August pulled away his shirt and inspected the wound to his side. Up to now they had all assumed the blood had come from Jimmy D.

"How bad?" James inquired his voice breaking.

"Ain't so bad thet he won't live, tha ball went clean though. Have ta get him home quick though, befo' poison sets in," August explained. "Jus' passed out, but he'll come ahroun' directly," he added, as they tied a bandage fashioned from his shirtsleeve over the wound.

"Jojo yo' here?" Jimmy D. asked, unaware of the commotion over his uncle.

"Yeah, I'm here Jimmy D." Jojo moved over to his wounded brother.

"Yo' make it through alright, Jojo?" Ain't hurt none?"

Ain't hurt none," he answered, kneeling close, and lightly placing a hand on Jimmy D's shoulder.

"Thet's good, I reckon thet injin kilt me right 'nough."

For Jojo it was unbearable, as he stared at Jimmy D's dry quivering pale lips, then at James. He wanted to scream out. Scream loud. He did not. Instead he forced himself to speak quietly to Jimmy D.

"Ain't such. Naw, he ain't kilt yo'. We get yo' back ta home an' yo' ma an' Miz Anna, they c'n doctor yo' proper lak."

Bones gently moved James away from his dying son, fearing Jimmy D. would realize his father's grief. James at first was reluctant, but understood after looking into the sheriff's face. Bones physically supported him, his fit of silent spasms, as he turned from his son. His convulsions ceased when hearing his dying son, and Jojo's quietly converse. He did not look however.

"Am I laying in water?"

"Naw yo' ain't. Why yo' want to move?"

"Naw jus' wonderin', but ain't wantin' ta die in water." His answer was extremely weak, testimony that his strength was leaving him.

"Jojo."

"Yeah?" Jojo forced himself to speak without choking.

"Tell me thet sayin' whut yo' said yo' pa always tol' yo' 'bout livin'. Yo' know it always made me laugh every time." The simple request to Jojo seemed so inadequate, coming from someone dying, yet attempting a smile. But from dry quivering pale lips unable to do so.

"Oh, yeah thet." Jojo glanced around at the others, confused over what to do. Even though he understood his friend's request.

James turned in time to see his son's slim body pull slightly. Silently he cried... His son had asked for so little in life. And now on the brink of death, ask only to be reminded of something amusing that he had shared with his friend. Bones shook his head slowly indicating it was permitted that Jojo honor Jimmy D's request. Once again James turned away his body jerking violently in silent sobs. August and Bones came over, each placing a hand on his back, moving him further from his mortally wounded son. As they expected, the effort failed to stop his tears or his body from convulsing. He took a place nearby on the ground leaning against a tree; Luke now recovered somewhat moved next to him. They listened to Jojo's words.

"My pa said, fight lak yo' always wonna win. Love lak' yo' never been hurt, and never trus' ah red headed woman," Jojo softly quoted his pa as he looked down and into the pale face of his dying brother.

"Thet's it. It make's me laugh every ti." Jimmy D. could not finish the sentence. With a thin smile pasted on his ashen lips, his head rolled to one side, his dull eyes stared vacantly toward the luminous rays of the rising sun, finding their path through the trees. He would never see the picture. Jojo began sobbing loudly, unashamedly, and like James his body began to quake uncontrollably, while squeezing his dead brother to his jerking breast; his flowing of tears drenching Jimmy D.'s waxen face.

With trembling fingers August drew the dead boys lids down over his unseeing eyes.

"Don' die, Jimmy D.!! Don' die! Yo cain' die! Please don' die! Yo' ain't never seen no whippoorwill. We wuz gonna do thet soon's we get home..." He wailed. "An' Miz Anna ain't never got time ta read tha res' of Moby Dick, an' me an' yo' ain't never been ta San-an-tone Texas. We wuz goin' there one day. Yo' 'member thet?" His loud wailing continued, rocking back and forth tightly holding his dead brother, close against his heaving chest.

"Easy boy, he's gone. He's done lef' us." August pulled Jojo away, practically having to pry the crying boy loose from Jimmy D' limp body.

Bones removed his coat and placed it over Jimmy D. before August helped him move his limp thin body from the wet ground to a hut. Jumper looked at the young Indian girl called Wanda Cypress. She as the others cried, feeling their pain plus her own, and fright of the unknown. Of what the whites might do to them especially after the death of the boy. Jumper moved closer and took her shaking hand, he didn't know what would happen either, but refused to display any fear. The dead boys father had spoken to him earlier, and indicated no set plan, other than they intended to take Iron Bull to Fort Pierce to be hanged.

With Jimmy D's death came a state of darkness for the living, leaving them as incapable of viewing the filtering sunlight, as his on once gaping eyes. None took notice as Caroline slowly made her way closer, to watch from the shadow of a tree. Still yet, they paid no mind, even as she left her place of concealment. And only until the pistol that Luke had left with her exploded, echoing over the death scene, did they notice. They spun facing the sound of the shot. Confused, their ears ringing. They saw the pitiful Caroline Thomas standing in the gray smoke left by the barking pistol. As if invisible she had made her way to where Iron Bull sat on the ground. His one leg, the knee blown away, lay twisted to the side; the other stretched out straight. Standing at his feet close enough to touch him, holding the heavy pistol with both hands, she had pulled the trigger. Even with shaking hands her aim was accurate, the round hitting the already tortured Indian directly in the crotch, the dull thud splattering his blood over them both

With inhuman strength and without a sound, Iron Bull broke the leather bonds that secured his hands behind his back. Wild eyed, yet silent, he grabbed his crotch with both hands. Deep red almost black blood oozed through his clutching fingers. A puddle of blood instantly appeared at his crotch. In silent pain he rolled to his side and began kicking his healthy leg as if attempting to run while still on the bloody ground. The onlookers stood paralyzed... Watching... Too late to prevent the horror. Who among them would have? They continued watching in indescribable shock, as Iron Bull forced his way back into a setting position, but quickly doubled over like a rag doll, his face in the bloody ground between his legs. Then suddenly as if immunized from pain he calmly sat up once again and with his finger dipped in his own blood, he drew a circle on his bare chest.

Holding the bloody fingertip in the center of the circle over his heart, indicating that he wanted Caroline to shoot him again. With hate, he stared into the woman's eyes and then replaced it with a taunting grin, intentionally reminding her that he was mostly responsible for the dreadful torment afflicting her. The tormented woman cracked an evil toothless thin-lipped grin that matched that of the Indian. As they watched unbelieving, unable to move, she took careful aim at the circle drawn in blood on his heaving wet chest. He squirmed on the ground before her, anticipating a swift end to his own suffering. Still pointing the heavy revolver with trembling hands she cocked it. All the while staring at Iron Bull's red mud covered grinning face, through lifeless deep sunken eyes. Her tight smile faded... Then vanished completely... But to Iron Bull's great disappointment, she cheated him by not firing and ending his agony. He screamed out apparent insults at her in his own language, once again groping his mangled bloody crotch. Eyes red with hate.

Her intended rescuers watched with continued crippling horror as she slowly but deliberately stuck the muzzle of the big forty-four into her mouth. Dry narrow cracked lips circled tight on the still warm blue steel of the revolver's barrel. Eyes opened wide, staring at the Indian... Leaning forward into the expected force, she pulled the trigger. A cloud of black smoke followed the explosion momentarily masking her head from view of the others. As if in slow motion, a mass of red goo discharged from the backside of the smoke. Blood coated flesh and bone painted the tree trunk behind her. Her body jerked, she fell squarely on top of the wildly kicking cursing Iron

Bull, preventing further movement of his weakening good leg. Iron Bull's strength had deserted him, leaving him unable to budge the limp, almost headless woman. The surprised and helpless Iron Bull started screaming. Not insults or curses now, but words of a terrified agonizing human being wishing to die. But not like this, screaming like the woman had done so many times before, caused by inhuman treatment, at his hands.

"Sweet Jesus!" August the nearest rushed over and pulled her body off the screaming Indian, stretching her out on the ground.

Iron Bull's limber body once again doubled over his face in blood, hers mixed with his own; the blood and mud muffling his screams. After grabbing a blanket from a hut and covering her body with slow deliberate movements, Bones slowly walked over to the still jerking Indian. Pulling his big knife from its sheath and with a studied movement grabbed Iron Bull's matted hair. The injured Indian just barely alive was unable to produce further screams, only wild stares. Bones drew the knife across the front of the Indian's hair, pulling the scalp free. Only a small amount of blood dripped from the raw flesh, as Iron Bull's body fell forward again. Bones tossed the greasy mass of hair onto the wet ground at his feet.

CHAPTER SIXTEEN

Even August was shocked at what had just happened. He considered that he had seen many things in his time, but nothing would compare to what he had just witnessed on this day.

"Whut manner of hell is this place we're in?" Luke gaped at the death scene before him. His hand pressed against his injured side, and his mind unwilling to register what his eyes portrayed.

James wiped a rough hand across his tear-streaked face, and looking into the brightening sky, as if for instruction on what to do next. Jimmy D's dying, and the woman's action of blowing the back of her head out with the forty-four, caused something in him to snap. Without comment, he walked over and took a defiant stance a few feet directly in front of Jumper. Firmly cementing his feet apart for balance, he drew his pistol and looked directly into Jumper's eyes, pointed the weapon and cocked it. Jumper stared directly into the black muzzle of the revolver being directed, and held steady between his eyes. With the barrel only a few inches from his nose, he kept his eyes open and waited for the shot that would send him to the spirits.

Wanda Cypress watched in horror, dropping to her knees as Jumper had done earlier. No one else moved, even as she began a high shrill chant, raising her arms toward the sky. She knew the white man would kill her next, as they had several women and even a few children scattered about the island, dead or perhaps dying. Jojo the nearest to James flinched as the pistol exploded. Jumper's head did not come apart as the woman's had earlier. James had fired the round into the ground between his own feet, sending mud into the air. He continued firing, maybe three times no one remembered, stopping only after hearing the clicks of several empty chambers of the pistol.

"My God, he'p us all!" Luke exclaimed. Thinking of nothing else to say.

"Come James we gotta leave this place. We gotta get tha dead home. Get Jimmy D. home to his ma." Luke guided James toward a log and sat him down, taking the empty pistol from his brother's hand and placing it in it's holster.

"Luke...tell me..." Looking directly into his brothers eyes. Luke's face told him he would get no reasonable answers. He looked toward the others, "somebody! Anybody!" Louder now. "Tell me how, I'm ta explain all this ta his ma... How I'm ta explain how he died. Him gutted lak ah fresh kilt hog...."

James collapsed against his brother's chest. Crying out, "God he'p her!"

Luke could barely hold James' jerking body. He grasped him tighter. "Don' talk such James. Don' say them things."

Bones teary eyed, placed an arm over Jojo's shoulder, sensing the boy needed to be held, but only patted his shoulder lightly with his rough hand. Bones Mizell could not think of anything else, but could not bear seeing the boy cry so.

August watched it all, helplessly. Turning toward Jumper, "tell tha girl not ta fret, we don' aim ta do her no harm, it's all over. They's been 'nough killin'"

"She has no fear of death now. She prays for the spirits of all the dead, and even this one." Jumper pointed toward Iron Bull's unmoving form.

"Jumper yo' come with us, we gotta check whut's out there, now thet tha smokes cleared," Bones said.

Wanda Cypress ceased wailing and regained her feet, watching Jumper leave with the two white men, wondering about the one with the sharp knife and rag on his hand.

Jumper followed Bones and August as he had been instructed, still very confused as to why James had not shot him. Even more confusing to him, was why Bones would put the talking marks in a small book. The names of the dead Indians as Jumper identified them, one by one. Bones attempted to explain that accurate records should be kept for history and maybe even for a news account.

"The marks that make silent talk soon will be carried by Johnson from one soldier house to another soldier house." the Indian stated matter-of-factly.

"Uh, yeah. Yo' ah knowing thet Acre Foot Johnson totes mail fo' tha government?" Bones was surprised, it seemed that every Indian knew or knew of Johnson.

"This I know, I know the giant, and know the story of how he wanted to strap a chair on his back to carry people while carrying the tracks that do not speak. But the white father would not let him use the chair to carry men on his back even though Johnson is strong like the mule."

"Yeah, politics I reckon."

"Politics? I do not know this word, Johnson taught me many, but never such a word."

"It's ta be crafty lak ah fox." August explained with a smile, " never knowin' if ah man speaks true," he added.

"Then the great father is politics?"

"Yep."

Jumper thought that maybe all whites were politics, tricky like the fox. The word still was confusing him. He considered it silly that the white father would not let Acre Foot Johnson carry people in a chair on his back while carrying the words. He had seen the giant do this with ease. To Jumper, even the white giant was strange, he had said he disliked Indians, yet he had shown him kindness. Even trying to teach him to read the words that made no sound, so Jumper could talk the sounds for his people, but there was no time for such lessons as reading. Two Ghosts had wanted to keep Cork for just such a purpose, as Jumper could not speak what the marks said. Jumper had been reluctant to learn the marks from the boy, knowing Two Ghosts would have killed Cork once Jumper had learned to read. Also it would have helped Two Ghosts make more war, by stealing mail, bring more soldiers. But the soldiers came anyway, and took most of his adopted people away. Now he was asked to name the dead left scattered in the smoke.

Jumper noticed August's hand had resumed bleeding once again after turning over a body for identification. Delaying their work momentarily, Jumper gathered a handful of deer moss growing thick on a dead log, applying it to the wound tying it with a bandana before continuing their unwholesome chore. Briefly Jumper considered whether he should continue helping the whites, after all they had killed many Indians. But they had not killed him or Wanda Cypress, even after what they had done to the woman and other whites. Jumper concluded that there was much good and evil in all people, he would continue to help them. Not all whites were politics, nor Indians either.

"Two Ghosts is not among the dead, he has gone with the children and squaws, and a few warriors. I do not know where, somewhere out there." Jumper pointed south toward the miles of swamp, after seeing the questioned look on Bones' face.

"I believe that Two Ghosts is not so brave. Strong yes, but not brave."

"Yeah, yo' probably right about thet, he sho' aint hung 'round long when the picnic started."

"Picnic?" The ever-curious Jumper questioned, but August didn't explain.

Jumper wondered why August hadn't bothered to explain the meaning of picnic; there were so many words to learn from the whites. He intended to ask Acre Foot Johnson the meaning of the word, if he ever saw him again. That is if Two Ghosts does not kill him soon. While Jumper, August and Bones were counting and identifying the remaining dead, Wanda Cypress had scrounged some coffee grounds. Coffee and salt were two things that the Indians wanted most from the whites, other than powder and shot.

Later, August explained to James and Luke how the Negro called Two Ghosts, had escaped with the surviving women and children. They had little stomach for eating the cornmeal cakes that Wanda Cypress had fried in pork fat to have with the coffee, but they forced themselves to eat a few. James and Jojo had no stomach for eating at all. They could only set and silently stare at the body of Jimmy D. lying cold in the hut. Nor could James escape the thought of how Polly would react upon receiving the news of her son. Both sons have gone now, one to spring sickness back in Georgia and another in a battle with Indians; a battle in a swamp, which the boy should never have been involved in. Polly had told him that much. He feared Polly might not survive such terrible news, at least with her same mind.

"James we bes' get movin', we got ta get Jim, uh, we got ta get on home." Luke started to suggest they get Jimmy D. back home for burying, but decided it best not to say it like that, instead stating it another way. "We gotta get from this place, so as we can reach tha' end of tha Devil's Crutch by good dark."

"Yeah, we c'n make the Peace River by breakin' light tomarrer," August added.

"C'n noon at Tater Bluff too." Bones was trying to lift their spirits, but could not, nothing would have accomplished the elevating of spirits, so no second effort was attempted.

"Yo' right, we gotta get on. Get Jimmy D back ta his ma fo' buryin'. Then send word ta Two Rivers Plantation 'bout tha woman." James declared, somehow having the capacity to say what the others would not speak of.

Try as he might, he could not dissuade James from helping with the most unpleasant task of preparing the two bodies for transporting. James argued that it was his responsibility to get his son home. His eyes glazed over becoming hazy as he helped lift his son's body and laid it on the canvas. He closed his eyes hard, causing tears to streak down his ruddy cheeks as they wrapped the two bodies in canvas tarps from the trappings found in the camp.

Wanda Cypress assisted Bones in wrapping Caroline's thin bloody body, the young girl knew well, the importance of keeping the spirits appeased.

Although she had no idea what she and Jumper would do with the other dead left on the island. She, like Jumper was not full blood Seminole, she however was part Seminole, the other part Negro. Her mother was an escaped slave, then enslaved once again by Johnny Tiger, one of the Seminole war chiefs. Eventually her mother became his wife, and very much loved. Johnny Tiger was her father. She knew that the decision would not be hers, Jumper would tell her what must be done. One thing was certain, Iron Bull would not be given a warriors burial, she decided, as she looked at his spiritless body lying cold and contorted on the ground. Jumper had nothing good in his heart for such a cruel man. Jumper was not a cruel man, but he was a brave warrior. He would not fight the whites. He generally liked the white people, and even thought he did not understand their ways, he did not fear them.

Jojo cut stout cypress poles, and constructed two litters for transporting the dead. Their plan to carry them until they could gather their horses changed, once Jumper informed them of two mules that Iron Bull had hidden nearby.

"My God James look! Them's two ah tha mules we dickered away ta Randle Thomas fo' them oxen!" Luke declared still holding a hand over his wounded side.

"It is fo' ah fac'. They in need ah fattin' up ah mite, an' them hoof's ah little soft from bein' in this swamp, but they 'ppear ta be fine otherwise." James walked around the animals feeling their legs and checking their hooves and teeth. After agreeing to the animal's soundness, the stretchers were secured to the mule's travois fashion. Jojo and August would depart first, assigned the task of retracing their steps back to where they had left the horses. Movement for them would be quicker than the mules dragging the travois. They would meet the others at the north end of the Devil's Crutch River.

"You will tell the giant man Johnson, he must be watchful like the turkey? Two Ghosts will try to kill him and eat his heart. Two Ghosts fears the white giant, and wants to steal his courage and strength, to eat Johnson's' heart will give him this." Jumper mentioned to Luke, as James proceeded toward the trail, holding the lead rope of the mule pulling his sons' body.

Bones took control of the other mule assigned to pull Caroline, Luke returned one of the rifles and a hand gun to Jumper before he followed Bones away, he would need them for hunting, and possible protection against Two Ghosts should they meet.

"We will tell everybody thet Jumper Three Toes and Wanda Cypress are friends to the whites. How yo' he'ped us, and thet yo' he'ped the boy 'scape an' all, an' done yo' best ta he'p tha woman." Luke spoke before turning away, then stopped, turned back when Jumper spoke again.

"That is good. When the moon draws close to the big star, the one you whites call the North Star. That pleases the animals, and makes them move the hunting will be good. The girl and me will come visit you soon by the big river that runs west. We will bring you a fat deer."

"Good, yo' an' tha girl will be welcome, them mules will be there fo' yo' when yo' come,"

"The mules are not for me, they are for the Little Panther."

"Yeah, I reckon thet tha boy do have claimin' rights ta them animals. Me an' James see to it thet he gets'm."

Jumper and Wanda Cypress watched their friends until they had made their way across the wide expanse of saw grass and entered the thick hammock. And only until they could no longer see Luke, the last to enter the shadows of the thick trees, did they begin the task of caring for the dead left on the island. Deliberately they walked around the crumpled body of Iron Bull, even refusing to gaze at him. Thereby avoiding the large dark damp spot at his crotch, his frozen twisted face, absent of any evil grin; now exhibited the silent anguish he suffered before death robbed his wicked soul. Even though Jumper knew the whites had not intended to kill any women children, that knowledge did little to lessen the sadness engulfing their hearts. Wanda carried the limp body of the small girl, crying as she made her way toward the burial hut. The child was the daughter of her cousin, not found among the dead. Alone, Jumper made four trips carrying the bodies of several women. It took both of them together, to manage the heavier warriors, fourteen in all. Exhausted, after the physical work, they sat close together on the ground before once again praying to the spirits.

Soon the flames shot high in the air from the burning huts, not just the ones containing the bodies, he had torched them all. Wanda followed Jumper to where the body of Iron Bull lay, and watched as he rolled the muddy corpse over on it's back, he drew his pistol and fired, then another. While the shots still rang in their ears Jumper, with the but of his pistol, hammered a short palmetto stick, cut and sharpened earlier, into each of Iron Bull's ears, and pulling it out in turn.

"With no eyes to see, he will not find his way to the spirit world of our ancestors," Jumper said, as they looked at Iron Bull's harsh bloody face, with the two black holes oozing crimson goo, where his cruel eyes once had been, and now shot out. "Always his ears will be open, to hear the cries of the dead, Indian and white, forever, the women and children." He spit on the mutilated body.

Before leaving, and before the smell of the burning flesh could reach them, they gathered an iron pot, and a large bag of salt. These things were wrapped in a couple of blankets, which Wanda carried on her back. Jumper picked up the two long guns and gathered the much needed shot and powder. They walked away, neither looking at Iron Bull as they pasted, leaving him for the buzzards after the flames would die away. Jumper had a fair idea of where the women had gone; they would go there first. He led Wanda south, and deeper into the great sea of grass. As they walked, he felt that he might soon die if he and Two Ghosts should meet. Although Ghost needed killing, he was unsure if he alone possessed the strength and ability to accomplish it.

Two Ghosts had always wanted to take Wanda Cypress for another wife, but had lacked the wealth to buy her. Plus previously, Wanda's father had refused Iron Bull's offer of the two stolen mules a few months back, just before the soldiers took him away. Jumper brooded over the thought, that Two Ghosts might think a trade no longer necessary in obtaining Wanda for a wife. He also speculated that Two Ghost's desire to kill Acre Foot Johnson was greater than his craving for Wanda as another wife. If true, it would give him more time to pray to the spirits for strength and guidance on the matter. Jumper Three Toes did not consider himself to be a coward nor a fool, but he knew that they would meet eventually. Death must visit one of them soon.

Luke thought he had heard two quick shots, but was unsure because it sounded so faint and far away. Turning he glanced back toward the direction they had traveled. "Look boys smoke, an' lots of it," Luke said pointing bach toward the horizon.

Clouds of gray smoke drifted straight up into the windless sky. Clearly the smoke was from the island.

"Thet injin's burnin' his dead," Bones explained, rubbing the side of his thin whiskered face, with a callused hand.

"'Pears he's burnin' tha whole island," Luke added.

"Reckon if any place call fo' burnin' thet place fits tha bill." James turned away, lightly tugged on the mules lead rope.

Jojo and August had made good time, locating the horses before losing the sun. Finding the hobbled animals still bunched, as they had feared otherwise. Enough light remained allowing August to retrieve the sack of grain secured

265

high in a tree, and fed them. By the light of the fire that Jojo had quickly started with pine knots, he skinned out the three rabbits they had shot earlier.

"Good fat rabbits, an' ain't seen no worms in nary ah one." Jojo secured them onto a green palmetto stick for cooking over the already hot fire.

The sizzling sound of fat dripping from the cooking meat, along with the frogs and crickets lent peacefulness to the otherwise violent purpose for their being there.

"August." Jojo sat hatless, shoes off on a log near the fire; the colors from the low flames, reflecting off his damp face.

"Yeah boy?" August responded from his place on the ground, his back resting against his saddle, as he pulled his makings to roll a smoke.

"I been studyin', an' reckon I ain't got it set in my mind. I mean tha why of it an' all." The perplexed boy brushed a mosquito from his nose as he spoke, maybe as a reason to do something, while waiting for a response from his companion.

August knew the boy's heart, and saw no reason for the boy to say more. In a fatherly way he spoke.

"Well son I ain't rightly sho' thet I c'n clear it up. I ain't one fo philosophi'n' an' all, but I reckon I been where yo' are now, more'n once," he answered. "Back in forty eight, me an' my younger brother rode together, an' me only a few years older then yo' now. Scoutin' fo' tha army all over west Texas, chasin' Comanches and runnin' down Mexican bandits," he continued, raising himself a little higher and looking over at Jojo as he spoke. "We got separated, an' two days passed before we foun' him after tha injins finished with'm. Now them injins out west ain't lak these here, they make this bunch look lak they at ah church social an' all. Ain't human." He stopped speaking long enough to light his cigarette.

"I reckon," Jojo replied, seeing August deep in thought. There was no need for August to explain further, about what had happened to his brother. Jojo didn't want to picture it, after today, he knew the capabilities of Indians

"I asked back then tha same thang yo' askin' now, an' I wuz young, but growed up man jus' tha same. Them soldiers I went to ain't got no answers fo' such," August declared. "Thet wuz until I asked ah young army lieutenant colonel. Commander ah tha Second Cavalry we wuz workin' fo'. Real smart feller, ah West Point man." He stopped talking, drawing smoke, before continuing....

"He tol' me thet they is ah fine thread thet separates us humans from animals, an' ah feller could drift an' break thet line most any time. Said we got ta keep ah good grip on thet thread, an' don' let go." August recounted in his own words what the officer had told him. "In ah hard ruckus lak we jus' went through, or hard times jus' tryin' ta live', ah human might loose his grip. Slip some, or tha string might break complete. Kinda lak tha Books family we met, but they ain't let go complete. Ain't nobody able ta say when or whut might cause ah body ta let go. Only God c'n say I reckon."

Jojo listened intently, poking into the burning coals with a dried stick, increasing the flame, for no reason. August watched the boys action with the stick for a moment, then took a short puff from his cigarette before continuing.

"It jus' lak Miz Caroline back there. I reckon tha string finally gave out, an' mayhap Bones los' his grip ah little. Mayhap we all slipped some. I don' know boy. But I ain't gonna judge, naw suh, ain't got tha right." Drawing on his cigarette, watching the end of the stick moving in the coals.

"Me neither, an' I ain't ever gonna let go ah thet string. It lak yo' say, I might slip some, lak ah body might, but I'm hangin' on, jus' lak Mista Jesse Bill an' them done." Jojo vowed. "Ain't gonna judge neither," he added.

"Thet's good boy, yo' hang on lak yo' say, an' yo'll get by," August advised. "Yeah suh, thet Robert E. Lee wuz ah good officer, tha bes' soldier thet ever rode through Texas. I calculate he tha bes' soldier in tha whole army. Yeah suh, I'd foller Bobby E. Lee right inta hell an' right out tha other side, if tha devil ain't caught me fust."

"Thet wuz ah right good story 'bout west Texas, me an' Ji.... I like hearin' yo' tell'm." He caught himself before mentioning Jimmy D's name. He thought it improper for now. "Sorrowful 'bout yo' brother though."

"It al-right boy."

Jojo wanted August to continue talking; talking about anything it didn't matter. That might prevent the horrid pictures of the island from creeping back into his head. The woeful scene of his brother lying on the ground, quietly and bravely fighting to hold onto that string that August had mentioned, fighting hard to live. Or the ghastly picture of the woman who had rejected life, and accepted death, causing the back of her own head to fly away and painting the tree behind her a muddy crimson. Cutting the string, on her own accord. Right now he could think of no other way of preventing those awful images from being etched deeply into his mind, other than hearing August talk.

"Yo' ever know my mamma?" The question was asked quickly, not giving August a chance to be quiet.

"Huh?" The question seemed to come from nowhere catching August completely off guard.

"My mamma, did yo' ever know her?" He repeated the question, looking directly into his older companion's eyes.

"Ah, yeah, I knowed yo' ma boy." Startled by the question, and recovering... "Me an' yo' pa worked out ah Fort King fo' tha army, we both knew her there before they got hitched. Yo' ma wuz ah gen-u-ine saint, an' purty as ah speckled pup." Shaking his head slowly, slight grin, as if getting a clear picture of the boy's mother.

He narrated how Jojo's mother had come from a poor family, a dirt farmer in northwest Florida, near Yankee Town on the Gulf coast. "Yo' pa traded her pa two injin ponies an' ah five pound sack ah salt fo' her. I know 'cause I wuz there, Nigger John wuz there too. We both he'ped him steal them ponies from them injins, whut he made tha trade with."

Jojo dropped his poker stick, his eyes shot toward August. "Yo' sayin' my ma wuz ah slave or tha lak?"

"Naw boy. It wern't lak thet. Them ponies wuz jus' so her pa would approve tha marriage. Yo' pa loved yo' ma."

Jojo picked up his stick again. Stared at his friend and listened intently as August talked. For the first time he heard the story of his mother's death. A small group of drunken Indians had done the dirty deed when he was barely a year old, yet he was left unharmed. With pride, he learned how his father had ridden to St. Augistine in a cold winter wind to purchase a burial dress, leaving his young son with neighbors.

"Yo pa said she ain't never had no new store bought frock befo', jus' hand me downs or made from flour sacks or some such, by her or her ma. Yo' pa had tha preacher's wife put her in thet purty white dress, an' she looked jus' lak ah angel." August continued the account. "It wern't yo' ma thet would have wanted tha dress. She never asked fo' much. Thet's why me, Nigger John an' him wuz away, when yo' ma got kilt. He wanted ta trap 'nough furs, pay fo' buildin' ah proper house fo' yo' ma. Only thang she ever ask fo', wuz ah book now an' again ta practice her readin'. He said it wuz jus' thet he wanted her ta be dressed up in ah store bought frock when she got ta heaven," August repeated the words of the boy's father. "Yo' pa ordered ah pure white casket from Jacksonville, said she deserved more'n ah plain wooden one made from cypress."

"He wern't one ah them bible thumpers, but he said thet wuz tha most important thang ah-bout it, her goin' ta heaven an' all. Yo' pa never wuz tha same after thet." Not looking into the boy's teary eyes.

August related to Jojo how in great anger his father, Nigger John and himself had located and killed the Indians, from whom they had stolen the ponies, traded for his mother. Two years had passed, and they knew well, that those were not the Indians that had been responsible for her death. But Indians had to be killed.

"It wuz Nigger John whut done most of yo' raisin', him an' ah ol' free darky woman whut used ta be ah injin slave. But yo' pa he wern't no bad man, it lak I say, he never wuz right after thet." He repeated himself. "It lak I wuz sayin' 'bout thet thread. His broke."

"I reckon." Was all Jojo said, remembering his father at the end.

"'Lo tha camp!" Bones called seeing his companions in the glow of the low fire, not taking any chance of startling them.

Jojo after wiping his eyes, filled his hat with grain for the mules as the others went to the fire. His thoughts were of a mother he had never known and wondered why God had taken her, yet grateful for the friends that had replaced her and his father. The other pictures were gone, at least for now.

I reckon I ain't ready fo' any chuck yet." Luke declared, after tearing a small chunk of meat from the leg of the rabbit, placing it into his mouth, not bothering to try any more.

Yet, he attempted to convince James to eat. He noticed James had not drank any water, and thought perhaps eating might make him thirsty. James like Luke had no appetite for the usually tasty rabbit, nor did the others. Instead, deciding to make their rest a short one, leaving the rabbit for the animals. It was only until now that they all discovered, that August had been injured, and he had said nothing.

"One ah tha bastards shot my finger off," was the only comment he made on the subject. Other than mentioning that Jumper Three Toes had applied the bandage.

In the darkness they mounted and rode due north for the Peace River, appreciative of the horses, as they had been afoot for some time. The party had the advantage of a bright moon shortly after departing their hasty camp, allowing August to locate a familiar if slightly overgrown hunters trail on the grass prairie, yet plain enough to follow leading in the direction of the river. But once reaching the heavy forest, the sparse moonlight penetrating the thick jungle growth, did little to eliminate the dark shadows that encompassed them, yet; sufficient enough however for slow navigation.

Dawn passed with the sun already hovering over the eastern horizon as James stepped from the shadows of the trees. After blinking a couple of times, adjusting his eyes to the bright sunlight he, with the mule trailing, moved further out on the open savanna. The others followed. This sea of waist high saw grass void of trees and would cover the remaining distance to the river. James removed his hat, held it up blocking the sun from his yet unadjusted eyes, squinting he scrutinized the northern horizon. Quick tiny flashes above a line of blue green cabbage trees far away caught his eye, then many more appeared as his eyes focused in on the area. With a tired almost limp arm, James pointed toward what he knew to be birds as the still rising sun reflected brightly off their large white wings.

"White cranes, hundreds of 'm," Jojo gazed into the blue sky.

"Yeah, can' see it but them birds is over tha river," Bones said, "figured us ta be close."

"Yep, I knowed it ta be only 'bout three mile," August declared as he watched the barely visible birds in flight.

With the heel of his boots James touched the sides of his horse urging him in the direction of the line of trees. Because of the dragging poles supporting the bodies of the dead they continued slowly. On a suggestion from August they agreed to continue on the trail even thought it was less direct, but certain it would be higher ground thereby avoiding deep mud. The path became smoother as they made their way closer to the river, and a more rapid pace became possible. Three hours later the silver ripples of the waters surface became visible, and the calls of the white birds could be heard.

Once reaching the river, James turned his horse west slowly following the now wide trail, until an hour had passed and he heard a horse move up closer behind him. James tugged lightly on his reins stopping his horse. Without turning he knew it would be Bones. The others moved in close around, with the exception of Jojo who was leading the other mule.

"James, reckon I bes' split off here and cross over," Bones said with a tired drawl.

"Reckoned thet yo' would." James removed his hat and wiped his forehead with a shirtsleeve.

"Jojo throwed in ta he'p me with tha woman, crossin' tha river an' all. He allowed if yo' ah min', he could go all tha way inta Tater Bluff an' fetch back ah wagon with thet mule. I 'llow it might be ah sight more proper ta tote yo' boy back ta his ma in a wagon." Bones looked back at Jojo securing the dragging end of the travois to the front of his horse.

"Well…. Heck, I don' knows it gonna make much of ah difference. His ma ain't gonna be payin' much mind on how he's brung in." James said sadly, not fully convinced. "Naw, it'll jus' delay us gettin' home. We jus' go on lak we are an' get Luke an' August doctored up quick."

"Yo' know bes', I'm on my way then. Proud ta be soldier'n with yo' boys, cain't say I ever seen better. Real sorrowful 'bout yo' boy though," Bones lamented.

"We be holdin' ah service fo' tha boy ah day pas' tomarrer, mayhap yo' c'n tell tha preacher, an' ask him he might handle it, say tha right words an' all." James watched Jojo finish with the litter almost intently, as if he wanted something else to think on.

"Be proud ta. An' yo' want me ta mention thet they bring ta organ wagon?"

" Huh?"

"Tha organ wagon. Thet wagon thet they tote thet organ 'roun' 'n. Yo' know how fond sister Oletta Dewalt is 'bout playin' them church songs at weddin's an' funerals an' such," Bones explained.

"Oh yeah, if yo' ah min' yo' c'n tell tha parson thet we'd be right proud fo' sister Oletta ta play. Polly would lak thet."

James looked at Bones as if he had something else on his mind, then asked. "Reckon she knows how ta play tha 'Rose of Alabamie'? Thet was tha boy's favorite tune, since he heard in on tha trail down. He ain't never learned tha words, but he'd play it on his harmonica an' Jojo'd play along too. Thet boy sho' wuz ah fool 'bout thet song. Kin' ah fond ah it myself."

"Yeah, I'm kinda partial ta thet tune my own self. But yo' reckon it ah fittin' song fo' ah funeral? I'll ask jus' tha same."

"Yo do thet, But tell tha parson we bes' ask tha boy's ma too if it's fittin'," James said.

The sheriff replaced his hat slowly turned his mount and walked it back to where Jojo was waiting. Bones moved his horse into the clear water, leading the mule and litter, as Jojo's pony carried the other end clear of the water. The waters depth never reached the belly of the animals allowing an easy and dry crossing. Once on the opposite bank, Jojo unhooked the litter from his horse's chest, said his good byes to Bones, and crossed the river, quickly galloping to catch the others.

Bones set a slow pace for town, allowing his mind to relax once on the more familiar trail. He recounted the engagement that had taken place between them and the Indians, later to become known as the "Skull Mound Skirmish." Somehow his dull mind created clear pictures of what had taken place. Even the shots could be heard as a picture of the woman came into view, placing the forty-four into her mouth, between blood-dried lips.

Along with the other realistic sounds replayed for Bones, came the metallic sound of the hammer falling, followed by the explosion. Then an ever so slow picture of the back of her head flying away, ending up hanging on a nearby tree. Unaware of his body jerking, as a portrayal of Jojo projected somewhere in the depths of his listless mind. Graphic wailing echoed, violating his brain, as vivid pictures of streaming tears on sun browned cheeks, all somewhere else and far away, long ago. But the confusion drew closer and louder, distorted whippoorwill calls mixed with yelling, "I'll learn yo' how, don' die" along with the dead boy's name, over and over and over until the sheriff shook off the picture of the distraught boy, and the ugliness of it all.

Determined, Bones dueled his own mind, refusing to allow additional reflections on the dead and dying, in its stead, he thought of the song James had mentioned, "Rose Of Alabama." Quietly he hummed the song over and over, until it too faded and someone else was humming it. Surly Sister Oletta Dewalt could play the "Rose Of Alabama" if she took a notion, but he had serious doubts as to whether she would. "Not one finger will touch one key of my Beckweth Grand Imperial Organ, unless it's to play gospel music in testimony for the Lord." Her muffled quote coming from far away rang in his ears, along with a reveling picture of the preacher's wife. That was another thing. Bones had once made the mistake of calling the instrument a piano, in front of Sister Oletta herself. And for a churchwoman, the wife of the preacher yet, the almost three hundred pound woman came completely unhinged.

"I'll have yo' know Sheriff Bones Mizell," she screamed, in no uncertain terms,

"This is not a piano." And then she proceeded in even stronger more certain terms, just exactly what it was. "An Organ, and not a common every day organ, thank yo' very much. It's a brand new Beckweth Imperial Organ, Mista. Sheriff, Bones Mizell!" She exclaimed with the greatest of pride, emphasizing loudly the mister. in her rebuke of the sheriff.

Bones took his admonishment over the organ like a gentleman should. But how was he to know what it was, he thought in his own defense. After all he had only seen anything like it once before, in a whorehouse in Fort Pierce. And then low and behold one comes rolling down the only street in Tater Bluff in the bed of a wagon. Upon first seeing it, the sheriff thought it was some kind of carnival wagon without the bright paint. He had seen a carnival wagon in Punta Gorda all brightly painted up. But then he recognized Sister Oletta Dewalt at the keys, playing "Jesus Loves Me."

The organ included a stool which fancied the same dark finish as the organ, but it would not hold her bulk, so in it's place was an industrial strength bench, the handy work of the parson, who's skinny balding self was driving the wagon being pulled by a small red mule. And every day since that day, Bones felt he was an expert on "Beckweth Imperial Organs." Why he sometimes felt he might even become a drummer for the "Beckweth Imperial Organ Company, " after he quits sheriff'n. He had actually read the catalog that came with the organ from start to finish, three times, with the reluctant permission of Sister Oletta. That very catalog would be passed around the audience during intermission if everyone agreed to handle it with care. Sister Oletta was not bashful in telling how she bought the organ through Sears and Roebuck right out of their catalog. But that, it had been shipped directly from the factory, to save shipping charges by way of Jacksonville.

That bit of information, the sheriff knew to be on page 209 in the catalog, along with the liberal payment plan; indicating money need not be included with the order. Quick to point out that, she had ignored the send no money part, and had sent sixty-eight dollars, plus four more for shipping the organ to Jacksonville. And that she and the parson drove all the way to Jacksonville and brought it home in the very wagon it set sets on today. As a matter of fact it had never been off the wagon since. The fear of it being dropped or even scratched prevented the organ from ever being moved from the wagon. Parson Dewalt along with handy man, Doodle Hix, simply constructed a hard top with canvas sides over the wagon, even extending it over his seat for additional traveling comfort. The sides would be rolled up and tied for ease in performing. And because the full five years no-nonsense warranty clearly spelled out on page sixty-two about the instrument getting wet, the canvas sides were never up unless the organ was being played.

So, God forbid, should a malfunctioning of the organ ever happen, she would take a solemn oath on the good book if necessary, that she had taken care of it. To say that Sister Oletta was real eccentric about the organ would be an understatement. And there were two things everyone knew about Sister Oletta, one was, no one was allowed to touch the organ, and the second, she would not play any dance songs on it. Holy Rollers they were referred as by some unbelievers; mostly because she and the parson didn't hold with dancing, with or without music.

And if anyone had ever doubted her conviction it was backed up without hesitation at the Tater Bluff Christmas Jubilee a few months past. The controversy yet lingers, over what had actually happened. One minute Sister Oletta was plopped on her oak bench playing and accompanied by a number of the town ladies singing loudly from their hymnals, "The Old Rugged Cross." The next thing, before anyone could say Beckweth Organ, and right in the middle of the song she left the organ and plopped down on the wagon seat right next to the preacher.

"Shut'er down Parson Dewalt, and quickly sir, for the devil is amongst us this day." And for absolutely no reason at all. For some, at any rate her decision was irrevocable. Like a good soldier the preacher carried out her orders. He jumps up, rolls the canvas sides down and away they went, right on out of town, the wagon noticeably tilting to her side.

Now needless to say, that left the town folk with alot of questions about what had happened. Why would she just up and leave right in the middle of "The Old Rugged Cross" like that? And to be more precise, right in the middle of the word "rugged." Many decided it was because of that squaw a cowboy named Toby Jones had invited to the jubilee. And apparently form her seat on the wagon while playing "The Old Rugged Cross"; Sister Oletta spied the squaw dancing. Not only did she leave in great haste; it was little wonder she had not had an attack, as her heart was pretty well taxed by her bulk as it was. A few bystanders said the squaw was not dancing, not that any argument would bring the organ wagon back that day. While others said she looked to be dancing, as her bare feet were certainly moving and lightly kicking dust in the sandy street.

The sheriff concluded; she might have been, but he could not be certain. And even if she were, there was no law against it, except for Sister Oletta's law. And he could not lawfully jail even an Indian for that. Anyway at the time in question, he was looking through the Beckweth Imperial Organ Catalog. At the exact moment of the questionable act, he was reading page two hundred and nine, memorizing pertinent information describing the liberal payment plan. His judgment as to whether or not the squaw had been guilty of the charge was based purely on the testimony of others. According to most accounts, she barely lifted her feet in rhythm to Sister Oletta's playing, while her arms dangled limply at her sides. The only movement was from her knees down. Admittedly Bones declared that's the way Indians danced, and he had seen many Indian dances. And apparently Sister Oletta had witnessed a few her self, although he couldn't imagine when or where.

But, he only got involved after the fact, after Sister Oletta demanded the return of her catalog, just before the wagon rolled out of town. Screaming at the top of her lungs something about expecting to see the immediate arrest of the Indian woman and Toby Jones as a contributory subordinate of civil disobedience, whatever that was, and blasphemy. In his twenty-five years of being a peace officer, he had never heard of a law called civil disobedience, blasphemy and contributory subordinate? "Whut tha hell wuz she talkin' about? It sounded like it might be against the good book all right, but he had never heard of anyone being incarcerated for it.

After further cogitation, Bones felt certain that Sister Oletta would refuse to play the "Rose of Alabama," at Jimmy D.'s funeral. And even he harbored a slight judgement about it being a dance song. No she would not. Sound asleep in the saddle; like all cow hunters, sleeping in the saddle came easy. Deep in slumber he rocked along dreaming of becoming a drummer for the Beckweth Organ Company, even if he had to relocate to Louisville. His eyes shut tight, page fifty-six manifested in black and white, illustrating the two factories that produced the organs. One in Louisville, Kentucky where Sister Oletta's organ had been shipped, and the other at St. Paul, Minnesota, was too far away for any savings on freight. This was all very important and required information, once employed by the company as a drummer.

The horse with the mule and travois in tow plodded slowly down the street to the far end of town, stopping directly in front of the livery. The sheriff had no clue until his sleep was disrupted when his horse snorted, clearing it's nostrils after picking up familiar scents from the barn. To say he was surprised would be an understatement, after blinking, enabling his dazed bloodshot eyes to focus. There surrounding the startled sheriff stood a core of Tater Bluff's leading citizens, including the mayor and a couple of pretty wide-eyed whores.

And were all shouting the same question at the same time; demanding to know who or what was wrapped in the tarp. Even in his exhausted state he noticed, and was grateful, that Sister Oletta Dewalt wasn't one of the gawkers. The whores at anytime were far easier to look at. Bones after promising to explain later chose volunteers, the mayor being one of them, for an important task.

"Willie Joe, yo' go over ta Mista Milo's Drug Store, an' see if he's got thet casket completed he's been workin' on. An' yo' tell him I got no time fo' no argu-ment, thet he c'n bill it ta tha town. I'll sign fo' it later. Y'all put tha re-mains in it and bring it ta tha jail." The first true clue as to what was concealed in the tarp increased the appetites for even more information.

The sheriff along with everyone else in Tater Bluff knew that Homer Milo in his spare time had been preparing the casket for his mother-in-law. He had been bragging about the fine cedar wood he had gathered for the project. Although his mother-in-law had not yet passed, she was near one hundred years old, and had been off her feed for quite a spell. Hopefully she would hang in there long enough to allow Homer additional time to produce another casket. With things under control the weary sheriff headed for his office and bunk located in the jail cell. As a reward, Willie Joe was posted in the jail to keep everyone out and away from the mysterious tarp-wraped body and snoozing sheriff. Feeling he had earned the right, especially after lying to Homer saying the sheriff would jail him on contempt or something like it, if he failed to turn over the newly completed casket. Later, Caroline Thomas was buried in the town's graveyard after Bones completed his short nap, and explained briefly what had taken place. Even though none in Tater Bluff had known Caroline Thomas, they all attended the short obsequies. Sister Oletta displeased because the town whores showed up, yet, still played her organ.

CHAPTER SEVENTEEN

After she and Cork had completed the chore of cleaning the chicken coop, Kara Sue sat in the shade of the front porch, being entertained by Cork and Tater. Cork would throw a dried stick, and then encourage Tater to fetch it, which the playful dog would do.

"Kara Sue! Yonder, look yonder!" Cork yelled pointing with his stick, instead of tossing it again.

"Whut is it?"

"Yonder! Yo' papa's ah commin' down tha road. An' it 'pears they got 'ah extra mount." The observant boy called running toward the gate.

"It is! Mamma, it's Papa! It's Papa!" Kara Sue cried out loudly to her mother in the house, as she followed Cork.

Polly and Anna stood together on the porch, both nervous and starring intently toward the figures moving across the open span of high grass yet; some distance away.

"Kara Sue y'all stay inside the gate now yo' hear."

"Yes'm." She and Cork jumped to the second rail of the fence, for a better view of the coming riders.

"I count five horses, Polly, I believe the last animal is a mule," Anna declared

"Yeah, six animals, 'pears ta be ah empty saddle. Oh my god! Empty saddle!" Polly repeated the statement as if it had not sunk in the first time, as she shielded her eyes from a bright sun.

"Sweet Jesus Anna, one's missing," Polly said unable to see the travois being pulled by the mule, and hidden by the tall grass

"Oh Lord. No! Lord no! She grabbed Anna's arm urging her to follow.

Promptly they passed the gate, hurrying toward the approaching men, both stumbling almost falling as they waded into the tall grass blanketing the uneven ground. Suddenly they stopped, glancing back, assuring that Kara Sue and Cork held their places on the fence. Hurrying on waving, the two uneasy women drew closer. The leading rider returned their greeting with his own wave, and even though the distance was yet far, Anna recognized the first rider.

"Thet's Luke in front!" Anna identified the rider who had waved. "An' August, an' Jojo next. Thet's James behind, an' looks ta be leadin' ah mule," Anna continued identifying the riders.

"It's Jimmy D! My God Anna, Jimmy D ain't with 'em!" Polly screamed. Terrified. Realizing for the first time, Anna had called everyone's name but her son.

"Now slow down Polly it looks, wait! That mule is dragging a travois or something."

The women could not bring themselves to stop and wait for the slow moving column to come to them; instead they kept their quick pace and soon were directly in front of Luke's red horse. Stepping to one side they allowed his horse to continue past. Luke reined his mount to a stop, looking down into Polly's face and understanding the deep terror in her eyes. Without speaking Polly returned his gaze, and even under his unshaven dirty face, realized his cloak of deep sadness. The alarmed woman choked out a low anguished gasp, her eyes welling in tears, as she covered her mouth with the back of her hand, shear terror masked her face. Turning toward Anna unable to speak, she reached clutching one of Anna's hands, squeezing hard.

Quickly releasing her grip on Anna, she proceeded for her husband with a flow of tears washing down her red cheeks. August Moon touched the brim of his hat yet declined to speak to the distraught woman as she passed him by. Luke held out a hand for Anna, and slowly shook his head back and forth as he looked into her questioning wet eyes. She grasps his gentle callused hand, not speaking but lay her head against his leg. In an awkward fashion she moved next to his slow walking horse toward the house sobbing, saying nothing. James removed his hat as Polly approached his eyes red and swollen looking into hers. He reached down taking her small quivering hand in his before speaking.

"It's our boy Polly, I brung him home fo' buryin' wern't nothin' else ta be done." Tears dropped from his eyes.

"Ohhhh God! Nooo Jesus!" Screaming, she fell to her knees, emitting sounds of anguish.

After speaking, James dismounted, dropped to his knees next to Polly, and held her tightly. He reckoned it such a cruel awful way of telling her. But he was at a loss as to how one should bring to a mother, the news of losing a child. There was no way of abating the pain of such dreadful news. Her agonizing cries caused the others to turn and look back. Anna released Luke's hand and started to go to Polly, but Luke grasped her shaking hand stopping her once again. Dismounting quickly, he placed a strong rough hand on her trembling shoulder and gently pulled her close, holding her trembling form firmly against his chest. Releasing her, taking her small hand.

"Naw girl, it's them whut's got ta talk it out. She's got a fierce hurt, so does he, they gotta get through it together, they'll need us more later." Still holding her hand tightly in his own, they turned toward the house, leading his horse.

"Mamma!! It's Jimmy D, ain't it?" Kara Sue screamed running by, Cork following, both unnoticed until now.

"Hold up honey. Don't go back there, you must stay with us, it will not do you any good." Anna grasped the girl's arm as she attempted to pass.

"But thet's Jimmy D's horse with tha empty saddle. Jimmy D's dead ain't he?" The girl began crying uncontrollably, and struggled to release herself from Anna's grip, but could not.

"Yes child, I'm so sorry, it is your brother. But you can't do any good back there. You've got to be strong for your mamma and papa. They're going to be needing you and all of us to help them." She attempted to calm the sobbing girl.

"Let's go home." Luke gently nudged them both along, glazed over eyes staring blankly at the house.

As Cork raced by, August reached down grabbing his overall straps placing the crying boy onto his saddle, with a light hand on the boy's leg, he attempted to pacify him.

"It lak Kara Sue sayin', Jimmy D. dead ain't he?" The boy blurted out sobbing once again, not waiting for an answer from August. "Miz Caroline, is she?"

The boy's thin body trembled so, it required both hands to hold him, as the horse continued walking.

"Yeah boy, she's gone too, reckon it best." The comment came softly, while still gently pressing the boy's slight trembling leg.

They continued on toward the house, leaving James and Polly alone in the field with the body of their son. James held his dejected wife tenderly as they knelt beside their son's stretched-out tarp covered corpse. Polly screamed uncontrollably as she pressed her face into her husband's chest. With his shirtsleeve he wiped the tears from his haggard face, still holding the rope of the nervous mule stamping its feet. It was difficult for the others not to look back and satisfy their curiosity after hearing Polly's continuous tortured wailing.

"Come girl we bes' get tha boy home." Tenderly he picked her up with his strong arms and placed her on his horse, holding her in the saddle. Walking next to his horse, holding Polly shaking and sobbing doubled over the horse's neck, they made their way to the house.

"Oh James, I cain stand loosin' 'nother chil', not lak this I will go mad. Did he?" She almost tumbled from the saddle; to weak for holding on, James caught her.

"Don' talk 'bout it now, les' jus' get him home. We c'n talk later."

Polly was put to bed, with a damp cloth placed over her swollen eyes, eventually she laid still and quiet, lacking strength for further crying.

"There's beans and hog back warmin' on tha stove, an' we got ah pan ah cornbread in tha oven. Yo' set yo'self an' I'll pour coffee." Anna spoke quietly to James.

"But, I got ta go see ta tha boy before," James protested, stealin a glance at his now quiet wife. Not knowing how long she would be so.

Polly appeared to be sleeping, but occasionally she would moan or move an arm, it was a restless time, a time requiring all her strength. James wondered to himself if he possessed enough of his own to support her, he wondered, he hoped. No doubt Anna was there for her too, but it was his place, and worse it was his doing.

"Don't be concerned James, Luke and August are doing that, they're putting him in the room in back of the barn for now. Jojo's agreed to stay out there tonight, an' watch over things." Anna explained, looking into James' gaunt tear stained face.

"I 'llow yo' need ta fin' August, he took some lead in his hand, James mentioned, as he watched her dress Luke's wound. "It 'pears ta be fine, but, mayhap gonna lose ah finger, needs lookin' too jus' tha same." Staring out the window toward the barn.

"Why James Nash, almost scolding him but refrained. "I never took notice of his wound, and he never mentioned a word." She poured more hot water in the pan, gathered aditional clean cloths.

"Ain't thinkin' clear I reckon."

"It's all right, I'll see to it right now. I will be right back, you rest easy."

Soon Anna returned with Luke and August, August sporting a clean white bandage over his left hand.

"Yo' gonna lose thet finger August?" James asked quietly without looking up.

"Naw, I'll be fit as a fiddle in ah day or two."

Eating appealed to no one; they sat quietly drinking coffee. James would on occasion look over at Polly, not expecting any change and honestly had no idea what to expect. Setting on a bench against the wall with Kara Sue leaning on her shoulder, Anna held her small hand the girl occasionally dozing. Cork sat on the floor his arms wrapped around drawn up knees.

"I reckon I'll go an' spell Jojo, might be he c'n eat ah bite." Unexpectedly, James got up and walked toward the door.

"C'n I go too, Mista James?"

"'Corse boy. Iffin yo' ah min'."

It was well past dark when James still exhibiting swollen red eyes, returned to the house without Jojo or Cork, explaining the boy had no desire for a meal, Cork wanted to keep him company. Later Jojo ate a piece of the cornbread and drank a glass of buttermilk that Cork had returned for earlier, and respectively insisted on being allowed to stay and help Jojo watch over Jimmy D's body. Even though the canvas wrapped body was well off the ground, they would take no chances with rats cutting through the tarp. The rats would come, and they all knew it.

James heard a low moan from Polly and looked over just as she sat up, wiped her face before looking around, with the damp cloth that had been over her eyes. Looking confused by the presence of the others, having no notion of time.

"Reckon I've been ah-sleep fo' quiet ah spell. Anna how's tha coffee?" 'Spect I'll do fo' ah cup befo' we talk."

Anna poured the coffee, admiring her strength, remembering her pain when her own husband was killed.

"We got plans to decide an' I reckon it's high time we cogitate on'm."

To unknowing ears, it wouldn't have sounded as though she was enlisting them in a discussion over burial plans for a son. Instead more like, solving a less drastic problem. More like, if we're going to have chicken for Sunday dinner, we best get it plucked and cleaned. But her appearance displayed otherwise. It was plain she was preparing her self for a sight more than determining which roosters' neck to ring and pluck for the stew pot. Sitting on the edge of the bed, she attempted to conceal her nervous hands by clasping them firmly on her lap, her anguished face however; could not be disguised from the others, even by staring at the floor. She would talk about it now, no matter how unprepared.

281

"I had tha sheriff notify tha preacher 'bout tha buryin' tha day after tomarrer. What day would thet be?" Looking toward Polly for any reaction to his statement. None came.

"Thursday. The day after tomorrow is Thursday, James," Anna answered.

"Is thet all right? All right 'bout telling tha parson I mean?" James asked, being sure his wife had heard him, but had failed to draw a reaction from her. "An I tol' Bones ta tell 'em thet it would be alright ta bring tha organ wagon too, fo' funeral music."

James thought he had best let Polly know about the organ wagon also. He decided however, it not to be a proper time bringing up the subject of playing the "Rose Of Alabama." As a matter of fact he wasn't quite sure of how to approach it, especially since he had no idea as to whether sister Dewalt would even play the song anyway.

"Thet will be jus' fine, sister Oletta Dewalt plays real nice gospel music." Polly answered after the long pause, and to James, seemingly making a clear and direct point of church music only.

"I been studin' on it, an I calculate thet where thet stand ah cedar trees between here and tha river, will make ah fine spot fo' our boy. Ain't seen no sign ah tha river ever reachin' thet high," James explained. "C'n see it from the porch too."

"Reckon I'll get on thet right away in tha mornin', to late now, mayhap have ta cut ah parcel ah them root's ta dig ah proper hole. Don't reckon it will harm them trees though." Luke wishing he had not said so much, and not thinking he might not be able to use a shovel.

Not much else was said for the remainder of the evening, now that the simple plans were set. Everyone seemed to find a place to sleep or slept where they were. It didn't matter about sleeping. Or eating, or anything else, none of it amounted to anything. Not anymore. Not now. So the night passed.

Luke enlisted Cork and Jojo in digging the grave. Jojo with axe in hand followed Cork carrying shovels, Luke leading the way to the cypress grove all were silent. Immediately, a large diamond back rattlesnake challenged their presence. The deadly snake coiled and sent its chilling familiar warning in defense of its territory. Luke reacted quickly by severing the reptile's head with the working end of the shovel he had snatched from Cork. He knew that he would hear from Anna about his bleeding again. Without conversation, Cork picked up the snake and hung it over a low tree branch, intending later to prepare the snake's hide for fashioning a band for a hat, as soon as he acquired a hat. Pondering on a snake band and a hat at such a time suddenly plagued Cork with a flash of guilt, which caused him to redirect his thinking, wondering what Jimmy D. would have thought. There was a time Cork remembered, when he had not thought much on death, never on life after death. But of late, he had considered much on the subject of living and dying, and knew well, that the living must continue on somehow. In his tender years he had already learned, that, one could take chances in life and die-hard. But by not gambling and not moving forward, one chanced dying agonizingly slow. Jimmy D. had taken a chance, as did the Thomas' and the Nash family. The price they paid was quick and extreme. Later many time over he would think on it.

By dark when Polly brought coffee, the casket lacked only a lid for completion, and she urged them to complete it the next morning with improved light. Waiting until she departed the barn, before they placed the body in the box and put boards on top substituting as a temporary covering. Toward the river the lantern cast a dim light through the low limbs of the cedar trees where the digging was being completed by its yellowish-red light.

"Ain't no need, them boys are doin' jus' fine. I 'spect they most finished now," Polly said to James about him going to help them. Later from a window, Polly watched the bobbing lantern as the diggers made their way toward the house. Wednesday night passed quietly… Somberly

It was very early Thursday morning and the preacher's day had already begun. Beating the sunrise by thirty minutes was not his choice, funeral or no. It had been his wife's decision. She had been making the decisions ever since they had bought the Beckweth Imperial Organ.

"You'd ah thought thet owning thet organ automatically gave her the wisdom of Solomon, or made her queen ah tha whole state or some such." The preacher mumbled under his breath, always under his breath.

Another thing that vexed him, other than getting rousted from his sleep so early, was his black eye. It happened a lot and everybody knew it, but it just didn't look right at funerals or weddings. He had mentioned to Sister Oletta before, about her jumping out of bed so quickly. Catching him un-alert and off guard. That's what was doing it, but she paid little mind. Every time she did it, he rolled off the bed bumping his head on a nearby table. More often than not it resulted in a big shiner as he now sported, rather than a big lump on his head, but always one or the other. At any rate, there he was out there in the barn fumbling around in the dark, one good eye, harnessing the little red mule.

He had intended getting oil for the dry lantern the day before, and went to the store for that purpose. But Sister Oletta spied a hat, which she said she would kill for. So they returned home with an empty oilcan and a new white hat. He, without saying so, considered the hat unattractive. She never had owned a new hat before, and pointed that fact out, when making the statement about killing for it. The preacher secretly wished that they had never bought the Beckweth Imperial Organ, things had been alot better before, but it was far too late for wishing. He completed the chore of harnessing the mule and walked the animal out of the barn just far enough to recheck his work in more light. As always the wagon was left under cover until Sister Oletta was ready for travel.

The preacher had one other assignment, and that was to wake up Sheriff Bones Mizell, he would be traveling with them to the funeral. Loud banging on the window bars.

"Huh? Whut? Who tha hell's out there?" Came the sleepy voice in the darkness of the cell.

"It's me sheriff. Parson Dewalt."

"Huh, Parson Dewalt? Whut tha hell yo ah doin' out there in tha middle ah tha night? Uh uh, I mean heck?"

"Ain't middle ah tha night. An' Sister Oletta sez we got ta start early on account ah tha Nash place bein' south ah tha river an all."

"'Course, I know tha Nash place is on tha south side ah tha Peace. Thet ain't no secret, but Parson, it still only twelve mile from here, river or no river."

"Sheriff, he continued talking through the bars, "Sister Oletta sez fo' yo' not ta be makin' her come an' fetch yo' herself. She smells rain in tha air. Sez if thet river comes up, yo' gonna have ta bring tha Nash family over ta tha north side fo' holdin' of tha service. She ain't 'llowin' tha organ ta cross tha river, take no chances if it rains."

"Alright, I'm awake might jus' as well get ready. I declare thet woman's been ah real tribulation since she come by thet Beckweth Imperial Organ." The sheriff spoke aloud as he stood scratching himself, attempting some degree of alertness. Out of respect, saying the brand name of the organ completely, but not Sister Oletta's.

Gettin Rita Lowrey out of bed early to start cooking breakfast would not set well with her either. Bones knew that she normally was not due to open her kitchen for another twenty minutes yet. And the Tater Bluff Cafe was the only place to get a hot meal in town, without being invited to someone's home. Waking Rita early was the only option he had, other than making the ride on an empty stomach. Sheriff Bones Mizell had no intentions of riding that far on an empty stomach and dealing with Sister Oletta Dewalt at the same time.

With his assigned chores completed, the preacher could now return home for his breakfast. There was ample light now for cooking, and he hoped that a pot of grits might be on the stove, and maybe even some bacon frying in the skillet. Heck even a cup of hot coffee would help.

Within the hour and after a plate of lumpy grits the parson and his bulky wife rode the organ wagon down the sandy trail for the Nash ranch. An unhappy Bones Mizell, still smarting from a tongue lashing from the equally disagreeable cook trailed. Mounted on his dapple stud lagging back so as not to hear her fussing at the preacher. Plus intending staying far enough from her to lessen the chance of her cracking him and inflicting an eye like the preacher now sported. Unconvinced by the preacher's story, about how it happened.

"Looky yonder Brother Dewalt, they's ah rider far ahead," after an hour on the trail.

"Where? I don' see nobody, but tha Lord did bless yo' with real good eyes."

"Well I do. One rider. Reckon it ah bandit? We ain't got but one dollar and twenty two cents lef' after buyin' my new hat. 'Course they's tha Organ." She quickly refused to consider that last possibility at all.

"Now Sister Oletta we ain't suffered no banditry here ah bouts in ah coon's age, 'ceptin ah chicken or mayhap ah hog gettin' took. An' ain't nobody ever heard of ah no bandit high-jackin' no organ wagon. 'Sides yo' forgettin' we got tha High Sheriff ridin' right with us." He argued as politely as he could.

"Sheriff my big toe," she answered in disgust. "Any fool knows we cain' count on Bones Mizell fo' protection from bandits an' assassins or tha lak. Special he spendin' mos' his time whorin' an' drinkin'. Or sleepin' jus' lak he's doin' now."

She committed with irritation, her usual mood when speaking of Bones Mizel. Especially since she heard he wanted to be a salesman for the Beckweth Imperial Organ Company. She had concluded long ago, that the only thing he was capable of selling would be a new mattress to a whore. The sheriff had not a clue, he was indeed sound asleep, and Sister Oletta didn't even have to look.

"Then again it mayhap be one ah tha Nash family comin' ta greet us."

"Nash family my big toe! An' it's far worser than bandits. It's thet no count Skeeter Moody. I c'n see thet big white feather he always got stuck in his hat. I c'n see it plain as day." She spoke with confidence, and spewed the name Moody, as if spitting a bug from her mouth.

"Well I'll be dern," the preacher declared. He still couldn't see anyone on the trial, let alone a white feather. But he had no intentions of arguing.

Sister Oletta had more than a strong dislike for the Moody's and there were plenty of Moodys' scattered about the Peace River Valley. They were to a man, prone to hard drinking, gambling and serious whoring. But as was said they were not afraid of work, they would sleep right next to it. And if that wasn't enough she added dancing every Saturday night. Sister Oletta Dewalt placed Skeeter Moody at the very top of her list for disliking. Considering him the worst of the lot. Especially after the things he said about her personally. And it was his best friend Delbert Jones, right in the middle of church service that had passed on that awful, and very personal information to and about her.

Delbert Jones was listed right under Skeeter and Bones Mizell for their sinning ways around Tater Bluff. That opinion borne one Sunday morning over six months ago, after a night of hard drinking for Skeeter, Delbert and others that Sister Oletta considered white trash. Cecil Moody owner of Moody's Saloon, the town watering hole and uncle to Skeeter, kicked them out of his place and into the street the next morning. Both men still under the influence of strong liquor, mounted to ride out of town. Delbert didn't get far only to the other end of town, where he toppled from his saddle, right at the church house door. Parson Dewalt considered it a miracle that God delivered this sinner to his church on a Sunday morning. Especially a Sunday service declared for testimonial and confession.

In his inebriated and confused state Delbert was dragged before the little congregation. Music from the organ wagon parked outside flowed through an open window, started the preacher praying for Delbert's deliverance from his sinful ways.

Then came time for Delbert's confession. Not enough time had passed for Delbert to become completely sober. While on his knees he admitted to his, "dancin', drinkin', gamblin' and fornicatin' with Tater Bluff's unfortunates." Bringing gasps from the women folk, with a few passing out completely. The preacher raised an eyebrow, believing he had heard an excessive number of amen from the men folk, but continued on with the serious work of devil banishment from this poor sinner.

"Drive tha' devil from this brother! Drive tha devil from here! Screaming the spiritual request several more times at the top of his lungs, all the while whacking the drunken Delbert on top of his head with his heavy bible. The combination of sermonizing, additional screaming and head banging brought about the most disturbing confession of all from Delbert.

He admitted to a great deal of laughing; "laughing until my stomach hurt," about things said about Sister Oletta by his drinking pal Skeeter Moody. It brought a host of amen from the congregation, but a question from the preacher.

"An' jus' what wuz it Skeeter said 'bout Sister Oletta my dear wife?"

"Skeeter said she wuz ah awful mean woman, special her bein' ah preachers wife an' all." Delbert declared.

That's when the music stopped floating through the window, and in its place howling from the incensed woman stomping her bare feet on the floor of the organ wagon. She had thrown her shoes through the window, an accurate shot too, cracking Delbert in the head.

"Lord loosen this sinners tongue an' save his soul today," the preacher caterwauled, pumping and swinging one arm in the air. Rubbing his head at the same time. The other shoe hit him. Again bringing more amen and praises for the Lord.

"Confess all brother Delbert! Confess all before God! Be saved from damnation."

"I will, I will parson, I laughed when Skeeter said, he bet Sister Oletta had ta take ah axe handle to tha privy with'er." Delbert tearfully confessed all.

"Huh? Why would he thank thet?" The preacher questioned, almost forgetting what was taking place.

"Skeeter allowed, she's so mean she might crap ah wildcat an' she'd have somethin' ta kill it with. Thet's whut made me laugh till I hurt. Everybody else did too, an I'm powerful sorry fo' thet." Delbert cried shamefully asking forgiveness for his earth shaking sin.

This brought about a momentous stir from the assemblage. Because of this Sister Oletta could not hear or understand what was taking place inside. She laid it all on the presence of the Holy Ghost coming to save Delbert. There was little doubt just how much power the devil had over Delbert Jones, at least in the preacher's mind. Screaming "Lord save us in the name of your son Jesus Christ!" Jumping high in the air, shooting out a stiff-arm palm out. The outstretched hand caught Delbert square in the face, forcing him backward. The startled, slightly injured and still drunken man fell, with his face ending up between eighty year old Sister Lizzie Mott's wide spread legs. Lizzie Mott also considered the Holy Ghost had Delbert in his grip. She screamed and with frail arms grabbed Delbert's head pushing it harder into her crotch, "Thank you, Jesus!"

In his half-drunken state, bleeding from a broken nose, Delbert could only assume that he was in the saloon fight of his life. Out of survival he slammed a fist hard into Lizzie's rib cage, eliminating all her air, causing them both to fall to the floor. Old man Lott, Lizzie's husband, half blind and near deaf began whacking Delbert with his cane. A few of the hard licks made contact with his wife's head, causing increased screaming. The congregation in the rear of the church believed a great battle-taking place between the devil and the Holy Ghost. And they had every intention of marching in ranks behind the Holy Ghost to defeat the devil. The ones still physically able leaped to their feet shouting. Some bouncing up and down on the benches, others rolled on the floor, praying, wailing, and speaking in tongues.

The preacher thinking Delbert in need of additional prayer pulled him off Sister Lizzie, dragging him kicking and screaming back to the altar. Because of the pain to his head and upper body, Delbert was convinced even more that, it was a life or death situation and decided to be more aggressive. Emitting piercing screams he began striking out with both arms and fists, one of which caught the preacher flat in the mouth. Several bloody teeth flew out the window and landed in the organ wagon, causing Sister Oletta to play with more vigor. Eventually exhaustion overcame them and they ceased wailing and jumping, and quietness settled over the congregation. The members, Sister Oletta included believed fully that the former sinner Delbert Jones had been saved. It had been a hard fought battle for Delbert's soul, knowing saving Skeeter would be even worse; they would need a long rest.

However Delbert's conversion didn't take, because the following Saturday night he had back slid, and wound up in Moody's Saloon, along with Skeeter and the others. But, whatever happened to Delbert Jones had no bearing on what Sister Oletta would do to Skeeter Moody if she ever got her hands on him. And Skeeter knew it; he stood just barely over five feet tall, and tipped the scales boots pistol and all about one hundred thirty pounds. Certainly no match for Sister Oletta's almost three hundred pounds. Skeeter's friends, Delbert included kept the pot stirred by their constant teasing on the matter.

"Why thet big red haired woman's gonna kick tha crap right outten yo' an' then kick yo' fo' crappin'." Delbert was heard to say on more than one occasion, especially after healing and a few beers.

After months of waiting Sister Oletta might get her chance to bring the wrath of God right down on that no-count sinning Skeeter Moody. The Lord had steered him right here on the trail to the Nash place. And if the good Lord would continue his steering just a bit longer Sister Oletta would do the rest without any further assistance.

"Blessed be tha Lord. It is Skeeter, white feather an' all, an' he be sound asleep in tha saddle." The preacher rubbed his eyes, as rider and wagon drew closer together.

"Sleep my big toe. He's drunk, same as them Moody's always are." She was griping the seat so hard her hands turned red. "Bring him on Jesus real close lak. An' I'll be on him lak ah duck on ah June bug. I'll learn'm ta talk vulgar trash 'bout good Christian folk." She whacked a big red fist in her opened red palm. Not only was it her moral responsibility, Sister Oletta Dewalt considered it her spiritual duty to confront sin wherever she met it. Even on a trail to a funeral, "an' it ain't gonna take no jawbone ah no ass either lak Samson had," she thought, "I'll crack his sorry face with my fist," she spit out.

"Now sister, we got ta pray fer Skeeter jus' lak tha good book say," the preacher explained.

"Yo' c'n do all tha prayin' yo' want parson. "Pull this wagon over off tha trail, then his horse'll come right to me, I'll pray thet I got power in my fist." At no other time would she have given such an order, a chance of endangering the organ.

"Cain do thet Sister," he protested. "Them saw palmetters'll cut our mule up somethin' fierce." then realizing that, a weak argument he added, " 'sides it liable ta dump tha Beckweth Imperial Organ right out on tha ground."

"Yo correct, then jus' stop 'er right here." Realizing she could inflict damage, without endangering the organ.

By stopping, Skeeters horse might try and squeeze by, at which time she could reach out and grab him by his suspenders. Then with or without a jawbone she planned to inflict multiple knots and abrasions on his head and shoulders. But that plan also failed, because Skeeter's horse stopped dead in the trail, nose to nose with the little red mule. It seemed to Sister Oletta, that the Lord was turning his attention elsewhere, and no longer interested in helping her punish a sinner. Determined, she would act alone to carry through with Skeeter's punishment.

"Skeeter! Skeeter Moody!" she shrieked as loudly as she could, surrounding her mouth with her fat hands intensifying the scream.

Skeeter's cow pony jumped high in the air, emitting its own scream and snatching Skeeter from his dead sleep, causing him to loose his grip on the reins. The terrified horse landed off the trail disappearing in the high palmettos. Skeeter grabbed the pony's mane staying in the saddle, shrieking loudly as he clung to his pony. His mount darted over and through the thick brush and palmettos at full gallop running under a low tree. The sheriff sat stunned in his saddle, watching Steeters pony run through the brush, Skeeter screaming loudly holding on.

"Thet'll learn yo' Skeeter Moody," Sister Oletta screamed watching his horse run under a limb of a tree, knocking Skeeter out of his saddle. And out. Waking only after the ruckus had started, the sheriff had no idea what was amiss. And he had no intentions of asking Sister Dewalt or the preacher. He guided his horse off the trail toward the tree where Skeeter had fallen. He would ask Skeeter, assuming Skeeter would be able to talk.

"Whut tha hell! Whut yo' doin' out here sheriff? Whut happened ta me?" How come I'm laid out in this scrub? Hurtin' too…feel lak my nose is broke." Flat on his back, looking at the Sheriff, his eyes blurred. The sheriff's explanation, or lack of, confused him even more.

"Danged if I know Skeeter; but yo' look lak yo' been bear huntin' with ah switch." Bones lifted Skeeter up. "We wuz on our way ta tha Nash boy's funeral. Reckon I wuz sleepin'. Next thing I knowed yo' pony come runnin' by hell bent fo' leather, run under thet limb. An' here yo' are."

Where's my horse? I could swear I heard thet ornery Sister Oletta Dewalt ah hollerin. Mus' ta been some kin'ah nightmare," he babbled.

"Lak as not yo' did, tha preacher and Sister Oletta Dewalt wuz with me." Instant fear showed in Skeeters eyes. Bones recognized it.

"Don' fret Skeeter they done went down tha trail."

"C'n yo' fetch my pony?" Skeeter was rubbing a large knot on his head, and dabbed at his bloody nose with a finger.

"Cain' Skeeter. It aint thet fer ta town. I got ta move on. Won't do fo' tha organ wagon reachin' tha ford befo' me. Never hear tha end of it."

Still rubbing the knot, and gingerly touching his injured nose, he watched the sheriff ride away chasing the organ wagon. He shook his head causing additional blood to drip from his nose.

CHAPTER EIGHTEEN

"Thet's Bones yonder 'cross tha river."

"Sho' is, Luke. An' I see tha organ wagon commin' up too, jus' commin' out ah them trees. I'll fetch tha others."

"Yeah yo' do thet August." From the front porch Luke watched Bones stop at the river's edge, opposite side, look back toward the wagon. The distance restricted any sound from across the river, only the gesturing, mostly provided from Sister Oletta, provided evidence of communication taking place. He continued watching until joined by the others.

"I'm crossin' I'm crossin'." The sheriff called after urging his mount into the river. "It ain't gonna get no deeper," he yelled back only after his horse reached belly deep water on firm bottom, then started his ascent.

The preacher lightly whipped the mule up and slowly followed the sheriff to the far bank. Once the mourners witnessed the wagon had reached a halfway point crossing the ford, they woefully made their way toward the gravesite and waited. Soft music drifted toward them from the wagon after stopping allowing Sister Oletta to take her place on her bench. For Polly and James, the day and the music brought unbearable sadness. The sun as expected, bright and warm still left the family cloaked in one of the darkest days ever. Like a heavy black blanket, depression overlapped them, making the shear act of breathing difficult.

Especially Polly and James, it brought painful reminders of a grave in Georgia where their eldest would rest for eternity. Taken by spring fever, not the results of a bitter fight with renegades. It mattered little to Polly, the method used in calling her sons, and she resisted questioning God's purpose. She tried. At first as a mother, she felt she had a right asking God. But the fear of questioning God overcame her need for answers. One son under hard Georgia clay, now her only other son ready to go under Florida's damp sand.

291

Surely God would not burden her heart with a greater weight than it could manage. No God would. Her faith said so; she could outlive the pain. She would prey that her husband could also.

The agreeable notes of Sister Oletta's Beckweth Imperial Organ hovered over them as the wagon gently rolled closer to the group of mourners. Continuing with no interruption as the mule tugged the heavy wagon through the white sugar sand, leading to the cedar trees. Sister Oletta's wide fanny unmoving on the bench, as the wagon gently stopped and the preacher dismounted.

"I am truly sorrowful to come among y'all fo' such ah sad, sad occasion," The parson bemoaned, as he went about shaking hands with the red eyed group. "Why jus' nigh on ta five year, since God called our own son ta heaven. Him falling from ah tree an' bustin' his neck, hit were ah awful dark day, jus' lak yo' facing yo' own self."

None could help but notice the presence of the big shiner and swollen left eye of the preacher, nor the vacant dark hole where two upper teeth had once been seated. The teeth lost during the sanctification of Delbert Jones month's back, and his early morning mishap, left him appearing more as a barroom brawler than a man of the cloth.

Sister Oletta refrained from playing while her husband spoke, considering herself a professional, and only continued after being signaled to do so, after taking his place near the coffin. With thin rough hands he opened his worn white bible to the book of "OBADIAH," chapter nine.

"Lord ain't nobody here got questions, 'bout yo' reason fo' takin' this brave young man, Jimmy D Nash, an' callin' him ta be with yo' in heaven. Jus' lak yo' done our own boy. But we askin' yo' ta deal harsh with them evil red heathens whut caused his sufferin', jus' lak yo' promises in tha good book. Jus' lak yo' caused thet tree thet our boy fell out of, ta be hit by lightin' and burn up." The words came uncommonly soft, but a slight hissing sound at the end of each word, caused by his missing teeth especially prominent, the ones ending with an "s." He patted his opened bible gingerly. Pulling a clean white handkerchief from a pocket of his rumpled black tattered coat. He wiped his face not bothering removing his large black hat, before reading in his slow voice.

1. "I saw ta Lord standing upon tha alter; an' he said, Smite tha lintel of tha door, that the posts may shake; an' cut them in tha head, all ah them: and I will slay tha last of them with tha sword: he thet fleeth ah them shall not flee away, an' he thet escapeth of them shall not be delivered." Raising a skinny arm into

the air pointing, revealing a frayed clean white cuff under his long coat sleeve.

2. "Though they dig inta hell, thence shall mine hand take them, though they climb up ta heaven, thence will I bring them down." This time tha same arm shoots downward.

3. "An' though they hide themselves in the top ah Car'mel, I will search them out thence, an' though they be hid from my sight in tha bottom ah tha sea, thence will I command tha serpent ta bite them."

With that Cork quickly glanced over at the dead rattler hanging stiffly from the tree limb, unnoticed by the others.

4. "An' though they go inta captivity before their enemies, thence I will command tha sword, and it shall slay them." Chopping motion. Stopping short of completing the fourth verse, he looked about the wet eyed mourners. The stern faced preacher, with the chopping hand, signaled his wife to play once again. Without hesitation she obliged. As sweat dripped from under her new hat down her plump face, and strands of wet red hair hung free, she played. Her short, fat, drilled fingers manipulated the keys, causing combined tones to fall among the small gathering as they watched the parson through clouded eyes. After gently pressing the last key and before the sound died away, Sister Oletta put her hands in her lap after wiping them of sweat with a rag.

Again the preacher, with bent knotty fingers, opened his bible and flipped the pages, he quoted from the book of "Job," chapter fourteen. Without actually looking at the pages, he hissed out the words from within.

1 "Man thet is born of a woman is of ah few days, an' full ah trouble."

2 "He cometh forth lak ah flower, an' is cut down; he fleeth also as ah shadow, an' continueth not." The parson let his eyes fall on the pages cocking his head slightly, forcing most of the effort of seeing, on his unimpaired eye... Continued quoting from memory.

13 "O thet thou wouldes hide me in tha grave, thet thou wouldest keep me secret, until thy wrath is past, thet thou wouldest appoint me ah set time, an' remember me."

14 "If ah man dies, shall he live again? All tha days of my appointed time will I wait, till my change come." Closing his bible, quiet, "Amen."

He stooped and scooped up a handful of dry sand, then resumed standing.

"Ashes to ashes, and dust to dust." Tossing the sand onto the casket. "In tha name of Jesus Christ, our Lord."

"Thet wuz ah fine service. Them wuz good words parson." James took the preachers skinny hand.

"I'm thankin' yo' brother Nash, proud ta be of service,"

"Thank yo' parson, be proud ta have yo' an' yo' dear wife stay fo' dinner." Polly passed her hand to him.

"Now Sister Nash I jus' don' know how we could say no." Firmly pumping her hand.

They made their way back to the house, with the exception of Luke, Jojo and August. Cork and Kara Sue quickly moved ahead, as prearranged it was their responsibility to chase down the rooster.

"Mamma said we got ta get thet big red one." Kara Sue pointed toward the big rooster with the long black tail feathers.

"An I ain't sad 'bout thet either. Thet ol' bird is ah real mean one, he run me out ah tha chicken yard las' week. No suh, I ain't sad one bit 'bout him in no stew pot." Cork grinned as the two attempted to corner the ornery rooster. As Polly had hoped, it took their minds off Jimmy D.

It was well into the afternoon when Sister Oletta took her place next to her husband on the seat of the organ wagon. As always causing the wagon to settle a little more on her side into the deep sand as it moved slowly toward the river. The Nash family waved their good-byes, and once again thanked the parson and his wife for the fine service, before Sister Oletta barked out orders for the return trip home.

"Bones Mizell yo' better check out thet water an' bottom before we roll in!" The demand could be heard from where the family stood by the grave.

"Sister Oletta we done jus' crossed thet river not more'n three hour ago, ain't no cause fo' yo' ta be ah frettin' 'bout tha organ wagon sinkin'." The sheriff protested what he considered an extreme precaution. Knowing her over vigilance like his protest was a waste of time.

"Sheriff Bones Mizell yo' ain't got ta tell me when we crossed thet river las'. I know my own self. 'Sides, it might be it come a squall someplace an' got thet water up ah sight deeper, or ah hole washed out. An' yo' responsible fo' public safety, yo' bein' tha sheriff an' all." Reminding the sheriff of his duties, in no uncertain terms, and not in a low tone

"If I wuz ta concern myself with tha public's safety right now, I'd pull my pistol an' shoot thet fat ass heifer right off thet wagon seat. Thet would be tha bes' thang I could do fo' public safety," uttering the threat to himself as he moved his horse into the water. "Mayhap get me ah raise or'lected mayor," still mumbling

Speaking of public safety, he reminded himself he might check on Skeeter Moody left dazed in the brush by the trail. As it turned out, Skeeter walked back to town. And to the great disappointment of Sister Oletta, recovered from his scrapes and cuts.

Little was done around the ranch for the next few days; just keeping up was accepted. However with each day passing, there arrived additional relief to the family's depression. Bringing with it another chore to be dealt with concerning Cork, and James found him cleaning the chicken coop.

"Cork.... Sheriff Bones Mizell tol' me he sent ah letter ta Two Rivers Plantation, where y'all wuz goin' befo' them injins took yo'. He tol'm 'bout Miz Caroline, an' 'spect they'll be ah comin' soon ta fetch her re-mains home fo' buryin'." He spoke with a soft tone to his voice.

"Yas suh Mista James, I 'spect too." He answered, continuing scratching one of Bacon's ears. Not looking up.

"Yeah... Well, whut I wanted ta say wuz thet, when them injuns took y'all, word is they aint burned tha wagon. Mayhap yo' freedom papers wuz kept safe in thet possible box yo' had."

That caught Cork's interest; he looked up at James for the first time, believing that James had more to say on the subject of his freedom.

"So whut I am tryin' ta say is thet yo' c'n come an' go as yo' please. Least ways after we get copies. Cain' nobody make yo' do otherwise." Awkwardly he explained to the boy. James removed an axe imbedded into the top of a sawed off stump and sat holding the axe, allowing himself to be closer to the boy. Looking into the Cork's dark round eyes, he waited for the boy to speak.

"Whut's tha good of it all Mista James?" Looking up then quickly returning his eyes toward the pig lying on the ground.

Even though James had been waiting for a response, the question caught him completely off guard. The plain words clouded his brain leaving him temporarily unable to answer... A long pause... Cork looked up... a puzzled look on James' deeply tanned face. Still desiring an answer to what he had considered a simple question, he stopped scratching the pigs ear, as if directing his full attention for the coming answer... None came.

"I mean whut's tha good of it all, ah little colored boy lak me bein' free? I ain't got no kin folk... I don' know nobody 'cept y'all. I ain't got nothin' 'cept them two mules thet yo' an' Mista Luke fetched back fo' me. An' I be purly obliged, but I don' even know if little colored boys 'llowed ta own mules an' tha lak," he lamented. "Do yo' know if I 'llowed?" He didn't wait for an answer. "An' whut I go traipsin' off an' somebody ketch me again 'fo' I get ah mile from this place jus' lak them Mista Rice brothers did?" The questions were coming much faster than answers. Questions that James could not give proper answers, so another long pause, then.

"I cain' rightly say 'bout them kinda laws boy. I ain't had much schoolin', an' I ain't never owned slaves. But, I reckon Miz Anna might know 'bout such," he attempted an answer, then realized it inadequate by the look on the boys face.

"Then there's Judge Johns, he'll be passin' through Tatter Bluff soon ta try Rat Davis fo' pig stealin'. I'll ask him 'bout yo' mules an' 'bout somebody ketchin' yo', he ah regular judge an' all. So don' fret 'bout them thangs."

"I'll be thankin' yo' Mista James," he responded, looking into James' eyes.

James noticed a look of concern still masking the boys brown face, and quickly thought back on the words they had just communicated. His main reason for wanting to talk to the boy had not been completely covered, as the boy's face indicated.

"Now tha main thang, whut I wanted ta say wuz, that they ain't no call fo' yo' ta be frettin' 'bout goin' 'less yo' wantin' ta be goin'. Yo' welcome ta be stayin' right here with us, if yo' ah min'."

"Lordy Mista James I sho' do! An I'll do ah mans work ever' day too."

"Know thet, yo' doin' thet right now. But, yo' stay close, if yo' go out an' fetch logs fo' firewood with them mules, yo' take Jojo 'case they's trouble. Least ways 'till we get ah letter from Judge Johns."

"Mista James.... Uhh... yo' reckon, uh, thet." Speaking with great difficulty, looking directly into James' eyes.

"Whut is it boy? Yo' c'n say it straight out."

"Yeah suh. Reckon I c'n. Mista James, yo' reckon I might borrow yo' name jus' lak Jojo borrowed yo' las' name? But I c'n use James too. An' I c'n tell folks my name same as yo'? James Cork Nash...."

"Well I be danged. Well... I 'spect thet will be all right if yo' be of ah min'." Startled over the request. Admiring the boy's boldness. Remembering Caroline Thomas mentioning Cork to be a very special boy. He was indeed.

"I sho be proud Mista James, powerful proud."

"Well then Master James Cork Nash, thet would make me proud too. I'll see tha judge c'n make up ah paper sayin so."

"James Cork Nash. I'll have three names, jus' lak white folks. James Cork Nash," he repeated.

"Mista James I ain't knowin' whut ta say. I ain't had nobody since them injuns hit our wagon. I ain't always knowin' proper words an' all."

"Heck boy ain't no cause ta say nothin'. Yo' got our name an' place. Yo' our family now." Placing a rough hand gently on the boy's narrow shoulder. "Now yo' go on ta yo' chores."

Putting out his hand. James accepted it and shook it, and could not help but notice the boy's wet eyes. "Run on now boy I got my own work to do." Sending Cork on, while yet in control of his own emotions.

Cork ran out, his excited shouts brought Polly to the back porch as he ran past, still howling in delight.

"James whut in tha world's wrong with thet boy? He ain't got hisself snake bit has he?"

The startled Polly peered around the corner of the house looking for Cork. But, he had already disappeared behind a tall patch of palmettos on a path toward the river.

"Naw, he ain't snake bit Polly, he's jus' excited 'bout some news, I'll explain at dinner," he said, satisfying Polly for the moment.

"Whut's ailin' thet young'n?" August called out, while repairing the wagon wheel.

"Nothin' August. He's jus' tryin' ta find his own peaceful little place, in ah big confused world." James held the wheel secure as August tightened the nut.

"Tha way he ah hollerin' I allow he found it. But he's commin' up ah little short on tha peaceful part."

"Mayhap, Come on, let's wash up fo' dinner."

James allowed Cork to reveal the news of the acquisition of the name James Nash as his own. August stole a glance toward James as the boy shared his exciting news, flashing a wide toothy grin, beaming bright eyes.

"Well.... Welcome to the family, Masta James Cork Nash," Polly said, causing his grin to widen even more.

Chapter Nineteen

The added addition to the family was not the sole reason for creating the festive mood during the noon meal; a planed trip into Tater Bluff shortly was another. Even though there had been many previous visits before, but they had always been on Saturday, this was Wednesday. And there were yet, several reasons for the trip no matter the day. Judge J. Wilmer Johns had agreed to draw up papers declaring Cork hereafter, to be James Cork Nash. Also an agreement between the Nash family and Captain Kormac McBean, transferring the McBean property including all stock too the Nash brothers. James, Luke and McBean had agreed earlier to the terms, of payments sent to McBean twice yearly, until the debt was satisfied.

McBean and the Rice Brothers, along with Mammer, were leaving for Nevada immediately after signing the contract agreement. McBean had read news articles of silver all over the territory of Nevada, simply for the taking, and he intended to get his share of it. An invitation from the eccentric Captain had been extended to the Rice twins, to join him in his adventure along with their mother. Mammer, reluctant at first to leave Florida, eventually grew to the idea. She like her sons had never been more than twenty miles from the banks of the Okeechobee. Not counting the trip the twins made to Punta Rassa, where they first met Captain McBean and his monkey Geechee.

Tatter Bluff expected other visitors today, a Wednesday. The visitors would fetch the remains of Caroline Thomas for burial next to her husband in Tallahassee. An obligation toward sending the brave woman home was felt by everyone in town, especially the Nash's. And they intended to satisfy that obligation, as soon as the last pan was washed and the men readied the animals and wagon for the trip. A sudden twinge of sadness plagued their minds as they mounted the horses and boarded the wagon. Knowing well the unbearable hurt that the Thomas family would be experiencing. Anna resisted the intrusion of sad feelings and forced a chuckle as she lightly slapped the reins, encouraging the two mules to ease the wagon down the gentle slope and into the clear running water toward the far bank.

"Whut's so funny?" Polly inquired after hearing Anna snicker as she guided the team on.

"Well I wuz just thinking about what folks must think, when the Nash family rolls into town now, all of us."

"Yeah, must seem 'bout as queer as ol' Capt'n McBean comin' down tha street with thet three legged pony ah his with thet monkey on his back."

"An' thet little ol' monkey wearing thet little red hat," Kara Sue said, "An' folks sayin' them two boy took ta dressin' up jus' lak thet monkey." The three laughed gaily causing the men on horseback to laugh along, putting all thoughts of sadness behind them. The lively mood continued with them into Tatter Bluff, especially after seeing the crowd.

August Moon allowed himself a moment of distraction from a game of mumbly peg between Jojo and a younger boy, and resident of the town. Jojo had just flipped his Barlow in the air; it landed vertically with its shinny blade penetrating the soft sugar sand. He failed to hear a response from either of the boys, regarding Jojo's winning accomplishment with the knife. The distracted man regained his feet, and with a deliberate slow movement brushed the sand from the knees of his britches, saying nothing, only pointing a bony finger toward the approaching wagon that had come into view.

"Thet's gotta be them," James said, as he watched the wagon clear the last curve in the trail approaching the north entrance of town.

"Yeah, it don' 'pear ta be folks from here 'bouts," Luke responded, about the wagon, yet some distance away.

Drawn by two gray mules, the wagon moved slowly down the street, pulled up in front of Moody's saloon and stopped. The un-kept two-story building stood alone separated from the rest of the town by a good hundred yards, at the insistence of the local women folk and town leaders. It wasn't the guzzling of whiskey by the cowhands taking place on the ground floor that disturbed the town ladies, but the activities upstairs with the sporting ladies; this anxiety created immense and constant pressure on Sheriff Mizell to run the whores out of town. His failure to do his duty was pointed out on a daily basis, mostly by Sister Oletta Dewalt. But it wasn't entirely the sheriff fault. The business longevity was owed mostly to J. Wilmer Johns circuit judge. It was a "Constitutional Matter, not a matter of kin," explained the judge, who just happened to be a third cousin of Pee Wee Moody, its owner.

"My Big toe! Them ain't no representative of the Thomas family!" protested Sister Oletta Dewalt from her seat on the organ wagon. She had the parson park the wagon directly in front of the dry goods store, believing it would be the pilgrims' first stop. "The Thomas' are quality folk. They ain't ah 'bout ta stop at no whore.... ah... I mean house ah sin." Choosing more proper wording to describe the business.

But just as Sister Oletta had finished speaking, the Negro driver of the wagon close enough now, that the observers could see the white man next to the driver, slowly shaking his head from side to side.

"My big toe if it ain't them! See there, them pilgrims comin' on right ta us," Sister Oletta changing her evaluation of the visitors in the wagon.

"Sheriff Bones Mizell, who made Oletta Dewalt a one woman welcomin' committee?" Yelled Liz Moody, another cousin of Pee Wee's. "'Sides ain't nobody said fo' her ta park tha organ wagon right here in tha middle ah town, blockin' everybody's view an' all." Liz Moody continued her protest.

Bones refused a response to Liz Moody's complaint, especially after noticing the evil look given him by Sister Oletta. Instead moving quickly and quietly away, to the opposite side of the street. Joining Luke and Cork standing together, as Sister Oletta began a loud rendition of Sweet Chariot on her organ. All the while Liz Moody continued her remonstrance to anyone in town willing to listen. She gained few willing ears. By now, they were more focused on the arrival of the strangers that would take the body home to its final resting-place.

"Uncle Caesar."

"Huh? How's thet boy?" Thinking Cork had spoken.

"Thet's Uncle Caesar in thet wagon." Cork spoke once again, not realizing he had said Uncle Caesar's name out loud the first time. To Cork, it was as if he had been only thinking to himself about the second Negro in back of the wagon.

"Uncle Caesar? Naw ain't so." Luke shading his eyes from the sun, attempting a better look at the Negro man in the back of the wagon.

"Aint it so, yo' said yo'self thet them injuns kilt thet ol' man?" Bones siding with Luke about the boy's confusion.

"I know I did right 'nough suh. But, thet's sho' 'nough him in thet wagon." The puzzled boy was sure of it now, as the wagon drew closer.

"Dang boy I believe yo' right. Sweet Baby Jesus it is him. Well go on boy, go on up there and give ol' Uncle Caesar ah proper welcome." Luke lightly slapped Cork on the back, urging him forward.

"Uncle Caesar! Uncle Caesar! It's me Cork!" Cork yelled excitedly, running for the wagon, as the Negro driver pulled the mules to a stop.

Somewhat confused by all the yelling, the tired old man cupped a hand to one ear to assist his hearing, an effort to determine what was happening. Who was yelling? At the same time Cork scrambled up the tailgate and into the wagon, the old man still looking toward the front.

"Who dat yellin' ol' Caesar?" Before realizing someone had climbed into the wagon.

"It's me Uncle Caesar, it's me. Cork."

"Cork! Lawd have mercy, I ain't 'llowed yo' ta be 'live boy. Thought them injuns kilt yo' 'long wid Miz Caroline." Reaching for the boy from his seat on the long wooden crate.

"No suh I be 'live right 'nough." Cork crawled to the old man. Eyes misting. "Though yo' wuz dead too. Seen whut thet injin done ta yo', tol' ever'body such, didn't know no different." Crying openly now.

"Thet all right boy, ain't no way fo' yo' knowin'. We here now, an' it look like de good lawd done look after us both. Thet all they is to it," he said, wiping tears from his dark wrinkled face.

For the old man there could be no other explanation for the two of them being alive, other than Gods interception. And he was left only to imagine what depraved cruelty Miz Caroline had endured at the hands of the savages, before her merciful death. All explained later; he chose not to dwell on it at present, but would much later.

"But, how yo' been gettin' on boy? I ain't knowed yo', yo' growed near ah man now. No suh I ain't knowed yo' ah-tall. How yo' been gettin' on?" Asking once again, squeezing the boy tighter.

"Yo' 'member Mista James an' Mista Luke Nash whut he'ped us 'cross thet river, well, they been lookin' out fo' me," he explained. "An' they all here with me now."

"Ain't thet ah caution? Right here wid de Nash family, day be real nice folk."

"Yeah suh, come on they be wantin' ta greet yo' too. We c'n go home now." Cork carefully helped the old man out of the wagon, with Luke's assistance.

Cork and Luke afforded Uncle Caesar extra support after noticing the bad limp, no doubt the result of what the Indian had done during the attack. As Cork had predicted the Nash family gathered, giving Uncle Caesar a warm welcome, again bringing tears of joy to the old mans eyes. With no thoughts

VIRGIL GRIFFIS

before, of finding Cork alive, Uncle Caesar had considered staying. Only feeling it his sad duty to make the trip and bring Miz Caroline home. That all changed after finding Cork alive. And with very little persuading from Cork and the Nash family, he accepted his new home.

After seeing to it that Miz Caroline's remains were placed in the wagon for the trip, and their legal business completed, the Nash family plus Uncle Caesar prepared for their trip home. What unfolded next was completely unplanned, catching the Nash's' even more off-guard. Had they been given an opportunity, their exit from Tater Bluff would have been much sooner. Four wagons departed town at the same time theirs included, producing a jamboree like atmosphere. First in line, the wagon transporting Miz Caroline's remains, followed by the Nash wagon with the addition of Uncle Caesar; August, Jojo, Anna and Luke on horseback. James handled their wagon, with the McBean wagon behind them. Certainly no one expected Sister Oletta Dewalt to join in. But the parson, his eye almost healed guided the organ wagon in behind, McBean. And if that wasn't enough, six drunken cowhunters loafing in front of PeeWee Moody's whorehouse, brought up the rear of the departing caravan. The whole business became an instant irritant to the Nash's'.

The local gossip, that the Rice twins had been attempting to look like McBean's monkey Geechee, proved correct. Setting on Roelon's head with a slight tilt just as Geechee's, was a similar hat. The newly acquired headgear was fashioned from an inverted three-pound lard can, painted red and sporting a white feather. The red paint used for the lard can left McBean's red wagon with one unpainted wheel. That was Roelon's assurance that there would be sufficient red paint remaining for his hat. However, Roelon had taken his imitation of the white-faced monkey a step further even yet. For the past three months he had insisted on wearing a white cotton mask created by Mammer, which covered the upper portion of his face night and day; especially during daylight hours preventing sunlight from tanning his face around his eyes. The ingenious functional mask did its work, because the skin around Roelon's eyes and nose, was as white as a magnolia flower, with the remaining portion left darkly tanned. Raelon on the other hand was partial to the monkey's little red britches, and little black belt. To his great disappointment, the store lacked enough red material for Mammer to fashion a pair of red shorts big enough for the larger twin. However they did have in stock a substantial quantity of red dye, and this Mammer used to color a pair of Raelon's overalls, after first cutting them off at knee length, exposing white legs never having seen the light of day.

Raelon was quite taken with his new red shorts, but was unhappy with the eighty-five cents he had to expend for the black belt required for completing his ensemble. His thinking was that he deserved a discount on the belt, considering the lard from the can had been returned unused, back to the storekeeper. At any rate they felt dressed to the nines, even Mammer sporting a new homemade red cotton frock, explaining the shortage of red material remaining in the store. With this, the four wagons rolled slowly out of town, Roelon with the similar looking Geechee on his shoulder, sat next to his brother managing the team of two mules. McBean and Mammer shared a box for their seat in the rear of the wagon, with the mynah bird perched on McBean's shoulder.

The little white three-legged pony also shared the back of the wagon, along with a large basket containing McBean's cobra. Nevada was too far for a three-legged pony to walk according to the Captain, and surly no one expected he would leave his snake behind. Both the cobra and pony were present over Mammer's objection. Mammer had an extreme phobia toward the snake. The white pony, she considered as useless as tits on a boar hog; plus she just didn't consider it proper to be sharing the back of a wagon with a horse; especially one with only three legs; and especially all the way to Nevada. She quickly overcame her resentment of both however.

"We on our way ta Navadie! We on our way ta Navadie!" Mammer screamed over and over, waving madly at everyone as the red wagon with one unpainted wheel rolled past. Then suddenly she had something else to scream about "Capt'n thet freak pony ah yourn done shit on my foot!" Mammer screamed out her grievance for all to hear, between yelling out their destination. Kicking her bare foot in the air, slinging the wet crap from her toes on bystanders nearby.

"We on our way to Navadie! Thet freak pony shit on my foot! This now from the mynah bird, loudly screeching Mammer's words exactly. Her audience being everyone in town, rolled with laughter; all that is except Sister Oletta Dewalt. Following behind the wagon, the drunken cowhands could barely stay in their saddles from laughing, as they watched the irritated Mammer kick the smelly wet manure from her bare foot. Sister Oletta played as loud as possible, so as to be heard over Mammer's screaming, and laughter from the profane cowboys and the screeching from the vulgar bird. To the disappointment of the town's inhabitants and visitors, the parade was too quickly out of sight, and soon after even Mammer's wailing could no longer be heard. For the Nash family, the turn off from the river taking the others north, was nowhere soon enough, but after traveling with the caravan for five miles they finally reached it. Raelon closed the gap left by the Nash wagon, as did the cowhands, who now had taken a place behind McBean. As for Sister Oletta, she intended on following the McBean wagon as far as possible, in hopes the cowhands would stay with them all the way to Nevada, beings half of them were Moodys', and everybody in Tater Bluff knew how much she dislike the Moodys'. Sister Oletta never once prayed over her feeling of hate toward the Moodys', she allowed God disliked them equally as much. They were heathens all.

She was fully aware that some believed that men descended from monkeys, although she herself didn't put one ounce of stock in such a primitive belief. Because she had placed her faith in another doctrine, radically different from that of men coming from monkeys, considering instead, those sinners as punishment, would turn into monkeys for another life. Even more now; because the proof of God's castigation was right before everyone, after seeing the Rice twins setting in their red wagon, looking much like that monkey belonging to that "half-wit Captain McBean," her judgement. God had actually communicated to her in a dream, this business of sinners becoming monkeys. It certainly was not just a silly reflection. Not just once but many times over the years. The last time a week ago, a Saturday night, in which she had received added information on the subject of sinners being made into monkeys. This new revelation was that, after all the sinners were changed to monkeys, which certainly included every cowman and whore in Tater bluff, God would send a massive swarm of locust to eat up all the banana trees on earth.

Even in sleep, this added disclosure about the sinning monkeys starving brought a smile to Sister Oletta's chubby cheeks. Oh no, not starve completely to death, no no no, just being hungry all the time, until the Second Coming of Christ.

Hunger was something Sister Oletta Dewalt was well aquatinted with, that is until she married the preacher. One would never know it by looking at her now, but as an adult, she didn't always weigh two hundred and fifty pounds. At Fort Christmas where the parson first saw her, she was very skinny and with her long red hair, he was quite taken with her. And after considerable dickering, her father agreed a bushel of new potatoes would be an equitable trade. The agreement being contingent on the preacher's promise to marry his not so comely skinny daughter. It was not an easy choice for the young parson, because new potatoes are his favorite vegetable, especially when boiled up with smoked bacon and green beans. Now after twenty years, she claimed the added weight gave her extra energy for prayer and playing the Beckweth Imperial Organ. Which she was presently doing with great zeal, in between praying that everyone in the McBean wagon would continue their progression toward "monkey-ism," a word God had conveyed to her, before reaching Nevada, including "thet bunch ah whore-mongerin' cowhands."

Soon Sister Oletta became disappointed that they had not grown long tails. So she instructed the parson to head back. The completions of monkey-ism would have to take place out of her sight, to her disappointment. Loudly playing the organ as the wagon turned toward home, thinking at least that, that no account sheriff Bones Mizell might be inflicted with monkey-ism before they reached town.

"Stop tha wagon Parson Dewalt. Stop tha wagon now!"

"Why? Yo' got ta relieve yo'self sister?" the parson asked, bringing the wagon to a halt.

"Yo' jus' watch me," she said, jumping from the back of the wagon, her bulk landing with a hard thud and loud grunt, up past her fat ankles in sand.

The parson couldn't believe his ears, she said "watch me." His wife had always been what he called "skittish," about such things. For the first eight months of marriage the only parts of her body he had seen, was her face and hands. But after those months, and he will always remember it, even today; he saw more than that, one steamy Fourth of July night. Because of the fact he had consumed over a gallon of lemonade during the festivities that day, his bladder became overly taxed during the night, and he awoke in need of the chamber pot. Ten o'clock at night, he had looked at the clock. In the moonlight from the curtain-less window, as he was peeing in the chamber pot he saw them, soft and white. He fought an urge from the devil to stroke them, lightly. He was frightened to do so, and did not. But the devil eventually won another battle, because he reached and pulled the sheet away, exposing more of her naked skin. He couldn't pee anymore; he had an erection. While still holding the pot in his left hand, Satan took full control of his right hand. He did it to himself as he stood at the foot of the bed staring at the milky skin of the soles of her bare feet.

Racked with guilt the following morning, he grabbed the hot coffee pot off the stove, holding it tight with the offensive hand, inflicting a severe burn to his palm. He felt better after that, even though it took almost two weeks before the hand healed enough to hold a knife for cutting his meat at mealtime. Sister Oletta refused to cut his meat for him.

"Only a fool would grab holt of ah hot pot with his bare hand," she scolded. But after that she became more mindful of using a rag when handling the coffeepot. Unwilling to gamble a chance of injury to her hands; and left unable to cut her meat at mealtime. No sir, stupidity would not cause her to miss any meals, especially after putting on the added weight, which helped her play the Beckweth Imperial Organ better.

But that was many years ago, and even now after all those years past, when they did it. The thing that married couples do at night, in the privacy of the bedroom, mostly in their younger years. Sister Oletta still insisted on removing her clothing in total darkness, under a sheet. And after they did it, which didn't take long, he was required to leave the room until she was dressed, leaving nothing exposed but her fat red face and fat red hands. The preacher was willing to bet a pot of boiled new potatoes, that the bottoms of her feet were red now, not pure white like they were that July night.

He was totally baffled now because it appeared to him, she was requesting he watch. At first, red faced at the prospect of watching his fat wife relieve her self by the trail, but now he became aroused, just like that forth of July night. With any luck at all she might request him to hold her frock out of the way, at which time he could squat down for a better look. He rubbed his rough hand between his legs, holding the mule steady with his other, watching his wife step toward a cluster of tall dark green banana trees.

"Huh? What tha?" She wasn't at all doing what he had pictured in his mind as he massaged his crotch. There was no wide snow-white bare butt flashing in the sun matching the mental picture that influenced what was taking place between his legs, and he sure as hell was not pulling her dress up for her. Instead, stooping slightly her butt aiming skyward, but remaining covered, while with both her chubby red hands, she grabbed hold and snatched an eight-foot banana tree completely from the ground. Roots and all. Tossing it aside, like she had just pulled a small weed from a turnip patch

"Praise tha Lord!" she screamed. "Say it with me Parson Dewalt," she hollered. She continued screaming, "praise tha Lord. Pray with me parson!" As she pulled more of the trees from the same clump, until she had pulled them all up, and tossing them aside, almost a dozen trees in all, height ranging from two to nine feet.

The astonished preacher had not the slightest idea what was taking place, why his wife had pulled up the banana trees instead of peeing beside the trail, and letting him watch, as he thought she had intended. He ceased rubbing his crotch, no need, feeling nothing now but the roughness of his black britches.

The perplexed preacher dropped to his knees in the wagon and begins praying as loudly as he could. Having no idea what his wife was petitioning God for, unless it was for more banana trees to uproot, it sure as hell wasn't for more strength, because all the trees were pulled. As far as he was concerned, he was convinced his dear wife Sister Dewalt was possessed with demons. Because he had never even known a man who could pull an eight-foot tall banana trees from the ground like that. Maybe Acre-foot Johnson could. But why would he? Unless he would became possessed too? His prayer was to have the demons driven from his wife.

With one eye slightly cracked he watched as his wife drop to her knees in the black dirt now void of any banana trees, praying louder than ever. The skinny preacher prayed until his voice had all but left him, then ended with an afterthought, "An' Lord, if them trees Sister Dewalt jus' pulled up belonged to any injins here 'bouts, mayhap yo' might strick'm blin', so's they cain' see they trees been pulled up. Then they want be 'nother war lak las' time over banana trees. Amen."

The preacher to his dying day never knew why she started pulling banana trees, he never asked and she never said. But she had only wanted to give God a little active support, thinking the locust he would send, might not be sufficient to eat all the trees. In the following months he prayed longer and harder to no avail, because she pulled out every banana tree she saw, until she injured her back in the process. Then the tree pulling stopped, especially after the threat of lawsuits from some of the locals, especially the mayor of Tater Bluff. One moonlight night Sister Oletta slipped out of the house and went directly to the mayors house where she pulled almost every tree he had until her luck turned bad. After that screaming in the darkness until help arrived, she was found sprawled spread eagle, face down on top of the pile trees she had just extracted. She would have gotten them all, but that's when she hurt her back, that was the bad luck. It took six men plus the preacher to carry her back home. The preacher mostly attempted keeping his wife decent, by tugging her gown down over her thick white knees, as the others struggled with her bulk. That was the last time she pulled any banana trees up. And with his prayers finally answered over her demons, he prayed long and hard over not being sued.

Back on the trail, shortly after Sister Oletta's initial tree pulling act, the McBean wagon rolled on and, Mammer felt dryness in her throat from all the yelling. And she had a sure-fire cure for a parched throat. The juice from a few China oranges would be fine. But Mammer was a sight more weary from all the excitement and screaming than she thought. And instead of reaching into the basket for a China orange, she plunged her hand into the similar basket containing the cobra. As would be expected the deadly serpent struck, injecting into Mammer's small hand ample venom for killing a healthy bull elephant. The startled tiny woman jerked her hand free of the angry cobra and out of the basket.

"Yeow!" she howled, "Capt'n thet dern snake ah yourn done up an' bit me good!" she continued screaming after pulling her hand out, and seeing the immediate swelling around the two small punctures in her hand.

"Huh! Mammer, what in the world did you annoy Adam for?" The surprised captain asked, as Raelon brought the wagon to a stop.

"Adam? I ain't knowed his name wuz Adam," as if that made a difference. "'Sides I wern't aimin' to vex thet varmint. I wuz jus' cravin' me ah Chinie orange fo' suckin' on fo' my parched throat an' all. Reckon I reached my hand in tha wrong basket," she added, shaking her wounded already badly swollen hand. "Aint been ah real good trip so fer. I done been snake bit, and ah horse done shit on me; an' we less than four hours from town. An' I still ain't had me no Chinie orange." She lamented.

The man in the front wagon transporting Caroline Thomas' body, and his driver puzzled by all the hollering, walked back, stood watching.

"Make way Jesus," his black driver said, "Dis snake bit white woman coming ta see yo' lawd."

"C'n we suck thet pisen outen Mammer's hand?" Skeeter Moody asked, riding up with the other hands after hearing Mammer's yelling.

"No boys. I'm afraid Mammer's done for. There is nothing to be done but make her as comfortable as possible until the end, which wont be long now. The venom from this viper is a deadly neuro toxin, unlike the hemo toxin of your indigenous rattlesnake. Her heart and lungs will cease to function quickly," he added.

Neuro? Hemo? The bystanders had no clue what in hell he was talking about, except that she was a goner for sure. A little old woman like Mammer couldn't take any more poison than a rabbit. Curious, they had never even seen a cobra before, much less seen a tiny old woman die from its bite.

"Thet flat headed bugger done got Mammer good ain't he? "She ain't got ah snow-ball chance in hell, is she?" Delbert asked the rhetorical questions

"Thet mean I ain't goin' ta Nevadie lak before?"

"No Mammer you wont be traveling to Nevada, at least not with us, and especially not like before," the Captain said, feeling it unnecessary to explain further.

"Raelon," her voice already weakening

"Yeah Mammer?"

"C'n yo' fix yo' ol' dyin' snake bit Mammer one ah them Chinie oranges tha way I lak'm?"

Raelon reached for an orange, unlike Mammer, mindful to dig into the correct basket. With his jack-knife, he cut a cone shaped hole in the stem end of the biggest China orange from the basket, and passed it to Mammer. In her faulty state, and ballooning hand, she lacked the strength to bring the orange to her mouth, let alone squeeze out the juice into her mouth. Roelon took the orange and squeezed the juice into a tin cup, picking out a few pits, not wanting Mammer to choke on one, and careful not to lose his lard can hat. He held the cup to his dying mother's lips allowing her to sip the sweet juice. The now sober cowhands removed their hats, as they watched Mammer pass into another world, even before she finished her juice. One tiny hand holding the tin cup, the other large and red, sticking straight up'

"She looks real nice don' she Raelon?" Roelon mentioned looking at his mother's wan face, blue thin lips twisted. "Special since she ain't got chapped lips lak usual, from suckin' on them Chinie oranges," he pointed out as they wrapped Mammer and secured the tarp with a length of hemp rope, face yet uncovered. They had discussed covering her face last, no special reason they could think of, other than Mammer never did like having her face covered.

"Hol' up ah minute." Raelon thought of something as he tied the last knot, and Roelon was about to drop the flap over her face.

"How come yo' stopped Raelon?

"Got me ah notion," Raelon answered.

He uncovered Mammer's tiny feet, and with a wet rag he cleaned Mammer's bare feet. "Reckon ol' Saint Peter get vexed if Mammer shows up at them pearly gates with horse shit betwixed her toes an' all. Don' reckon they got horse shit in heaven, an' tha Rice's' ain't gonna be tha fus'ones bringin' it in an' track it all over them golden sidewalks," Raelon explained, before re-wrapping Mammer's wet feet.

"Lord we are sending on to your care a good Christian woman, who raised her son's the best that she knew how, in an unforgiving country. Better known to all that knew her as Mammer. And we will not question your judgment in taking her, especially before she reached Nevada, and knowing she has never been more than twenty miles from the Okeechobee Lake" almost criticizing God for not allowing Mammer to go another few more miles, before allowing the cobra to kill her. "And that snake, well, it was just one of your creations, and as for Mammer, she just had a craving for another of your wonderful creations, a sweet China orange. Barefoot in death as in life, but clean feet now." With that Captain McBean slid the small bible into his coat pocket.

Raelon nudged his brother, they had both helped her enjoy her very last China orange before dying, he spoke, "Oh yeah one large hand, but mayhap it will go down befo' she reaches yo'. An' she ain't got chapped lips lak usual." With the addition of Raelon's words the short ceremony was concluded. "Ashes to ashes, dust to dust." The Captain sprinkled sand over Mammer's canvas covered corpse. They covered her with black dirt.

Roelon retied Geechee's hat back on before securing his own. Standing together around the grave on the sand hill not ten miles from Tater Bluff, Skeeter Moody looked around, and decided that this was without a doubt the best funeral he had ever attended. The fact that he and his friends had been sucking on a canteen, containing a mixture of water and liquor had no bearing on his thoughts. He especially enjoyed seeing Geechee setting on the back of the three-legged pony holding his red hat. Adding to his enjoyment, the fact that Roelon was still wearing the white cotton mask he had put on shortly after leaving town. The simple service ended, Miz Caroline's escort walked away, the Negro driver was heard to say, "Lawd I ain't never seen tha lak it, ah white woman kilt by ah snake named Adam, an' her boys dressed lak monkeys an all."

The cowhunters remained talking, making no effort to mount up, as the others prepared to depart. Something was clearly on their minds. Eventually they mounted and rode up next to the wagon.

"Capt'n me an' tha boys been talkin' an' all, an we lak ta say thet them wuz real quality words yo' said over Mammer." The reluctant lean cowman nervously shifted in the saddle.

"Well I thank you Delbert, it's kind of you to say so. Well lets be on our way," he said to Raelon.

"Ah Capt'n ah, thet ain't all. Me an' tha boys here been wonderin' if yo' might do us ah Christian kindness."

"Well I don't know, if it won't take too long. You boys are aware that we have a long trip ahead."

"Ah yeah suh we aware. An' it won't take long Capt'n." One of the other boys named Spud Townsend spoke up.

"Yeah Capt'n it 'bout them words yo' said fo' Mammer, we got ah frien' whut ain't never had quality words said over'm," Delbert said.

"Are you saying your friend is dead?"

"Yeah suh Capt'n, deader'n ah las' Christmas turkey. Kilt by ah Spanish bull whut gored'm," another explained. "Thet's his brother there, Little

Willie Harold." The young one pointed out, and Little Willie shook his head affirmatively.

"Well boys I don't quiet understand."

"It ain't far from here Capt'n, ain't hardly ah mile." Delbert Jones pointed up the trail.

"All right boys lead on." The Rice boys looked one last time at Mammer's grave marker, a crude red cross, fashioned from a board kicked from the wagon. The young cowmen moved their horses around in front of the wagon, leading out. Just as one had said, they reached a cutoff from the main trail, which actually was as cleared as the main trail. The boys lead them off and slowly traveled for another twenty minutes, eventually reaching a clearing surrounding a huge tall pine tree. Raelon stopped his team after guiding them to the edge of the clearing.

The perplexed old seaman looked around, seeing nothing in the needle-covered clearing but the bleached out skeleton of a long dead bull. At least from the long horns it appeared that it had been a bull. Upon further inspection he saw what seemed to be the equally bleached bones of a horse. But nothing indicating a grave; no marker of any kind.

"Boys just point out the grave and we will have a proper funeral." Holding his small bible as he jumped to the ground, as did Roelon, Raelon and Geechee, plus the pony helped down by Raelon.

"Well I reckon y'all wanted to wait for the proper time for installing the marker. Huh boys?

"Naw Capt'n ain't gonna be no marker he's there," Skeeter said, pointing high in the tree.

The extremely confused Captain followed the pointing finger toward a limb high in the pine. What he saw only disconcerted him further. His eyes focused on a human skeleton draped over, and secured to the limb by rope. The bones were bleached white like the bones under the tree. Raelon and Roelon stood gawking too; Roelon even lifting his mask for a better look, thinking it interfering with his sight.

"Bless me boys, I don't understand. I assume that is your friend up there," he declared, staring at the skeleton, still wearing his brogans, his faded hat hanging on a string about his neck bones, plus a few pieces of ragged fabric blowing in the breeze.

"Right as rain Capt'n thet's our frien' Buck Harold, an' thet's tha Spanish bull whut kilt him." Spud pointed to oblivious pile of bones, on the ground.

"I shot him myself after he gored my brother," Little Willie responded.

"I must say Little Willie this seems a bit irregular. Why would you hang your dead brother in a tree like that?"

"Well suh it wern't our idea. It wuz Ol' Buck hisself whut come up with it. We all thinkin' it wuz a real queer idea," Spud explained for Little Willie. "We laid him under this tree here whilst he wuz ah dying. Then he made High Pockets fetch his bible he totes in his saddle pocket."

"High Pockets cain' read much but he always got thet bible," Spud further explained.

"I see." The Captain rubbed his chin, as Raelon and Roelon still slack jawed eyed the skeleton, both wondering if maybe they should not have hung Mammer in a tree.

"Thet's right Capt'n he made us swear on tha good book, thet we would do lak he said afore he died from thet horn in his gut," Skeeter explained.

"I see." Repeating his earlier words.

"When a feller swears on tha good-book, he's obliged ta do whut he swears to. Don' he Capt'n?" The youngest, called Splinters Wooten spoke for the first time.

"Well that is correct. When you take an oath, you're bound to keep it."

"Thet's zackly right, an' thet's why we had to haul him up there. But before we done thet, he said we got ta cut tha seat of his britches out, drawers an' all," Delbert added.

"You don't say." Was the only response the perplexed Captain could muster. "But did he explain why? I mean it seems a very queer request for a dying man to ask of his friends.

The Rice brothers having second thoughts about hanging Mammer in a tree with her ass hanging out, plain a day. They were glad now they had not done that, instead followed the more traditional burial.

"Yeah suh he sho did. He said we do thet an' haul him way up there an' tie him," Skeeter pointed up into the tree.

"Thet way, when any ah them bible thumpers from Tater Bluff take ah notion ta come by fo' ah visit they c'n kiss his lily-white ass," Little Willie further explained the reason his brother Buck being tied in the tree.

"An' thet's why we want proper words said fo' ol' Buck. He ain't had none 'ceptin' whut thet wagon load ah whores we brung out here las' Christmas said over, uh, under him." The shy Splinters spoke again.

"In that case I suppose we should get on with the service."

"Lord I never had the pleasure of meeting Buck Harold, but you knew him better than any of us or even his brother Little Willie. His companions state that he was the best cowman in the state. They declared him the best pistol shot too, as they witnessed his killing an Indian that was stealing Delbert's pony one night. Shooting him straight in the ear from forty yards away." The Captain ended the service with amen, and then started again. "But Lord I hope you won't be to critical of his friends, because of Buck's final resting place. The boys decided he would be closer to your kingdom than he would have been in the ground." Adding an explanation for the peculiar method of his final arrangements. The service for Buck was over.

As the wagon prepared to roll away, the Rice brothers renewed their thoughts, wishing once again they had tied Mammer in a tree, only keeping her ass covered. Mammer deserved a shorter walk to heaven too, she always did complain of bad feet.

"Them wuz quality words fo' ol' Buck, we beholdin' Capt'n," Skeeter called.

"All right boy. We're on our way to Nevada. Good luck boys." He called back.

Buck's companions spent the remainder of the day and night under the tree, drinking whisky by a low fire, discussing the exciting events of the day and fighting off mosquitoes. Still not believing they had attended two funerals the same day and wondering if some day they might convince Sister Oletta Dewalt to bring the organ wagon out and play Buck's favorite song, "Camptown Races." Fat chance.

CHAPTER TWENTY

"It's ah plumb miracle thet Uncle Caesar survived them Indians." Polly spoke quietly, unwilling to wake Uncle Caesar, as the wagon bumped along paralleling the river, and almost home.

"Yeah, 'special after they cut tha back of his legs leaving him lame an' all."

"Whut we gonna do with ol' Uncle when we start tha cow hunt?" Polly asked, looking back at the old man leaning against the side of the wagon, a blanket over his legs.

"Well, we sho' cain' leave him at tha ranch alone. I been studin' on it some. Been figurin' on lashin' thet ol' rocker in tha back ah Anna's wagon, so's he c'n ride in comfort. In good weather mayhap he c'n sit by tha cook fire an' he'p Kara Sue. Her bringin' tha pine knots an all, him chunkin'm on tha fire," James explained.

"Reckon thet will do jus' fin'. An' we c'n put ah bed ah hay in tha wagon fo' ah pallet. Thet ort ta be good sleepin', even if it should come ah cool night," Polly added.

Later Uncle Caesar and Cork continued chatting, and making the most of their miraculous reunion. The mules required no guidance from James as the trail altered its direction turning away from the river and thick saw grass, edging its bank for miles. The animals would exert slightly more effort, as the hard packed black dirt changed to a layer of sand, trailing through the higher elevation of the piney woods. In spots where the tall pines allowed the warm sun permission to enter, it created a blue green reflection from the palmettos crowding the white sandy path.

Songs from the mocking birds, and calls from blue jays replaced squawking calls from the large river herons. James pointed out a doe and her fawn in a grassy clearing some distance away. The buck, concealed in the shadows of a large oak watched them pass.

"I got me ah new name." Cork waiting until the doe and fawn had disappeared into thick brush, and Uncle Caesar was more alert before speaking.

"Huh? Yo' mean yo' ain't Cork no mo'?" Uncle Caesar somewhat confused by this revelation.

"Nah suh. I mean, it jus' thet I got me other names ta go with it. Mista James said I c'n take his name.

"It ain't so!" Total disbelief in his voice. He knew of such things happening in the past, freed slaves taking the name of their previous masters.

"It so, right 'nough. I'm James Cork Nash now. Mista James had tha judge in Tatter Bluff make ah paper fo' me sayin' so. Miz Polly said thet I c'n still go by Cork if I'm ah min'. Reckon I will.

"I do declare boy, yo' ah sho' caution. Here I is calculatin' all dis time dem injuns kilt yo'. 'Stead here yo' is, livin' wid ah nice family. An' din takin' on ah 'nother name jus' lak white folks, legal lak too. Miz Caroline, God res' her soul always say yo' ah special boy. An' gonna grow ta be a special man someday." Ah pure saint she wuz, an' set great store in yo'. Wide smile exhibited on both.

"I plum' weary now boy. 'Spect I bes' lay back fo' ah spell. Don' get on lak I use to, befo'." Cutting the sentence short.

Cork assisted the old man in lying back into a soft layer of hay once again; a tear in his eye as he pulled a blanket over the prone figure, gently patting him on the shoulder.

Looking about he spotted Luke, Anna, and Jojo along with August riding ahead on the trail, as it returned once again toward the river.

"It's jus' beautiful James." Polly's eyes engulfed all the colors, the blue of the sky to the purple shading in distant tree line across the river.

Ahead, Luke reined his horse to a stop, stood in his stirrups looking back at the wagon. He pointed toward the south bank of the river. James and Polly could barely make out his broad grin, because of the distance separating them. James stood after stopping the wagon, waved an arm signaling them to cross over. The distance was not so great as to muffle the wild yells, as they raced into the cool clear water toward the south bank.

"Me an' Luke been watchin' thet bunch ah cows an' them springers fo' nigh on ta ah week now."

Polly shaded her eyes, better to see the cows with their calves that had been born over the winter; over a dozen animals in the small jackpot herd.

"Mista James."

"Yo' jus' as well go on an' he'p boy. Take my horse. Pay min' them animals gonna be wild, take some doin' gettin' them outten thet brush." Cork looked at Polly.

"Go on, we'll look ta Uncle Caesar. An' yo' pay min' ta what Mista James said 'bout them wild cows," she cautioned him again.

"Yes'm I will Ma'am."

James looked west toward the sun, calculating another three hours before dusk. With any luck at all, he knew Luke and the others would have the small bunch in the holding pen. The pen had been constructed about a mile down river, from the house. It's intended purpose other than to secure the animals for branding was a sweet-potato patch, once the cows were turned out. They watched from the wagon until Cork had disappeared into the brush, where the cows had taken refuge, before James urged the mules forward. Then forced to ease back a little on the reins slowing them, they were getting close to home and the mules sensed it.

"James!"

"I see'm. Lay thet scatter gun 'cross my lap."

He had seen the tall figure standing in the trail just as Polly had. James shaded his eyes from the sun and could tell the figure was moving toward them. Pulling on the reins he stopped the wagon, and passed the reins to Polly. Making the gun ready, by checking its load.

"Wait ah minute. Thet ain't no bandit or tha lak, thet's ol' Acrefoot Johnson. Ain't nobody else stands thet tall 'round here, animal or man. I reckon ah feller cain' be too careful though." He set the gun down and took the reins once again.

Polly noticed his large friendly blue eyes, and could detect a smile even under a thick black beard covering the lower half of his face; as usual, his shirt splitting at both shoulders from the strain of being forced to cover his muscled upper torso. The only visible weapon was a large knife secured to his waist by a length of rope.

"Hello Mista Johnson. Ain't 'spectin' ta be runnin' into yo' on tha trail this late."

"Howdy Mista Nash, Miz Nash." Slowly raising a massive hand, touching the brim of his hat, as he passed the verbal greeting.

"Well I'm ah might tardy on ah 'count ah tha books I'm totein'," showing no strain from the large pack strapped across his wide back.

"Books?"

"Yea suh. Sears and Roebuck catalogs. Started from Orlando with nigh three hundred pounds. Got shet ah some, now down ta mayhap two hundred pounds, I reckon."

"Gracious me, Mista Johnson. Why don' yo' get yo'self ah mule?"

"Mule? Shucks no Miz Nash, slow me down too much, stopping ta feed an all; 'sides mules cain' swim too good with all this weight. I jus' hol' my pack up an' walk 'cross most rivers, keep tha mail dry, me bein' so big an' all." Speaking as if they had not recognized his height.

"Well I reckon yo' got ah good argument ahgin ah mule at thet," Polly answered.

"Yes'm." He removed his burden, setting it on the ground. "I calculated strappin' ah chair ta my pack fo' toting' sight-seers at tha same time. Lots ah British folks come through Punta Gorda, cravin' ta see our beautiful land, but tha gove-ment say no tha thet. Well pleasure visitin' with ya'll, but I bes' be goin',"

"Yeah, us too. But yo' pay min' Mista. Johnson, I be plumb sorry 'bout lettin' thet renegade Two Ghosts 'scape from us. 'Special after knowin' he's aimin' ta cut out yo' heart an' eat it an' all." James apologized for allowing the Negro to slip away during their skirmish.

"Don' yo' fret none ah-tall Mista Nash. If I run inta thet assassin, I reckon I'll jus' snap him lak a dried out stick." Twisting his huge hands together, simulating breaking a twig.

"Reckon we be movin' on too, but pay min' Mista Johnson."

"Good evenin' Mista Johnson, Lak James sez walk cautious."

"Ma'am." Touching his hat brim once again, after lifting his pack effortlessly and placing it on is back.

With a clicking sound and a light slap of the reins, James started the animals down the trail once more. Turning, Polly checked on Kara Sue and Uncle Caesar. Both were sound asleep, and had missed the short visit with Acrefoot Johnson. She smiled at the two before stealing a last glance toward Mr. Johnson, walking away with a stretched stride in the opposite direction. For the first time she noticed the enormous man being barefoot; and that his trousers were far too short for his long legs. It occurred to her that he probably could not purchase britches with a proper fit, and only homemade would accommodate his massive bulk.

As if feeling her watching, he turned one last time, and waved. She returned his gesture. Deep imprints of his immense bare feet remained in the sand behind him, and Polly could see them far ahead in the trail where he had walked. She shuddered thinking how easy it would be for the renegade Negro to trail him, should he cut the giants trail anywhere.

"I fear fo' Mista. Johnson," Still eyeing his deep tracks in front.

"No cause. Thet Nigger fears Acrefoot. Otherwise he would've already come at'em. An' I doubt he c'n scare up any he'p from any ah them other injuns whut got away."

"I 'spect yo' right. If he did, it won't be straight on. He'd back shoot 'em."

Polly shuddered once more at the thought. Before turning her attention across the river as they approached the ford. On the other side she watched Luke and Anna moving three or four head of cattle into the pen. Distracting her of any further thoughts of harm befalling the giant barefoot mailman.

"Ain't thet ah sight? Looks to be they got ah few calves already."

"Yeah. August calculated we got mayhap fifty springers to get mamied up. Thet's countin' tha stock we picked up from McBean. All got ta be ear marked an' branded. An' lak as not we c'n hunt out some ah them wild long horns whut's been runnin' tha scrub. Mean animals, throw back from thet Spanish stock."

James held the mules at the water edge, allowing them to drink before crossing. Across the ford they could see Anna and Luke setting on the top rail of the holding pen. Then noticed the others one at a time clearing the scrub, herding additional cows.

Observing the activity on the far side invoked a rare cloak of calmness in Polly. For the first time in awhile, she conjured agreeable thoughts of their future. She and Anna had discussed them visiting the McBean place after the cow hunt was completed. Now she smiled, thinking once again of such a visit. It was a small cabin, but she knew it to be sound, made of thick cypress planks. In addition, was a separate cookhouse of the same materials, with both having a fireplace constructed of brick.

Anna had shared with Polly her the dream of a marriage with Luke, and moving into the McBean cabin. On rare occasions Luke had hinted the same, but only in a playful way.

"I swear Polly, at times, Luke Nash makes me so angry I could jus' spit."

That conversation from the past was as close to vulgarity as Anna's upbringing would permit. The picture being presented on the far side, led Polly to believe Luke was as anxious as Anna to have the cow hunt finished.

"Now Anna, yo' stop yo' frettin' 'bout such," Polly would argue. "Luke will come 'round, thet's tha way ah them Nash's'. I 'llow it took James nigh on ta two year ta muster tha spine ta pop tha question. An' me ah pushin' as hard as ah body could," Polly assured her.

"An' his ma said tha same 'bout his pa."

Those conversations with Anna, concerning Luke and wedlock, amused her. Speculation of it actually happening pleased her. She smiled.

Glancing at James, she could tell, he was also deep in thought; their past and their future. His tanned face displayed contentment, and confidence. She could remember very few times when it did not, even in the most trying of times. She refused to dwell on those.

"James."

"Yes, Ma'am," came a simple reply, without removing his gaze from the far side of the river.

"I'm awful ashamed 'bout some feelin's thet's been comin' on me." Maintaining her own observation across the river, focusing on nothing in particular.

"Whut kin' ah feelin's yo' got ta be 'shamed 'bout girl?" Turning and facing his wife, perplexity replacing the contentment on his face, he stared at her.

"They's been times ah my heart an' min' givin' in ta this hard land. Special since we crossed thet river. Lak at times we wuz in ah deep hole in tha sand. An' tha sides cavin' in, or some such." Not wanting to face James, instead staring at the back of one of the mules. "Special, after some tribulations we done experienced. Times I jus' wanted to give up." Her blue eyes glazed over, with maybe a hint of shame forming. "I would've give in ah long time back James, if yo' had not had enough strength fo' tha both ah us. Times I feared we should cut an' run back ta Georgia, other times I feared we would. Shame got ah real holt on me.

"Yo' jus' hol' on girl. Ain't no cause fo' yo' feelin' mortification over such." Attempting to sooth his wife. Knowing the tribulation she mentioned was the death of their son. "No ma'am. Ain't no cause ta fret 'bout such. Why I reckon I had my full share ah doubt, my ownself. It wuz me whut got our boy kilt, pure an' simple." James made his statement in a very shaky voice. "An' I 'spect tha good Lord gonna pile another trial or two on us. Thangs we only heard of an' ain't yet seen. Lak them great swarms of skeeters, whut come every spring. Tha ol crackers tell they so thick, they clog tha windpipe's an' choke tha animals." Covering his lower face with a hand, crudely demonstrating his point.

"Then they's always them marsh fires thet mayhap burn fo' weeks on end. Hurricanes blowing away dwellin's an' drownin' stock. If thet ain't 'nough yo' c'n throw in bandits or two an' a few injuns, lak thet Two Ghosts still roamin' 'bout. No ma'am, they aint no cause fo' feelin' shame ah fearin' all them thangs." Taking one of her small hands in both of his, after stopping the team and dropping the reins.

Polly felt strength through his rough hands as he gently gripped hers. Even more strength, as he ever so tenderly kissed away a teardrop on her cheek.

"They's ol' timers here thet's been through all them tribulations an' more. An' with guts an' tha grace ah God, they still here. Least ways they kin is, an' still building. Jus' lak us, together. Makin' this ah good land."

As he spoke, he held both of her hands giving her all his strength and love, at the same time, drawing on her trust and love.

"This river... Tha Peace River... Beyond it there." Freeing one of his hands and Pointing. "Nash Land... With Nash blood in it. No, ma'am, we ain't goin' nowheres. No matter whut comes, we Nash's gonna meet it head on, God willin' jus' lak always."

His gentle comforting words drew a flashing smile from her, which matched his, after seeing the shine on his face and the conviction of his eyes. She continued smiling placing her calm hand on one of his. James guided the wagon into the Peace River toward the far bank, where the others waited in the dusk. The dimming light from the setting sun would guide them.

"Les' get on home."

THE END

Printed in the United States
69664LV00003B/21